NO
ADAM
IN
EDEN

by Grace Metalious

TRIDENT PRESS *New York* • *1963*

THIS BOOK IS FOR THE PEOPLE WHO HAVE
GIVEN ME MORE HAPPINESS THAN ANYONE
ELSE IN THE WORLD:

My husband, *George Metalious*

and my children,
> *Marsha and Edward Dupuis*
> *Christopher "Mike" Metalious*
> *Cynthia "Cindy" Metalious*
> *Suzanne "Suzy" Roy*

and the frosting on the cake,
my grandson,
> *William Edward "Billy" Dupuis*

Book One

1

It took Armand Bergeron a long, long time to die and even then there was no dignity to his dying. Perhaps it was because he was still a relatively young man. He lay alone in the middle of the double bed that he had shared for over twelve years with his wife, Monique, and in his moments of lucidity he reflected sourly that the bed was no colder now than it had always been. It was a big bed and quite the most hideous Armand had ever seen in his life. It was made of golden oak and highly varnished. Monique liked things to shine and in her house everything made a reflection.

Shiny, thought Armand. Shiny and clean and antiseptic. Like Monique herself.

The bedroom smelled of disinfectant but underneath that there was the hint of vomit and blood which never quite went away in spite of Monique's scrubbings and airings.

Armand smiled deep inside himself. Last night—at least it seemed as if it had been only last night—Monique had come into the room. It was very late and Armand had thrown up again. She began to clean him and she talked aloud to herself.

"Pig," she said. "I should leave you to drown in your own filth."

Armand kept his eyes closed so that she should not see the laughter there.

"Pig!"

She washed him and changed his nightshirt and all the while he made himself stay limp and heavy. And then in her passion for cleanliness, she began to strip the bed. It was difficult to maintain the pretense of sleep while Monique worked, but Armand steeled himself. He did not really know which was the harder to do. To keep from moaning aloud under his wife's rough handling as she yanked at one sheet and put another in its place, rolling him back and forth like a ball, or to keep from laughing like a madman at the sight of her blackly enraged eyes and her rigid mouth.

But at last she was finished. She aired the room again and the cold wind coming through the window lashed at Armand until he thought that surely now a shiver would betray his wakefulness. Yet once Monique had finished her cleaning of him she did not even glance his way again. She went back and forth from the bedroom to the bathroom carrying her basins and cloths and then she took a final look around. She lowered the window a little, but it was still open a good six inches, letting in the miserable cold of February, when she clicked off the light and slammed the door behind her.

It was then that Armand stopped laughing to himself.

He hadn't fooled Monique for a minute, he realized. She knew that he had been awake and now she had left him for the night to freeze alone in bed. She had always known how he hated an open window during the winter.

Armand did not know how long he lay there shivering, the pain like hot coals in his belly, but he knew that he must have groaned and cried out. The bedroom door opened so silently that he did not even realize it was open until he saw the shaft of light from the hallway. A little figure in a white nightgown crept toward the window and closed it.

4

Armand could smile again now, he could let it show. The little figure was his daughter, Angelique, and she was the only human being Armand loved or had ever loved for many, many years.

"Mon ange," he murmured and the child came and stood next to the bed. With a great effort, Armand moved his hand and Angelique took it in both of hers.

"Mon petit ange du ciel," he whispered.

But his voice made no sound. Only his lips moved. The child put his cold hand against her cheek.

"Papa. Papa," she said.

He felt hot tears on his skin.

"Non, non, ma petite," he said. "You must not cry for me."

Angelique stood quietly, holding his hand for a long time until she felt him growing warmer. Then she kissed his fingers and lowered the hand gently to his side.

The door closed without a sound and the room was dark again. Armand let himself drift into the place between sleep and non-sleep. His whole body was warmer now and the pain not quite so sharp. Fragments of sound seemed to come to him from the corners of the room, and beneath his closed eyelids bits of forgotten pictures came into focus. This phenomenon had been happening to him more and more frequently of late and tonight he almost welcomed it.

"Tonight I will look at the pretty ones only," he told himself. "Tonight I will not listen to any ugliness nor look at anything unbeautiful."

But, he realized, it was not always as easy as all that. Sometimes the sounds and pictures seemed to have a life all their own and in the end they usually did what they pleased with him.

Armand Bergeron had been born and raised on a farm in the southern part of the province of Quebec, Canada, and until he was fifteen years old he had not really believed that a world existed beyond the nearest village of Sainte Thérèse. Oh, he knew the world was there all right because his grandfather, Zenophile, subscribed to the newspapers from Montreal and sometimes strangers passed through the village of Sainte Thérèse on their way to one pursuit or another on the Saint Lawrence River. But Armand was not particularly interested in newspapers and strangers were mostly a matter of curiosity and good for only a moment or two of idle speculation. The village, the farm, the neighbors and, most of all, his own family were his life, and until he was fifteen these were all he wanted or needed from the world.

Armand was the seventh-born child in a family of six boys and five girls and they were a big, brawling, loud-mouthed group. There was a saying in the village that everything about the Bergerons was big. Not that there was anything unusual in a French-Canadian family producing eleven children. There were the Paquettes, on the next farm down the river from the Bergerons, who had fourteen children and in Sainte Thérèse there were the Turcottes. Marie Rose Turcotte had borne seventeen children before Armand Bergeron was born and before she reached the menopause at the age of fifty-one she had achieved a grand total of twenty-two little Turcottes.

No, it was not in the size of the family that the Bergerons were big. It was in other ways. Old Zenophile Bergeron was six feet tall and his son, Alcide, topped him. So did his grandsons, Edouard, Pierre, Christian, Jacques, Armand and Antoine, although the old man hated like hell to admit it. All the Bergeron men had enormous shoulders and arms knotted with muscle. They had legs and thighs like tree trunks and their strength was the strength of bulls. It was quite a sight to see them all trooping into church of a Sunday morning.

Heaven only knew, said the people of Sainte Thérèse, that the church was small enough to begin with but when the

6

Bergerons came in everybody and everything in the building was dwarfed into insignificance.

The Bergerons were impressive enough in church but that was nothing compared to when all of them stood up in the Town Hall to dance a quadrille at the Saturday night socials. Then the whole building quivered to its very foundations and everybody had to laugh at the sight of the eight big men who laughed and clapped and yet were strangely graceful as they moved.

It was a terrible thing to boast, said the people of Sainte Thérèse, but after all the truth was the truth and the truth of the matter was that there were no handsomer, stronger men anywhere. Not even in Montreal were there men like the Bergerons. No, not in Montreal or Quebec City or the whole province.

In addition to their size and strength, the Bergeron men had big voices. They shouted, laughed and cursed in tones that people said could be heard all the way to Ottawa. It was a town legend that once when the youngest son, Antoine, had broken his leg while hunting in the forest, it had been his lungs that saved him.

Antoine had gone out with his gun early in the afternoon. There was a light snow falling and he had hoped to find a few deer tracks. No one had worried about him until after the snow had turned into a blizzard and darkness fell.

"I have a bad feeling," Berthe finally said to her husband, Alcide. "You must take your father and the boys and go to find Antoine."

"Ah, *ma petite,* you worry yourself over nothing," Alcide had answered.

Berthe Bergeron stood five feet ten inches tall in her bare feet but from the day he had begun to court her Alcide had always called her *"ma petite."*

Now she folded her arms over her big, soft bosom and stood

straight and strong in front of the iron cookstove. "Not one mouthful of food for any one of you until you come back with Antoine. I have a bad feeling."

Alcide threw back his big, dark head and laughed. Then he went to her and picked her up by the elbows, just as if she did not weigh one hundred and seventy pounds. He kissed her firmly on the mouth and gave her a resounding smack on the behind.

"And what kind of a feeling does this give you, *ma petite?*" he had asked as he pressed her hand against his crotch. "Eh, tell me that, *ma petite*. What kind of feeling?"

Berthe pushed him away.

"You are a dirty old man, Alcide Bergeron. Performing like a young stallion at your age." But she had to smile at him and for a moment the frown of worry was gone from her face.

"Ah, so it is a good feeling, eh?" he said and began to play with one of her breasts. He could feel her nipple hardening at once through her rough cotton dress.

"Go, Alcide," she said and moved away from his touch. "At once now. I mean it. I am afraid for Antoine."

"Ah, you are like an American," said Alcide in mock disgust. "You are like one of those skinny sticks from the States with the look of ice on your face."

But he called his father and his sons and they all went out to look for Antoine.

The snow was very deep now and still falling in a heavy, slanting curtain. The lanterns that the men carried seemed to cast no more light than a single candle as they made their way through the woods, and after an hour even Alcide began to feel a certain uneasiness. They had gone more than five miles into the woods before they heard Antoine shouting.

"He is over this way," Alcide called to the others and they moved toward the voice.

They found Antoine half covered with snow, his right leg twisted under him and his face scarlet with rage.

8

"Goddam son of a bitch," cursed Antoine methodically as he struggled to move himself. "Goddam son of a whore."

Alcide stood over his youngest son and began to laugh and in a second the others joined him.

"My poor fool," roared old Zenophile. "Why are you lying there screaming like a woman with your gun still in your hand? You could have let go with one shot and we would have heard you an hour ago."

"Yes, indeed," said Edouard. "Do tell us, little brother, why you are lying there in the snow like that?"

"You son of a bitch," shouted Antoine. "It's my fucking leg. Now give me a hand before I blow your goddam head off."

"Ah," said Pierre. "It is a good thing that Maman cannot hear her baby talk in such a fashion. She would take down his pants and spank his bottom for sure."

"Just wait, Pierre," yelled Antoine. "Just wait until I can stand up and I'll kick the living shit out of you."

"Naughty, naughty," said Armand.

They hoisted Antoine up on their shoulders, and laughing and singing dirty songs, they carried him home.

In the meantime, Berthe, with her "bad feeling" going strong, had sent to Sainte Thérèse for the doctor, and as it turned out it was well that she had, for Antoine's leg was broken in two places.

"Well, you're lucky it is no worse," Dr. Girard said. "The way this bunch of roughnecks brought him in here, it is a miracle the whole leg is not smashed to bits."

The doctor had set the leg while Antoine kept up a steady stream of cursing for which his mother, this once, did not reprimand him. When it was done, Berthe dished up the supper and afterward the men sat around the warm kitchen and got drunk.

Years later, as he lay there dying in a cold, clean bed in a small town in New Hampshire, Armand Bergeron tried to remember if the day his brother broke his leg had been the first time he had ever got drunk.

"Could it have been that day?" he asked himself. "No, certainly, that could not have been the day."

He did not really know when the drinking had started. In fact, when he stopped to think of it he couldn't remember a time when he had not been a drinker. But then so had his father and his grandfather and his brothers and no harm had ever come to any of them. Every year the making of wine from grapes and dandelions and berries had been an integral part of the life of his family. The women canned the fruits and vegetables and smoked and salted the meats, while Armand and his brothers, together with their father and grandfather, attended to the making of the wine. They also made beer and cider and whiskey from potatoes and corn, and brandy from cherries and apricots. Alcohol had always been there, as much a part of the Bergeron table as milk and butter and meat.

It was good to look forward to that first dark, foaming bottle of beer after a hot, hard day in the fields. And at the evening meal Armand had always extended his glass with the others when his mother said, "Here. A bit more wine to wash down the last of your meat."

In the village of Sainte Thérèse there was one saloon. It was called Le Pechoir and it was here that the men from the farms and the town congregated on Saturday nights both before and after the weekly dance at the Town Hall.

Everybody got drunk on Saturday night, Armand remembered. Ah, but what marvelous singing and joking and fighting! Never had there been fights in the whole world to match the brawls that started at Le Pechoir on a Saturday night. And if there were cuts and bruises and big heads the next morning at Mass, the night before had made it well worth while.

All these years later it seemed to Armand that he could still feel the lump on the back of his head where one of the

Cormier boys had once smashed him with a chair. But that one had got his in the end. Armand had knocked him out cold and it had taken three men to carry him home.

Ah, those were sweet times, Armand thought. But at once the happy memory vanished and he remembered now the doctor who came to see him every day, sometimes twice a day. The doctor who had warned him years ago that drink was going to kill him.

The old fool, thought Armand. He never knows what the hell he's talking about anyway.

Old Dr. Southworth didn't mind a taste of the bottle himself and that was a fact. And after all, how could one expect a dried-up old Yankee like Southworth to understand about the juices that ran through the blood of a French-Canadian like Armand Bergeron?

No, it would take a lot more than a little drinking to kill a Bergeron. Why, just look at old Zenophile. Now there was a man. Old Zenophile had swilled liquor like a pig and he had died at the age of ninety-one. And he hadn't died of liquor either. He had died of influenza, which he had picked up on a trip to Montreal. And what about Alcide, who could drink even more than Zenophile? Liquor certainly hadn't killed him. He'd drunk like a fish all his life and had been killed at the age of seventy-six while cutting down a bothersome maple tree. The damned tree had fallen on him and Alcide had died of a broken neck. Not of liquor. No. Old Dr. Southworth just didn't know what the hell he was talking about.

On Armand's fifteenth birthday, he remembered, which fell on the third of August in 1914, his grandfather had come home from Sainte Thérèse with the Montreal newspapers. Zenophile had sat quite still at the kitchen table while Berthe poured him out a cup of hot, strong tea.

The old man drank and then set his cup down very gently.

"France is at war with Germany," he said at last.

11

For a long time no one had spoken and then Alcide had gone to stand by his father's chair. He had put one of his big hands on Zenophile's shoulder.

"You said it would come, Papa," Alcide said. "For months now you have been saying it."

"Yes," replied Zenophile. "I said it, but all the while I was hoping it would not be so."

Berthe Bergeron had not spoken but had gone to stand at one of the kitchen windows which overlooked the fields. It would be the time of harvest in a few weeks and the land was green and gold with promise. The fields promised food and warmth for her family, money for the new parlor curtains and a beautiful wedding for her daughter, Aurelie, who was going to marry Omer Cormier after the crops were in. She turned and looked at her husband and her father-in-law.

"It has nothing to do with us," she had said at last.

Zenophile turned to her and it seemed to Armand, who was watching from across the table, that in the space of a few hours his grandfather had turned into an old man.

"It has everything to do with us," said Zenophile. "With me and with Alcide and with the boys. And with you, Berthe. And with your daughters. The blood that runs through your veins is as French as the blood in mine."

"No," Berthe had cried and to Armand it seemed as if the words had been torn from her mouth. "It is not true, Papa. I was born here. Not ten miles from this very house. I am a Canadian, not a Frenchwoman. I am a Canadian and therefore I am English, and England is not at war."

Zenophile had looked away from her.

"Wait until tomorrow, Berthe," he said. "Tomorrow or the day after. Then England, too, will be at war."

"And even then it will have nothing to do with us," said Berthe and turned away to look out the window again at the fruitful fields.

"What do you want us to do, Papa?" asked Alcide.

Berthe almost ran from the window to put her hand on Alcide's arm. "I tell you it has nothing to do with us, Alcide," she said and for the first time in his life Armand saw tears in his mother's eyes.

"What can it matter to us?" she demanded. "France and England are thousands of miles away. Across the ocean. Let the war stay there. Let it stay far away from you and me and the children."

Alcide pulled away from her.

"That's enough, Berthe," he said roughly. "This is a decision that will remain with Papa."

"No," she cried. "The decision is not up to Papa. You are not married to Papa and he is not the father of my children. This is my home and you and the children belong to me and I will not listen to any more talk of war."

"This was Papa's home long before it was yours," shouted Alcide. "Now I say that you have spoken enough and I want you to be quiet."

Zenophile went to Berthe and put his arm around her shoulder.

"No, Alcide," he had said gently. "Berthe is right. This is her home. It has been hers since the day you brought her here as your bride and she has done well for you. She has given you strong sons and beautiful daughters and she has shown me nothing but love and respect." He turned her to face him. "But, Berthe, France is my country. I was born there and I married there and I cannot help but feel more French than English."

Berthe began to cry and Zenophile had tried to rest her head against his shoulder but she pulled away from him. She stood with her fists clenched at her sides, tears pouring down her face.

"They will take my husband and my sons," she said, her voice shrill, "to fight for a people they do not know in a country which they have never seen. Perhaps to die. And for

13

things that do not concern any of them. The fields will run red with blood and my sons will be dead in a strange land."

"Berthe, Berthe," Zenophile said, trying to comfort her. "War is not all killing and brass bands and glory and flags flying. It is also food. There is an old saying that an Army travels on its stomach. That is what we can do. We will raise and harvest the food for the men who will do the fighting for us."

"Yes," wept Berthe. "We will feed an army of savages while my children starve. I tell you I will listen to no more!"

She had run from the room and Armand heard a door slam on the second floor. He was stunned. Never, in all his years, had he seen his mother go to her room during the day except for the occasions when her time had come and she was to be delivered of a child. He stared at his father, waiting to see Alcide run after her, but Alcide stood quietly and looked down at the floor.

"Come, Armand," he had said finally. "There is work to do outside. We have rested long enough and the others will be watching for us."

Armand followed his father outside, Zenophile with them. For the first time in his life Armand had really looked around him. Now he, too, saw the fields in all their green and golden beauty and far away the black dots that were his brothers working on the land. The fruit trees were heavy, their branches bending under the loads of fruit, and Armand wondered why he had never really stopped to look at them in the springtime when they were tall-stemmed balls of white, soft-smelling fluff.

The earth seemed to have a sponginess beneath his feet and he had an almost irresistible urge to bend down and press his hands against the green grass. But his grandfather was watching him and he was overcome with shyness. In the meadow behind the house he knew that the cattle would be grazing, their bodies fat and brown and white, and in the lower pasture the pigs would be rooting and grunting in their pens.

It was as if his head were a series of compartments, he thought, so that he could see the fields in front of his eyes, but could also see the animals and the fruit trees and the vines heavy with grapes, the jars of food in the cellar and the bottles of wine in the racks. The racks his father had made with his own hands. He felt the hot August wind on his face, but somehow he could also feel the warmth of the kitchen stove in January and the mud of early May beneath his feet.

The fields will run red with blood . . .

He ran to catch up with his grandfather.

"Grand-père!" he called.

The old man stopped and turned to him.

"Yes, Armand?"

Armand, who could run for miles without even breathing hard, came up to the old man, and although he had hurried for only a few yards he felt a tightness in his chest as if he had been running for hours.

"Will it come here, *Grand-père?"* he asked.

Zenophile did not answer at once. He just stood and looked at his grandson.

"Today you are fifteen years old," he said at last. "It does not seem possible that you are still a boy and yet I have to raise my eyes to meet yours."

He sighed and again Armand had had the strange feeling that his grandfather was old. An old, old man. And that, too, did not seem possible.

"In a war," said Zenophile, "anything is possible. Suppose the Germans take France. Then who is to stop them from taking over the whole of Europe? Maybe I am an old sentimentalist, but I truly believe that if France goes to the Germans, it is the end for the whole Continent. It would not be hard then to take the one tiny island that is England."

15

"But England has not been invaded for hundreds and hundreds of years. You told me so yourself."

"There is always a first time for everything," said Zenophile. "And remember, I did say 'suppose.' Now, again suppose that the Germans took England. It would not be difficult to take Canada then, would it?"

"But we would still have the United States," protested Armand.

Zenophile spat on the ground.

"The United States. Hah! A nation of factory workers and storekeepers. No, my boy, do not depend on the United States. They will stay behind their own borders, they will never endanger themselves. Remember that in the United States it is not like it is here. Down there they do not have a king. They have a president who is elected by the people and if he gets the people involved in a war he runs the risk of not being re-elected. No, do not look to the United States to help the world. They are far too busy looking after themselves."

"Are you coming?" called Alcide.

Armand looked up and saw his father, far ahead of them now. Alcide was like a big black shadow outlined in green and gold.

The fields will run red with blood . . . And what if the big, black shadow was not Alcide but a German officer?

Armand began to run and he did not stop until he reached his brothers.

That same night all the Bergeron men went into Sainte Thérèse and met with their friends at Le Pechoir. It was the first time Armand had ever been to the village during the week and he was surprised to find that the streets looked just as they did on Saturday nights or Sunday mornings, except that now there were no women and the only lights came from behind the windows of the saloon. The same men sat at the

16

same tables so that Le Pechoir looked the same as ever, but tonight there was no laughing and no singing and Armand had known that tonight there would be no fist fights either.

Armand sat down with his brothers and his father and grandfather and soon some of the other men came to join them. Maurice Lemay, the proprietor, pushed tables together and soon everyone in the saloon was sitting with everybody else. The talk was only of war and of France and Armand and his brothers had sat still and listened to the older men.

But the peculiar feeling of being able to see more than one thing at a time had still remained with Armand. He looked at his older brothers, especially Edouard, and while he watched, Edouard picked up his glass and drank. Armand could see the movement in his brother's throat and he saw his big hand, a hand so big that the glass was almost hidden in it, but he could also see Edouard lying in a field of blood with his throat cut and a gun clutched uselessly in his hand.

But the war will not come to Canada, thought Armand. We will stay on the farm and raise food for the troops just as *Grand-père* said and our fields will not run red with blood. Maman was not herself today.

Maurice Lemay put down more drinks for everyone and then he sat and joined the conversation.

Perhaps Maman is going to have another child, thought Armand. Yes, of course. That must be it.

He smiled and felt better than he had all day.

Yes, of course. Maman was going to have another baby. Always before, when she had been carrying a child, Maman had been out of sorts and short-tempered in the beginning. But as soon as she began to show, everything was all right again. Then Maman sang and laughed and made little night-gowns out of flannel and his father went around like an oversized rooster, while the girls clucked like hens and did most of the cooking and his brothers made jokes.

"I swear to God," said the boys, "every time Maman

17

is with child, we lose twenty pounds. The meals are fit only for the Women's Guild of the Sacred Heart at the church."

Yes, thought Armand, Maman is with child and that is why she was not herself today. Perhaps she will have another girl and then things will be even. Six boys and six girls. There is nothing to worry about. The war will not come to Canada.

" . . . and even though she was seven months gone with child—seven months, mind you—the filthy pig raped her."

Armand's head snapped up and he looked down toward the end of the table. His grandfather was listening to Louis Primeau and nodding his head.

"That is the way it has always been with the Germans. Pigs. War-mad swine."

"But we are all behaving like a bunch of old women," said Edouard.

It was the first time one of the younger men had spoken all evening and now everyone turned to look at him.

"After all," continued Edouard, "we are underestimating France. The Germans cannot possibly take over a whole nation of people who know they are on the side of right."

"You are a child, Edouard," said Zenophile coldly. "You are the size of an ox and strong as a bull but you are a child."

Edouard flushed red and Armand knew that his brother wished he had not spoken.

"But France—" began Edouard again.

"The French are not a nation of warriors," said Zenophile. "The French are a nation of lovers."

"Yes," agreed Louis Primeau righteously. "Can you imagine a Frenchman attacking a child? Striking a woman?"

The comforting thought that his mother might be pregnant left Armand.

If the Germans should come to Canada, what would happen to Maman and the girls?

Again, although Armand was looking at the men at the

18

table in Le Pechoir, he could see the dining room at home. It was not yet nine o'clock and his mother would be sitting with his sisters around the big table. She would be mending clothes and his two older sisters, Aurelie and Yvette, would be hemming the sheets that Aurelie would bring to her new home when she married Omer Cormier. Adrienne, the third oldest, would be working at her embroidery, the needle plunging lightning quick through the material within the wooden hoop. She was embroidering pink roses on the pillowcase that would belong to Aurelie. The two little girls, the babies as they were called by the others, would be bent over their schoolbooks. Armand felt a vicious pain in his chest when he thought of Michele, who was eight years old, and of Marie, who was barely seven.

The talk went on and the drinks seemed to be coming closer and closer together and bits of sentences swam in Armand's mind.

Pigs. They raped her and she was seven— What had Louis said? Seven years old and raped by a German? No. No, it could not have been that. Seven months along?

Maman!

Armand stood up abruptly, spilling his drink and making the table sway.

"What is it?" demanded Alcide impatiently.

"I want to go home," said Armand.

"Well, go then," snapped his father. "You will have to walk alone because the rest of us are not ready to leave."

He had turned back to his conversation with Louis and Zenophile and did not even look up as Armand had gone out the door.

The road that led away from Sainte Thérèse was a narrow, winding one and tonight it seemed to be endless as well. The air was still hot, uncooled by the big, bright moon, as Armand walked, half stumbling, toward home.

It must be the drink, thought Armand. For never before

had he imagined that he could feel the tall grass against his thighs as he walked fully clad in the middle of the road. Never before had he fancied that he could smell apple blossoms when the trees were in full fruit or hear the sound of sleigh bells in the heat of an August night. He wanted to run but his legs were too heavy. In fact his whole body felt as if it weighed a ton, and all that he wanted to do was to lie down somewhere to rest, not to think or feel.

He could see lights up ahead now and he knew that he was coming to the farm of Jean Duplessis. He would wait until he had passed the house and then he would lie down in the field beyond. Just for a few minutes, until this heaviness left him. He noticed a light behind a second-floor window in the Duplessis's house. The light came from Cecile Duplessis's bedroom and he wondered what she was doing. Perhaps she was preparing for bed. Brushing her long, black hair in front of a mirror perhaps, with her little pink nipples showing through her nightgown.

Armand laughed aloud and when he came to the field beyond the house he threw himself on the ground and laughed even louder.

It was more or less understood by both the Bergerons and the Duplessis that Armand and Cecile were courting and that one day, perhaps after his older brothers were married, Cecile and Armand would be wed.

It was really funny, thought Armand as he lay on his back and looked up at the undulating sky. Maman and Papa, his brothers, Mr. and Mrs. Duplessis, everybody in Sainte Thé-rèse thought that Cecile was such an angel. They should have known better. It had taken Armand only one look at her and he had known.

Cecile Duplessis had eyes as black as her hair and a fine-grained, white skin that looked thick, like the meringue Armand's mother put on the tops of her lemon pies. She was not big like the Bergeron girls. The top of her head reached only to Armand's armpit and her waist was tiny. She looked like the virgin she was and would remain until she married but Armand knew that this state of affairs was not of her choosing. Little Cecile Duplessis was as hot as a firecracker and she was also a tease. If she wasn't careful she would get herself raped one of these days. God only knew that Armand himself had been tempted more than once.

Armand sat up quickly and the whole world swayed so that he had to press his hands hard against the ground to steady himself.

If Cecile was not careful and the Germans came to Canada . . .

He clipped off the thought and lay back down on the ground very slowly.

But he could not help remembering that way Cecile had of looking up at him out of the corners of her eyes and the way a pink flush showed through her skin when she danced a quadrille with him. He thought of his hand against her little waist, sliding slyly upward until it touched the underslope of her breast and of the way Cecile pretended not to notice.

Oh, she was a firecracker all right, that one. One could lead her out of the Town Hall between dances and down to the sweet-smelling meadow behind and Cecile would let a man do almost anything with her.

He could see her now, lying on the grass, but the man with her was not Armand. The man was a German. An officer who wore a black uniform much decorated with gold and his skin, too, was gold and his hair and his hands were long and slender. Armand could not help himself. He gagged and began to throw up and even when it was over and he lay still on the ground, his sweat like chips of ice all over his body, he could not erase the picture of Cecile.

Her hot little tongue circled his mouth and it took hard, deep kisses to silence her sounds of passion. Armand knew well the feel of her and the sounds she made. It took a long

21

time of kissing, with his hands tangled in the mass of her black hair, pulling, pulling back hard until she began to whimper. Only then would she let him open her bodice and give him her breasts. The sounds never stopped and what she cried out was, "Harder. Harder with your mouth. With your hands. Oh, don't stop."

Her little belly was round and soft and she loved to have it played with. She loved his tongue tickling her navel and the soft, biting kisses.

"Don't stop. Don't stop!"

And then, "That's enough. Stop. Do you hear me? Stop!"

Her arms would look very white in the moonlight as she raised her hand to her head to smooth her hair. The light would gleam on her teeth and she would be laughing.

"It is time to go back to the dance," she would say.

But what if the man with her were not Armand? If it were a German officer and he pushed her back down on the ground? His knee would be hard and hurtful between her soft thighs and Cecile would not be laughing now. She would be screaming but no one could hear. The German would rip into her and move faster and faster and the fields would run red with blood.

Armand turned over on his stomach to shut out the sight and he covered his ears to deaden the sound, but he could not stop the feeling of his body pressed hard against the hot ground.

In and out. In and out. Faster and faster.

His head was pounding, and his heart, and in a few seconds it was over. He fell asleep in his own warm wetness.

An hour later his father spotted him, lying there near the side of the road.

"Well, I'll be goddamned," he said to Zenophile. "I never thought he was *that* drunk."

Edouard and the other boys began to laugh.

"Well, after all, it's his birthday."

They picked him up and put him in the wagon and Armand never stirred.

"He's gone and thrown up all over himself," said Pierre. "Maman will have a fit."

"We'd better clean him up a little before we bring him into the house," Christian said.

"To hell with him," said Jacques. "I don't feel so good myself that I want to wipe up anybody else's puke."

Nevertheless, they stopped at the pump behind the house and attempted to wash him. He awoke then and his brother Antoine began to shake him.

"For God's sake, Armand, take hold of yourself," said Antoine. "Do you want Maman to see you like this?"

They brought him into the house as quietly as possible but it did no good. Berthe was sitting in the kitchen and as soon as she heard them she lit a lamp.

"Well, this is some sight," she said angrily. "All of you drunk and Armand the worst of the lot. All of you should be ashamed of yourselves!"

Armand was dimly aware that his mother was speaking and that he was in the kitchen of his own home.

So. The Germans have not yet come to Canada, he thought.

"Maman," he said. "Maman."

"Just look at you, Armand," said his mother. "You are worse than a pig in his trough."

"Maman," he said again. "Maman, are you going to have a baby?"

Berthe drew herself up to her full height and then she gave him a solid slap across the face.

"Get to bed, you disrespectful boy," she said angrily.

Alcide shrugged. "He's drunker than I thought," he said. "Come on, Edouard. Give me a hand with him."

The next morning, for the first time in his life, Armand

23

sneaked to the sideboard in the dining room and took a drink before breakfast. The liquor settled his stomach and helped to calm his quivering nerves but the heavy depression of the night before would not leave him. He forced himself to work side by side in the fields with his brothers and he made himself smile when they teased him.

"What happened, little brother?" demanded Edouard. "Was all the talk and the drink at Le Pechoir too much for you?"

"You are a little pale today, Armand. Are you not well?"

"What is it, little man? A touch of the grippe, perhaps?"

On the way back to the house for the noon meal, Alcide gave him such a slap on the back that Armand thought his head would surely fall off and roll away.

"Your mother is still sulking at your rudeness, my boy," he said. "You'd best make your apologies before you sit down at the table."

"What are you talking about?" demanded Armand.

"Do you mean to tell me you don't remember?" asked his father.

"Remember what?"

Alcide began to laugh and gave Armand another crack on the back.

"You'd best leave the drinking to the men of the family in the future," he said. "You were indeed drunker than I thought. You were worried about Maman."

"Oh?"

Alcide gave him a dig in the ribs. "Maman is not in the family way," he said. "More's the pity."

Armand was shocked. "Do you mean to say I asked her? Right out to her face?"

"That you did, my boy," said his father. "And you'd better make your peace with her now if you know what's good for you. Ah, a cold bottle of beer is going to taste good."

You cannot imagine how true that is, Papa, thought Armand as they went into the house.

24

Two days later, Omer Cormier came to call on Aurelie and brought the news from Sainte Thérèse. England was at war with Germany.

"France, England, Italy, the whole goddamned world is at war," said Zenophile. "Where will it end?"

Armand's days were filled with the terrible facility he had acquired for seeing many things all at one time. He worked the black soil and saw blood and when he looked at his brothers, vibrant with strength and life, he saw corpses. He watched his mother and sisters as they served food and did their sewing and he saw them lying under the bodies of German officers, their mouths open in soundless screams. His restless nights were a series of horrible dreams from which he awoke exhausted and drenched in his own clamminess. Fear had come to Armand Bergeron for the first time in his life and it took him a week before he realized what he must do.

The next night he took his savings and left the house soon after midnight. He walked all the rest of the night and part of the next morning until he reached the town of Saint Jean Baptiste, where he boarded a train for Montreal.

By four o'clock that afternoon he had been sworn in as a soldier in the British Army and it was only then that he sat down to write to his mother.

He confessed to her that he had lied to the recruiting officer about his age but he said also that he knew she would understand his need to go to war.

"If the Germans come to Canada, dear Maman," he wrote, "they will have to kill me before they can harm a hair of your head or lay one filthy hand on my sisters."

After he had posted his letter he felt well and happy for the first time since his grandfather had told him that France was at war.

Now he was part of it. Part of the strength that was France and England too. He would wear an iron helmet and a uniform and carry a gun and he would kill every German he laid eyes on before the enemy even knew himself to be in danger. It would be rather like stalking deer in the woods, he imagined. All it would take was patience and the ability to move quietly and then bang, bang. The Germans would die like flies. The war would soon be over and Armand would come back a hero, covered with medals, and then he would walk right up to the front door of Jean Duplessis's house and announce that he had come for Cecile. He would marry her and put an end to her teasing forever and he would build himself a house on the acreage his father had always promised would be his.

Much later, Armand remembered those dreams he had dreamed on the day of his enlistment. The British Army had played a good joke on him. At the training camp they found that he had a punctured eardrum and his eyesight was not all it should be. So they sent him to school and made a baker out of him and the closest he ever came to the Germans was when he baked bread at a hospital far behind the front lines in France.

Armand Bergeron did not return to Canada a war hero. And he never married Cecile Duplessis either.

2

It was taking a long time, thought Monique Bergeron. Much too long. According to Dr. Southworth, Armand should have been dead a year ago and still he hung on. An obscenity in her bedroom, a stink in her house, a defilement upon her and her child.

If he had one single ounce of pride left in him, she thought, he would stop this stubborn fighting and die cleanly and quietly. To save the face of his daughter, if for nothing else.

God only knew she expected no consideration at all for herself from Armand but for Angelique, whom he professed to love, he might have shown a little thoughtfulness.

Monique scrubbed savagely at the basin she had used to clean up the mess Armand had made. She scrubbed until her hands were red and sore and the disinfectant had made a hurtful sting on her skin.

It was eleven o'clock at night and she was nowhere near finished with her work. It would be another two hours at least before she could finally turn out all the lights and go to bed.

The miserable pig, she thought. Why won't he get it over and done with? It is going to happen anyway. Why not now? Tonight. But oh, no. Not Armand. No matter what she did he would stay alive. Out of spite if nothing else. Merely to plague her.

She bent and began to wring out the sheets and cloths she

had put into the bathtub to soak and when she was finished she carried them to the kitchen and put them into a tub on the stove to boil. The fire needed stoking and she went to fetch the coal scuttle from the back porch.

It was bitterly cold and she smiled as she thought of Armand shivering in the bed upstairs. The day had not yet come when he could fool her. Especially when he feigned sleep just to make her cleaning up and changing of the bed more difficult.

Monique Bergeron never swore out loud but her thoughts were something else again. Now as she carried the coal scuttle into the kitchen she glanced up at the ceiling and thought of the open window in the bedroom above.

Freeze, you bastard, she said silently.

She piled coal into the big, black stove and then adjusted the draft controls. There was a thin trail of coal dust between the stove and the door and after she had returned the scuttle to the porch, she began to fill a pail with hot water and soap to scrub the floor.

Everyone in town said that Monique Bergeron was the best housekeeper anyone had ever seen, and it was true. But what no one ever realized was the savage anger with which she attacked her chores. There was no love in the care that Monique gave her things. When she polished her furniture she looked upon each piece as a dangerous enemy ready to attack her with filth and germs until she had scrubbed and waxed it into sterile submission. It was the same with her floors and woodwork, with the clothes her family wore. Angelique, her daughter, was the only child in school whose dresses were changed three times a day.

Monique never read a newspaper, let alone a book.

"Who has time for such nonsense?" she had demanded when Armand once asked her why she never looked at the paper he brought home from work every day.

"Who would keep this six-room house clean and neat if

I didn't?" she cried angrily. "Who is going to see that your clothes are washed and ironed if I don't? You'd go to work looking like a filthy pig if I didn't watch you like a child."

Armand sighed. "Pig" and "filthy" were Monique's favorite words.

"Don't you think I'd like to be sprawled out in an easy chair reading the paper the way you are right now?" she asked.

He looked at her for a long moment, seeing her thin body in its spotless starched house dress.

"No, Monique," he had replied. "I don't think you would."

She finished washing the kitchen floor and then, while the sheets and washcloths boiled on the stove, she went upstairs and began to scrub the bathtub. Two hours later she was finished with just about everything. The washing had boiled and been rinsed to her satisfaction and now she put on her coat to go out to hang it on the lines behind the house. She did not put on her gloves and the cold wind cut as she hung up the sheets, which froze as soon as the air hit them.

Everyone in town said the same thing about Monique Bergeron, even Dr. Southworth, who detested her.

"You can tell she's a worker, Mrs. Bergeron," they said. "You have only to look at her hands. She must work like a galley slave in that house."

The only two people who never made comments of that sort were her husband and her daughter—Armand because he could not and Angelique because she never noticed. If Monique had been a weaker woman the tears of pity might have welled up into her eyes now. But she did not cry. She picked up the empty clothes basket and as she moved toward the house she paused and looked up. The bedroom window was closed.

Angelique, she thought angrily, but her anger was not at the child alone. It was for Armand as well. Armand, who, no matter what he did, managed to make the child love him.

29

Monique hung up her coat neatly and then she went to the sideboard in the dining room. She picked up a full bottle of whiskey and made her way silently past Angelique's door to the bedroom where her husband lay.

"Armand," she whispered. "Armand, are you awake?"

He muttered and opened his eyes and the first thing he saw was the bottle in her hand.

She came close to the bed and leaned over him.

"It is such a cold night," she said. "I thought you might like a little drink to warm you."

He tried to raise his head from the pillow as he watched her pour liquor into a water glass on his night table but he could not move. She had to help him. Very quietly and gently she put her arm beneath his head and held the glass to his mouth. He gagged twice but that did not stop him from swallowing.

"Ah," he whispered when the glass was empty, "ah, that is so much better. It is warmer in here now. I was so cold."

She watched his mouth moving and her own mouth tightened in disgust but she kept her voice very low and gentle.

"Yes, Armand," she said. "Now you will sleep."

She waited, unmoving, by the bed until his eyes closed and his breathing became as regular as it ever did these days and then she went silently to the window and raised it as high as it would go. She moved back to the side of the bed and bent over Armand again, making doubly sure that he was asleep, and then she pulled the heavy blankets down to below his knees. She straightened up and looked down at him, smiling, and then she left the room as quietly as she had entered it.

After she had returned the bottle of whiskey to the dining room and before she lay down on the bed in the spare room off the kitchen, she set her alarm for five o'clock. Angelique was never awake before six and that would give her more

30

than enough time to go back to the bedroom, close the window and cover Armand. It would also give the room a chance to warm up before the child went in to pay her father her first visit of the day.

Dr. Benjamin Southworth arrived at the Bergeron house at ten the next morning. Monique saw his car as it turned the corner, which was not at all surprising since she had been standing in front of the parlor window with her coat on ever since Angelique had left for school. She ran out the front door, across the porch and down the steps. She pretended not to see the doctor climbing out of his car as she ran down the walk.

"Monique!" he called after her. "Hold up, Monique!"

She stopped and turned, then ran up to him.

"Oh, dear God, hurry," she cried hysterically. "I was just going to get you. I think he must be dying, Doctor. There is blood all over the room!"

Dr. Southworth pushed her aside and ran into the house and a few minutes later, with his fingers on Armand's wrist, he turned to her.

"You had better go down to the school and fetch Angelique," he said. "He has slipped into a coma and I doubt very much that he will come out of it."

"But it can't be!" said Monique.

"Go for Angelique if you want her to see her father before he dies!"

Monique ran until she was out of sight of the house and then she strolled toward the school. Her explanation to Angelique's teacher was long and involved, for Monique's English was broken and heavily accented. In the end the teacher, a Miss Plankton, sent Monique into the hall and called Angelique out of the class.

The child came, her face scarlet with shame. Her mother was the only woman in the whole town who could not speak

31

English properly. Her explanation to Angelique was rapid and in French.

"I have to go home, Miss Plankton," said Angelique. "My father is very, very sick."

Miss Plankton was immediately sympathetic and very helpful about getting Angelique buttoned into her coat and overshoes while Monique stood by helplessly, wringing her hands.

That poor, poor woman, thought the teacher as she watched the child and her mother leave the building. Poor Mrs. Bergeron. She's had to put up with a lot.

Monique held firmly to Angelique's hand, trying to force her to walk slowly, but the child broke away from her and began to run.

"Papa, Papa," screamed Angelique as she came into the bedroom.

She ran to the bed and would have thrown herself across her father's body if Dr. Southworth had not stopped her.

"Hush, child," he said gently, holding her back. "Hush."

"How is he, Doctor?" asked Monique.

"He is still alive."

"How long?"

"I don't know. Perhaps an hour, maybe less. Maybe more, too. Armand is too stubborn for his own good. You'd better get some rest, Monique. I'll call you."

"No," she said. "I'll stay with him. You have other patients to see."

"There is nothing urgent," the doctor said. "He is my friend. I'll stay with him."

"But there is no need—" Monique began.

The doctor looked at her sharply and put his fingers back on Armand's wrist.

"Go somewhere and lie down, Monique. I'm staying."

He breathed a sigh of relief when she had left the room. His French was much better than Monique's English but it had never been a language in which he felt comfortable and a conversation with Monique always exhausted him. He sat down in the armchair next to the bed and took Angelique into his lap.

"Don't cry, little angel," he said to her. "Don't cry. You see, he is only sleeping."

Of all the foolish, goddamned trite things to say, he thought angrily. What will I tell her when it is over? Don't cry, Angelique. He is not dead. He has just gone away. Oh, Christ.

He smoothed the child's fair hair back from her forehead and wished to hell he had a drink. A double, preferably, without benefit of ice or soda.

Downstairs, Monique lay down on the bed in the spare room but she knew she would not sleep. She made herself lie very still until several minutes had passed and she was sure that the doctor was not coming downstairs for any reason. Then she got up and went to sit in a chair by the window. It was starting to snow. Monique stared out at the slow white flakes for what seemed to her hours and then she turned away and looked down at her hands. They were red, with thousands of tiny cracks in them from cold and wind and disinfectant and soap. Ugly.

Really, she thought, it is time that I started taking better care of myself.

Eventually she stood up and went to her bureau. She rummaged around in the top drawer until she found a fingernail file and then she sat down again. She was humming a little as she began to work on her nails.

3

Monique Montambeault was born in Montreal, Canada, the first child of a couple named Toussaint and Claudette Montambeault, who had never wanted to have children in the first place. Their reasons for this were many and varied but primary among them was the fact that they were second cousins. Besides, in his trade as a blacksmith Toussaint was not particularly well paid, and there was also the circumstance of Claudette's unusually frail health. While none of these reasons, except possibly the first one, would have made any difference in the eyes of most French-Canadian families, they were very important to the Montambeaults.

Within his particular circle of friends and relatives Toussaint was considered to be a bit above himself in his hopes and aspirations. He had been born and raised on a farm outside Sherbrooke, and a not very successful farm at that, and his two brothers worked as miners at Asbestos.

"You have to give it to Toussaint," said some members of his family. "He thinks big."

"He thinks too much of himself, if you ask me," answered most of the others. "Perhaps he imagines that one day he will be a big important businessman in Montreal."

"Ah, it is not all his fault. It is Claudette who is the cause of it."

"Yes. Claudette and her Parisian mother!"

"I swear to God if I hear any more from her about the

34

Champs Elysées and the little dressmakers in the Faubourg Saint Germain, I'll throw up!"

"Yes. If the old lady loved it so much in Paris, why the hell didn't she stay there?"

"Well, if she had, it would at least have spared us Claudette and her fancy talk."

When all was said and done it was really Claudette's way of speaking that annoyed the Montambeaults. She spoke a true French taught to her by her mother and not the bastardized patois used in the towns and villages of French Canada. What was worse, she had taught Toussaint to speak properly and soon his friends and relatives were bitterly sure that he was lost to them forever.

"He is getting above himself," was their favorite expression when the conversation came around to Toussaint. It did not matter that most of his relatives were also related to Claudette.

"Only on her father's side," they hastened to reassure one another. "A good honest man, Claudette's father. A hard worker and just like the rest of us. It was his wife's airs and fancy ways that put Jean Montambeault into an early grave."

But it was not Claudette who had first fired Toussaint with ambition. As far back as he could remember he had wanted something better than the run-down farm of his father or the asbestos mines where his brothers worked. Claudette merely strengthened and extended his dreams for a better future.

"There must be more to life than just this," Toussaint had said when he first met Claudette.

She looked at his father's ill-kept acres and nodded her head.

"There is," she answered.

After they were married they went to Montreal and moved in with Claudette's mother, Henriette.

"You will see," said Claudette. "Soon you will own the

35

blacksmith shop where you now work. And then later you can buy another and another and eventually there will not be a horse in all of Montreal that has not been shod by Toussaint Montambeault."

"Or one of his employees," laughed Toussaint.

Claudette had many long talks with her mother and she understood perfectly what must be done to ensure their future with Toussaint. The insurance money left by Jean Montambeault was not going to last forever, nor was the small legacy willed to Henriette by her parents. They must be careful, said Henriette, and prepare well for their old age.

"Toussaint, are you sure you don't mind about not having children?" asked Claudette.

He kissed her fondly. "What do we need with a passel of brats screaming around the place?" he replied. "No. I had enough of that at home."

But they had been married less than a year when Claudette discovered that she was pregnant. She wept hysterically and fainted so often that Toussaint was afraid she would miscarry, while her mother hoped sincerely that she would hurry up and do so.

"You must be mad, the two of you," said Henriette. "Don't you realize, Toussaint, what can happen when cousins reproduce themselves?"

"I know," replied Toussaint. "But let us not remind Claudette of that."

"There is no need to remind her," said Henriette grimly. "She is already much aware of it."

Claudette continued to weep and faint all through her pregnancy and Toussaint lived with fear and his mother-in-law's predictions of doom.

It was into this household that Claudette was finally delivered of a five-and-a-half-pound daughter. The parish priest from Sainte Marie's came to the house to baptize the baby within an hour of its birth for it was unheard of for a child that small to live. Claudette named her daughter Monique and fully expected her to be dead before the day was over.

But Monique did not die. She grew into a fat, rosy-cheeked child who had naturally curly dark hair and none of the symptoms which are supposed to be the mark of an offspring born of second cousins. For the first time in her life Claudette, who had been an only child, had someone to think of besides herself. She watched her baby develop and wondered at the marvelous sense of accomplishment that filled her.

"We have been blessed," declared Claudette.

"You've been lucky," said Henriette sourly. "And no clever human being pushes his luck."

"No, Maman," replied Claudette docilely.

Toussaint was happier than he had ever been in his life. While it was true that his wife had remained weak for a long time after the birth of Monique, by the time the child was a few months old Claudette had regained her strength and was blooming like a rose. She had not kept the weight put on during her pregnancy and her waist now was as slender as a young virgin's. Just to look at her made Toussaint feel like a young boy.

"Sometimes when your husband looks at you," said Henriette, "I cannot help but be reminded of a stallion."

"Yes," replied Claudette and blushed prettily.

"You'd better watch yourself," said Henriette.

"Of course, Maman," said Claudette, as docile as ever.

Monique took her first steps when she was only nine months old and even Henriette had to acknowledge that this was something of a miracle. That evening the old lady broke out a bottle of her best wine to celebrate.

"Thank God we've come out of this with a normal child, at least," she said.

Claudette drank two glasses of wine with her meal and then promptly fainted.

"It is the excitement," said Toussaint.

37

Henriette looked down at her pale-faced daughter lying on the sofa where Toussaint had placed her.

"It is like hell," she said bluntly.

"What do you mean?" Toussaint demanded.

Henriette sighed. "I'll wager the best pair of matched horses in all of Montreal that she is that way again."

"It can't be," said Toussaint, frightened.

But it was and the three of them went through it all again. The weeping, the fainting, the fear, until Toussaint thought that he would lose his mind and took to lighting a candle at Sainte Marie's every morning on his way to work. He had never been a religious man but when Claudette was eventually delivered of a second daughter, who proved to be frail but normal, Toussaint went to Sainte Marie's and lit every candle on the rack. The child was baptized Antoinette and Henriette began her lectures on birth control all over again.

Claudette nodded and said, "Yes, Maman." She smiled and blushed, but a year later she gave birth to a son, who was christened Ansele. He was born stone deaf. She never seemed quite to recover from the birth of this third child and when Ansele was six months old Claudette died, of what the best doctors in Montreal said was consumption.

"It is all your doing!" Henriette screamed at her son-in-law. "She had everything to live for. Youth, beauty, a nice home. But oh, no. That wasn't enough, was it? She had to produce young like a rabbit. Like a stinking rabbit in a hutch! Look at what you have caused, Toussaint Montambeault!"

Toussaint continued to live in Henriette's house and to work in the blacksmith shop, while Henriette, with the air of a martyred saint, looked after the children. Before too many months had passed, Toussaint began to notice that the children cried a lot, more than they had ever done before, and that Monique, who had been a happy, outgoing child, was turning into a sullen, temperamental little girl. Within a year the situation had become intolerable and Toussaint knew that he would have to do something, not only for his own sanity but to protect his children.

In the minds of most French-Canadians, the United States of America was simply a place on the map located to the south of Canada. It was a never-never land into which a few of their countrymen had migrated, never to return. But by the time his son, Ansele, was a year and a half old, the United States had become the one hope left in an almost hopeless world to Toussaint Montambeault.

Surely, he reasoned, there were as many horses in the United States as there were in Canada. And these horses would be as badly in need of shoeing as they were anywhere else. In the United States, too, there would be farm equipment in need of repair and iron fences to be built.

Toussaint had a friend, Aristide Jolicoeur, who had gone to America a few years before and had never come back. At first Aristide had written letters to Toussaint but Toussaint had not replied after the first few times and eventually Aristide stopped writing.

Now Toussaint hunted through the trunk full of things he had brought to Montreal from his father's farm and at last he found one of Aristide's old letters. That same night he sat down and wrote to his old friend.

"There is opportunity here such as you have never dreamed of," Aristide wrote back. "You must come at once. It is true that I remember your wife's branch of the Montambeault family and you have my profound sympathy. You must come to the United States at once."

Aristide wrote also that he had begun his life in America as a mill hand in the textile factories and in five years he had managed to save enough money to open his own grocery store.

It seemed like a miracle to Toussaint. In only five years his friend had risen from a lowly employee to the owner of his own business. But what was even more important, Aristide concluded his letter with the words Toussaint wanted most desperately to hear.

"You must come to us with your children," wrote Aristide. "Jacqueline and I have six of our own so three more will not make that much difference to us. You will stay with us until you secure a job and then I will help you find a place to live. Hurry, old friend. It has been too many years since we have seen you."

And so, on the tenth of August, 1900, Toussaint Montambeault had a rousing vocal battle with his mother-in-law. He packed his things and those of his three children and boarded the train for a place with the unimaginable name of Livingstone, New Hampshire. When he arrived at his destination he had two very grimy little girls who trailed wearily behind him, and a crying baby in his arms.

He also had seventeen dollars in his pocket and a box of blacksmith tools.

4

The house in which Aristide Jolicoeur and his family lived was a two-and-a-half-story building of gray clapboard located halfway between Sherman and Eastman Streets. Eastman Street was the main street of Livingstone, New Hampshire, and it was here, on the choice corner where Eastman was bisected by Atwood Street, the city's second most important business street, that Aristide had his grocery store.

America was indeed a marvelous country, Aristide told Toussaint, when all a man had to do was roll out of his bed in the morning, eat his good breakfast and then saunter only a block away to his place of business. And it would be just as wonderful for Toussaint too, for there was a forge located only two blocks away from the Jolicoeur house.

"You will see, Toussaint," said Aristide. "You will thank God that you came to the United States. It will be a whole new life for you."

And it was. Within two days after his arrival in Livingstone, Toussaint had a job with the Cartier Forge and Iron Works Company at almost twice the money he had been earning in Montreal, and in even less time than that his family had settled down and become a part of the Jolicoeur household.

"Don't worry about space, Toussaint," said Jacqueline. "Above these two floors there is an attic and we will put beds up there for the older children. Ansele can sleep in the bed with Jacques in our room and you can have a bed in the room with three of our boys. You will see, everything will be perfect."

So it happened that years later, when Monique Montambeault tried to recall her first conscious memory of her life in America, she thought of a dark attic room which she shared with her sister, Antoinette, and three of the Jolicoeur girls, Annette, Beatrice and Marguerite. She remembered the way the light from the kerosene lamp cast frightening shadows on the walls and she would hear Antoinette crying. Antoinette imagined great monsters with two heads in the shadows, monsters who had huge, sharp-taloned claws and who waited only for her to climb up the stairs into that attic before they grabbed her.

It seemed to Monique that in her memory Antoinette was always crying, but at least Antoinette cried only in the dark when she was frightened. Her brother, Ansele, was something else again. Ansele cried all the time and he cried loudly as if, knowing he was deaf, he also wanted the whole world to know it.

By the time she was six years old and enrolled at Saint George's Parochial School, Monique had developed a deep hatred for small crowded rooms and for all small children. It was not until she was seven that she began to hate all grownups in general and men in particular. It had been when she was seven years old that her father decided that what he needed was a wife for himself and his children. Monique overheard him, one night, discussing it with Aristide and Jacqueline Jolicoeur and both of them could not have agreed more heartily with Toussaint.

"You are still a young man," said Aristide and slapped Toussaint across the back. "It is not right for you to be alone."

Jacqueline laughed. "Aristide is right, Toussaint. After all, it you wanted to spend your life alone you could have been a priest, eh?"

"I have never had the least desire to be a priest," said Toussaint and he, too, laughed.

Monique listened and wanted to run at them and beat all three of them with her fists.

Why were they making fun of the priests? she wondered angrily. She saw priests every day when she went to school. They lived in the rectory right next door to the church and they were always clean. At morning Mass their surplices were blindingly white, starched and ironed so that there was not a wrinkle anywhere, and on Sundays they were of white lace, made with painstaking care by the nuns, and their white collars never showed a single smudge. Every single day when Aristide came home at noon his apron was covered with blood and filth from the grocery store and at night Toussaint had to stand on newspapers and change his clothes in the kitchen because of the black dirt that covered him. Even on Sundays Toussaint's fingernails were black and the smell of dead chickens never quite left Aristide.

The house itself smelled, thought Monique, but the rectory where the priests lived was different. The Jolicoeur house smelled of baby urine and throw-up and it smelled of cooking and dirty clothes and too many people in too little space. But once a nun had sent Monique to fetch one of the priests and she had waited for him in the little office off the hallway in the rectory. The room smelled of furniture polish and incense and soap and to Monique it was the most wonderful aroma she had ever breathed.

Someday, she told herself, I am going to live in a house like that. It will smell good all the time and everywhere you look things will shine and look back at you. It won't be like this, she thought. And I won't be like them.

"You must go to Montreal," Aristide was saying. "I will arrange everything with Cartier at the forge."

"It will be a good thing," said Jacqueline. "Your children need a mother and while God only knows that I could not love your little ones more, it is not the same."

"You are right," said Toussaint decisively. "Aristide, you

go to Cartier and tell him there has been a death in the family and that I will have to be gone for a few days."

Aristide laughed and pounded the table and Jacqueline poured wine.

"You old bastard, Toussaint," roared Aristide. "A few days indeed! Just listen to him, Jacqueline, the old cock. A few days and he will come back to us with a bride!"

"Well, after all, why not?" said Jacqueline. "Look at him. Strong, handsome, still young. What woman could resist him, eh?"

Monique peeked around the corner of the doorway. It was true, she thought. Her father *was* strong and handsome. But he was other things too. He was dirty and he was a liar.

Children have no sense of time. Not even French-Canadian children in attic bedrooms. Every day seems long to them and a year is an unimaginable stretch of weeks that will never end.

Monique Montambeault did not really remember just when her father married Georgette Delacroix except that it was during the year that she was eight years old. It seemed to her that one day there had been a great deal of company in the Jolicoeur house and all the men got drunk and then the next day she and Antoinette and Ansele had moved into a house on Pine Street together with Toussaint and his new wife, Georgette.

This house was no different from the house of Aristide and Jacqueline Jolicoeur. It was the same two-and-a-half-story gray clapboard, of the type which had originally been built by one man to house one family. But with the great influx of French-Canadians who had come to Livingstone to work in the Northeast mills, the men who owned these houses had seen an opportunity to make money, a lot of it. Most of the houses had been converted into two-family and in some cases even three-family dwellings, when the landlord had been clever enough to utilize the attic. The Jolicoeurs had been for-

44

tunate in having a whole house to themselves but they were the rare exception. Not one family in a hundred had an entire house. These converted buildings came eventually to be known as "tenements" and in many, many cases the first English words a French-Canadian child learned to read were those on the white-lettered blue card in the window of an empty dwelling: "Tenement to Let."

To Monique Montambeault the only difference in her surroundings was that now the family occupied a single floor and she and Antoinette no longer had to sleep in an attic. She and her sister and her brother slept in one bedroom while Toussaint and his new wife occupied the other. There was also a parlor with stiff, dark furniture that Georgette had brought with her from Canada and a kitchen with a big wooden table and straight-backed wooden chairs and a black stove that was used for both cooking and heating. The toilet was in the back hall and the Montambeaults shared it with the Ladieus, who lived on the second floor, and the Guilmettes, who occupied the attic.

All the rest of her life Monique carried the memory of needing to go to the bathroom and of having to wait until someone else had finished.

Toussaint Montambeault and his family lived just the way every other French-Canadian family in Livingstone, New Hampshire, lived before the First World War. The one thing that set him apart was that he worked as a blacksmith instead of a mill hand, but in all other respects his life conformed to the accepted pattern. He worked from six o'clock in the morning until six o'clock at night from Monday through Saturday and his Sundays were given over to going to Mass and to visiting his friends or receiving them in his own home. His wife, like every other wife, put in the same long hours as her husband, with the added burden of cooking enormous meals on the Sundays when her family did not go visiting.

Like all the others, the Montambeault children went to a

French Catholic school. The exception, of course, was Ansele, but even with his handicap there was a certain niche into which he fitted. Ansele belonged to the group of children made up of the unfortunates—the deaf like himself, the blind, the crippled and the retarded, for whom the French-Canadians had an idiom all their own.

"Il n'est pas tout là," they said about such children. "He is not all there."

It was into this last category that his own particular world placed Ansele, for along with being deaf he also could not talk. It never occurred to anyone that Ansele was far from being mentally retarded, that it was simply because he could not hear that he could not talk. His only path to knowledge was through observation and for a child alone in a silent world this is a dark and difficult road indeed.

And so Ansele Montambeault, like the others of his kind, did not go to school. He helped Georgette around the house with the tasks that did not demand intelligence, like wringing out the wash and scrubbing floors. He learned to amuse himself in his own mind and was very used to being ignored.

The only time anyone ever paid any attention to Ansele was when they looked at him and said, "He's not all there, that one. He won't live long. They never do."

By the time Monique Montambeault was thirteen years old, Georgette and Toussaint had produced three children, all girls, whom they named Helene, Francoise and Therese, and Monique had decided upon her life's vocation. She was going to be a nun.

"But, Monique," protested Antoinette, who was the only person in whom Monique confided, "it's not any fun to be a sister. You have to stay locked up in the convent most of the time and you have to wear a black habit. I'll bet those things weigh a ton and you have to wear them all the time. Even when it's hot in the summer. And when they do unlock the door and let you out you have to have another nun with you every single minute so you can't even go to the store for an ice cream or anything. So who wants to be an old sister anyway?"

"It is the divine will of God," replied Monique piously.

Antoinette laughed. "What are you talking about?"

"I mean exactly what I say," Monique answered without the trace of a smile.

"You mean you had a vision?" asked Antoinette, awed into seriousness. "Like Joan of Arc?"

"Yes," whispered Monique. "That's what it was. I had it in a dream. God told me to be a nun."

She told this story to Antoinette so often that in the end she came to believe it herself and it became a cloak to hide the ugliness of her existence.

Nuns lived in clean, sweet-smelling, shining convents where no noise ever intruded. At the end of each day a nun went to chapel. She did not stand in a back hallway sweeping the dust and filth off a man before he was fit to enter the house. She did not have to change babies nor wash their stinking diapers nor give her breast to them when they screamed. In the convent there were none of the hard, grunting sounds that Monique could hear almost every night coming from the bedroom Toussaint shared with his new wife, nor did nuns grow periodically fat and ungainly in order that they might eventually produce a bloody, slimy baby who cried and dirtied itself and took up space.

Monique's dream of salvation carried her through all the distasteful tasks she was forced to perform. It helped her bear the sounds of fornication made by her father and Georgette and it saved her from fear when Georgette lay in her bed screaming and writhing and being delivered of a child. It kept her warm in winter and allowed her to be detached all through the hot, noisy, bad-smelling summers. It lasted indeed until she was fourteen years old.

On the afternoon of her fourteenth birthday, Georgette told her to get dressed in her Sunday clothes.

47

"But whatever for?" asked Monique. It was unheard of to get all dressed up during the week.

"Because we are going downtown," Georgette answered impatiently. "To the City Hall."

"To the City Hall?" echoed Monique stupidly.

Like every other child, she knew what the only reason was for anyone to go to the City Hall. Nobody ever went there except to get a work permit.

"Of course to the City Hall," said Georgette. "You are fourteen years old. Did you think you were going to laze around and go to school for the rest of your life?"

That same evening, after supper, Alphonse Cartier, for whom Toussaint worked, came to the Montambeault house. He looked at Monique as if she had been a side of beef in Aristide Jolicoeur's market.

"She's skinny enough."

"But she's strong," said Georgette quickly. "Strong as a horse."

Cartier sighed and shrugged.

"I don't know," he said. "She doesn't look very strong to me."

"But she is," protested Georgette. "She is. Here, Monique, lift something and show Mr. Cartier how strong you are."

"Never mind. Never mind," Cartier replied. "I'll speak to Leroux at the mill. He's second in command in the spinning room. Maybe he can use her."

"Oh, thank you, Mr. Cartier," said Georgette. "Thank you very much."

"Papa!" cried Monique. "Papa!"

Toussaint looked at her and shrugged.

"We need another pay coming into the house, Monique," he said. "And you are the oldest."

The next day Monique went to work as an apprentice spinner at the Northeast Manufacturing Company. It was the end of her dream and the end of her childhood.

5

He is going to die today, thought Dr. Benjamin Southworth as he looked down at Armand Bergeron. He cannot possibly come out of this again. It just goes to show that you never can tell. Yesterday afternoon he seemed a little better and now today he is going to die.

The doctor continued to stare at his friend. In his lap the child Angelique was quieter now, although she too stared fixedly at the man in the bed.

Jesus, I wish I had a drink.

He laughed at himself.

Even with this pitiful example staring me in the face, he thought, I still want a drink. I'm a bigger fool than Armand ever was.

Benjamin Southworth had been born, raised and had lived all his life, except for the years of his schooling, in the town of Amity, New Hampshire. He knew every single person in town by his first name and he also knew the most intimate facts about each of them. But he had never been able to understand why Armand Bergeron had come to live in Amity with his French-speaking wife. In his trade as a baker Armand could have worked in any city at twice the money he earned here and his wife could have lived among her own kind. Yet Armand had come to Amity and had lived there for more than a dozen years. Eventually he had become manager of the Sunny Day Baking Company, which sounded much grander than it actually was. Sunny Day was a very small company which supplied bread and pastry to Amity and its surrounding towns and it was less than a quarter the size of a bakery in almost any small city.

The Bergerons were the only French-Canadian family in town and Monique its only French-speaking woman. There was not even a Catholic church in Amity and on Sundays Monique lit candles and she and Angelique said prayers at home. Once a month a priest came up from the nearest city, Franklin, to hear their confessions and to serve Communion, though Armand would have no part of what he called these shenanigans. Monique Bergeron had never even bothered to learn to speak English, nor had she ever become a citizen of the United States. It was enough, she said, that her husband had.

So why live in Amity? the doctor had often wondered. Why live as strangers in a small Yankee town rather than in a city like Livingstone, where Monique could have belonged to a particular group who spoke her language and attended her church?

"It's the way she wanted it," Armand had once told him.

"Don't misunderstand me, my friend," the doctor had replied. "It's not that I want you to move away. Hell, who'd stay up nights and drink with me if you left? It's just that I can't help but be curious because I know damned well that Monique does not feel at home here. She has no friends. She never goes anywhere. It must be lonely as hell for her."

"Who knows the mind of a woman?" Armand had asked. "Especially a woman like Monique. Come on, let's forget it. Have another drink."

The doctor had dropped the subject then and there but he still sometimes wondered. It never occurred to him that he was asking the wrong person. He should have gone to Monique. She could, if she had so chosen, have put his mind at rest.

50

6

In the year that Monique Montambeault went to work there, the Northeast Manufacturing Company was more powerful than it had ever been. Fifteen thousand of the city's forty thousand inhabitants depended on the mill for their livelihood and a great number of Americans everywhere depended on its gingham and chambray, its tickings and towelings and shirtings and its worsted and other dress goods. Every single weekday, the company's million spindles spun out one mile of cloth every minute and in Boston the financiers and bankers sat on their bony behinds and counted the profits with their thin, dry fingers and congratulated one another through narrow, vinegary lips. They had built more than a city on the banks of the Merrimack River up there in New Hampshire. They had shaped the destinies of thousands of people but they were content to enjoy their power in anonymity. Not one out of a thousand of the company's employees knew that their very lives depended on a group of men who sat behind mahogany desks in far-off Boston, Massachusetts. To the average mill hand, the men who "owned" the mills were the Archibalds, the Atwoods and the Eastmans. The men who lived in houses as big as palaces on North King Street and along the North River Road.

The ancestors of these men had built the original mills back in the early eighteen hundreds but as time passed the need for expansion came and it was then that the descendants of these founding fathers went to the Boston bankers. The mills that had been known as Northeastern Fine Cloth became the Northeast Manufacturing Company, and the Archibalds, the Atwoods and the Eastmans were merely stockholders to whom was left the actual physical running of the mills.

But in the year 1912, all three of these families were sure that the death knell of Northeast had been sounded, for in that year all the paternal rules, written in almost Biblical language by their forefathers, were suddenly scrapped.

Old Ezekiel Atwood had written:

"Any single person who comes to be employed shall be sent to board in one of the Company's boardinghouses, where he shall live in an atmosphere at once moral and pleasant."

And old Peregrine Archibald had decreed:

"The Company will not employ any person who is absent from public worship on the Sabbath, nor one who uses profane, indecent or questionable language in the mills or elsewhere, nor one who uses ardent spirits as a beverage."

But it was old Harvey Eastman, for whom the main street of the city had been named, who had really set the pattern which was most effected:

"At four-thirty in the morning," old Harvey Eastman had established, "the mill bells will be rung to awaken the keepers of the boardinghouses. It shall then be their responsibility to sound the call to breakfast at five-thirty and it shall be the responsibility of every employee to be at his machine at six-thirty, when work will begin. At high noon the Company will give to each and every one of its employees one half hour to be used to partake of the noon meal. The employee is expected to be back at his machine promptly at twelve-thirty in the afternoon and any defection of this rule is grounds for immediate dismissal from the Company's employ. At seven-thirty in the evening the mills will close for the day and every employee shall leave the premises within ten minutes of

52

the dismissal bell. He shall then proceed to his particular boardinghouse, where he will receive his supper at eight o'clock. All lamps and candles shall be extinguished in the boardinghouses at no later than nine-thirty in the evening."

And then, as one of the present "owners" put it, the bottom fell out of the boat. The state enacted a law that limited the work week to only fifty-five hours and there was gloom in the houses of the Archibalds, the Atwoods and the Eastmans.

"We will be bankrupt within a year," they all said.

"The workers will grow so lazy we won't be able to get a decent day's work out of them."

"Well, we shall have to make the best of it," said Lawrence Archibald. "It is the law."

Lawrence was the eldest member of any of the three families and he regarded himself as forward-looking, progressive and something of a poet. Every year, on the day before Christmas, he closed the mills one half hour earlier than usual so the employees could gather in the main mill yard to listen to the speech that he himself had written for their spiritual uplift. The name of the oration was "The River" and he always introduced it in just that way.

" 'The River,' by Lawrence W. Archibald," he would announce in tones loud and ringing enough to echo over all the heads assembled before him.

"And so it came to pass that the mighty Algonquin Indian bent to his task at the whirling pools of the mighty Falls where he gathered up his winter's store of fish. Then he transported his squaw and his papoose in his birch-bark canoe across the smooth surface of the River to lose himself in the mighty forest where his tepee was hidden. Little else disturbed the even tenor of the River's way. But times changed with the coming of the white man. Then the mighty Merrimack, formed by the junction of the Pemigewasset and the Winnipesaukee at what is now the city of Franklin, New

53

Hampshire, was subdued and its mighty powers forced to do its master's will.

"But it was not the River alone, but rather the great and mighty Falls, where the water tumbled over the ledges and roared defiance to all intruders, that determined this site as a proper place for manufacturing. Here, then, because the mighty power of the River could be most practically developed, were born the Northeast Manufacturing Company and the mighty city of Livingstone."

As soon as Lawrence Archibald finished speaking, the mill hands looked at one another for a moment and then broke out into a roar of enthusiastic cheering, whistling and hand clapping. In all the years that Lawrence gave his little speech it never once occurred to him that he was speaking to a crowd made up almost entirely of French-Canadians, Greeks and Poles who had not understood one single word he uttered.

"You did beautifully, dear," Louise Archibald said to her husband each year.

"Thank you, my dear," Lawrence would reply. "It gives them something to ponder over, I think. A lot of poetry there, and a little geography."

"I suppose so, dear," Louise would reply, "although I must say that I've never heard of a mill hand with a penchant for poetry."

Louise would have been surprised indeed to meet one Patrick Joseph Noonan. Patrick was an immigrant Irishman and he, too, was a poet. Sometimes on Saturday nights when he got drunk enough he would recite his poem for his friends:

> If your nose is close to the grindstone enough
> And you hold it down there long enough,
> In time you'll say there's no such thing
> As brooks that babble and birds that sing.
> These three will all your world compose
> Just you—the stone—and your goddamned nose.

54

Monique Montambeault had worked in the mill for over three months before she discovered that there were people who actually dreamed of getting away from what she regarded as her red-brick prison. While it was true that the employees of the Northeast Manufacturing Company were French-Canadian by an overwhelming majority, there had been an influx during the past few years of Greeks, Poles and Irish who settled in Livingstone and eventually came to work for the company.

The Greeks worked with a singleness of purpose. To make money. The Greek ate lunches of black bread soaked in olive oil and he usually lived in the poorest place he could find and he lived alone. He had left his family behind while he came to America to make his fortune. The Greek saved his money with almost maniacal care and one day Monique found out why. The Greek saved his money so that one day he could return to what he called "the old country" and buy an olive grove.

In his broken English the Greek explained, "I will have an olive grove of my own and in the eyes of my countrymen I will be a millionaire."

Monique, who very, very seldom spoke to anyone, went out of her way to question the man who worked on the spinning frames next to hers.

"Zephrin," she asked, "what are you going to do when you stop working in the mill?"

Zephrin Bolduc looked at her as if she had lost her senses.

"Are you crazy?" he demanded. "Why should I stop working in the mill?"

"I thought that perhaps you wanted to return to your village in Canada one day."

"You *are* crazy." Zephrin laughed. "Go back there? My girl, you have been spoiled by this short work week. When I first came here we worked seventy-five hours a week and it was still paradise compared to the hours I worked on the

55

farm. And it was not even the farm of my father, you understand. No. I worked for an old bastard named Hector LaPointe who worked the ass off me and paid me twenty-five cents a day. Oh, yes, the son of a bitch gave me my meals too. Bread and lard at noon and fat meat and greens for supper. Go back to that? As I said, you *are* crazy."

"But I didn't mean to go back like that," Monique said. "I meant if you saved up your money and bought your own farm."

"And who is going to save money with ten children to feed and a wife who wants a new hat every time she goes to the store, eh? No, my girl. I'm not going anywhere. In fact, I am going to become a citizen next month."

"But then you'll never escape," cried Monique.

Zephrin finished the bobbins on one of his frames before he turned to look at her.

"Escape from what, for God's sake?" he asked in exasperation.

"From this," said Monique and gestured toward the spinning frames. "From all this."

"Ah," said Zephrin. "You are talking like a Greek or one of those goddam Polacks."

"They are not the same thing, the Greeks and the Polacks," said Monique and went back to her work.

It was true. While the Greek wanted to get out not only of the mills but also of the country, the Pole was content to eat his lunch of bread and salt pork and to save his money to buy a piece of land on the outskirts of the city.

"Just a small piece of land," said the Pole. "Then I will have a garden and a place to keep a couple of pigs and a cow. And someday I will not work here in the mill. I will be a farmer and every day I will bring fruit and vegetables to the market to sell."

The Irishman, too, was different. All he wanted was to

56

save up enough money to buy a saloon and then he would spend all his time in a white apron behind a polished bar and make so much money he would be able to live like a king forever.

But I am not a Greek or a Pole or an Irishman, thought Monique. I am a French-Canadian and I cannot eat black bread and olive oil or salt pork and I cannot run a saloon. I cannot wear filthy rags next to my skin nor live in a cellar and I will never get out. Never!

She stared down the long aisles between the spinning machines and the frames seemed never to end. She would live in a world where the floors beneath her feet always shook and where one had to shout to make oneself heard.

Standing next to her, Zephrin Bolduc coughed and brought up a great gob of phlegm, which he swirled around in his mouth and deposited neatly on the floor between two of the machines. Monique's stomach turned over and she felt like crying.

On the day that the United States of America declared war on Germany, the Archibalds, the Atwoods and the Eastmans got together and gave a party. The men came scandalously close to becoming what Louise Archibald referred to as "tipsy" and the women laughed a great deal at the antics of their men.

Surely there was just cause for celebration, for America was certainly in no danger of losing the war and now that the Northeast Manufacturing Company would work day and night, twenty-four hours around the clock, the United States government would pour money in an unending stream into the mills. At last things would be back to normal, the way they had been in the old days before any ridiculous state laws were passed to pamper the workers. Everything would be as it should be. For the Archibalds, the Atwoods and the Eastmans.

To Monique Montambeault, and others like her, it seemed

57

as if the war would never end. She had never realized how many women there were in the city of Livingstone. There were women in the mills, uoing the jobs that men had always done before, and there were hordes of women on the streets, in the shops, in the churches. She worked with women who wept almost constantly and who took to buying newspapers for the first time in their lives. These were the women who bought Government bonds and scanned the casualty lists, who wept and wept so they could not do their jobs properly.

Will it never end? thought Monique, for whom the war was a series of petty aggravations. No sugar, poor clothing and the incessant clatter of knitting needles on the streetcars.

But, of course, it did end and with the end of the war came Monique's salvation.

What saved Monique from the mills, her wretched home and a life she hated could have been put into one word, and that word was "influenza."

In the autumn of 1918, influenza, like one of the four horsemen of the Apocalypse, galloped into the northern hemisphere of the world. From their pulpits Catholic priests urged the need for confession, Communion and constant prayer, while the Revivalists screamed: "Repent and be saved!" The doctors merely preached cleanliness and isolation.

In October, 1918, Dr. Maxwell Thompson, who served part time as the company physician, went to see Lawrence Archibald.

"Lawrence," said the doctor, "you've got to close down the mills until this epidemic is under control."

"Maxwell," Lawrence replied, "you are talking like an old woman. Just because there are a few sick people in town doesn't mean that there is an epidemic. We will keep the mills open as usual."

"Forty per cent of Livingstone's population is down with influenza," yelled the doctor. "Is that what you call a few sick

58

people? A lot more than a few people have already died and a great many more are going to be dead before this is over. You *must* close down the mills."

"Listen here, Maxwell. The country is in dire need of the cloth we manufacture. The nation is tired of war and of uniforms and of doing without. Women want gingham to make into pretty dresses and men want worsteds to be made into suits. The mills are working two shifts as it is and we still can't keep up with the demand. I tell you no and for the last time. We *must* keep going and we *will* keep going."

The doctor sat down tiredly and it was no wonder. Like doctors everywhere, Maxwell Thompson often went without sleep for sixty hours at a stretch. His whole body was sore with weariness, his head pounded with it and his nerves trembled with it.

"Lawrence," he said, trying hard to keep his voice calm, "you are taking a terrible responsibility upon yourself. You know that, don't you? Influenza spreads through a community by the transfer of germs from sneezing and coughing. It spreads from the excretions of the respiratory tract or by what is called snot and spit by your mill hands."

"For God's sake, Maxwell!" Lawrence performed a fastidious pursing of his lips.

"Shut up, Lawrence, and listen to me. How long has it been since you took a long walk through the mills?"

"You know very well that I go to the mills every single day, Maxwell."

"Yes," said the doctor. "You go to your nice, clean, carpeted, uncrowded office. But tomorrow you are going to come with me. We'll walk through the spinning rooms and the weaving rooms. We'll go down into the dye house and the shipping rooms and you'll watch the men who blow their noses through their fingers and the ones who spit out their chewing tobacco on the floor. You'll watch the women who

59

don't take their hands off the work for a minute to cover up a sneeze or a cough and you'll feel the wet heat in those rooms. When we're finished I guarantee that you'll be able to hear influenza growing and spreading, spreading into every last corner of your mills!"

"You're mad," said Lawrence, but he had grown pale. "I can't close the mills, Maxwell. The decision is not mine to make in the first place. Remember the stockholders—"

"Fuck your goddamned stockholders!" shouted Maxwell Thompson. "Do you think I give one jolly—"

"Thompson," Lawrence said icily, "you might remember that my wife is in the next room."

"I don't give a shit about your wife or anybody else's wife," roared the doctor. "I'm concerned with fifteen thousand people who are in desperate danger because you're worried about your goddamned stockholders."

"That will be just about enough," said Lawrence and stood up to terminate the interview. "The Northeast Manufacturing Company has never closed its doors and it is not going to do so now! Good day."

"I am not a religious man, Lawrence," said the doctor as he headed toward the door. "But I would not want to be in your shoes today. Surer than Hell or Heaven you will be punished for what you are doing."

"Good day, Maxwell," repeated Lawrence Archibald.

"God help you," Maxwell Thompson replied.

The first member of the Montambeault family to be struck down was Therese, the youngest child of the union between Toussaint and Georgette. Within three days of the time she first fell ill she contracted pneumonia, and less than a week later she was dead. At the age of six, Therese Montambeault became a statistic, one of the 548,000 people who died in the flu epidemic.

Along with the other members of her family, Monique had taken her turn in caring for the sick child but forever after, the true horror of the whole thing, to Monique, had not been in nursing Therese or in watching the poor child choke to death. It had been the sight of the little body in its white coffin laid out in the Montambeault parlor for five days awaiting burial. To have a solemn requiem High Mass sung in a Catholic church in Livingstone, New Hampshire, in the autumn of 1918 was almost as difficult as getting an appointment with the President of the United States. On the fifth day, when Therese Montambeault was finally buried, there were six funerals in Saint George's Church before hers and when it was over, Father Rolland, who had conducted the Mass, dropped in his tracks and was rushed to the hospital, where he died that same night.

A week later Georgette and all the children except Antoinette and Monique had contracted influenza. Antoinette, who had been working in the mills with her sister for the past three years, was elected to stay home and care for the sick.

"Antoinette will stay home," Georgette told Toussaint from her sickbed. "Monique gets a better pay and God only knows we need every cent she can make. Now let us pray that neither of you come down sick."

For three days Monique fought the fever that burned in her body. Her legs ached so that she could scarcely stand in front of the spinning frames and her arms hurt so much that tears came to her eyes when she tried to reach the topmost bobbins on the machines. On the fourth day she fainted and lay on the floor for over an hour because no one wanted to risk infection by touching her.

Dr. Maxwell Thompson found her as he was making one of his unending rounds through the mills.

"Another one," he said hopelessly and picked her up. "Dear God, where is the end to this thing?"

The doctor took her home and then turned his helpless rage on Toussaint.

"Do you know that your daughter has been walking around with influenza for three days?" he demanded. "Do you have the faintest glimmering of an idea of how many people she may have infected in that length of time? What the hell's the matter with you Canucks anyway? This girl may die. In fact, it's a miracle that she isn't dead already."

Silently, Toussaint led the doctor to one of the two bedrooms in the house. He opened the door and let Dr. Maxwell Thompson look in at his wife and the rest of his children.

"Oh, sweet, suffering Jesus!" said the doctor.

Monique, fortunately, was much stronger than her frail body would have led anyone to believe. In less than a week the fever had left her and she began to recover. But life in the Montambeault household was like a vicious merry-go-round. Monique was soon well enough to help Antoinette with the others and finally Georgette was back on her feet. But Ansele grew sicker and sicker and Helene and Francoise were so weak that they had to be spoon-fed.

"Ansele is going to die," Antoinette told Monique.

"Well, he would not have lived much longer in any case," said Georgette.

The next day Antoinette fell ill and on top of everything else, as Georgette put it, the letter came.

The letter was from a solicitor named Henri Perron in Montreal and it was addressed to Toussaint.

The city of Montreal, said the letter, was in the throes of a great influenza epidemic and one of those afflicted was Henriette Montambeault. One of her family must come to the city at once to care for the old woman, who refused to go to a hospital. Not that her refusal amounted to much, for even if she had wanted to go, the hospitals of Montreal were filled to overflowing and it was doubtful that there would be room for her anyway. So one of her family must come, and quickly.

Georgette laughed hysterically when Toussaint read the letter to her.

"What kind of fool is this Henri Perron?" she demanded. "So they have influenza in Montreal! What does he think we have here, a mild case of the sniffles?"

"Monique must go," said Toussaint.

"Are you crazy?" Georgette cried. "Monique must go back to work as soon as possible. What do you think we are going to do for money with only your pay coming in?"

"Henriette is Monique's grandmother," said Toussaint stubbornly. "She once took care of us and now Monique must go to her. We owe it to Henriette."

"Well, I, for one, do not owe Henriette one blessed thing," shouted Georgette. "Monique will stay here and help me with the others and then she will go back to the mill!"

"Monique is going to Montreal to take care of her grandmother," repeated Toussaint. "I will help you here and soon Antoinette will be well enough to go back to work."

"I tell you Monique is staying here!" screamed Georgette.

Toussaint stood up and looked at his wife.

"You have said enough," he said in a calm, cold voice. "If you say one more word, I shall beat you until you cannot stand."

He turned to Monique.

"Pack your things," he said. "You will take the midnight train to Montreal."

7

Henriette Montambeault's house was a three-story Victorian monstrosity made of yellow-painted wood with turrets and round windows and countless tortured-looking carvings stuck onto every available inch of space, but to Monique it was the loveliest thing she had ever seen. She could not remember ever having been in such a fine house and yet all the rooms seemed to have a vague familiarity that reached out to her in a way that was wonderfully comforting. From the moment she stepped into Henriette's house, Monique felt that she had come home at last. It was the first time she had ever had this particular feeling in her whole life.

There was room to spare in this house. One could wander up and down stairs, from one room to another, without encountering a single other person. She was alone in the house with her grandmother and an old woman named Celeste, who did the cooking. Another woman, named Blanche, came in every day to clean and twice a week Blanche brought her husband, Normand, with her. Normand washed and waxed the floors and he scrubbed the woodwork and polished the windows. In addition, he was Henriette's gardener and stable boy.

Truly, I have died and gone to Heaven, thought Monique. But it will not last, she amended hastily. Soon this will be over and I'll have to go back.

Quickly she put the thought from her mind and ran up the stairs to her grandmother.

Henriette Montambeault was desperately ill for six weeks and even her doctor, René Gendron, did not think she would recover.

"Your grandmother has had a heart condition for ten years," he told Monique. "Influenza in a woman of her age and poor health is almost always fatal."

Do not die, *Grand-mère,* prayed Monique. She prayed constantly while she tended the old woman. Live, she prayed. Please, please live.

When Henriette began to rally, everyone, including Dr. Gendron, said that it was a miracle. Everyone except Monique. She believed that God had saved Henriette for the express purpose of giving Monique the gift of time.

Henriette's convalescence was a long one and as Monique sat with the old lady day after day she began to know another woman intimately for the first time in her life. Henriette Montambeault was a great talker and Monique had had the habit of listening for a long, long time.

"Tell me about your father and that woman he married," demanded Henriette. "A Delacroix, wasn't she?"

"Yes," Monique answered and she began to tell her grandmother about Georgette. She was not even conscious of lying.

Georgette Montambeault had never been either more or less than others of her kind. She was a hard-working French-Canadian wife who kept her house as clean as possible and her family as well fed as circumstances would allow. Regularly she lay on her back without argument or pleasure for the convenience of her husband and bore his children without complaint. All she expected from life was that those around her be as diligent and patient as herself and it was only when she had to put up with what seemed to her a lazy or duty-shirking child that she lost her temper.

But in Monique's mind and therefore from her lips now

65

came a picture of Georgette as the epitome of the wicked step-mother.

"She went so far as to argue with my father," Monique said to Henriette, "because she did not want me to come here to take care of you when you were dying. All she could think of was that she would lose my pay every week. She did not care at all that you were dying."

"Peasant," muttered Henriette. "That is the word that describes every last Delacroix I've ever known. Peasants every one." She sipped at the broth that Monique had brought to her. "Tell me, child," she went on, "did your father ever tell you how much you resemble your dear mother?"

"Never," said Monique. "Papa never speaks of Maman at all. It's as if—"

"Go on, Monique," prodded Henriette. "It's as if what?"

Monique looked down at her hands. "As if Maman had never been at all," she said. "As if Papa had always been married to Georgette, as if Antoinette and Ansele and I belonged to her."

"Well, you don't belong to her," replied Henriette. "You have your mother's blood in you and it shows. The same delicacy of bone. Tell me, Monique. What are you going to do when you leave here?"

"I never, never want to leave here," said Monique passionately. "I want to stay forever!"

"Well, you can't," Henriette replied practically. "This place is too big for me. I've always known it but never realized the expense of it until this sickness. You can't imagine what it takes to run things around here. Celeste and Blanche and Normand don't work for nothing, I can tell you, and those two horses of mine eat more than five men. No, I'm going to sell this house just as soon as I can find a buyer and even that isn't going to be much help. I owe a fortune in back taxes. No, neither of us can stay here much longer. It was different when you were small and lived here with your father and sis-

66

ter and brother. Then there was still a little money from my poor husband and the legacy from my parents. But, alas, it costs a great deal just to live."

"I knew it was too much like Heaven," said Monique. "And there is no Heaven here on earth. I knew it would have to end and that one day I would have to go back to Livingstone. Back to Georgette and the dirt and the mills."

Henriette looked at her granddaughter for a long time, studying her carefully.

"Monique," she said at last, "you are now twenty-one years old and you are very good-looking. Not as beautiful as your mother, perhaps, but very pretty all the same. Why is it that you never seem to have given a thought to getting married?"

"Married!" cried Monique and stood up so abruptly that her chair tipped over. *"Grand-mère,* I could not bear to be married. Oh, the thought of it is too horrible!"

"Whatever is the matter with you, child?" demanded the old woman. "Every girl wants to be married someday."

"Not I!" said Monique. "I could not bear it."

"Well, what then?" asked Henriette. "A convent, perhaps? How do you want to end up? As an old maid or a nun?"

"Yes," breathed Monique. "I've wanted to be a nun ever since I can remember."

"You are a fool, Monique," Henriette replied. "Nobody ever gained anything from the world by hiding from it. Come now, be sensible. What is it that frightens you about marriage?"

When Monique could neither look at her nor answer, the old lady began to smile.

"It is the idea of being with a man, isn't it, Monique?" she asked. "That is what frightens you."

"Yes," whispered Monique without looking up from her clenched hands. "I could not bear for a man to touch me. Not even a little. I would be sick. I'd die from it."

Henriette Montambeault began to laugh.

"It is not as bad as all that, Monique," she said. "Now sit down and listen to me. I've been through it all myself and I watched your mother go through it. Believe me, it is not as bad as you think. Now hear me."

The old woman began to talk and Monique listened. At first she was horrified at the words that came from the lips of her refined grandmother but then, as she began to feel a little less ashamed and embarrassed, what Henriette was saying began to make a certain amount of sense.

"My dear," said Henriette, "the average man is stupid. As long as he is comfortable, he is happy. It is as simple as that. And there are many different ways of making sure that a man is comfortable. Give him plenty of good food and wine and a warm house. Let him root around in bed until he has convinced himself that he is a strong bull and he is happy."

She looked sideways at her granddaughter and smiled.

"And, Monique, remember that the woman a man takes to bed does not have to be his wife. You must understand, my dear, that your mother was not like us. If Toussaint had ever been unfaithful to Claudette she would have screamed and raved and carried on like a little bourgeois shopgirl. She loved being in bed with your father. She could not get enough of it."

Monique's face was scarlet. "That is terrible," she whispered in a shamed voice.

"No," said Henriette, "it is not terrible. It is merely true. Some women are like that. They love to be fondled and handled. They pant like animals when a man looks at them. Claudette was like that but I never was. And I don't think you are either. But you must tell me the truth. Have you ever felt eager for the touch of a man, Monique?"

"Never! Oh, never. I cannot even think of it."

"Well, you are going to have to begin thinking of it right now," said Henriette flatly. "Listen to me. The easiest, safest way of life for a woman is marriage. Take a look around you, Monique. How do you think I achieved all this? By remaining an old maid? No. I married Jean Montambeault and I made sure that he made the best of himself. Jean would have been content to grub around in the dirt on a farm, but there is no money in that. I told him so, right from the first. But there was money in buying food from other farmers and reselling it to markets, hotels, restaurants. Jean protested at first but in the end he saw it was the best way. We managed to make a very nice living for ourselves in the wholesale food business and that is why I have this house and have managed to live with a measure of peace of mind. I had one child and my husband left me only once—to go to his grave. Ah, yes, there are ways, my dear."

"But I don't understand," said Monique. "What do you mean, 'there are ways'?"

"Ways to be married and have all the advantages of marriage without, shall we say, any of the unpleasantness. Yes. All one has to do is to make a good home for a man, feed him, make sure his clothes are in order, perhaps give him a child for the sake of his pride."

"But what about—"

"Hush," said Henriette and put up one hand. "Sooner or later even the most stupid man gets the idea that it is depraved to ask his wife to give in to his lust. That is when he finally takes a mistress, and when he does, the clever wife keeps her mouth shut, a smile on her face as she thanks God on her knees every night out of sheer relief."

"But the shame of it!" cried Monique.

"What shame?" demanded Henriette. "Believe me, the last thing a man wants is for his wife to find out that he has taken up with another woman. You can be sure that he will go to great lengths to be careful and discreet. In fact, it is very amusing to watch at times. Besides, what does it matter if a few people suspect and begin to gossip? I promise you,

I never cared. When Jean was sleeping with his little whore in some dingy room I was sitting in my parlor entertaining interesting guests, wearing a beautiful, unmussed gown and drinking good wine. No, I certainly never cared about Jean and his panting, whimpering little friend. When he was with her he was leaving me alone and that was what I wanted. I was a lot better off, happier than he ever was."

That night, Monique lay awake for a long, long time. She wondered how many women planned their lives as carefully as her grandmother had done and she decided that there were not very many. That was why the slums of Livingstone and other cities like it were filled with women like Georgette Montambeault and Jacqueline Jolicoeur, who lived in dark, dirty, overcrowded tenements and had a child every year. A child who would eventually be pulled out of school to go to work in the mills so that more and more children could be fed and clothed. Women like Georgette and Jacqueline grew old too soon and died young after living lives filled with nothing but dirt and drudgery, piggish husbands and squealing children.

But not I, thought Monique. Please, God. Not I!

Almost in a panic, she got out of bed and ran to look at herself in the mirror.

I am young, she thought. And *Grand-mère* says I am pretty. Her heart slowed its frightened beating as she looked in the glass.

It's true, she thought, almost coldly. I am pretty. I could get a man if I wanted to. I could get married and have a pretty, clean house all my own and then I'd never have to go back to Livingstone, to my father's house. I'd never have to look at the inside of a mill again.

The next morning Monique carried her grandmother's breakfast tray into the old woman's bedroom and waited quietly until Henriette had had her first cup of coffee.

70

"I lay awake most of the night, *Grand-mère,*" she said finally. "I was thinking about all the things you told me yesterday."

"And?" asked the old lady.

"I'm sure that all you told me is true."

Henriette looked at her granddaughter, whose skin was fine and smooth even in the bright early-morning sunlight, and then she began to laugh.

"We shall have a party," she said. "Yes. A big, gay party with a great number of guests. It will be my way of announcing my recovery and introducing my lovely granddaughter from the United States to all my friends. We shall have a very grand party indeed, my dear. God only knows that since the end of the war Montreal is crawling with attractive young men. Now run downstairs and fetch Celeste. We shall begin to plan at once. And tell Blanche that I want to see Normand as soon as he gets here. Hurry, child. Hurry."

But as Monique ran to the door, Henriette called her back.

"Wait," she said. "There are things you will have to learn before this party. Things I can teach you myself."

"What things?" asked Monique.

"Things like how to attract a man and make him crazy for you," answered Henriette and this time her laugh followed Monique all the way down the stairs.

Monique Montambeault had never even dreamed of such a party nor of the gown that was to be hers. Henriette's own dressmaker came to the house to make the dress. It was white silk, embroidered with roses, and it showed her shoulders.

"My God, it is unbelievable," said Henriette. "You have skin just like your mother's."

Downstairs there were flowers in all the rooms and platters of small, sweet pastries and wine in Henriette's crystal glasses. There was a buffet spread with more kinds of food than Monique had ever imagined and there were three fiddlers to

71

play for the dancing. There was even a piano player and a drummer and a man who played the accordion.

Henri Perron, Henriette's lawyer, leaned toward her and whispered in her ear.

"You are quite mad, my dear Henriette," he said. "You can no more afford a party like this than could your poor relations who have come up from the farm for this affair."

"You are so right, Henri," replied Henriette. "But I've always been something of a gambler as you very well know. And this is my last gamble. If it doesn't pay off it's out of here and to the poorhouse with me."

"You are not only a gambler but one of the shrewdest women I've ever met. You are not quite so badly off as you'd have the girl believe and we both know it, eh? Come now, Henriette. Tell me the truth. The whole idea of this party is to get the girl married off to a man who can afford to keep both of you, is it not? You have a little money left but you don't want to spend it if you don't have to. Right?"

"As usual, you are absolutely right, Henri."

"Does the girl know?"

"But of course," said Henriette. "I may be shrewd and all that, but I am not a sneak."

"Unless it is to your advantage," added Henri Perron.

"You are an impossible old man."

"Perhaps, but I've known you a good many years," replied Henri. "Look, who is the handsome young man to whom Monique is speaking now?"

"And you are also very good at changing the subject," said Henriette. She looked across the room. "That is Armand Bergeron. He was in the army with one of my cousins from Sherbrooke. He is indeed very handsome, isn't he?"

Henri Perron laughed. "I can well imagine that you know everything there is to know about this Bergeron," he said. "Including his weight, height and how much money he has in his pockets at this very moment."

Henriette continued to watch Monique and Armand Bergeron. Monique was actually laughing up into the face of her
partner and the excitement of the party had brought color to
her normally pale cheeks. The girl looks quite beautiful,
thought the old lady. She has learned the lessons I taught her
well.

"Remember, Monique," she had said. "There is really nothing to attracting a man. It is all very well to be pretty, and it
certainly helps, but more men want to jump into bed with a
warm personality than with a mere pretty face. You must
smile and pretend to each poor fool that he is the most
marvelous thing alive."

"And what about after he is attracted?" Monique had
asked.

Henriette had told her that she would teach her about that
after the party.

"Armand Bergeron is the son of a farmer from Sainte
Thérèse," Henriette said to Henri Perron. "His father owns
his own land, which will one day go to his sons. The boy
learned to be a baker while he was in the army."

"A baker!" said Henri Perron. "A man with such a modest
trade was not what I imagined you had in mind for Monique."

Henriette turned to look at the lawyer. "I needn't point
out to you that we are not the cream of Montreal society,"
she said coldly. "There is nothing at all the matter with a man
who makes his living as a baker. Besides, the farm land that
will one day be his is some of the best land on the Saint Lawrence River. It should certainly be worth something some
day. And not only that. Monique isn't getting any younger.
She doesn't have the time to wait for a man to go to college
and become a lawyer."

"Who doesn't have time," asked the lawyer, "Monique
or you?"

"Shut up and go fetch me a glass of wine," demanded
Henriette. "It's hot in here and you always did talk too much."

Later that same night, Henriette and Monique sat in the old lady's bedroom. Monique was brushing her long, dark hair. The movement of her arms was almost languid and Henriette smiled.

"How did it go?" she asked.

"Armand Bergeron," murmured Monique. "He will be the one."

Henriette began to laugh.

"You don't waste any time, do you?" she said. "Why have you made up your mind so quickly?"

"It was not I," replied Monique. "It was he. He has already decided."

"Ha! Listen to her," said Henriette. "One party and she already has a man at her feet."

"Yes," replied Monique and continued to brush her hair slowly.

She had never known this feeling of strength and power before and the taste of it was sweet indeed. She had known that Armand Bergeron wanted her from the moment he looked at her and without knowing how she knew, she realized that the way to keep Armand attracted to her was to appear unattainable. For a while, at least.

"He does not want to remain in Montreal," said Monique. "He has it in his head that he wants to go to the United States."

"Well, what's wrong with that?" asked Henriette. "I certainly wouldn't mind."

Monique put down her hairbrush.

"I am never going back," she said passionately. "When I marry it will not be to return to Livingstone and the mills and the filth. I would rather stay here and live on a farm with Armand's family than go back to that."

"Don't be a fool, Monique," replied Henriette impatiently. "Livingstone is not the only place in the United States, you know. There are towns and cities in America that have never

74

even heard of textile mills. Does this Armand Bergeron intend to follow the baking trade?"

"Of course. It is the only thing he knows, except farming."

"I'll write to some of my friends in America," said Henriette. "We must look into the possibilities of the baking business. Don't worry, little one. You won't have to go back to Livingstone."

Armand Bergeron was convinced that Monique Montambeault was the most beautiful creature he had ever seen. More than that, she was a lady and he was positive that she was a virgin.

"And what makes you so damned sure of that, Armand?" asked his friend, Ezdore DeBlois. "I've heard stories about those girls from the States, you know."

"How would you like to hear your teeth cracking against my fist?" demanded Armand.

"Don't be so touchy, Armand. All I asked was what made you so sure that the fair Monique was an uncorked bottle of wine?"

"You are one blind son of a bitch if you can't tell it just by looking at her," Armand replied heatedly. "You have been ruined for life by the whores of Europe with their big, flabby tits and the rancid smell that comes from them when they spread their legs for you."

"Maybe so, Armand, but I'd give a week's pay for one of them this minute. No churchgoing little virgin could relieve my heavy balls today. Not even a prize like Monique Montambeault."

Armand struck his friend full in the mouth and Ezdore went down on his back, spitting blood.

"You crazy bastard!" yelled Ezdore. "I was only having a little fun with you."

Armand reached down and helped his friend to his feet.

"I apologize, Ezdore," he said. "But you see, I am in love with her."

"Then it is I who must apologize to you," answered Ezdore. "I didn't realize it had gone that far this soon. Come on. I'll buy you a drink."

"No," Armand said reluctantly. "I am going to call on Monique and she hates the smell of liquor on a man."

"Then you are not the man for her, my old friend," replied Ezdore. "You, the prize boozer of the whole British Army!"

"Don't worry about it," said Armand and laughed. "It will just take a little time, you'll see. In the end I'll have her thinking my way."

"That idea has been the downfall of more than one good man."

"You have no faith in me," said Armand. "Just you wait and see. Soon I'll have her eating out of my hand like a little kitten."

"Yes," replied Ezdore. "But please remember one thing, dear friend. Kittens turn into cats and cats sometimes scratch."

Monique Montambeault allowed herself to be courted in a manner that was most respectable but entirely maddening to Armand Bergeron. When they went walking and he tried to take her hand she pulled away from him, and once, when they had been dancing, he had squeezed her so hard to him that he could feel her whole body against his. She had pulled away from him angrily and run out of the room and when he had rushed after her she would not speak to him.

"What is it?" asked Armand. "Please, tell me. What have I done to offend you?"

Monique's face was white.

"I am not some woman off the streets that you can take liberties with," she said.

"But Monique," he answered. "I love you. I only wanted to hold you and feel you near me. I was not insulting you."

76

That same night Henriette brushed away Monique's reservations.

"For God's sake," she said, "let him squeeze you a little. Do you want to drive him away entirely? It is all very well to play hard to get, but you must not make it impossible!"

So the next time Armand tried to hold her hand she did not pull away, and she let him put his arm around her shoulder very gently. She did not even stiffen when he put his lips against her hair.

She is young and shy, thought Armand. I must try to remember that she is not one of those Parisian girls who let a man do anything the first time around.

Two months later Armand Bergeron asked Monique to marry him and she accepted. That same night he looked up his old friend Ezdore and the two of them went out and got roaring drunk.

Soon it will be different, thought Armand through a haze of whiskey. Very soon now. Then I'll teach her what a man is for. I'll have her on her back begging me to give it to her.

"Well, it is done," Monique told Henriette. "Tonight he asked me to marry him and I said yes."

Henriette hugged her granddaughter. "Good for you!" she said. "Now we must get busy."

During the weeks between the announcement of the engagement and the day of the wedding there were a few things that came up which were, as Henriette put it, a nuisance. For one thing, she received a letter from Toussaint, who wrote that Ansele was very near death and that Monique's presence was needed at home.

"Don't let that worry you," Henriette told Monique. "I'll have Henri Perron write to your father."

And she did too. She had her lawyer write that she, Henriette, was still very ill and could not possibly be left alone. Ansele, on the other hand, had his whole family at his disposal. Toussaint Montambeault did not reply and when Ansele finally died, two weeks before the wedding, Henriette shrugged.

"We knew it was bound to happen sooner or later," she said to Monique. "Ansele's kind never live long. He is better off in Heaven, poor thing."

"What shall I do now?" asked Monique.

"Nothing, of course," replied Henriette. "Why take a chance on ruining everything? Don't say a word to Armand about this. What he doesn't know can't keep him awake nights."

But Monique felt compelled to write to her sister Antoinette, and Antoinette, sweet and compassionate as always, wrote back that although she would love to come to Montreal for the wedding, it was impossible. She and Toussaint were the bread-winners for the rest of the family, for although Francoise, their half-sister, had started working a month ago in the mills, she was still not making enough to amount to anything.

She is trapped, thought Monique. She will be like all the others.

Monique was genuinely sorry for Antoinette but she could not avoid a feeling of gratitude that it was Antoinette and not herself who was trapped.

So none of the Montambeaults came to Montreal for the wedding, though all the Bergerons were there.

Zenophile toasted his grandson and his new granddaugh-ter-in-law, and he shivered.

"What is it, Papa?" asked Alcide.

"Nothing, nothing," answered Zenophile. "Too much wine, perhaps. I felt chilled for a moment."

"Well, then, have another drink," said Alcide. "This one will warm you."

Perhaps, thought the old man. But what in the world is to warm Armand?

I have seen many things in my lifetime, he thought. I have

been with many women, both good and bad, and warm and cold. But never have I seen such coldness in the eyes of any woman as that which I see in the eyes of this woman poor Armand has taken to wife.

"I don't like her," said Armand's mother to his sister Aurelie.

"But Maman, we hardly know Monique. How can you say such a thing?"

Aurelie was heavy with her third child and was inclined to be placid and pleased with herself.

"I cannot help myself," said Berthe. "I have a bad feeling."

"Oh, Maman. Don't talk like that," answered Aurelie, but she felt a little less comfortable. Maman's hunches were seldom wrong.

By eight o'clock that night all the men were drunk and Armand, although not so far gone as his brothers, was a long way from being sober.

Monique took him aside.

"How much longer is this disgusting performance going to go on?" she demanded.

Armand laughed and lifted her up off her feet and swung her around.

"It is our wedding day," he answered. "A day of joy and revelry. Come. Let me pour you some wine."

"Put me down at once," she commanded coldly, and when he had done so she stood and looked at him with eyes of such iciness that for a moment Armand felt almost sober.

"What is it, my darling?" he asked.

"You may stay here if you wish," replied Monique, "but I am leaving."

Armand grabbed her wrist, knowing that he was hurting her.

"You will leave when I leave," he said. "You are my wife now. It will be best if you begin to realize that."

79

She tore away from him and even as he stood there she ran to pick up her wrap. In seconds she had run out the door.

"Ah, she will take some taming, that one!" yelled Armand's brother Antoine. "You had better run after her, Armand!"

"Yes," said Armand and tried to match the laughter of his father and his brothers.

He did not even notice that his grandfather had not laughed, nor had his mother and his sister Aurelie. The other girls giggled nervously and as soon as the fiddlers began to play again they were whirled off to dance.

As Armand strode down the street toward Henriette Montambeault's house, he had never felt such anger. Not even during the war. He would tame Monique all right, he vowed. Tonight he'd teach her a lesson she'd never forget.

The house was dark except for a light in one of the second-floor bedrooms, so Armand knew that Monique must have run all the way to have got there before him. The old lady had given her cook the night off and she herself had gone to stay with friends so that the newlyweds might have the house to themselves. Armand went up the walk and twisted the knob of the front door. It was locked.

Armand did not even hesitate. He went directly to one of the first-floor windows and smashed the glass with a rock. Then he entered and made his way through the dark rooms, stumbling against furniture and banging himself painfully against the newel post of the stairway. When he reached the bedroom door, he did not even try to open it. He rammed his shoulder against it until the lock gave way and then stood in the doorway looking at Monique.

She was sitting very quietly on a dark-red velvet chair and she had not even removed her wrap.

"Now look at what you've done to *Grand-mère's* door," she said. "You will have it repaired the first thing in the morning."

Then, very slowly, she stood up and took off her wrap.

"You will have to help me with my dress," she said. "It unbuttons down the back."

Armand moved forward as if wading through mud and his fingers seemed wooden against the silk of her dress. He thought fleetingly that he must have had more to drink than he imagined to feel this heaviness all through him.

"Thank you," said Monique when he had finished. "Now, please go into the other room while I prepare for bed."

Once Armand had seen an idiot walking on the street in a French village and as he moved out of the bedroom now he remembered how the man had shuffled along. He realized that he was moving in exactly the same way.

I'm drunk, he thought. And now that my anger has left me I am weak.

But after he had undressed and waited for more than a half hour for some sign from the next room, his rage began to return.

What kind of woman is she? he asked himself as he paced back and forth.

At last he went to the bedroom door with the broken lock and looked in. The room was in darkness and Monique was in bed.

"Goddamn you!" shouted Armand. "You are my wife and you leave me waiting like a fool while you lie there laughing to yourself."

"Don't curse, Armand," Monique answered. "And go to bed in the other room. You are drunk."

She did not have a chance to move before he was at the side of the bed.

He tore at the bedclothes and he tore at her nightgown and in the end he tore at her body until he was exhausted. He knew that he had hurt her and he waited for her cries of fear or pain and finally of submission but they did not come. When he finally got up and turned on a light she was lying on her back very still. She was lying with her torn nightgown

81

crumpled around her and the bright red stain of blood showed against the sheet. She was lying there, staring up at him with her dark eyes of stone.

"Well?" he said at last.

She continued to look up at him for a long time and he could only stand there and wait for her to speak.

"You are a pig, Armand Bergeron," she said finally. "A filthy, drunken pig."

A week later Armand and Monique Bergeron moved to the town of Amity, New Hampshire, where, Henriette's friend and doctor, René Gendron, had learned from an American colleague, Dr. Benjamin Southworth, there was an establishment in need of an experienced baker. The plan was that as soon as Henriette sold her house in Montreal, she would come to Amity to live with them. Armand reflected sourly that for the second time in his life the joke was on him. He had delivered himself into the hands of these two like a package, all neatly tied up, and from which there was no escape.

But perhaps the joke was on Henriette Montambeault, too, for she never lived to enjoy the results of her planning. She was dead of a heart attack before the Bergerons had been married a month and she never did get to see the United States. From the money that Henriette left, which was considerably more than anyone had ever suspected, Monique inherited nine thousand dollars, most of which she used to buy a house in Amity. She paid for it in cash and then she and Armand moved in. And there they had stayed.

8

Angelique Bergeron watched Dr. Benjamin Southworth as he stood by the bedside of her father. The doctor looked very old and tired, Angelique thought, and his fingers shook as he touched them to Armand's wrist. It was very hot in the room and there was a smell that the child had come to know so well that now she scarcely noticed it.

It is all very sad, thought Angelique and sighed. To die in a hot room with no fresh air. Poor Papa. To die at all and leave a little girl behind. It is very, very sad. She could feel the tears burning just behind her eyes but try as she would she could not squeeze them out.

The truth of the matter was that now that she had recovered from her initial fright she no longer believed that her father was dying. But she felt as though she should feel something at the sight of him lying there, asleep, helpless, with his wrist in the doctor's hand. Yet she could not cry any more so she just sighed.

The doctor turned and looked at her sharply but Angelique did not notice. She was staring down at her hands, folded in her lap, and her hair fell forward and covered the sides of her face.

When Angelique sighs like that, thought the doctor, she sounds exactly like her mother. Monique is an expert at the deep, mournful martyr's sigh.

Angelique was a thin, small girl with dark-brown eyes in a high-cheekboned face. She had long, fair hair that reached halfway down her back and her mother spent hours brushing it. Every week, after she had washed it, Monique brushed and brushed until Angelique's hair was dry. She never rubbed it roughly as she did her own, and every night, after the child had undressed for bed, Monique came into her room and brushed her hair again, for a full ten minutes.

Monique did all this out of a sense of pride. No one was ever going to be able to say that her child was not the best cared for child in Amity.

Armand loved Angelique's hair too. Sometimes in the evening she sat in his lap, although her mother had been saying lately that she was too big for that, and then Armand would run his fingers through her long hair.

"Ma petite blonde," he would say and kiss the back of her neck.

"Armand, for the love of God," Monique would call to him. "The child is twelve years old."

Armand would glance at his wife and continue to play with Angelique's hair.

"She is a baby," he would say. "She is *mon petit ange,* aren't you, darling?" Then he would kiss his daughter again. *"Mon petit ange du ciel."*

"She is not a baby," Monique would cry angrily. "She is twelve years old, she is a young lady."

"Now I ask you, Angelique," Armand would demand seriously, while all the time she could see his eyes laughing, "are you or are you not my baby?"

She would snuggle in his arms, her face pressed into the wonderful-smelling place between his neck and his shoulder.

"Yes, Papa," she would whisper. "Oh, yes."

"Angelique," Monique would say and sigh deeply, "go upstairs. It is time to do your lessons."

"Yes, Maman," Angelique would say dutifully, but she would smile at her father because she knew that he would come up to her room and kiss her good night before he went out. When he came home again he would tiptoe up to her bed to make sure she was covered and sometimes when he came

84

home very late she would wake up and find him sitting on the edge of the bed whispering foolish things to her.

"Tonight I have solved the problems of the world," he would say. "I am mightier than the President of the United States and the King of England put together."

"And now that you are mightier than the President and the King what will you do?" she would ask.

"Hmm-m," Armand would murmur, and stroke his chin. "Let me see. Ah. First of all I will declare next Saturday to be a holiday. But a holiday only for all little girls of twelve who have long blonde hair and big brown eyes and are named Angelique."

She would begin to giggle.

"Sh-h," he would warn. "We do not want the Treasurer or any member of the Cabinet to find out about this. It is a state secret."

Angelique would hide her face against him and smother her giggles in his coat.

"I love the way you smell, Papa."

Her father smelled of shaving soap and cigars and whiskey and it was of these she thought first when she thought of Armand. The heavenly smell was all mixed up with the sound of a gentle, soft voice and a big, roaring laugh that showed white teeth and the feel of stubble rubbed against her cheek. But it was the fragrance of her father that really intrigued Angelique.

Once, when she had been very little, she was peering out the front window waiting for Armand to come home from work and when she saw him turn the corner and walk toward the house she had jumped from her chair and run toward the door.

"I smell Papa coming," she shouted to her mother, but Monique had not turned from the stove where she was preparing the evening meal.

"No doubt," said Monique.

The child stopped, not at the words but at the tone of her mother's voice.

"What did you say, Maman?" she asked.

"I said 'no doubt,' " replied Monique. "Even a dead man could smell your father. The fumes rise from him; he is like a walking saloon."

"What, Maman?"

Monique turned and looked at her daughter's uplifted face and for the millionth time since Angelique had been born it occurred to her that she did not even like the child. Perhaps if she had been left alone with her it might have been different, but from the day of her birth Angelique had been Armand's child.

"I said it's no wonder you can smell your father," said Monique harshly. "Even a dead man could smell him."

"Oh."

Angelique was puzzled and felt that she should stand there and ask her mother to explain but her father was at the door and she could wait no longer.

"Papa!"

Armand picked her up and swung her in the air.

"And who am I if not a king?" he said. "Don't I have a princess waiting to greet me?"

Angelique screamed with excitement as he swung her in a great, sweeping arc.

"Armand!" Monique shouted. "Put the child down. Do you want to get her stomach all upset before she eats?"

Armand put her down and Angelique could feel the rubber band beginning to stretch between her parents. The rubber band was always there, always tight, never slack, waiting to stretch tighter and tighter.

"Angelique," said her mother. "Go wash your hands."

Angelique could feel her throat beginning to hurt and her eyes burned.

"Yes, indeed," added Armand. "Hurry and wash because as soon as you do, I shall tell you of a marvelous invention."

"What is it, Papa?" asked Angelique, her near tears forgotten.

"Ah," he said. "It is an invention I can describe only to little girls named Angelique who have very clean hands." He paused and looked at her glistening eyes. "But I shall be gracious and give you a little hint. It is an invention that has something to do with transportation."

"A car!" cried the child and began to hop up and down.

"Angelique," said Monique and sighed. "Why is it that you never mind your mother? I told you to go wash your hands. At once."

"Yes, Maman."

"You don't have time for that," said Monique as she saw Armand go for the bottle of whiskey on the sideboard in the dining room. "We are ready to eat. Hurry and wash up."

"I have time," said Armand. "I always have time."

"No doubt," replied Monique.

And the rubber band tightened and continued to get tighter at the tone of Monique's voice. Angelique wondered if the rubber band would ever stretch so tight that it would snap apart. The thought frightened her so that she turned and ran to the bathroom.

Angelique did not consciously make up her mind but after that day she never again told her mother that she could smell her father coming. In fact, she very seldom told her mother anything at all. The life she led with her mother was composed of clean clothing, spotless rooms and substantial food unimaginatively cooked, though Angelique had no part in the physical preparation of any of these.

Monique said, "You must not spoil your hands. A lady is always judged by her hands. I never want anyone to be able to say that I have not turned out a little lady."

Or: "It is a sin to be dirty. The good Lord has made the body as the temple for the soul. Can you imagine a dirty church? No. Then it is the same with people. A person who is dirty is committing a sin against God."

Angelique and her mother did not have conversations. When Monique talked, Angelique listened with one ear and only half her mind. Her mother never had much to say that mattered anyway. She only talked about the house and her grandmother, Henriette, or the new dress she would make for Angelique, none of which interested the child at all.

Shortly before her twelfth birthday, Angelique awakened one night to pain and the feeling that she was wrapped up in some sort of horrible wet stickiness. She turned on her light and threw back the bedclothes and then she saw that her nightgown and the sheets were covered with blood. She ran downstairs screaming and her mother took one look at her and turned away in disgust.

"It has come," said Monique.

"What has happened to me?" Angelique screamed, but her mother would not look at her.

"Go wash yourself."

"But I am dying!" cried Angelique.

In a panic, she sped out of the house and she ran and ran until she reached the home of Dr. Benjamin Southworth, where she knew her father was. She darted up the front steps and pounded at the door.

"Papa! Papa!"

Armand himself opened the door with the doctor right behind him.

"What in the world?" he said. He could not believe that he was seeing his daughter lying on the floor of the doctor's front porch, crying. "What has happened?"

He picked her up.

"I am dying, Papa," sobbed Angelique.

"For God's sake," said Benjamin Southworth.

But Angelique did not care any more. Her face was against her father's neck and his arms were very gentle. If she had to die she wanted to die right where she was.

"You are not dying, my dear," said the doctor.

The two men cleaned her up and Dr. Southworth went to fetch one of his own nightshirts for her.

"Here you are, Angelique," he said gently. "We'll just throw this dirty old thing away."

"No," said Armand. "Nothing dirty has happened."

And so Angelique Bergeron learned about the menstrual cycle. She sat warm and safe in her father's lap and listened. The two aspirin tablets the doctor had given her had erased her cramps and the few drops of brandy in a glass of warm milk which her father had prepared for her made her drowsy. She was almost asleep when her mother came into the room.

Monique picked Angelique's soiled nightgown up off the floor and turned on her husband.

"What have you done to her?" she demanded.

Angelique kept her eyes closed but she heard the coldness in her father's voice.

"We have told her what she should have been told some time ago."

Monique picked up the half-empty glass of milk and sniffed it.

"Just as I thought," she said. "You are two of a kind all right, you and your drunken friend. Angelique! Wake up."

"Monique." Armand did not raise his voice but it seemed to Angelique that he was shouting. "Shut your mouth."

Angelique heard her mother gasp.

"Because you have had a head full of crazy ideas about the functions of women all your life does not mean that you are going to pass your poison on to the child. I will not allow it. You had better believe me."

"Who do you think you're talking to?" demanded Monique. "One of the hired hands down at the bakery?"

"I am talking to you, Monique," said Armand in the same level tone. "You are not going to twist the mind of my child."

"Your child!" cried Monique. "And I suppose she is not mine as well?"

"Yes," replied Armand, "but through no fault of yours."

He wrapped Angelique, who still pretended to be asleep, in his coat and carried her all the way home and up the stairs to her bed.

"You can open your eyes now, darling," he said. "She is downstairs."

Angelique smiled up at him and he stroked her hair and kissed her.

"Sleep now," he said. "We will talk tomorrow."

A short time later Armand told his daughter about men and sex and babies. He told her very gently but accurately and that, too, was part of the life she led with her father. When Armand spoke he talked with her, not at her, and he listened to her as if her ideas and opinions mattered. Sometimes they carried on very serious conversations but more often they played wonderful games of the imagination which they were very careful not to let Monique overhear.

In recent years Dr. Southworth had purchased an automobile which he had taught Armand to drive and which Monique both hated and feared. But to Armand and Angelique, the doctor's car was more than a mere means of transportation. It was the chariot of Ben-Hur, the wings of the gods, a magic carpet.

"Since the doctor taught you to operate that machine, I have not had a single moment's peace," declared Monique. "I do not want Angelique riding in that thing. It is dangerous and it is dirty."

In the end, Armand and Angelique stopped mentioning the car in front of Monique. Instead, in the evening after supper,

90

Armand would sometimes take his daughter by the hand and say, "Would you like to go for a little walk, my darling?"

Then he and Angelique would hurry to Dr. Southworth's house, where the marvelous automobile waited. They drove around and around Amity's few paved streets, and it seemed to Angelique that she was flying through space like a bird and she never wanted to stop.

"Do not worry, darling," her father would say when the ride was over. "There will be other, better times. I promise you."

The better times usually came after Armand had been drinking heavily for many days, for it was then that he would declare that he felt mightier than the President of the United States and the King of England.

Then he would take Angelique on a little trip. Sometimes for an afternoon, sometimes for the day, and a few wonderful times for a whole weekend. By the time she was twelve years old, Angelique had been to Boston and even as far as Providence, which was more than any other child who attended the Amity Town School could say. She had slept in a hotel overnight and had her breakfast in bed the next morning while her father read the newspaper aloud to her and made her laugh because of all the different voices he could assume.

He bought her a velvet coat with a muff to match and she felt like the finest lady in all of Boston as she walked by his side into the glittering hotel dining room. At dinner she ate very exotic things, like fresh fruit salad topped with whipped cream, apple pie à la mode and even coffee with a lot of cream and two lumps of sugar, while her father ordered absolutely disgusting things like raw oysters.

"An oyster is to chew," Armand would say, "not to swallow whole. Here. Try it my way."

But Angelique could not do it so her father held his

napkin very discreetly so that no one could see her spit the oyster into it.

"Oh, Papa," she said, "I wish we never had to go home. I wish that we could move to Boston and live right here in this hotel forever and ever. Just the two of us."

Armand Bergeron did not look up from his plate and he felt enormously relieved when the waiter came up to the table.

"More coffee?" he asked.

"Yes, please," answered Angelique importantly.

Twice her father had taken her to the ocean. At first she had been frightened for she had never seen the ocean before and it was much bigger and colder and fiercer looking in real life than in any picture she had ever seen. But the second time she loved it.

"It is like a magnificent giant, Papa."

"Perhaps," said Armand and laughed. "But what I love about it the most is that it is just there. It roars or washes up gently onto the beach. It can be calm or a killer, depending on its mood, and no one on earth can do a damned thing about it."

Both times they had gone in the winter, for Armand did not like the seashore in the summertime. He said that it was too crowded and noisy and that people left half-eaten sandwiches on the sand in the summer.

When they returned home, Monique did not ask many questions about where they had been and even the simplest answers satisfied her.

"Oh, we had dinner in a restaurant," Angelique would say. "I had a salad."

"That's nice," Monique would answer. "And what did your father have?"

Angelique knew what her mother wanted to hear. She was waiting for Angelique to tell her that Armand had eaten nothing, that he had spent the whole time drinking.

"Oysters," Angelique would say. "Maman, do you like my new coat?"

"Yes, of course." Monique sighed. "It must have cost a pretty penny and so impractical. Velvet always is."

She does not have to sigh like that, thought Angelique. She could have come along if she had wanted to. She *wanted* to stay home.

It was true, for Armand never took Angelique anywhere away from home without also inviting his wife. But Monique almost always had a stock answer ready. She had too much ironing to do, or washing; the floors needed polishing, or she was working on a new dress for the child.

Once or twice, though, she had gone along with them and the result had been very unhappy. Monique did not want to walk in the Boston Common and feed the pigeons. The prices in the hotel restaurants were too high and she could have cooked better food anyway for much less money. The train was noisy and filthy and hadn't those men in the rear of the car been drinking? Her feet hurt. When did the next train leave for Amity? For the love of God, what was there to see in Boston? The place was filthy.

Angelique could never keep herself from holding her breath when her father planned one of their excursions.

"I'd like to take the train down to Boston next Saturday," he would say. "Would you care to join me, Monique?"

"No. I've far too much to do. Besides, the expense is foolish."

And then Angelique would let her breath escape in tiny little wisps that no one else could hear.

"And what about you, my angel?"

"Oh, yes, Papa. I'd dearly love to join you."

It did not seem to Angelique that her father drank either more or less on their trips than he did at home. She knew that he always packed a few bottles in his suitcase when they were going to be gone overnight, but she never gave it much thought. Armand did not drink in public when he was escorting a fine lady.

He drank when they were alone in the hotel room and on the train he made a lot of trips to the men's room. Sometimes when they were just walking he would take his beautiful silver flask from his hip pocket and drink from that, but he never did so if there were other people around.

Once Monique had come right out and asked Angelique if Armand drank when he was away from home.

"Why do you ask, Maman?" Angelique hedged.

"Why?" demanded Monique. "Because it is against the law, that's why. Now tell me."

Angelique was puzzled. "What do you mean it is against the law?"

"I mean just what I said," replied Monique impatiently. "It is against the law in this country for a man to drink. It is called the Prohibition and to break that law is a bad sin."

"Is it also a sin when Papa drinks here or at Dr. Southworth's house?"

"Yes, but at least then there are no strangers to see him. Now answer me. Does your father drink when he is away from home?"

Angelique looked her mother straight in the eyes.

"No," she said.

It was the first time she could remember ever having told a deliberate lie to either of her parents.

Drinking might be against the law and a sin to boot, Armand thought in moments of guilt, but, my God, a man had to have something. A little warmth, a little kindness, the gentle strength of a woman's arms when he wanted to retreat from the world for a little while. If the need for warmth and kindness and gentleness was a weakness, then he was weak indeed, for he had tried to do without these things and he knew that he could not.

At first he had hoped that things would improve as Monique's pregnancy progressed. After all, his own mother had been cross and out of sorts at the beginning of each of her pregnancies and perhaps, as with Berthe, time would work a miracle on Monique. But it did not.

In the eyes of the world, Monique performed the externals of marriage to perfection. Even Armand had to admit that no one could beat her at that. His house and clothing were immaculately kept and if his food was uninspired it was palatable and filling. But sometimes as he ate, Armand remembered his mother's kitchen and the wonderful smell of garlic and leeks and the bite of hot sauces against his tongue. Monique did not believe in spicy food. She said that it was bad for the stomach but what she really believed was the old wives' tale that spices aroused the sexual appetites of men.

So Armand grew used to meals that tasted very much alike, and one morning after he had downed his second glass of wine he thought: I am drinking too much, I should slow down. But he filled his flask with whiskey all the same. After all, a man had to have something to carry him through the day. A little warmth to shut out the coldness of his life.

"Why do you drink that stuff?" demanded Monique.

Armand held up a pacifying hand.

"It gives me a certain amount of pleasure, my dear," he replied.

But he was thinking: not another argument. Not today. Please God, not today.

"Pleasure!" Monique said the word as if it were an obscenity. "That's all you can think of, isn't it? Never mind my wishes. Oh, no. Never mind your wife and your unborn child. You can't be bothered to spare us a thought, can you?"

"That's not true, darling," Armand answered and reflected that if there was one word that did not fit his wife and very probably never had, it was the word 'darling.' "I think about you and the baby all the time."

"Don't make me laugh," she said harshly. "You never think about anyone but yourself, nor about anything except your own degenerate pleasures."

Very deliberately, Armand poured himself out two fingers of straight whiskey and drank it down.

"What pleasures are you talking about, Monique?" he asked. "Whiskey? Sex? Or both?"

Suddenly she covered her face with her hands.

"Just never mind, Armand," she said. "Please, just stop talking and leave me alone."

He was quickly and thoroughly ashamed as he looked at her bowed head and then at her swelling abdomen. He put down his empty glass and tried to take her in his arms.

"No. Don't do that, Armand. Please. Just leave me alone."

"Monique. Monique, darling. Let's not fight today. Let me—"

She ripped away from his hands.

"Leave me alone," she screamed. "Don't touch me!"

The one small part of himself that was not completely taken over by rage sensed the anger that pounded through his blood. He could feel it pulsing against his temples, in the big veins inside his elbows and at his wrists. But most of all he could feel it in the palms of his clenched hands and this frightened him because he remembered all the times that he had felt anger there before. Before a fist fight in a saloon, before he had gone into the Army, before he knocked down one of his brothers. And he knew now that he wanted to hit his wife. He made himself turn away from her, but the anger persisted and even though he could now control his hands he could not his mouth.

"I have got myself married to the most unreasonable, most immature, coldest fish of a woman in the whole goddamned world!"

She whirled away from him to run out of the room and he

tried to catch her arm but missed. She ran up the stairs to their bedroom and when she got there she tried to slam the door in his face. But he put his foot in the crack and forced his way through.

"No you don't," he said. "You've locked enough doors in my face to last me a lifetime. You're not ever going to get away with it again."

She was not crying. She merely stood, straight and tall, staring out the window, and Armand thought fleetingly that from the back no one would ever have guessed she was with child. He looked at her, feeling the hollowness that follows deep anger. He did not know what to do with his hands so he stuck them in his pants pockets and stared down at the rug, wishing that he had a drink.

"Monique?"

She would not turn to him and she did not answer.

"Couldn't we just sit down and talk to each other instead of chasing each other around all over the house like a couple of children playing hide and seek?" He spoke as gently as he could.

Without turning, she said, "Any man with any sensitivity at all would have realized long ago that I don't want to talk to you about anything."

"All right, all right," he said. "But, Monique, I'm trying to understand. I know how difficult it has been for you—"

And then she did turn. "How very kind of you," she answered with heavy sarcasm. "How very saintlike of you."

"Please, Monique." He took his hands out of his pockets but in a few moments he felt the anger returning and he put them back. "I know that it is difficult for a woman carrying a child. But it will be over soon and in the meantime I don't think you should take your discomfort out on me. I am as gentle and patient as I know how to be, but I'm goddamned if I can stand living like this."

"*I, I, I,*" she said. "That's all you can think of, isn't it? Only yourself. Your liquor, your comfort, your gentleness and patience, the way you want to live."

She marched past him and went out the door.

"Wait a minute," he called.

Monique walked down the stairs and into the kitchen and Armand followed. He came up behind her. He tried to swallow but it hurt his throat and his need of a drink was almost desperate.

"Now, you listen to me," he began.

"Oh, Father in Heaven," cried Monique. "Will you please put on your coat and go to work? You're late as it is."

He could stand it no longer. He went quickly to the sideboard in the dining room and poured himself a glass of whiskey. He gulped quickly and then went back to her, carrying the not yet empty glass.

"You know," he said, grateful for the warmth that began to fill him and make swallowing easier, "there's something wrong with you, Monique. Something radically wrong."

"And there's one thing wrong with you," she said. Her eyes went over him and she moved as if he were something dirty in the street that she wished to avoid. "The thing wrong with you is that you are disgusting."

The rage came back, throbbing so loudly that Armand was surprised she could not hear it. He wanted to reach out and grab her, to begin slapping her face back and forth until her head lolled on her neck. He wanted to hurl her across the room, away from him. He raised his glass and finished his drink.

"Oh, you've never been able to hide it from me, Armand," she went on. "Perhaps you have managed to from the rest of the world, but I've always known about you. Right from the beginning. You were born disgusting and you'll die the same way!"

"Then why in hell did you ever marry me?" he shouted.

Monique's voice was calm and quiet. "Because my grand-mother wanted me to," she said. "Because I wasn't getting any younger and I wanted a husband. Because I was fool enough to think that in time I could make you into a decent human being. I thought that with a nice home and a family you'd stop wallowing in filth. I thought I could make you into something I'd be proud to take home to my family in Living-stone, but I don't even dare ask them here for a visit. I was wrong about you all the way, but you needn't think that just because I'm trapped now I'm going to wallow in your filth with you."

"You, trapped!" yelled Armand. "You, trapped? That's the greatest laugh of all time!"

"Yes," said Monique and now her voice was ugly. "Yes, I am trapped." She made her hands into fists and clenched them against her belly. "Take a good look at yourself and tell me I'm not. Just look at you. Drunk more often than sober, rooting around like a pig with your drunken friends while I'm trapped here, in a house you could never have provided without my grandmother's money, in a town where I don't want to be but am forced to live because I'm too ashamed to let my relatives see you. Trapped because I'm being forced to have a child I never wanted, a child put into me because of your drunken lechery. Yes, I'm trapped all right, Armand, and don't think I don't remember it every single minute of every single day. And don't expect I'll ever forgive you either, because I never shall. You'll pay for this. If it's the last thing I ever do I'll make sure that you pay and pay and pay."

Armand put his glass down very carefully and picked up his coat and put it on. He went to her and stood directly in front of her and stared hard into her distorted face.

"Goddamn you," he said. "Goddamn you to hell, Monique."

Nor did things improve after Angelique was born. In fact, in one respect they worsened, for before the birth of his daughter Armand had been able to dream of escape. He did not do this consciously, but sometimes late at night, especially when he was good and drunk, the thought would come to him and he would be helpless against it.

I can run away.

But no. The Bergeron men simply did not go off and leave their pregnant wives helpless.

She would not be helpless. Not Monique. As long as she had her house and her scrubbing powders, she would be happy and fulfilled.

I could go home to the farm. I could send her money.

I'd never have to see her again, nor listen to her, nor watch her hating me.

I could run and run and run.

But on the night that Dr. Southworth presented Armand with the pink-and-gold baby that was Angelique, Armand knew that he would never again think about running away. He smiled down at his beautiful sleeping daughter and reflected almost happily that now he was bound to Monique forever. Bound with the chains of softness that his daughter had forged.

"It was a breech birth, Armand," said Dr. Southworth. "We were lucky. Both of them are going to be fine but I must tell you now that there is never going to be another baby for Monique."

"Thank you, my friend," Armand answered, kissing his daughter's soft cheek. "Thank you for giving me this one."

Monique was unable to nurse her child, so it was Armand who got up during the night to feed the baby.

"It's a shame about Monique," said Benjamin Southworth. "Every woman wants to nurse her baby."

"Yes," Armand replied, but he thought: how can Monique give milk to a baby when her breasts are filled with vinegar?

But the years went so quickly.

Before he knew it Armand no longer had to feed his daughter. Before he could snap his fingers she was walking and then running and he could actually feel the crack in his heart.

Don't run so fast, my darling. Don't run away from me. Stay.

Then it was time for her first party dress and Armand took her to Boston for it. He bought her a blue velvet frock with white lace trim.

"Now you really look like a princess," he told Angelique. "A princess with the whole world at her feet."

Monique cried, "Are you a complete fool, Armand? Do you want her to grow up believing that foolishness?"

"Yes," replied Armand. "Yes, I do. I want her to know that she is someone special, someone who is wanted. A miracle, if you will. And in a way it is true."

"Just what do you mean?"

"I mean that it is somewhat of a miracle that a child conceived in hatred, a child carried and borne by an unwilling woman, should turn out as beautiful and sweet as Angelique. That probably makes her one of the most unique human beings in the world. Don't you agree, Monique?"

He looked at her with a bitter smile.

But the years went so quickly.

Before Armand could close his fist to grasp the times that were so precious to him, Angelique was ready to go to school. In the evening she was busy with her lessons and now she had playmates, so that Armand was lonelier than he had ever been.

The men who owned the Sunny Day Baking Company were the scions of a family named Everett. The only interest they ever showed in the bakery was when their attorney showed them the profit statement twice a year. Charles and Lester spent their winters at Palm Beach or in the south of France and their summers in Canada or Denmark or Sweden. They were content never to set foot in Amity, New Hampshire, where their father had originally built the bakery because he had a summer home in the vicinity and had seen the need for local bread and pastry. The family's main interest was in wood pulp, paper and Canadian mining and except for the profit statement the boys were very apt to forget that Sunny Day even existed.

Long ago Armand had learned that a good executive is the one who knows how to delegate authority and he had learned his lesson well. The bakery could run without him so long as he had good men in his employ, and Armand made very sure that he never hired any man who was lazy, stupid or a drunkard. He soon discovered that if he put in an hour a day at his office things ran like clockwork. By the time Angelique was seven years old, Armand Bergeron lived in a world where his job made no demands on him, his wife never needed him and his daughter was rapidly growing away from him. It was in Angelique's seventh year that he took a mistress.

Her name was Diana Dickinson, or at least she said it was. At one time she had wanted to be an actress but now she was thirty-five years old and running to fat, so she had settled for a career as a combination hostess and singer of sorts in what passed as a speakeasy in the city of Hubbard.

Hubbard, a very small city whose principal mainstay was a factory which manufactured shoes, was conveniently located only fifteen miles from Amity.

Armand paid the rent on Diana's kitchenette apartment and whenever he traveled to Hubbard, Diana began to sing "The Man I Love" the minute he walked into the speak. Then she sat and drank with him until he was ready to go to her apartment. Her breasts were always ready for his hands and mouth and her legs opened for him at his merest suggestion.

As soon as it was over, Diana got up and began to brush her hair and she always said, "You were great, honey," as

102

Armand got up and had another drink to wash away the taste of ashes from his mouth. Then she said, "I gotta go back to work, honey," exactly fifteen minutes after their love-making. So then Armand always put on his coat without a word and went back to Amity.

"What the hell's the matter with you, Armand?" yelled Dr. Benjamin Southworth. "That woman's nothing but a whore. She's fucked all of Hubbard, half of Amity and the entire male population of Tilton and Franklin."

"I know it," replied Armand.

"Well, then, for Christ's sake—"

"Oh, sit down and have a drink," said Armand, breaking the seal on a bottle. "This is the real stuff. From Canada."

"I know," answered the doctor. "I saw Pugueot today myself."

Pugueot was a narrow-eyed little thief from Montreal who acted as a bootlegger for the whole of northern New Hampshire.

"Well, then. Sit down and relax," said Armand.

"Don't try to distract me, Armand. I was talking about that Dickinson woman."

"Don't," replied Armand. "I have just come from Hubbard and I've had my fill of Diana for the time being."

"You're an ass, my friend," said the doctor. "Suppose Monique finds out?"

Armand took a long drink and then sat staring at the liquid that remained in his glass.

"My dear Benjamin," he said at last, "I will tell you something about me and Monique. Something about our life together."

Benjamin Southworth had had more than his share of curiosity about the Bergerons ever since they'd come to Amity. All he had known of them when he replied to Dr. René Gendron's letter of inquiry was that Armand was a veteran, a married man who had learned the baker's trade in the Army.

But Dr. Southworth also had the natural reticence of the native New Englander.

"Armand," he said. "Forgive me. I did not mean to pry. What you do is your own business."

Armand laughed. "Now you sound like one of those bloody English from Toronto. They never, never pry. But no, *mon cher,* you are not prying. What I am going to tell you will be good for you. It could even enhance you in the eyes of your profession."

"Please, Armand," said the doctor, embarrassed.

"No, no," protested Armand. "Listen to me, and one day perhaps you will write a very learned article for one of the medical magazines. My wife and I," he said and stopped. "Or should I say Monique and I? In any case. We don't sleep together."

"What the hell do you mean?" demanded the doctor.

"Patience, my friend," Armand replied and put up one hand. "Patience. Oh, we occupy the same bed on occasion. I'm sure that you have noticed that we do not have separate rooms and I imagine you saw that there is but one bed in our conjugal chamber. But that bed is not the bed of a man and his wife."

"Armand, you're drunk."

"Well, I should certainly hope so. I've been working at it all day. No, listen. Monique has a very unique system. Perhaps you also noticed that in our house Monique has arranged a small room for herself on the first floor which she calls her sewing room, eh? And you saw that there is a sofa in that room, eh? Well. On the very few nights when I go upstairs to bed before she does, Monique remains downstairs and sleeps on the sofa in her sewing room. But that is not what is interesting, my dear friend. It is the other evenings that will fascinate you. For on these nights, the many, many nights when Monique goes to bed before I do, she climbs into the big double bed in our room and she lies there like a stone.

When finally I go to bed myself, she does not move but continues to lie very still, pretending she is asleep. You see, it is a matter of pride with her. She got into the bed first and has therefore established squatter's rights, so she will not move, not even when I climb in beside her."

Armand poured more whiskey into his glass.

"She finally goes to sleep and I lie on the opposite side of the bed and sometimes it is a long, long time before I, too, go to sleep. Perhaps it is a matter of pride with me also. For I will not go downstairs to sleep on her little sofa in the sewing room."

"Armand," said the doctor softly and put a hand on the arm of his friend.

"Oh, I know what you must be thinking," said Armand. "You are wondering how we ever managed to achieve a child, Monique and I. Well, I'll tell you that too. On our wedding night I raped her and made her pregnant. As far as I know, it is the only constructive thing I've ever done in our married life and so far as Monique is concerned, I am absolutely certain that bearing a child is the only creative act she has ever performed. I have never touched Monique again, from that first night to this."

The two men were silent for a long time and then Armand looked at his friend.

"There is something else you could put into your article for the medical journals," he said. "It is something I've been thinking about for a long time and now I shall give you the benefits of my long hours of thought. There are children who come into the world with only one arm, one leg. There are babies who are born deaf or mute or blind. These are the ghastly mistakes of nature, the oversights. It is as if someone had not taken enough time in their formation. But, my friend, over the years I have come to another conclusion. Does it not follow that if nature can make such errors in the physical shaping of human beings, it must be possible for mistakes to be made in the forming of their insides as well? Of course it follows. I know because that is what happened to Monique."

"Frankly, I don't know what the hell you're talking about," said the doctor. "Monique is made the same as any other woman. The fact that she cannot have another child—"

"Wait," interrupted Armand. "I am not talking about a physical defect. The mistake that nature made in Monique was not in her body. It was in leaving out warmth from her heart, love from her soul. In whatever deep place the emotions are stored inside a woman, that place is empty in Monique. She has filled it with nothing and then locked the door so that nothing more can ever get in."

"Armand, you must not say these things," the doctor protested. "I am sure that Monique loves your child, as well as you."

"Love?" replied Armand. "Monique has no more love for Angelique than she has for her house, her furniture, the linens in her closets. All of them are objects to her, nothing more. Objects to be kept clean and polished, so that no one may find fault when looking at them."

"If all this is true," said the doctor, "you should have left her years ago."

"I used to think about it," Armand admitted. "Before Angelique was born I used to dream about running away. But I never thought about it again after you placed the child in my arms the day she was born. And, too, there is the matter of Monique's religion."

"A child does not compensate for everything," said the doctor. "A child does not make up for the love of a woman. Surely you could have found happiness with someone other than Monique."

"Even if I did not love Angelique more than my life," Armand answered, "I could not abandon her to Monique. I don't want the child to grow into a woman like her mother. I

106

want everything to be magnificent for her, with so much love to give and receive that it will encompass her whole world."

"Then you have sacrificed yourself for Angelique," said the doctor. "And I, for one, have never been a great believer in the grand gesture of self-sacrifice."

"But I have not sacrificed anything," replied Armand. "I have merely said good-bye to a few things."

He filled their glasses but when he raised his to drink, he paused with it halfway to his lips.

"Benjamin," he said. "Benjamin, do you know the apple orchards of my village? In the spring when they are in blossom? They stretch in endless rows of impossible white, looking even whiter than they really are because of a tinge of pink. Their flowers have little yellow centers and when a honeybee goes to one, he sucks at its heart with such gentle passion that it is like a young boy kissing his sweetheart. Do you know the first wild strawberries of the season? So tiny that it takes two of them to cover the nail on your small finger? You eat them with cream so heavy that your spoon stands up by itself and you don't even need sugar, for the berries provide their own.

"There are mornings on the farm near Sainte Thérèse when you wake with the first light. And when you look out of your open window the beauty makes your eyes mist and you want to run outside in your bare feet to get as close as you can to the earth. It makes a pain in your groin and you are suddenly aware that somewhere in the world there is one person waiting to share all this with you. One woman to whom you would not have to say a word, but who would stand next to you and feel the same agony at the same time.

"Benjamin, do you know that on a rainy night in Paris the street lamps cast a light on the pavements that is like no other light in the world? In Paris, on such a night, a young girl feels boneless in your arms, pliant, bending into your body as if she were part of it. The dawn comes early into the little bedrooms in the houses off the Boulevard Saint Germain. It comes in a deep blue light, and the woman next to you awakens with the tips of her breasts already swollen and the inside of her thighs already lubricous with waiting for you. A girl does not thrash about or scream on such a morning. She barely moves as you play with her and she breathes softly, gently against your skin and makes little sounds you can barely hear. But under your lips you can feel her heart beating until it must surely break away from her, and it is then that you know that your greatest pleasure comes not from your own joy spilling into her but in hers coming to you. I wonder, Benjamin. Sometimes I wonder where they have all gone—the apple blossoms and the wild strawberries and the little, blue-lighted rooms of the world."

Armand had leaned back in his chair and his glass fell to the floor, but the doctor did not hear it break.

Dr. Benjamin Southworth was quietly crying.

9

It was shortly after Angelique Bergeron's eighth birthday that Dr. Southworth began to worry seriously about his friend Armand. Over the years he had repeatedly cautioned Armand about his drinking but Armand had only laughed.

"Benjamin, if there ever was a case of the pot calling the kettle black, this is certainly it. You're as big a boozer as I."

"With two significant differences," replied the doctor. "I don't drink during the day and I always make damned sure that I have a full stomach before I start in at night."

"A waste of good liquor, my friend," said Armand. "Everyone knows that there is nothing like a good stiff jolt on an empty stomach."

"Yes," agreed the doctor, "and it gives your liver a goddamned good jolt too."

"Stop talking like an old woman, Benjamin," Armand answered coldly. "You are beginning to sound like Monique and God knows I don't need that from you."

On several occasions the doctor had gone so far as to refuse to drink with Armand. But even this did no good, for Armand would either come to visit him and proceed to get drunk alone, or else he would get drunk in Hubbard and stay there until the doctor came to pick him up.

"Look, Benjamin," said Armand. "If you don't want me in your house, all you have to do is say so. I don't have to come here, you know. I can always go over to Hubbard where everybody isn't so goddamned busy playing Carrie Nation."

"All right, all right, Armand," Benjamin Southworth replied. "We have been friends for much too long to start quarreling now. But believe me, I'm only thinking of you and your insides."

"Now you sound more like an old woman than ever," said Armand. "Come on. Give me your glass."

So the doctor drank with his friend, but he noticed the little spiderlike veins that had crawled across Armand's cheeks. Sometimes he saw Armand press his hand against his upper right side and then remove it quickly as if it hurt him to touch himself there, and the doctor was frightened.

One evening he said, "Armand, why don't you let me give you a checkup? You look like hell."

Armand slammed his glass down on the table.

"Will you please leave my physical well-being to me?" he shouted. "When I need you professionally, I'll send for you. In the meantime, this is supposed to be a social visit, remember?"

Armand began to put on weight but it was not the kind of fat that comes from overeating. It was soft, bloated, and every day it became increasingly difficult for him to make himself go down to the bakery to put in even his one hour of work.

"You look more like a pig than ever," said Monique. "Just look at you. You can't even button your trousers properly any more and your shirt collar is choking you."

"I began to choke years ago, my dear Monique," Armand replied, "and shirt collars were not the cause of it."

Every morning now, when he awoke, his heart pounded so hard that it was difficult for him to breathe and it took every ounce of his energy to walk downstairs to pour his first drink. Finally he began to leave the bottle under the bed so that in the morning all he had to do was to lean over for it.

"A little eye-opener," he told himself. "A man has to have a little something to wake up on."

110

When Monique discovered this she flew into such a rage that Armand thought she would have a stroke.

"Isn't it enough that you drink everywhere else in the house?" she screamed. "Must you bring the filthy stuff right into our bedroom?"

"And what is so goddamned sacrosanct about our bedroom?" demanded Armand. "Are we to keep this room as a sacred altar to celibacy?"

He raised the bottle high.

"I propose a toast," he said. "Here's to the act of love. Come over here and help me toast the act of love, my saintly, super-clean darling."

"You're drunk," cried Monique. "You have not even set a foot out of bed and you're drunk."

"Oh, Christ," Armand answered softly. "Oh, Christ, I hope so."

Monique ran over to the bed and snatched the bottle away from him. She ran to the window and began to pour out its contents.

"Pig!" she screamed. "Pig! Pig! Pig!"

Armand did not realize that he could still move so fast. In a second he was at her side and had wrenched the half-empty bottle away from her. With his other hand he pushed her so hard that she reeled backward and fell heavily to the floor.

"You ever do that again, you black-hearted bitch, and I'll kill you!"

She lay on the floor, staring up at him.

"So," she said when she could speak, "it is not enough that you shame me, degrade me, now you must beat me."

"I should have beaten you years ago," answered Armand. "Now I couldn't even be bothered."

Monique pounded her fists against the floor. "Oh, you are rotten," she shouted. "Rotten and diseased and filthy."

Armand took a long pull from the bottle. "You'd better get

111

up," he said. "There may be a speck of dust on the floor; you'll soil your hands."

"Get out!" she screamed. "Get out of my room! Get out of my house!"

Armand stepped over her. "Gladly, my dear."

"Run!" cried Monique. "Run to your whore and drink in her bedroom!"

Armand turned very slowly. "What are you talking about?"

"You know very well what I'm talking about," she screamed. "I'm talking about the whore you keep over in Hubbard. The slut who sells herself to you for room rent and a few drinks."

"So you know about that," said Armand and smiled.

"I've known about it since it started. You couldn't even take a mistress properly. Everybody in town knows about it."

Armand stood absolutely still.

"The child?" he asked. "Does she know?"

Monique got up off the floor and began to brush at her skirt.

"Not yet," she said and smiled, "but she will. Don't you worry yourself about that!"

Armand advanced toward her and for a moment she cringed at the look on his face.

"If you ever tell Angelique anything about that I will kill you," he said. "I mean it, Monique. I'll kill you with my bare hands!"

Monique brushed past him to the door.

"Don't make me laugh," she said. "Already this morning you have threatened to kill me twice but you haven't the strength left to kill a fly. It takes everything you've got just to raise that filthy bottle to your mouth."

Armand set the bottle down on a small table.

"Don't be too sure, Monique."

They stood facing one another for a long moment and then they heard the sound of feet running toward the closed door.

"Papa," called Angelique. "Papa, are you in there? I have to leave for school."

Monique did not move or take her eyes away from her husband. It was Armand who turned away.

"You see," she whispered viciously. "You are not only a pig and a drunkard. You are also a coward."

Armand straightened his shoulders but he did not look at his wife.

"I am here, my darling," he called. "Come in."

As the years passed, the times when Armand Bergeron was comparatively sober became fewer and fewer, until it reached a point where he was sober only when he took Angelique away on a trip, and even then he was not wholly sober. When he was with his daughter he managed to keep from being sick or falling down and he made certain his speech sounded normal to the child, but his trips to various men's rooms became more frequent. And he always awoke before she did and drank enough to be able to face the long day ahead.

One night, soon after Angelique had turned eleven, Armand arrived at Dr. Benjamin Southworth's and drank until he passed out. The doctor lifted him onto a sofa and stood for a long time looking down at his friend. At last he unbuttoned Armand's trousers and pulled up his shirt and bent over him. The whole story was written on Armand's abdomen. The big, blue, snaky-looking veins were like a road map to the doctor, and beneath his gently probing fingers Armand's liver was hobnailed to the point where it felt like an old boot. He did not waste words on Armand but did the only thing he felt there was left to do. He went to Monique.

"What are you doing here?" she asked coldly as she showed him into the parlor. "Armand isn't home."

"I know," replied the doctor. "I came to talk to you."

113

"Well, what is it?"

"Monique, I know that you and I have never been friends," he said. "But tonight I have come as a friend."

She did not answer him but merely stood with her hands folded in front of her, waiting, and suddenly Benjamin Southworth got a small glimpse into the life of his friend Armand. This woman was made of stone. There was no warmth in her, no compassion, and surely no forgiveness.

"Armand is going to die," he said bluntly, wanting to shake her, to smash through her iron cocoon.

Even then she did not move but continued to look at him.

"From what?" she demanded. "What ails him?"

"Cirrhosis of the liver."

"Doctor," she said calmly, "you needn't try to impress me with the jargon of your profession. Come to the point, please. Just what is it that makes you say Armand is going to die?"

"Liquor," said the doctor. "Whiskey, booze, whatever you choose to call it. It is killing him."

"And that surprises you, Doctor?" asked Monique with a little smile. "If it is liquor that is killing Armand, it is a wonder that he hasn't been dead for years."

"It's a combination of too much liquor and too little food," the doctor replied. "Unless he stops drinking completely, and immediately, he is going to die."

"You must pardon me if I seem confused," said Monique, "but I am not quite clear in my mind. What is it you want of me?"

"You must make him stop drinking," said the doctor. "You must make him eat. I made up a diet for him before I left the house. I'll leave it here with you. He must follow it to the letter."

"Sit down, Doctor," said Monique with more cordiality than she had ever before extended to him. "Now. Have you told any of this to Armand?"

"I've tried to a thousand times. You know how he is. He merely laughs and tells me not to be an old woman."

"There is your answer," replied Monique. "If he won't listen to you, what makes you think he'd listen to me?"

"You are his wife."

"And what does that have to do with it?" asked Monique. "I've been trying to make Armand stop drinking ever since the day I married him. It never did any good, you know. The talking, the pleading, nothing ever helped. It runs in his family."

"I don't care about his family," said the doctor. "I do care about Armand."

"I remember our wedding day," Monique said, as if he had not spoken. "Drunk. The lot of them. His grandfather and his father and all his brothers and his sisters' husbands. I wouldn't be surprised if the women drank right along with the men. And Armand was the drunkest of them all."

"But that is in the past," answered the doctor. "Now we must help him."

"Again, I must ask you, Doctor. What do you want me to do?"

"I'll talk to him again," said the doctor. "I'll tell him exactly what I've told you and then you must begin to take care of him."

"What do you mean, begin?" demanded Monique. "I've been taking care of Armand for years. I've made certain that he had clean clothes to wear, that his meals were ready on time." She shrugged. "Is it my fault if he only picks at his food? No, Dr. Southworth. I have done everything humanly possible for my husband. There is nothing more to be done now."

"You must!" cried the doctor. "For God's sake, can't you understand what I'm telling you. He'll die if you don't help him. Do you understand that much? If he keeps on the way he is, he'll be dead in less than a year!"

115

Monique stared at him.

"Start from the beginning," she said quietly. "Explain this disease of Armand's to me."

Painstakingly, for almost an hour, the doctor explained cirrhosis of the liver in the simplest terms possible. Later, after he had gone, Monique continued to sit very still in the chair.

It was odd, she thought, that both times salvation for her had come in the guise of disease. Years ago, right after the war, it had been influenza which had made possible her escape from Livingstone and the mills, and now, when she was locked in her present trap, Armand's illness just might free her again.

She got up and went to the stove in the kitchen and began to make a pot of tea, but her movements were those of a sleepwalker.

If Armand were to die, she thought, I could take Angelique and leave Amity forever. I could go back to Livingstone, but this time I wouldn't be living in a slum and working in the mills. I would buy a little house, just big enough for the two of us, and I could begin to raise Angelique properly, without the filthy influence of her father. We would be alone, just the two of us, with no one to bother us. Perhaps I could do a little hand sewing for the rich ladies in Livingstone. Just the two of us. It would be like paradise.

If Armand should die, she could sell the house in Amity and with the money from that, plus Armand's insurance, she and Angelique could be very comfortable for a long time, perhaps even until it was time for Angelique to marry. Even beyond that.

Monique sprinkled tea leaves into the pot and she caught herself only after she had dropped in two spoonfuls too many. She had not been thinking of what she was doing. She had been thanking God for all the years she had gone without things in order to pay what seemed to her the enormous premiums on Armand's life insurance.

It was shortly after this that Armand Bergeron began to sense a subtle change in his household, but the feeling was so vague that he could not quite put his finger on what it was that seemed different.

Monique Bergeron had not changed any specific thing in her routine to a point where it was actually noticeable. It was simply that these days supper was never quite ready when Armand came home, so that he always had time for a couple of extra drinks. Sometimes he even had time for five or six drinks and after that what little appetite he might have had was completely gone. Nor did Monique ever scold him if he did not touch what she set before him. She did not even put away Armand's bottle as she had previously done. Whenever he came into the house there it was, always in plain sight on the sideboard in the dining room, and sometimes they were bottles that Armand could not remember having bought himself.

Oh, well, he thought, perhaps Pugueot was selling a different brand this month.

But in this, Armand was badly mistaken.

On the outskirts of Amity there lived two brothers by the name of Gamsby who specialized in the making of gin and a particularly bad whiskey. Very few people knew the given names of the Gamsby brothers for they had always been called Tweedledee and Tweedledum. Like a lot of others in Amity, it was to these two that Monique Bergeron went for her supply of liquor. She did not even have to speak English to Tweedledee and Tweedledum. She merely had to point to the bottles that lined the walls of their greasy tar-paper shack and then hand over the money. And there was no problem in getting Armand to drink the stuff; Armand would drink anything, especially when his bootlegger friend,

117

Pugueot, couldn't make it down from Canada right on schedule.

Oh, Monique knew about Pugueot all right. Just as she knew about Diana Dickinson. Diana Dickinson! What a ridiculous name.

Whenever Monique thought about Diana she was filled with a great resentment toward her dead grandmother, Henriette, though she told herself over and over that such a feeling was unreasonable and unfair.

Things had worked out just as Henriette had said they would, hadn't they? Armand had taken a mistress and left his wife alone. Just the way she and Henriette had planned. Monique had her nice home, the insurance was paid up, she had a child and even though she refused to learn English she knew that the people in Amity respected her for what she was. A hard-working, clean, religious woman of good character and morals who had a lot to put up with but who saw her duty and did it.

Whenever one of these moods came upon her, Monique gave herself a good mental shaking.

It was not Henriette's fault that Armand had picked out a saloon whore for himself, was it?

Monique kept telling herself that she would never have felt as she did if Armand had picked a good, clean, decent woman. But then, what good, clean, decent woman would have had anything to do with him? Her grandmother should have warned her about the kind of women men like Armand took up with. Henriette should have told her, all those years ago, back in Montreal. As it was, she had had to find out for herself, the hard way.

Monique felt again the terrible shame of boarding the train for Hubbard to discover where it was that Armand spent his time, then seeing him with his whore clinging to his arm and leading him to her grubby little flat. She remembered only too well standing in the cold, dark street, lighting matches to

118

look at her wrist watch to see exactly how many minutes her husband had spent with his filthy saloon woman. Surely Henriette should have warned her about the feelings of shame.

During the months that followed her talk with Dr. Southworth, Monique began to correspond regularly again with her family. Where previously she had written to them only at Christmas and Easter, she now began to send a letter almost every week. Her father, Toussaint, answered her as if nothing had ever happened between them, and Monique's sister, Antoinette, who was married to a mill worker by the name of Joseph Ledoux and had four children, was overjoyed to hear from Monique. In her letter she suggested an exchange of visits. Perhaps Antoinette could come to Amity if Monique had room for her and the four little ones? Or was it possible that Monique would prefer to come to Livingstone? None of her family had ever seen Angelique and snapshots were not very satisfying.

"Do not tell Papa or the others," Monique wrote back, "but the truth of the matter is that my husband is very ill. The doctor says he has cancer so you can see why I don't want you to come or anyone else to know. Perhaps later, when he is better, you can come for a visit or I will be able to visit you in Livingstone."

Antoinette read her sister's letter and was horrified. She did not even show it to her husband. Cancer was on a par with a venereal disease or mental illness and as a favor to her sister, Antoinette burned Monique's letter. She did not say a word to anyone, even when Armand was taken desperately ill only two weeks before Christmas and Monique wrote that she feared her husband had not much longer to live.

10

Dr. Benjamin Southworth went to the bed and, for what seemed to him to be the millionth time, put his fingers on Armand Bergeron's wrist.

It will be today, he thought.

Outside, the February sky was dark and heavy with the clouds that dropped a lovely white burden of snow. It was going to snow all night.

It shouldn't be today, thought the doctor. Armand always hated the cold and the snow. If it must happen it should be in June, with everything in blossom. Christ, if I don't have a drink soon I'm going to fall apart.

Angelique had begun to cry again, but silently now, as if in hopelessness.

"I'll get your mother, Angelique," the doctor said softly. "You just sit still and I'll fetch her."

He went downstairs and knocked softly on the door of the sewing room.

Monique's hideaway, he thought. The bastion of goddamned purity.

"You'd better go up, Monique," he said as she opened the door.

"Armand?" she asked quickly.

"Not yet," he replied. "It's Angelique. She needs you."

Monique ran up the stairs and he heard the bedroom door open and close quietly. He went to the sideboard in the dining room but there was nothing on top except Monique's china coffee service. He bent down and opened one of the low cupboards as he had seen Armand do so many times.

Thank God, he thought, as his fingers closed around the neck of a bottle.

But when he saw what he held he did not even take a drink. He stared down in horror at the bottle. It was one of Tweedledee and Tweedledum's specials and it was still half full of whiskey. The doctor pulled out the cork and sniffed.

"Doctor," called Monique from upstairs. "Please come quickly!"

Benjamin Southworth did not move. He could not take his eyes off the bottle in his hand.

Never, he thought. Drunk or sober, even if he'd been dying for a drink, never would Armand have gone to the Gamsby brothers. Then who? How?

"Doctor! Hurry!" cried Monique.

Benjamin Southworth turned toward the sound of the voice and then he knew. He was still carrying the bottle when he entered the upstairs bedroom and he set it down very gently on a bureau before he went over to the bed. Monique was watching him with eyes gone suddenly flat.

"Angelique!" called Armand. "Angelique!"

It was the first word that he had been able to articulate for days.

"Angelique!"

The child took his hand.

"I am here, Papa. I am right here."

"Be careful!" Armand cried. He thrashed around weakly and the doctor put a restraining hand against his shoulder.

Armand's chest heaved with the effort.

"Angelique!"

"Yes, Papa."

The tears fell from her cheeks down onto his arm and she tried to brush them away with her hand.

"Yes, Papa."

"Be careful!" said Armand. "Your mother. Watch out! Watch out!"

The child began to sob.

"Don't worry yourself, Papa," said Angelique. "I'll watch out for Maman. I'll take care of her always."

"No! No! No!" screamed Armand. "That's not what I mean. Watch out for her or she will destroy you!"

And for the last time in his life the bitter joke was on Armand.

He thought he was screaming a warning but no sound came from his mouth. His lips barely moved as a string of saliva ran down his chin. There was a great roaring in his ears now, a sound like the sea during a storm, and he could hear Angelique, from very far off, saying over and over again, "Don't worry yourself, Papa. I'll take care of Maman."

"No. No! *No!*"

The last big wave in the ocean had a high crest of foam and it was iridescent, so that it shone in the sun with a million different colors.

Book Two

1

Everyone who was invited said that the wedding of Angelique Bergeron and Etienne de Montigny was the most beautiful ever held in Saint George's Church and that the reception
which followed was the grandest ever held in the city of Livingstone. Those who had not been invited claimed that both
were ostentatious, overdone, cheap and far above the station
of a widow like Monique Bergeron, who had to take in sewing
to make ends meet. People in the position of the Bergerons
had no business putting on such a display. Especially at the
height of a great national depression.

The truth of the matter was that if the wedding and reception had been given by one of the first families from the north
end of the city, it would have seemed like a modest affair
indeed. But the French-Canadian population in the neighborhood where Monique and Angelique lived was unaccus-
tomed to any attempt at grandeur and they were therefore so
impressed with the Bergeron wedding that for months afterward they talked about little else.

Angelique had spent weeks pouring over Emily Post's book
on etiquette to be certain that everything was arranged to
perfection.

Her gown was white satin with a long train and featured
innumerable yards of white veiling. She forced her eight
bridesmaids to wear simple dresses of pastel organdy and
when they protested tearfully that they wanted something much
more elaborate, she soothed them with big, floppy-brimmed
picture hats.

"It is bad taste for bridesmaids to be overdressed," said Angelique and the eight girls could do nothing but nod in agreement, for Angelique was the cleverest girl they had ever known.

She had read books that none of them had ever even heard of and no one in Livingstone called *her* "Frenchie." Angelique's English had not a trace of accent, not even when she used words with the horribly difficult *th* in them.

No, it was best to do whatever Angelique told you to do, the girls agreed. Angelique was clever. She could do anything just like an American.

The bridesmaids' bouquets were of pink roses and sweet peas, while Angelique carried a huge sheaf of calla lilies. It did not matter that no one attending the service had ever seen a calla lily and therefore believed them to be artificial paper flowers. Calla lilies were traditional at fine weddings.

It had taken Angelique a solid month of pleading, threatening and weeping, but in the end she had her way and Etienne de Montigny, the groom, wore a rented cutaway coat and striped trousers.

"She can wrap Etienne around her little finger," said all Angelique's friends when Etienne finally capitulated, "and no wonder. Any girl who looks like Angelique could charm the Pope himself."

But it had been Etienne's mother, Simone, who had prevailed upon him to give in on the matter of the suit.

"A girl marries but once," said Simone, "so let her have her way, Etienne."

"But I'll look like a fool, Ma," replied Etienne.

If you are fool enough to marry her at all, you may as well look the part, thought Simone. She did not say these words aloud. She had said them often enough in the beginning when Etienne had first announced his intentions.

"She is not for you, Etienne," Simone had said.

"Ma, I'm going to marry her. I'm crazy about her and

that's that," Etienne answered. "What have you got against her anyway?"

"Nothing," replied Simone. "But I know you. You are a bread eater and you will soon tire of cake. You are a mechanic in a garage. Angelique dreams of a prince in a castle and in spite of your fancy last name, you're no prince."

"Aw, come on, Ma," protested Etienne. "Angelique is young. She'll get over her silly ideas. Wait and see."

"If you hold your breath waiting for that day, you'll be a long time blue in the face," said Simone sourly. She might have said more but she was grateful to her son. Etienne could easily have looked at her and asked, "What about you, Ma?" And he would have been perfectly justified.

Simone de Montigny had been born Simone Pichette in the village of Saint Pierre, in the province of Quebec. She was the eldest of fourteen children, only nine of whom lived to see maturity, and when her mother, Jeanine, died during the delivery of the last baby, the care of the family fell upon Simone, who was then fifteen years old. Her father, Ovila, owned a small farm where he raised fruit and vegetables but his mainstay was hogs, which he raised, slaughtered and sold to the big markets in Quebec City. Simone was sixteen years old before she found out that the whole world did not smell like a pigsty, for it was in her sixteenth year that she met Georges de Montigny.

Georges de Montigny was a Parisian. He had been born and raised in the French capital and had fully intended to spend the rest of his life there, but when he was twenty years old he impregnated the daughter of a minor police official.

Georges' mother, Giselle, had carried on at great length, weeping and fainting with clocklike regularity, when she heard this news but in the end she had agreed with Georges and his father, Charles. Escape was the only answer; after all, she did not want the big-hipped daughter of a gendarme in the family. So Georges fled to Montreal, where the de Montignys had relatives who were only too happy to receive their Parisian nephew.

From the moment Georges arrived in Montreal, he was a smashing social success. Women could not keep their eyes off him and yet he had a way about him that made men his fast and immediate friends. What Georges de Montigny had for women was the appeal of a scoundrel; for men, the appeal of the adventurer. He was tall and slender with very dark hair and blue eyes and he had beautiful hands and feet. He could dance like a professional and he could punch like a prize fighter and his sexual appetites were tremendous and constant. Within three months of his arrival he had slept with no less than twenty-four French-Canadian girls and in the end he got the daughter of an English Member of Parliament with child. He went immediately to his aunt and confessed.

"But my God," said Florence de Montigny. "She is English!"

"Oui, ma tante," replied Georges.

"And a Protestant!"

"Yes," answered Georges and hung his head in shame.

"Are you sure it is your child, Georges?" asked Florence hopefully.

Georges de Montigny had never been one to disappoint a lady. Although little Agatha Clemens had been a virgin when he had taken her, he now raised his head and looked his aunt straight in the eye.

"No, I am not sure," he said. "I may have been drinking a little, but I was not so drunk that I did not realize I was not the first."

Florence sighed happily and smiled at her handsome nephew.

"Well, then," she replied. "We are safe. There is nothing to worry about."

"Ma chère tante," answered Georges gently, "you do not understand the situation. The old devil has said that if I do

not marry Agatha there will be trouble. Not that he is so crazy about having a French son-in-law, mind you, but Agatha is twenty-seven years old and he knows he will not have an easy time marketing used goods. The name of de Montigny is an old and honorable one and he is willing to settle for it."

Florence de Montigny looked at Georges. The skin was drawn taut over his lovely high cheekbones and his beautiful blue eyes were filled with apprehension. Her heart contracted in pain for him.

"I will speak to your uncle," she said. "He will think of something."

But Ulysses de Montigny was not quite so taken with his brother's son as was his wife.

"You goddamned fool," he shouted at Georges, "have you no sense at all? The daughter of a Member of Parliament! You are insane, that is all there is to it!"

"Please, Ulysses," pleaded Florence, "we must help him. She is a Protestant, for the love of God! Think of something!"

Finally it was decided that the family would give out the story that Georges had gone to the United States.

"It is a big country, the United States," said Ulysses de Montigny. "Even Joshua Clemens would have a bitch of a time finding you there."

In a matter of hours, Ulysses made arrangements for Georges to go to the village of Saint Pierre, where Ulysses had a third cousin by marriage.

"That should dry up some of the juice in your glands," said Ulysses. "The village of Saint Pierre is the crossroads of the ends of the earth and if you have one ounce of brains left in your head you'll stay there for a good nine months. You'd be wise to find yourself a wife while you're up there too. Even Joshua Clemens can't force you to marry his daughter if you are already married. Now, get the hell out of my sight. You are a black spot on a good name."

Saint Pierre was the epitome of all tiny French-Canadian

129

villages and within a week of his arrival there Georges de Montigny was bored to distraction. The village had one store, one saloon and one Catholic church and the people who lived there were extremely clannish and suspicious of strangers. The only thing that saved Georges from being totally ignored was the fact that he was a relative of an old and honored native. Ulysses' third cousin by marriage was the wealthiest farmer in the region.

But the worst thing about Saint Pierre, to Georges' mind, was the female population. The girls all seemed to be huge, oxlike types who worked in the fields and most of them had ghastly dark shadows above their upper lips.

Good Christ, thought Georges, is it from among these mustachioed sows that I am to look for a wife? No, by God, I'd rather go back to Montreal and face the old man and his horse-faced daughter.

He had been in Saint Pierre for over a month when he saw Simone Pichette for the first time. He came upon her in church, where he had gone one Sunday morning because he had absolutely nothing else to do.

Simone was little; her head would barely have come to his shoulder. Her dress was old and too tight for her and he could see her small rounded breasts, far different from the overblown udders he had noticed on most of the Saint Pierre women.

Georges examined her as closely as possible. No, there was no hair on her face. She was young too. No more than fifteen or sixteen years old, he judged, and a virgin, he was sure. Georges de Montigny felt the old familiar hardening in his groin and he was very careful to hold his topcoat in front of him.

"Dominus vobiscum," chanted the priest as Georges leaned toward Ulysses' third cousin by marriage.

"Who is that girl?" whispered Georges.

"Simone Pichette," replied the cousin.

130

"Who are all those children with her?"

"Her brothers and sisters. The mother is dead."

"What about the father?"

"Sh-h," hissed the cousin as the priest turned to give his final blessing to the congregation.

"Let's get out of here," whispered Georges. "I want you to introduce me."

A few minutes later, on the church steps, Georges de Montigny was formally introduced to Simone Pichette. He gazed deep into her eyes and bowed over her hand and said he was enchanted to make her acquaintance.

As for Simone, she looked at him and immediately felt a burning all through her body. In less than one minute she fell completely and irrevocably in love with him.

"The daughter of a pig farmer!" cried Georges when Ulysses' cousin explained the Pichette family to him. "It is impossible!"

But the very next day he received a letter from his Aunt Florence, who wrote that Joshua Clemens had not been fooled for a minute by the story of Georges' flight to the United States. The old man had gone so far as to check with the shipping lines and when he found that Georges had not gone back to France, he had decided that Georges was still in Canada and he meant to seek him out.

"If he finds you and you refuse to marry his daughter," Florence de Montigny wrote, "he means to kill you. He said so to your uncle."

That same night, Georges borrowed the cousin's horse and buggy and went to call on Simone Pichette. He could smell Ovila's farm when he was still half a mile away and his stomach knotted in disgust.

Well, he would just have to make the best of it. Better Simone than Agatha Clemens. His father and mother had the patience of saints but this tolerance would never extend to the point of accepting a Protestant, English daughter-in-

131

law. Georges was completely dependent on his parents for money; he had never learned to earn his own living.

Within a month Georges and Simone were married. They were married in the church in Saint Pierre and, as the natives put it, nine months and ten minutes later a daughter was born to them. They christened her Josephine and when the child was six weeks old, Georges moved his family to the United States.

Anything, thought Georges, anything is preferable to this stinking pig farm. Even the United States. Even a city like Livingstone, New Hampshire.

Now, years later, Simone de Montigny studied her first-born son, Etienne, who was a year younger than his sister, Josephine.

He looks just like his father, she thought. But he is not like him inside. His father would never have protested at wearing a cutaway suit. He would have loved every minute of it.

Simone sighed and went back to work on the dress she would wear for her son's wedding to Angelique Bergeron.

No, she could not blame Angelique for falling in love with Etienne. He looked so much like his father.

For her daughter's wedding, Monique Bergeron wore a girdle and a brassiere for the first time in her life. She did so without grumbling, although she thought this bit of vanity a little obscene in a woman her age. She also wore a blue-and-white print dress and a little flowered white hat in which she felt like an idiot. But her daughter had informed her that these things were in good taste and good taste, it seemed, had become very important to Angelique over the years. At least that was what she called it. Good taste. It was Monique's private opinion that her daughter merely liked to put on airs to impress her contemporaries.

Her father did this to her, thought Monique. He put fancy ideas into her head. She loves to think of velours drapes and

132

raw oysters on ice and a man in a ridiculous black suit pouring chilled champagne.

Monique Bergeron did not like her daughter any better than she ever had and in the years since the two of them had left Amity she realized that she knew her even less than she had imagined. Angelique was an ungrateful, spoiled child whose foolish, Yankee ideas were totally impossible, but for all that it had not taken the girl very long to whip her mother into line. Monique remembered her daughter's fourteenth birthday with bitterness and stored-up rage. Now that the wedding was over she looked at her daughter dancing with Etienne and smiled maliciously to herself. She wondered if Angelique would have as easy a time with her new husband as she had had with her mother.

Probably, thought Monique. Etienne is a fool, just like any other man.

But there were no doubts in Angelique's mind. She gazed up into Etienne's eyes as the strains of "The Beautiful Blue Danube" floated up and over and around her and she smiled radiantly.

Oh, Etienne had done his share of champing at the bit before the wedding all right, but everything was going to be different now that he was all hers. She had suffered her few moments of humiliation at his hands, but nothing like that was ever going to happen again. Etienne would have to be made to see how wrong he had been. No one humiliates a princess.

Angelique smiled. It was going to take a bit of doing to make Etienne into what she expected him to be. It would take time too, but she had plenty of that. Angelique was barely seventeen years old.

Everyone commented on what a beautiful bride Angelique made. Slim, blonde, well made, and those incredible eyes! Etienne was indeed a lucky man to have found such a prize.

But if Zenophile Bergeron had been there, perhaps he might

133

have been the only one to see deep into those incredible eyes! Perhaps he might have looked deeply enough to notice the hard little glint hidden in them. A glint as shiny as tinsel and hard as diamonds. And perhaps he would have said, "Poor Etienne," as years ago he had said, "Poor Armand."

Simone de Montigny was not looking into Angelique's eyes. In fact, she was not looking at her daughter-in-law at all. She was staring at her son, who looked so much like his father. Simone's eyes did not fill with tears, they merely shone very brightly as she glanced down into her glass of untasted champagne.

Georges, she thought. Georges, where are you today?

Monique Bergeron stood next to Simone de Montigny, looking taller than she really was next to Simone's shortness. She was trying to look into the future.

It is done, she thought. It is true that I will be living in the same house with her and Etienne but now he will be the one who will have to put up with her. I wonder how he will cope with everything.

"Hurry, hurry," someone called. "Angelique is going to throw her bouquet!"

Etienne de Montigny stood at the bottom of the stairway and watched his bride toss down her flowers, then run to the room where she was to change for their wedding trip.

His brother, Christophe, who had been his best man, clapped him on the back.

"Come, bridegroom," said Christophe. "It is time for you to get out of your rented finery."

"Yes, I'm coming," answered Etienne, but he turned and looked up again at the closed door of the room where Angelique was changing.

Soon, he thought as he walked away with his brother. Very soon now.

2

Angelique de Montigny sent her bridesmaids away as soon
as they had helped her slip out of her wedding dress, and
when they had left she locked the door behind them. Then
she finished undressing slowly, pausing occasionally to sip
from a glass of champagne. When she had finished she went to
the bathroom and began to fill the tub.

Thank God for naturally curly hair, she thought, as the
steam began to rise.

She poured eau de cologne into the water and then lowered herself into the tub. Slowly. Dreamily.

Now it was done and she did not have to hurry at all. Let
Etienne wait. It would be good for him.

Angelique ran her hands up over her flat belly and cupped
her breasts, pinching the nipples until they stood straight up.

Well, how do you think it went, Papa? she asked silently.
Yes, I did look like a princess, didn't I? Everybody thought so.
Not that Etienne and that stupid family of his would know
a princess if they fell over one, but they know that I'm something special all the same. Everybody says that Etienne is
very, very lucky to get me.

Angelique laughed out loud and played with her nipples
gently. She moved her lower body slowly and sensually in the
hot water. The steam smelled delicious.

Well, it's true. He is lucky, isn't he, Papa? And don't you
worry, I'll make sure he appreciates me. I remember all the
things you told me and I learned a few things for myself too.

135

Do you know that the greatest attraction a woman can have for a man is to withhold herself, Papa? But I guess you know that all right, don't you? I'll bet that's how Maman got you. Maman. You don't have to worry about her either, Papa. I never have any trouble with Maman any more.

Angelique stretched her legs as far as they would reach in the hot water and then she closed her eyes drowsily as her muscles began to loosen.

The funeral had been long and tedious but not so much so as the period before it when Monique had been busy with all the arrangements so that Armand Bergeron could be properly laid out in his own parlor. Angelique could still smell the flowers that filled the front room of the house in Amity and she could still see the coffin standing stark against one wall. A dark, mahogany coffin with silver handles and a white satin lining.

Everybody who came to the house to pay his respects had said how natural Armand looked. Why, he didn't look dead at all. He looked as if he were asleep.

Angelique sat in a straight-backed chair and did not look at anybody. Her black wool dress made her itch and the starched white collar scratched her neck. Besides, why should she look at anybody anyway? Everyone in the room was a fool. Her father wasn't dead. He was right there beside her, laughing at all these idiots.

Look at that fat one over there, *mon ange,* said Armand, the one with the roses on her hat. She is the wife of Amos Shute, who runs the dry goods store. I don't think she ever spoke ten words to me in her entire life and now look at her, simpering at Benjamin Southworth. What a foolish woman!

Ah, my little princess, everyone here expects you to cry and carry on but don't you do it. You hold your beautiful head up high, as befits a princess. Don't be one of them, my darling.

136

The house was filled with Bergerons from Sainte Thérèse and with Montambeaults from Livingstone. It was the first time Angelique had ever met any of her grandparents or aunts and uncles.

What shall I do, Papa?

They are good people, my darling, replied Armand. But they are not our kind. You are so far above them that they cannot really see you. But one day, when you are older, they will. They are farmers and mill hands and always will be, but one day you shall walk with kings.

Papa. Papa, what about the other thing? I want to ask Dr. Southworth—

Hush, my angel. Not now. Don't think about it now. It is not the time. Quickly now. Lift your head. Everyone is looking at you.

"It is not good, Monique," whispered Antoinette. "The child has not shed one tear. It is unnatural."

"I know," replied Monique. "The doctor thinks that she is in some kind of shock."

"But she was just smiling," said Antoinette. "I saw her myself. She was looking down at her hands and smiling. I tell you, it's unnatural. After all, her own father . . ."

"Yes," answered Monique and dabbed at her eyes with a lace-trimmed handkerchief.

"Oh, my poor sister," said Antoinette. "I have been talking too much. Come. I'll make you a nice cup of hot tea."

Angelique did not cry once during the three long days that Armand's body reposed in the parlor. And every time the front door opened and she caught sight of the spray of flowers that hung there, tied with a purple ribbon, she smiled.

Isn't that the most ridiculous thing you ever saw in your life? asked Armand. In fact, the whole ritual for the burying of the dead is ridiculous. A pagan festival if you ask me. Did you know that when a child dies, they tie the bouquet of flowers on the door with a white ribbon? It's supposed to

137

symbolize purity or some such thing. Well, mine is purple. You may draw your own conclusions from that.

Angelique stared down at her hands and began to giggle.

"Angelique!"

"Yes, Maman?"

"Please go to your room at once."

"Yes, Maman."

"Be careful, Monique," said Dr. Benjamin Southworth. "The child is suffering enough."

Monique Bergeron drew him into the kitchen where they could be alone. When she had closed the door behind them she turned to him.

"I want you to get out of my house," she said coldly. "I mean right now. You have no business here and you are certainly not entitled to tell me how to talk to my own child."

"Be careful, Monique," warned the doctor. "Don't make me angry."

"I don't have to be careful with you any more," replied Monique. "The death certificate is already signed and it would be a little awkward for you to reverse yourself now, wouldn't it?"

"Perhaps," said the doctor. "But don't forget, Monique. You and I know what should have been on that certificate, don't we? I wonder what would happen if I should start a little whispering campaign in Amity? Rumor travels quickly in a town like this."

Monique smiled.

"You won't," she said.

"What makes you so damned sure of yourself?" asked the doctor angrily. He had been drinking all afternoon and now his head hurt. "What makes you so goddamned sure?"

"The child," answered Monique calmly. "You won't say a word because of Angelique."

Neither of them had heard the door open, so intent were

138

they on staring into each other's eyes, and Dr. Southworth actually jumped when he heard the voice behind him.

"I want a drink of water," said Angelique.

The sun was shining the day they buried Armand, and Angelique was glad of that.

Are you very cold, Papa? she asked as she followed her mother into the cemetery.

Not at all, *mon ange*. I'm snug as a bug in a rug.

I'm glad, Papa.

Angelique had not wanted to leave Amity, but before Armand had been in the ground a month, Monique had sold the house.

"But *why* do you want to leave Amity?" asked Angelique. *"Why* do we have to move to Livingstone?"

Monique looked at her sharply. Ever since Armand's death, the child had spoken hardly at all and when she did it was usually in a whining, complaining voice that rasped against Monique's nerves like a file. She spent long hours alone in her room and when she was not there she sat in the front parlor, as close as possible to the wall where Armand's coffin had lain. Monique found her behavior morbid and depressing. The child was more irksome than she had ever been.

"Because there is nothing for us here," said Monique. "We never had any friends in this town and there's not even a decent church here. A priest had to come all the way from Franklin to attend to your father and I've had enough of the inconvenience of living here. Besides, your grandfather has found a very suitable house for us in Livingstone. We will be comfortable there and our family will be near."

"I have friends here," Angelique replied. "Papa had friends here."

"Some friends!" said Monique with a little laugh. "Your little playmates' mothers laugh behind my back because I

139

don't speak their language. And as for your father, the only friend he ever had was Dr. Southworth and only because the doctor loved to have someone weaker than himself to booze with!"

Angelique closed her eyes and her hands began to tremble. Every time her mother mentioned Dr. Southworth's name, Angelique's heart began to pound and she felt all shaky and weak inside.

"Maman," she said, "Dr. Southworth said something to you about Papa the night Papa died. He was shouting as if he was angry and—"

"Nonsense," answered Monique quickly and more gently than she usually spoke to Angelique. "You were upset and imagined things. Dr. Southworth was upset too, for in spite of all his faults he was truly fond of your father."

"But he was shouting," said Angelique. "Loud."

"Come," replied Monique, "you must help me pack. The moving van is going to be here at seven o'clock in the morning and we have a million things to do."

"But there was something—"

"Angelique," said Monique sharply, "that's enough. Now get to your room and start sorting your things so that I can pack them. Hurry!"

The house that Toussaint Montambeault had found for his daughter Monique was in the middle of the French-Canadian neighborhood of Livingstone. It was different from every other house there, however, for it had been built before the advent of the Northeast Manufacturing Company. It stood on the southeast corner of Pine and Chestnut, where it caught the sunlight all day long, and it was surrounded by several feet of lawn on three sides. It had a generous back yard.

"The back yard will be a good place for Angelique to play," said Toussaint Montambeault. "With so many automobiles these days, the streets are no longer safe for children."

"Yes," replied Monique. She did not tell her father that Angelique no longer played outdoors unless she was forced out of the house by her mother.

The house was a six-room cottage with a full bathroom and in the Great Depression of the early thirties it cost forty-seven hundred dollars. Monique paid cash for it and after she had done so she still had fourteen thousand dollars left over from Armand's insurance and the sale of the house in Amity. It was a great deal of money for a widow with only one child in that depressed neighborhood, but Monique never told anyone that she had it. Instead, she had little cards printed announcing that she would do fine hand sewing at reasonable prices, and these she mailed to the women of all the best families in Livingstone.

Soon Monique Bergeron was absorbed into the French-Canadian society of her family and her neighborhood. She was once again one of them and on Sundays she and Angelique dined with Toussaint and Georgette or with Antoinette and her husband, Joseph Ledoux, and their four children. Toussaint's two daughters by his marriage to Georgette were now married and occasionally Monique went to visit Helene and Francoise. But she never felt really close to them. They had married mill hands and both lived on the west side of the river. Helene had five children and Francoise seven. Both families lived in squalid, overcrowded tenements that depressed Monique.

"Soap is still cheap," said Monique to her sister Antoinette. "You'd think Helene and Francoise would use some on themselves and their children."

Antoinette sighed. "Nothing is cheap these days. If the mills don't pick up soon, I don't know what any of us will do. Papa is lucky. He doesn't have to depend on Northeast."

Georgette Montambeault said that she thanked God on her knees every night that Toussaint had never gone into the mills but had had the brains to realize that the automobile was the

141

coming thing. He had begun to fool around with cars while he was still working as a blacksmith and once the automobiles became a reality instead of a crazy, fly-by-night dream, Toussaint was ready. Now he was employed as a mechanic at the Main Street Ford Garage and did not have to worry about the passing of the horse or the slashed workweek at the Northeast Manufacturing Company.

Angelique Bergeron hated her Aunt Helene and Aunt Francoise because they were dirty and their hair hung in strings. She hated her Aunt Antoinette because Antoinette was such a fuss-budget.

"The child is so pale," said Antoinette. "Why don't you make her get out in the sun, Monique?"

"Angelique is so thin, Monique. You should make her eat more bread and potatoes. She looks like a skeleton. If she lived with me for one week I guarantee you she'd have some meat on her bones!"

Angelique hated her cousins because they yelled and jumped and pulled at her when she came to visit.

"Viens jouer, 'Gelique," they shouted.

"I don't want to play with you," Angelique would say, pulling away from their grubby hands.

"Regardez," they'd yell. *"Elle parle Anglais. Petite Irlandaise!"*

To most French-Canadian children in Livingstone, all children who did not speak French were Irish.

"Don't be so stupid," Angelique would cry and run away to hide.

But most of all Angelique hated her grandfather. It was all because of him that she was enrolled in a French Catholic school.

"C'est terrible," said Toussaint to Monique. *"Un enfant qui ne peut pas parler sa langue."*

"It is because of her father," replied Monique. "He al-

142

ways spoke English to her and whenever I speak to her she refuses to answer in French, although she knows perfectly well what I'm saying. But no. She always answers me in English."

"If you ask me," said Georgette Montambeault, "what that child needs is a good whack on the behind. It's unnatural for a child her age to be hiding in her room all the time, refusing to speak when she is spoken to. She needs a damned good licking."

Monique sighed, "She has not got over the death of her father," she replied. "He spoiled her rotten."

Angelique was graduated from Saint George's Parochial School when she was thirteen, which made her unique in the neighborhood. Most children did not finish grade school until they were at least fourteen or, more often, fifteen or sixteen. Another thing that made her unique was the fact that she was going on to high school.

"What for?" demanded Toussaint when Monique apprised him of this. "What good will it do the girl? I tell you, Monique, you are making a mistake. All high school will do is to make her think she's better than she is. Angelique has enough fancy ideas now. You'd better put a stop to it before she gets even worse!"

But Monique stood firm, although she did not tell her father the true reasons.

"She is frail," she told Toussaint. "In another year she will be stronger. Then I can take her out of school and send her to work."

But the truth of the matter was that Monique did not want Angelique to end up in the mills. She hoped that if her daughter went through high school she would one day be able to get a job as a secretary. So Angelique was enrolled in Saint Antoine's High School for Girls.

But on the day after her next birthday, she was transferred

143

by her mother to the Livingstone Central High School, which was not only coeducational but, as the French-Canadians put it, Protestant.

"It was time Angelique had a change," was the only explanation Monique ever gave to her outraged relatives.

And change Angelique did. Soon there was color in her cheeks and her figure began to fill out into curves and she smiled more than she ever had since coming to Livingstone. She no longer went to visit her relatives with her mother on Sundays and now the only times they ever saw her was when they came to Monique's house.

"What ails the girl?" they demanded.

"She merely likes to keep to herself," replied Monique, but she found it increasingly difficult, these days, to look any member of her family in the eye.

On the evening of Angelique's fourteenth birthday, Antoinette had come to visit, and without her whole family for a change. Since the day fell in the middle of the week she said that Joseph and the children needed their rest. She brought Angelique a dozen chocolate-frosted cupcakes and a pair of the most hideous cotton stockings Angelique had ever seen.

"Thank you, Aunt Antoinette," Angelique said.

"It is nothing," replied Antoinette, pleased. "But in these hard times it is all I could afford. Come. Sit down and talk for a minute. Tell me about high school."

"I can't," Angelique answered. "I have to do my homework."

She escaped to the dining room and spread her books out on the table. Her homework had been done hours ago but she did not want to sit in the kitchen and gossip and drink tea and eat cake. Angelique opened a book and started to read, but she could hear Monique and Antoinette, talking, talking, talking.

About everything and everybody, thought Angelique in disgust.

She did not know how much time had elapsed before she became aware that they were talking about her father. They had lowered their voices and now Angelique could catch only a word here and there.

"Cancer," Monique was saying.

"Awful, awful," replied Antoinette.

Angelique felt her palms getting damp and the trembling started throughout her body.

Papa!

But he did not answer.

Papa! Papa!

"Drank," said Monique.

"Awful, awful."

"For the child's sake—"

Angelique jumped up from her chair and went to the doorway to the kitchen.

"But what is it?" cried Antoinette. "Monique, look! The child is white as a sheet!"

"It's nothing," replied Angelique faintly. "I just have a headache."

"It's all those books," said Antoinette. "Too much studying is bad."

"Do you want some tea, Angelique?" asked Monique.

"No. No, thank you. I'm going to bed."

Angelique undressed and put on her nightgown, then took two aspirins, but the trembling would not stop.

What was it? It was something that she should remember but though it was quivering right on the edge of her mind, she could not recall what it was.

Papa, help me.

I have to remember, Papa.

Lie down, said Armand. Lie down, my darling. Sleep. Sleep.

In Angelique's dream there was a huge door and the knob was so high that she could not reach it. She tried and tried but something like mud kept holding her back. Somebody was behind the door, shouting. She had to reach the knob and open the door. Her life depended on it. Hurry. A little higher. Almost. Almost.

"Murderess!"

"Drunkard!"

Her fingers closed on the knob but the door was so heavy. She tugged and pulled as hard as she could but it would not open.

"Murderess!"

At last the door yielded to her and swung open as if its hinges had just been freshly oiled.

There was Dr. Southworth, tall and straight. So tall that his shadow was immense on the wall and she could see the outline of his raised fist.

And there was her mother, standing as if she had been carved of marble, only her eyes alive.

"You killed him!" shouted Dr. Southworth. "Just as sure as if you'd held a knife to his heart. You killed him!"

"You are a fool," said Monique and her voice was as cold as the marble that made up her body. "You are a fool and a drunkard."

Dr. Southworth's other hand came up and now he was holding a bottle.

"Armand had not moved out of his bed in weeks," demanded the doctor. "Where did this come from?"

Monique's marble figure did not move. Only her eyes.

"I've no idea," she said.

"You goddamned, miserable liar!" yelled the doctor. "It came from the Gamsby brothers and you bought it. You've been buying their poison for weeks!"

"You are a fool," Monique repeated.

"And I say again that you are a liar. I got it out of Tweedledee himself, not an hour ago. You bought this bottle and you've been doing business with them both since

146

before Christmas. You killed your husband. You killed him with this."

Dr. Southworth shook the bottle in her face but Monique would not move.

"With this!" shouted the doctor. "With this and your inhumanity and your lack of love and your cold body and your black, evil heart."

Monique Bergeron moved at last. She leaned toward Benjamin Southworth and spoke directly into his face.

"Yes," she said, "I went to the Gamsby brothers. I bought their poison and I fed it to Armand as often as he was conscious enough to gulp it down. And every minute I prayed. I prayed that every swallow would be his last and that he would have the decency to die."

"You black bitch," whispered Dr. Southworth.

"And do you know why?" asked Monique, as if he had not spoken. "Because for years Armand shamed me. He even turned my own child against me."

"That's a dirty lie!"

"What do you know about it?" demanded Monique. "All you know is what Armand chose to tell you and you can bet that he was never the villain in his stories. He was filthy—a pig, a drunkard and a liar—and I'm glad he's dead!"

Papa. Papa.

Angelique stood in the doorway and tried to scream. But her mother and the doctor could not hear her.

"And you can put it on the death certificate too!" said Monique. "Go ahead, write it down. He is dead and his wife rejoices."

"No," said the doctor and sat down.

Monique was triumphant. "Now get out of my house," she said. "I never want to set eyes on you again."

"A slow bleeding of the soul," whispered Dr. Southworth. "That's what it should say on that certificate. My friend died of a slow bleeding of the soul."

147

Papa. Papa. Papa.

Angelique awoke and sat bolt upright in bed. Her trembling hands fumbled for the lamp but even then she still trembled, and her body was soaked with perspiration.

Two years, she thought. It had taken her two years to remember and now she remembered everything.

When she had finally cried out and made herself heard that night, Monique and the doctor had turned just in time to see her fall unconscious to the floor. She had had to stay in bed all the next day and at the time she did not know why. Dr. Southworth came and gave her pills and when she asked why, he told her not to talk, to rest. The pills made her sleep, but once, when the doctor was talking to Monique, she heard him say, "You're lucky, Monique. The child does not remember what she heard."

Remember what? All this time she had tried to recall what it was that she must remember and now she knew.

Angelique sat in her bed with the blankets pulled up tight around her neck until the trembling stopped.

Is it true, Papa? she asked.

Yes, replied Armand. Do you think I would have left you otherwise?

A great calm began to come over her and then she knew what she must do.

Everything is within your grasp, said Armand. Hurry. Go downstairs. Hurry.

Very deliberately Angelique got up and put on her bathrobe. As she brushed her hair she smiled at her reflection in the mirror.

At last, Papa, she said as she opened her bedroom door and went downstairs.

Monique was in the kitchen, ironing.

"I see your headache is better," she said.

"Yes, Maman."

Angelique went to the stove and put on the water for

tea. Her movements were slow and studied and she felt as if she were acting on a stage. When the tea was ready she poured herself a cup and turned to Monique.

"Tell me, Maman, how did you feel after you killed my father?"

Monique Bergeron's iron stopped in the exact center of a white pillowcase and in seconds it had turned yellow.

"What are you saying, you wicked girl?" asked Monique. But her hands trembled and her voice shook.

"You heard what I said," replied Angelique in the same even tone. "How did you feel after you killed my father?"

Monique slammed her iron down on the board and advanced toward Angelique, her hand raised to strike her.

"Don't you dare touch me," said Angelique. "You murderess."

Monique lowered her hand. Her face had turned very white.

"Angelique!"

"A slow bleeding of the soul," said Angelique. "Tell me, Maman, what does that mean?"

"You are a bad, wicked girl," whispered Monique in horror.

"But I am not a murderess," said Angelique. "You are. You killed my father."

"No. No. You don't know what you are saying."

"I know exactly what I am saying. You killed him. I heard you confess it to Dr. Southworth the night Papa died. I heard every word."

"You were sick that night," said Monique. "You had just had a terrible shock and you fainted. You don't know what you're saying even now."

"Oh, yes I do," replied Angelique.

She smiled and her voice grew theatrically taunting. "My, my. I wonder what Aunt Antoinette would say if she knew you killed Papa? or *Grand-père?* What do you think he'd say? And Georgette. She doesn't like you, you know. I'll bet she'd love to hear how you killed Papa."

"Shut up!" cried Monique. "I won't listen to any more of this nonsense!"

"Don't, then," replied Angelique. "But the others will."

"No one would ever believe you," said Monique, and feeling that she had had the last word, returned to her ironing board. "No one would even listen to you, you silly child."

"Well, there's only one way to find out," answered Angelique. "I think I'll go visit Georgette tomorrow after school. We'll see whether or not she listens to me."

Georgette Montambeault had never forgiven Monique for many things. She still remembered Ansele and how Monique had not even come to the funeral. She remembered how Monique had gone right ahead and got married while her brother still lay in his coffin. Moreover, Georgette suspected that Monique had a little money put aside. Money that Monique would not talk about or share with her relatives. Oh, Georgette would listen to Angelique all right. With bated breath, hungry for the smallest detail.

"You can't prove a word of this," said Monique.

"Oh, come, Maman! You know better than that."

Angelique was right. She wouldn't have to prove a single word. All she'd have to do was plant one small seed of suspicion and Georgette would do the rest. It was all so unfair, Monique thought, just one little doubt and she'd be an outcast again. A woman who had probably murdered her husband. Where there's smoke there's fire. If it weren't true, why would a child say such a thing? And against her own mother? No, there must be something to the story. Monique could hear everyone talking, and she could not control her shaking hands.

"Of course, it would depend on what school I was going to," said Angelique.

"What do you mean?"

"I mean that if I were going to Livingstone Central, start-

150

ing tomorrow, I might not feel like going to visit Georgette."

And so, in Angelique's fourteenth year, it began. What Angelique wanted she got, and Monique's relatives said it was a crime the way she spoiled that child. Why she worked her fingers to the bone for Angelique. Look at how thin she was getting. God only knew that she had never been plump to begin with, but these days she looked positively haggard. But Angelique had never looked better.

"She is finally getting over the death of her father," said Monique's relatives.

"It's high time. There is a time for mourning and a time for forgetting."

Still, the public high school was not necessary. Monique would live to regret that, all right.

Livingstone Central High School was comprised of two big buildings of yellow brick, and over a thousand boys and girls attended classes there.

"You'll hate it, Angelique," said some of the girls who had attended Saint Antoine's High School for Girls with her.

"It's so big, you'll get lost."

"And all those dreadful boys."

"I heard that a girl got in the family way from going to that school."

"My father says that the boys who go to Central are all going to grow up to be gangsters."

"Only Protestants go there."

It was true that Livingstone High was big but that did not disturb Angelique. She had a certain anonymity there which pleased her because it gave her a chance to look around and listen. Everyone at Livingstone High spoke English and English without the terrible Canuck accent of her friends and relatives. The students at Livingstone Central spoke English like Armand had spoken it, the way Angelique herself spoke it, as her father had taught her from the time she had been a little girl.

151

No, no, my angel. Not "dem." *Them. Th.* Put your tongue between your teeth. Now say it. *Them. Th. Th.* Now say *these. They. That. Theater.*

Within a month Angelique had fitted herself into a group. Her girl friends no longer had French names; girls named Linda and Martha and Jane, with last names like Baker and Brown and Bates. They went to the movies together on Saturday afternoons and giggled over ice cream sodas afterward. They spent hours washing and styling each other's hair, giving one another manicures, and they exchanged clothes, movie magazines and sexy novels. But none of these activities ever took place at Angelique's house. In the very beginning, when she had realized that visiting back and forth was part of belonging to a group, Angelique decided that honesty was her best bet.

"My mother is high-strung," she said to her new friends. "She can't stand a lot of people in the house."

"What's the matter with her?" asked one of the girls. Angelique could make her lovely face look very sad.

"She hasn't been the same since my father died," she replied.

And her new friends, who had hard-working, affectionate parents, understood and did not think it at all strange that they never were introduced to Monique Bergeron.

When Linda and Martha and Jane were not talking about movie stars or hairdos, they talked about boys.

"That Robbie Hoyt. I could sure go for him."

"You bet. He's got K.L."

"What do you mean, K.L.?"

"Kissable Lips, you sap!"

"I'd rather have Donald Grover. Mm-m. Those shoulders!"

"Yes, Donald's big all over. I bet he could crush the breath out of a girl!"

"It makes me get goose bumps all over just to think of it!"

152

The first big dance of the year at Livingstone High was always in early October. It was given for the benefit of the athletic department and Angelique was invited by Jamie Marsh, who was on the basketball team. Jamie Marsh was seventeen years old, with blond curly hair and a heavy mouth, and he had his own car, which made him quite a catch for any girl. Angelique had hoped to be asked by Bill Endicott, who was the star halfback on the football team and a straight-A student besides. But Bill had a steady girl by the name of Jill Robbins, who was considered by many to be the prettiest girl in school.

"Are you crazy?" demanded Linda Baker when Angelique confessed this to her. "Why, Bill and Jill are a team. Even their names go together. They've been going steady ever since grammar school."

"I can't help that," Angelique answered flatly. "I want him."

"Don't be an idiot," said Linda. "You'd better settle for Jamie and be glad of it. I'm going with Ray Kelley, and you know what a nut he is. Believe me, if Jamie Marsh asked me to the dance I wouldn't be wasting my time thinking about Bill Endicott! Why, for heaven's sake, Bill doesn't even know you're alive. He's a *senior,* for heaven's sake!"

"He'll find out," replied Angelique.

"Who'll find out what?"

"Bill Endicott," said Angelique. "He'll find out I'm alive."

"Oh, for heaven's sake! Will you please forget about Bill?"

But Angelique did not forget. She spent two hours getting ready for the dance, and she was not fussing over herself for Jamie Marsh. She was thinking of Bill Endicott.

Jill Robbins is not as pretty as I am, Papa.

Of course not, my darling. Nobody is.

She even has *black* hair.

How unfortunate for her, said Armand.

Angelique smiled into the mirror and brushed her long blonde hair.

153

You'll see, Papa. He'll find out that I'm alive tonight.

I'm sure of it, replied Armand.

Good night, Papa. I'll tell you all about it when I get home.

Monique Bergeron stood in the living room, waiting for her daughter to come downstairs, and she shook her head impatiently when she found herself thinking the words "living room." "Parlor" or "front room" had always been good enough for her and everyone she knew, but Angelique had picked up a lot of fancy ideas since she had transferred to Livingstone High. When she heard Angelique on the stairs, she called out to her.

"Come in here, Angelique," she said. "I'm in the parlor."

"Living room, Mother," replied Angelique.

"Why isn't this friend of yours calling for you here?" demanded Monique. "Why must you go out to meet him like a little tart on an assignation?"

Angelique put her coat down on a chair along with the little purse and gloves she was carrying. She fixed her mother with the cold look that Monique had come to know and fear.

"It is immoral, I tell you," said Monique.

"Listen, Mother," Angelique replied, "we might as well have this over and done with right now. I don't want my friends coming to this house. I am ashamed to have them meet you."

Monique stood as if she had been slapped across the face.

"You are a bad girl," she said because that was all she could think of to say.

"And you are a stupid woman. You have never even bothered to learn English. You are a tight-fisted old penny-pincher who takes in sewing when you don't have to. Besides that, you are a sneak and a liar."

"What are you talking about?" demanded Monique.

Angelique sighed. "Don't you think I've seen the statements that come from the bank every month?" she asked patiently as if she were talking to a retarded child. "Don't you think I know about the money Papa left?"

154

"Your father never had a cent to his name," shouted Monique. "That money is mine, inherited from my grandmother. He never had a cent, I tell you!"

"I suppose all that insurance was on your sainted grandmother," said Angelique with another patient sigh. "Oh, Mother, please don't be such a complete fool! And do me the honor please of not taking me for one."

"God is going to punish you," said Monique impotently.

Angelique gave her a cold, hard look.

"Why should He?" she asked. "He never punished you for taking my father from me."

Monique did not answer and Angelique went out the front door and down the steps to the street. She was smiling because, of course, neither Monique nor anyone else in the whole world could know that Armand had not gone away from Angelique at all.

Her father was always with her, waiting for her to talk to him. Tonight she had left him in her room but she knew full well that he would show up at the dance later if she needed him. If everything went well for her, though, and she didn't, he would be waiting in her room when she got home, eager to hear all about everything. Angelique had never told anyone that her father was still with her because he had asked her not to.

It will be our secret, my angel, he had said. I can trust you not to tell, can't I?

Why, Papa, what a thing to ask! You know very well that I've always been able to keep a secret.

Her father laughed because, of course, he'd been joking with her. Her father never found fault with her, or disagreed with her. His approval of everything she said and did was constant and unwavering.

Jamie Marsh was waiting for Angelique in his car at the corner of Bridge and Ash Streets. He felt rather dashing and brave to be meeting a girl this way. It was the first time in

155

his life he'd ever done such a thing. The parents of all the girls he had ever dated always met him at the door whenever he called and then engaged him in inane conversation while he waited for their daughters. The parents of the girls Jamie took out always knew his mother and father.

"How is your mother, Jamie? And your father?"

"They're fine, thank you."

He saw her hurrying toward the car and he leaned forward to open the door.

"Good evening," said Angelique formally.

"Hi," answered Jamie Marsh.

Oh, she was something all right, this Angelique. There was something different about her. She never screeched like other girls, but spoke in a soft voice. And she smiled to herself a lot, as if she had some secret that was the most amusing thing in the world.

"What's so funny?" Jamie had asked her more than once, but Angelique only continued to smile.

"Nothing, Jamie. Nothing at all."

It was probably just as well that his folks didn't know that he was taking Angelique to the dance. Not that there was anything the matter with her but his folks *were* inclined to be a bit stuffy. And he had to be honest, Angelique *was* different from any girl he had ever dated. Jamie Marsh had the distinct feeling that his folks wouldn't understand about Angelique, so he had told them that he was going to the dance "stag."

"A lot of the guys are going to this time," he explained to his mother. "Just for a change."

"Oh," said his mother, relieved. One of the greatest fears of her life was that one of her children might turn out to be unpopular.

"All set, Angie?" asked Jamie.

"Of course," replied Angelique. "But please don't ever call me 'Angie' again."

156

There. That was one of the ways she was different from other girls. She could say a thing like that, calm and cold as ice, but a guy couldn't get mad at her. He just felt as if he'd been put in his place good and proper, but he didn't get mad.

"Okay," said Jamie and put the car in gear. "What shall I call you then? Angel?"

She gave him that sweet smile of hers.

"Yes," she answered. "If you like, you may call me Angel."

The gymnasium of the Livingstone High School was decorated with crepe paper and autumn leaves and huge cutouts of footballs and basketballs and baseball bats. At one end of the big room there was a group of eight boys on a raised platform, Petey DeRocca and his Dixieland Seven, and if they did not play altogether on key or in tempo, they could at least play loud. Petey DeRocca was worshiped by every boy and girl at Livingstone High.

Angelique danced with Jamie and Jamie thought that he had never held such a smooth, cool girl before. But she was soft too. Her blue dress was made of silk and it felt soft and slippery under his fingers. Her hand in his was not clammy the way other girls' hands were and when he put his chin against her temple her skin there, too, was perfectly dry and cool.

He moved his hand down her back and felt the narrow strap of her brassiere. He began to wonder if her bare breasts would feel cool and dry or if the flesh would be warm and quivery under his touch. He missed a step and stumbled against her.

"God," he said, "it's hot in here."

"Oh?" answered Angelique. "Really? I hadn't noticed."

His hands began to tremble and he could not think of a single thing to talk about but apparently Angelique didn't notice anything.

"Who's that big, tall fellow over there?" she asked. "The one dancing with that black-haired girl in the yellow dress?"

157

"Him?" said Jamie in relief. "Why, that's Bill Endicott. I thought everybody knew him."

"I don't know him," replied Angelique.

"Good grief, he's the best football player in this school," said Jamie. "In fact, he's probably the best football player in any school in this whole state!"

"All I know is that he's in my Latin class."

"Oh?"

"Yes," answered Angelique. "Listen, Jamie, will you do me a favor?"

"Sure."

"Introduce me, will you? Let's swap partners for the next dance."

"What for?" demanded Jamie, quickly resentful.

Angelique looked up into his eyes and smiled.

"Don't be silly, Jamie," she said. "I only want to ask him a couple of questions about the next Latin test. I'm having a little trouble and you know how strict Mr. Evans is. You wouldn't want me to start getting bad grades, would you?"

"Of course not," replied Jamie and felt ashamed that he'd been jealous. "Come on."

Jill Robbins was short and dark, with a pointed little face and a disposition that made her the most popular girl at Livingstone High. She and Bill Endicott had grown up next door to each other and had always planned to get married. Some day when they had both graduated from college and Bill had a good job and they could afford to settle down. They had gone together for so long that they took each other for granted, like a couple that had been married for twenty-five years. Neither held any surprises for the other and they liked it that way. The only thing left to them was to sleep together and both of them doubted that even this would be much of a surprise.

"See you tomorrow," Bill would say every evening after they finished their homework.

"You bet," Jill would answer.

Friday nights they went out to a dance or a movie and afterward they always parked in Bill's father's car. The ritual never varied. They spent exactly one hour in the woods at the edge of the city. On those nights Bill and Jill kissed with their mouths open and Bill played with Jill's breasts. Then he'd open his fly and Jill would play with his penis while he put his hand between her legs and manipulated her until they both reached a climax. Then they wiped themselves off with tissues from a box that Bill kept in the glove compartment of the car, combed their hair and went home.

"How about swapping around?" said Jamie Marsh after he had introduced Angelique to Bill and Jill.

"You bet," said Jill. It was her favorite expression but she delivered it with so much good will and friendship that no one ever became annoyed at its constant repetition.

The minute that Bill Endicott put his arm around her to dance, Angelique felt as if she had been lifted up off the floor. Her heart pounded and her legs felt heavy, but her face was as cool and calm as ever. She even managed to send a smile of triumph across to Linda Baker as she danced by in the arms of Ray Kelley.

The look of surprise on Linda's face seemed to clear Angelique's head and she managed to frame some very intelligent questions about the conjugation of Latin verbs.

"I know what you mean," said Bill Endicott. "I had an awful time myself at first. But look, don't get discouraged. I'll help you. How about if I come over to your house tomorrow? We could go through the book together."

"No," replied Angelique, "my mother is having guests tomorrow. It would be just impossible to study in a house full of chattering women."

"Well, how about the library then?" asked Bill. "I could pick you up around two in the afternoon."

"No," Angelique said. "I have some errands to do downtown. But I could meet you."

"Okay," Bill answered. "I'll see you at the library at two o'clock then."

Angelique bit back the impulse to say "You bet."

"Thank you, Bill. I certainly appreciate your going to all this trouble."

Bill Endicott smiled. "No trouble," he said and took her back to Jamie Marsh.

The rest of the evening seemed interminable to Angelique. Jamie's erotic visions of her would not leave him and he perspired like a stevedore. He kept clutching at her with his wet hands and stepping on her feet and his chin felt sticky against her face.

"You're right," said Angelique finally. "It *is* warm in here."

"Yeah," replied Jamie. "How about leaving?"

"Fine."

He took her to the Pilgrim Ice Cream Parlor for a soda. But when they got back in the car he felt even more ill at ease than he had at the dance.

"Where do you want to go now?" he asked.

Angelique turned to stare at him.

"To the corner of Bridge and Ash Streets, of course," she said. "It's late and I have to get home."

With any other girl in the world, Jamie Marsh would have shouted, "What the hell do you mean, you have to get home? I take you out and show you a good time and what do I get for it? Not even a good-night kiss?"

But he could not say any of this to Angelique, which infuriated him. He shoved the car into gear and pulled away from the Pilgrim with a squeal of tires. When he reached the intersection of Bridge and Ash, he slammed on the brakes.

"What's the matter?" asked Angelique.

"Nothing," replied Jamie sullenly. "Nothing at all."

160

She put the cool, cool fingertips of one hand against his hot cheek.

"What is it, Jamie?" she asked softly. "Why are you cross with me?"

What, wondered Jamie helplessly, could a guy possibly say at a time like this to a girl like Angelique? He turned his head and looked out the car window.

"I'm not mad, Angel."

"Yes you are," said Angelique. "Now come on. Tell me."

Her fingertips traced a cool little path down the side of his jaw.

"Oh, Angel," said Jamie and turned and put his arm around her shoulder very gently. "I'm crazy about you, can't you tell?"

He hadn't meant to say it but before he could stop himself the words were out of his mouth and he realized with a pang that was half fear that he *was* crazy about her.

"But, Jamie—"

"Sh-h," said Jamie and tilted her head up and kissed her on the mouth.

It was the first time that Angelique Bergeron had ever been kissed by a boy and she found the sensation strangely pleasant. Her lips began to tingle and she felt herself wanting to press them harder against Jamie's. His hands cupped the sides of her face as he kissed her and then moved down to her shoulders and she found that very pleasant too.

But what Angelique liked best about kissing Jamie was the way he breathed. He breathed as if he had been running for a long time and his hands trembled on her shoulders. Angelique was not trembling, nor was she breathing any differently than she always did. The sensation she felt was rather like that she experienced when she stepped into a warm bath. Pleasant. Warm. Caressing. But certainly nothing to pant or tremble over. But Angelique liked the idea that kissing her made a boy like Jamie short of breath and nervous.

161

"Oh, Angel, Angel," he repeated over and over as he kissed her mouth and her cheeks and finally her throat. "Angel, Angel."

His face was sopping wet and when she put her hands up to the sides of his head, she found that his hair was damp too. She put her arms around his shoulders as if to embrace him but what she was really doing, as she seemed to caress his back, was drying her hands on his coat.

"Angel, Angel."

He kept kissing her and all of a sudden she was bored. The pleasant, bathtub feeling was replaced by one of annoyance and she pulled away from him.

"Please, please," he muttered, groping for her.

"Jamie."

Her voice stopped him cold.

"Jamie," she said more gently. "I have to get home."

He sat back in the seat, trying to catch his breath.

He was sweating like a pig, he thought, in self-disgust. His belly hurt and his genitals were swollen to the point of explosion.

Goddamn her, he thought savagely. Goddamn her to hell.

Angelique was crying.

"What's the matter?" asked Jamie, stunned by her tears. "What's the matter, Angel?"

"I'm frightened," said Angelique.

"Oh please, Angel." He put his arm around her. "Honest to God, I didn't mean to scare you."

"It's just that I've never known a man of such passion," she said, keeping her head carefully turned away from him.

Jamie almost beamed, his sore belly forgotten. A man, Angelique had said. A man of passion.

"I couldn't help myself, Angel," he said. "Honest. It's just that I'm so crazy about you."

He reached for her again, but she moved more quickly and opened the car door.

162

"Oh, no," she pleaded. "No more, Jamie. I just couldn't stand it. Please. Let me go. I must get home."

"Tomorrow night?" he asked.

She was standing outside the car.

"I don't know if I can," she said, "but I'll try. If you drive by here around eight tomorrow night I'll be here if I can."

"I'll be here for sure," Jamie replied. "Please try very hard, Angel."

"Yes, Jamie."

She watched him drive away, her eyes perfectly dry. She put away the handkerchief she hadn't needed and began to walk home. But she was too elated to walk and in a few minutes she began to run. She ran all the way home, smiling. Tonight Jamie Marsh. Tomorrow Bill Endicott. She couldn't wait to get to her room to tell Armand.

Bill Endicott was waiting when she walked into the Livingstone City Library at two-thirty the next afternoon.

"I thought you weren't coming," he said. "You said two o'clock."

And Angelique, who had been standing across the street from the library for the last half hour, looked up at him and smiled.

"Oh, I'm so sorry," she said. "I had these errands to do for Mother and they took longer than I had anticipated."

Jill Robbins, or any other girl Bill knew, for that matter, would have spent a half hour explaining her reasons for being late. Angelique had merely taken longer than she had anticipated. Bill grinned at her.

"Well, let's get to it," he said.

They worked over their Latin books for an hour and when they had finished Angelique smiled at Bill and put a hand on his arm.

"I truly can't tell you how much I appreciate your help," she said. "Thank you."

She was like no other girl he knew, thought Bill again. She did not have to make wisecracks when she was grateful. She merely said a simple thank you. And she didn't have the tough, almost boyish air that other girls had. Even Jill sometimes looked more like a boy than a girl with her tiny breasts and her bobbed hair. Angelique's hair was drawn back from the sides and top of her head and tied with a ribbon so that it hung almost to her waist. She was wearing a navy-blue dress with a little white collar and she looked immaculately blonde. You could tell that Angelique had breasts and hips too, and when she stood up the curve of her behind was pronounced and lovely.

"How about some coffee?" asked Bill.

He took her to a small diner down the street from the library but Angelique ordered tea. As they sat at the white-topped counter Angelique looked as if she were sitting in a lovely drawing room pouring tea into her cup.

"What do you do on Sundays?" Bill asked.

"I go for walks," replied Angelique.

"Oh? Where?"

"I never really decide that in advance," answered Angelique. "Especially in October. Everything is so beautiful this time of the year. Sometimes I just start walking and I don't stop until I'm tired. Tomorrow, though, I think I'll walk up toward Deer Park. The trees will be lovely there."

"I might just be up around there myself tomorrow," said Bill.

Angelique stirred her tea. "That would be nice."

That same evening, Angelique walked to the corner of Bridge and Ash Streets and hid behind a tree. From where she was hidden she could see Jamie Marsh's parked car and Jamie getting out every five minutes and looking up and down the street. He stayed there for over an hour before he finally drove away. Angelique laughed all the way home.

Boys like Jamie and Bill always thought they should have

164

their own way, she told Armand that night. They were important boys, from good families, who lived in the north end, and they were star athletes too. Well, they'd soon find out that Angelique wasn't going to fall into their arms as easily as all that.

They'll have to fight for me, Papa, she said.

You're certainly worth fighting for, replied Armand just as she had known he would.

The next afternoon Angelique walked to Deer Park, which was situated at the eastern outskirts of Livingstone, more than two miles from the Bergeron house. She carried a small basket of sandwiches and a book of English verse, both of which she detested. But the sandwich basket was made of straw and went very well with her tan skirt and the book had a dark-blue cover which she fancied made her look more intellectual than she actually was. When she arrived at the park, she selected one tree carefully for its size and color and she was sitting there with her back against the trunk, the open book in her lap, when Bill Endicott drove up.

He stopped the car and sat staring at her, thinking that he had never seen such a lovely sight in his entire life. Angelique seemed to be a part of the surroundings, rather than separate from them. Her clothing blended with the autumnal landscape and yet she stood out against the green fall grass and the colors of October seemed to make a halo of fire around her. The sun struck her hair and turned it into the finest threads of pure gold and her skin was like warm cream. Bill Endicott felt a slow pounding in his chest, like the excitement he felt just before a big football game, and he almost hated to get out of the car for fear of frightening Angelique. She might change her position or the look of rapture on her face.

"Hi," he said, more loudly than he had intended, and sure enough, she moved, startled.

"Hello," she called. "I didn't hear you drive up."

"That must be a pretty interesting book," said Bill and he approached until he was standing over her.

"Yes," she answered. "Won't you sit down?"

"Thanks," Bill replied. "What's in the basket?"

"Sandwiches. I planned to spend the day here."

"Oh," he said. "I didn't bring anything."

"That's all right." She looked him straight in the eyes. "I brought enough for two. I was hoping you'd come."

They read for a while from Angelique's book of English verse, and then they ate and leaned back on the ground watching the glow of leaves against the blue sky. When they decided to walk, Bill took her hand to help her up and somehow he did not drop it as they began to stroll.

As they walked along the narrow, leaf-covered paths Bill said, "I almost hate for next year to come."

"Why do you say that?" asked Angelique.

"Because next fall I won't be here. I'll be away at college."

"But that's wonderful," said Angelique.

He looked at her. "I suppose so," he replied. "But I'm sure going to miss old Livingstone High and playing football and all the kids."

"Aren't you going to play football at college?"

"Listen, to play on the team at the University you have to be really good and I don't kid myself that I'm *that* good."

"Of course you are," replied Angelique. "I saw you play last Saturday against Concord and you were absolutely marvelous. Why, you won that game singlehanded."

"Baloney," said Bill, but he felt warmed and pleased by her words. "Football is a team game. No man wins a game alone."

As the weeks of October faded and turned into a cold, windy November, Angelique continued to see Bill whenever she could. She also saw Jamie Marsh whenever she felt like it but Jamie tired her with his constant need to touch her,

166

although she still got a sort of thrill when she knew he was sexually excited.

"My God, Angel," said Jamie. "You're driving me crazy. You're all I think about. All the time."

So occasionally Angelique let him kiss her and fondle her a little. But only a little.

"Listen," demanded Jamie one night when she had excited him until he ached. "What is it with you anyway? Is it some other guy?"

"Don't be ridiculous, Jamie," answered Angelique coldly. "It's just that I don't like to be pawed all the time. And lately it seems to me that's all you think about."

"I heard you were in the Pilgrim having a soda with Bill Endicott the other day," said Jamie sullenly.

Angelique turned on him. "Yes, I was," she said. "But it wasn't a soda I was having, it was tea and toasted English muffins if you must know. And now, what business is it of yours who I see or where I go?"

"Aw, Angel, don't get mad. I was only asking. After all, it doesn't look too good, you know. Being seen with Bill, I mean."

"I don't know what you mean and I don't think you do either."

"Well, Bill, I mean. He belongs to Jill Robbins."

"No one in this world belongs to anybody," answered Angelique, rage in her voice.

Jamie had never seen her angry. "Hey, Angel, calm down. I didn't mean anything. But after all, everybody knows about Bill and Jill."

"Not quite," said Angelique. "I don't recognize anything about Bill and Jill and I'm somebody."

But people were beginning to talk. Angelique thought she detected a certain coolness in Linda and Jane and Martha these days and as usual it was Linda who spoke up first.

167

"How come you went to the movies with Bill Endicott last Thursday night?" she asked.

Angelique laughed but her three friends did not laugh with her.

"What am I faced with here?" she asked. "An inquisition?"

"I don't think it's so funny," replied Linda. "After all, you know perfectly well that Jill has been going steady with Bill for years and years. They're going to get married some-day."

"Linda, for heaven's sake," said Angelique. "I just happened to be downtown and I ran into Bill on Main Street. I wanted to see the movie at the Lyric, so he asked me to go with him."

"Maybe Jill wanted to see it too," answered Linda.

"Oh, don't be so silly," said Angelique, no longer laughing. "Can't a boy and a girl be just friends without everyone making a big thing about it? And that's all there is between Bill and me. We're just friends."

"Why didn't you get Jamie to take you to the show?" asked Linda. "After all, *he's* supposed to be your boyfriend."

"I hate that word 'boyfriend,' " answered Angelique, dismissing Linda. She turned to Jane and Martha for sympathy. "What is all this anyway? You don't even like Jill Robbins. You told me so yourself, Jane, and so did you, Martha. Now, all of a sudden, all you can think of is poor little Jill Robbins. How come?"

Martha and Jane looked at one another and shrugged and again it was Linda who answered.

"Liking or not liking Jill isn't the point," she said. "The point is that Bill Endicott is Jill's steady and everybody knows it. You've got no right to try to take Bill away from her."

"All right, all right," replied Angelique. "You don't have to get mad at me over nothing, do you? I won't bother with Bill Endicott again. Okay?"

The three girls smiled.

"Let's walk downtown and get a soda," said Linda.

"Sure," replied Martha and Jane. "Come on, Angelique."

Angelique wanted to smack their smiling faces and tell them where they could go in a hurry. But that time wasn't yet.

Just wait, thought Angelique. Just you wait. All of you. You'll see.

The right time came a week before Christmas. There was a holiday dance at Livingstone High and Angelique went with Jamie. She wore a new dress of holly-berry red and she knew that she had never looked better. She danced with Jamie but she watched Bill Endicott. He couldn't keep his eyes off her and Angelique knew that all she had to do was wait.

There was an overflowing crowd in the Livingstone High gymnasium that night and somehow, during the first intermission, Angelique managed to get herself separated from Jamie. She tossed her coat over her shoulders and went outside and within minutes Bill Endicott joined her.

"Please," said Bill. "Come sit in the car for a minute. I've got to talk to you."

Angelique looked him over coolly. "Why, Bill," she replied, "I couldn't do that. I came with Jamie and right now he must be wondering where I am. I've got to get back inside."

"Listen," pleaded Bill, "where are you going after the dance?"

Angelique laughed. "As usual, Jamie will take me to the Pilgrim for an ice cream soda."

"Listen, I know it's a nervy thing to ask, but could you meet me afterward? After Jamie takes you home, I mean?"

"Nice girls don't have late dates, Bill. You know that."

"Please. Please, I've just got to talk to you."

Angelique looked at him for a long moment. "All right," she said at last, "but don't pick me up at my house. I'll meet you."

"Where?" asked Bill urgently. "Just tell me where."

169

"Do you know Bridge and Ash Streets?"

"Of course."

"There," said Angelique. "I'll meet you there at twelve."

"I don't know if I can get Jill home by twelve."

Again Angelique gave him a long look. "Well, that's too bad," she said. "I'll be there at twelve and I'll wait five minutes."

"I'll be there," Bill answered. "Somehow."

That evening Angelique Bergeron developed a headache around eleven o'clock and Jamie, all concern for her well-being, took her home. Or at least as close to her home as Angelique would ever allow him to get. He let her off at the corner of Bridge and Ash.

A few minutes after Angelique and Jamie left the dance, Bill Endicott was suddenly taken with a gripping stomach-ache.

"I have to get out of here," he said to Jill. "Honest to God, I feel as if I'm going to throw up any second."

On the way home Jill Robbins was very quiet.

"Is there something bothering you, Bill?" she asked.

In the dark, Bill felt himself flushing. Jill sounded quiet, and serious and upset. It was almost unheard of for her to be any of these things.

"Of course not," answered Bill. "I just feel rotten, that's all. Any crime in that?"

"No." And then Jill added, "It's just that I guess you've been feeling rotten for weeks now."

"For Pete's sake, what makes you say a thing like that?" demanded Bill.

"You haven't been yourself," answered Jill flatly. "I've known you for too long not to know what's happening inside you."

"My God," Bill said, "things have come to something pretty awful when a guy can't even have a bellyache."

When they arrived at Jill's house she did not linger. She got

170

out immediately and then looked at him through the car window.

"Good night, Bill," she said. "If you feel like talking tomorrow, I'll be around."

Jill turned on the light in the front hall. Her parents were in bed sound asleep, secure in the knowledge that their daughter was safe. After all, she was out with Bill Endicott and Bill would never let anything happen to Jill.

Jill tiptoed out to the dark kitchen and watched through the window. Bill did not make his usual U-turn at the end of the street and drive down to his own house. He sped off down the road as if a mob of gangsters was after him. Jill went upstairs to her room very slowly. Her legs felt heavy and the peculiar feeling in her stomach was one she had never before experienced. It was fear. She went to bed and tried to imagine a life for herself without Bill but no coherent image would come to her mind. She simply could not visualize herself without Bill at her side.

Bill arrived at the corner of Bridge and Ash at a quarter to twelve and in the fifteen minutes that he waited for Angelique he smoked three cigarettes, which made him feel more headachy and edgy than ever. He usually smoked an average of three cigarettes a week and only when he happened to think of it. He heard a steeple clock nearby tolling midnight but he did not hear Angelique until she opened the car door.

"Hello, Bill," she said, just as if it were the middle of the afternoon.

She got into the car and sat down and Bill reached across her to shut the door on her side. Then he leaned back and lit another cigarette.

"Angelique," he said, "I'm going to say this straight out with no beating around the bush."

Angelique laughed softly. "My goodness," she answered, "you sound as if you were about to sentence me to prison or something."

171

"Angelique, I want you to be my girl. My steady girl."

There was a long, long silence and then Angelique said, "May I have one of those cigarettes?"

"Are you crazy?" asked Bill. "A kid like you smoking? You'll get sick."

"No, I won't," replied Angelique matter-of-factly. "I've smoked before. At home in my own room."

"What does your mother have to say about that?"

"Nothing," replied Angelique. "Have you told Jill?"

During the past weeks Bill had become accustomed to Angelique's swift changes of subject.

"No."

"Isn't that rather odd?" asked Angelique quietly. "How can you ask me to be your girl when you already have a girl?"

"I'll tell her," said Bill. "Tonight just didn't seem to be the right time, that's all."

"That isn't true," replied Angelique flatly. She puffed on the cigarette. "What you really mean is that you didn't tell Jill because you wanted to be sure I'd say yes first. Isn't that so?"

"No," objected Bill. "I just couldn't tell her tonight. But what difference does that make? I want you to be my girl. Not Jill."

"Why?"

"Why what?"

"Why do you want me to be your girl?"

"Because I can't think about anybody else. I don't want to be with anybody else. Every time I am, you're all I can think about."

"You have to tell Jill," said Angelique.

"I'll tell her," replied Bill. "Just say yes, Angelique. Please."

"No."

"But don't you like me even a little?" asked Bill. "All these weeks I've thought you liked me."

"I *do* like you," answered Angelique. "But I'm not going to

172

say I'll be your girl until you've told Jill. Then maybe I'll say yes. I'd have to think about it."

"I'll tell her."

"When?"

"Tomorrow."

"Tomorrow when?"

"Tomorrow afternoon."

"Are you sure?"

"Yes, for God's sake. Will you, Angelique?"

"I told you I'd have to think about it."

"How long will you have to think about it?"

Angelique laughed. "Why, until tomorrow night, I suppose. Tomorrow night after you've told Jill."

"You know I'm crazy about you, don't you, Angelique?"

"Don't use those words," replied Angelique sharply. "Why don't people ever talk about love? Why must it be that people are always 'crazy about' each other?"

"All right then. I love you."

He reached for her and drew her to him gently but his gentleness was an effort and this confused him. He wanted to grab her, hurt her and yet he felt this overwhelming love for her at the same time. Her lips were soft under his and yet he sensed a hunger there, a latent strength, so he kissed her harder. He felt her gasp and in the next moment his arms were around her, holding her crushed against him, feeling her go soft and pliant. His hand cupped one of her breasts and he could feel its rigid nipple right through her clothing. His other hand came up from around her and held her face tightly so that he could have her mouth where he wanted it. He felt her body arching against his as if in a spasm.

"Oh, God," he said against her mouth.

She broke away from him and moved to the far side of the car.

"No, please," she pleaded. "You're frightening me."

He tried to hold her again but her body would not yield and

173

she kept her head turned away as if she did not want him to see her tears. But he could hear her sobbing.

"I never dreamed that there could be a man of such passion," she said. "It frightens me. Please. You'll have to be very patient with me, Bill. You'll have to teach me."

His hands reached out. "Don't be afraid, Angelique."

"No. Don't," she said, turning away from him.

For some crazy, unaccountable reason he found himself thinking of Jill, with her tiny, almost flat little breasts and the way she opened her legs so methodically and matter-of-factly for him.

"I don't want to frighten you, Angelique," he said. "I'll be very careful, I'll never frighten you."

She was out of the car. "Tomorrow, if you tell Jill, come here. I'll meet you." Her voice was muffled by the handkerchief she held in front of her mouth.

"I'll be here," said Bill. "Eight o'clock."

"No, make it eight-thirty."

"All right," he said. "Eight-thirty."

"Andgaleek Burdgaron!" cried Bill Endicott's mother, Paula. "Who in the world is *she?*"

"Just a girl, Mother."

"Just a girl!" cried Paula.

"I met her at school," said Bill wearily. He thought he'd fall over and die if he had to go through a scene with his mother now after the hour he had just spent with Jill Robbins. Not that Jill hadn't been a good sport about the whole thing. You could always depend on Jill for that. It was just that she had looked so funny. Her skin had gone sort of white and she'd looked pinched around the mouth.

"I understand, Bill," she'd said. "I knew there was something bothering you."

"Honest to God, Jill, I'm sorry."

174

"I know you are, Bill," she replied. "Now I wish you'd go home. Please."

"Why, sure, Jill," he answered. "Anything you say."

So he'd come home to face his mother and father.

"But whoever *heard* of such a name!" said Paula Endicott. "It sounds like one of those foreign names like those people who work in the mills. Andgaleek Burdgaron indeed!"

"Her father is dead," answered Bill patiently, as if he were reciting a lesson. "But her mother doesn't work in the mills. She stays home."

"Well, what do they live on?" demanded Paula.

"I don't know."

"Well, how much *do* you know about this—this Andgaleek?"

"I want her to be my girl," said Bill.

"Are you out of your mind?" asked Paula shrilly. "What about Jill?"

"I've already told her."

"Told her *what?*" demanded Paula, and it occurred to Bill that his mother almost always spoke in italics. "Told her that you're throwing her *over?* And for a girl that none of us has even ever *heard* of? Bill, you are talking absolute *nonsense.*"

"Mother—" Bill began, but his mother would not let him finish.

"I won't listen to *another* word of this foolishness. I just *won't*. Frederick, *talk* to him."

Frederick Endicott was a heavy-set man who always seemed to be in need of a shave. He was the general manager of the Livingstone Power and Light Company, and he was also given to telling dirty jokes and putting his point across with an elbow to the ribs of his listener. Frederick Endicott smoked Havana cigars, belonged to every club in Livingstone and thought of his wife as a pure vessel given to him to bear his children and keep his house. But that didn't mean that he

175

had a narrow mind. Not by any manner of means. Why, at any out-of-town convention, Fred Endicott was the life of every party. You could always depend on old Fred to know where the strip shows were and what telephone numbers to call when a few girls were needed to liven things up a bit.

"Now listen here, Paula," said Frederick Endicott to his wife. "You leave this to me. Come on in the den, son. It's high time we had a little talk, you and I."

Bill Endicott knew that his father drank too much at parties and that he talked too much and that he was inclined to give other men's wives a free feel whenever he could talk one of them into going into the kitchen with him for ice cubes. But his father was also respected in his job, had more friends than he could count and made a good living for his family. He was, therefore, someone to be looked up to and listened to. Everybody said what a fine man Frederick Endicott was.

"Now listen here, son," said Frederick Endicott when the two of them were seated in his den. "You want to go away to college next year, right?"

"Yes, Dad."

"You want to be a lawyer some day, right?"

"Sure, Dad."

"And you know how important family relationships are in business, right?"

Every time Frederick Endicott said "Right?" he jutted his cigar out into Bill's face until all of a sudden Bill wanted to yell at him.

For Christ's sake, he wanted to shout, will you put down that goddamned cigar?

"Yes, Dad."

"Now look, Bill," said his father, smiling now and tolerant. "I know how you feel. Every young stud has to sow his wild oats. I understand that. There's nothing wrong with a guy wanting to fool around with girls. Hell, I'd be worried about

176

you if you didn't. Think there was something wrong with you. But nobody gets serious over the girls they fool around with."

Again Bill was struck with the image of Jill with her open thighs as he had been the night before. And then he thought of Angelique, who was frightened into tears over just a few kisses and his hand on her nipple.

"Angelique isn't the kind of girl a guy fools around with," said Bill.

"Now, Bill," said Frederick Endicott, "I've lived in Livingstone all my life and believe me I know something about those little Canuck girls from the south end." He paused to relight his cigar and gave a little chuckle at the same time. "They're something all right, those little Canuck pussies."

Bill felt a little sick as he looked at his father.

"Please, Dad."

"No, now you listen to me, son," said Frederick Endicott. "A little good advice never hurt anybody, you know. Say, how'd you like a little drink? If you're old enough to rip off a little piece of Canuck tail you're old enough to drink. How about it?"

"No, thanks, Dad."

His father fixed a drink for himself and sat down opposite Bill again.

"Listen, son, you can be honest with your old man. You got it from her, right? And you like a little nookie, right? Come on, boy, you can tell me."

Two years before, Bill had been at a summer camp with a boy named Frank Bourne who came from New York City. Frank had a whole collection of sex books and when he read aloud from one of them he got a look on his face like Bill had never seen before. Frank got this same expression when he described his own sexual triumphs or listened to those of others or when he was instructing someone like Bill on the niceties of sexual techniques.

177

"Listen, kid," Frank would say. "Here's what you do when you get a girl's pants off, see."

Or Frank would say, "Tell me, kid, how do you feel when you think about being with a girl, huh? Come on, kid, tell me."

And now Bill Endicott, sitting opposite his father, saw the same expression on his face. The Frank Bourne look on the face of his own father.

"It's nothing like that, Dad," he said, swallowing. "I just— I just like her a lot, that's all."

Ever since Bill had been born, Frederick Endicott had been telling himself that he would never neglect the needs of his son in any way. When Bill had begun to mature, Frederick Endicott had planned that someday, before Bill went away to school, he would take his son along with him to one of his conventions.

"When a young buck begins to think about it," Frederick Endicott often said, "it's time for his old man to do something about it. When my kid's old enough I'll take him down to Boston or New York or some place like that and lead him straight to the best whorehouse I can find. Let a good whore teach him what he needs to know.

"Take a kid to a good whore," said Frederick Endicott, "and he doesn't go around looking for some nice girl to lay. The kid is satisfied and our young girls are protected. I tell you, if every man did that the shotgun would go out of style."

Frederick Endicott was looked upon by his contemporaries as being very civilized and modern in his outlook.

"Listen, son," said Frederick Endicott, "how about going down to Boston with me next weekend? I know a few girls down there who'll give you all the ass you want with no strings attached. No son of mine has to fool around with some little Canuck tramp."

Bill could stand no more. He jumped up and faced his father.

178

"I told you it's not like that," he shouted. "Do you have to dirty up everything with your filthy mind?"

Frederick Endicott flushed a deep red.

"There's no need for that kind of talk, Bill," he said coldly. "But just let me tell you something. You want to fool around with some girl, go right ahead. But remember this. We don't marry girls like that, so watch your step. The Endicott men don't marry Canucks."

The next evening Angelique was exactly twenty minutes late. She did not say a word as she got into the car. She merely sat and looked at him.

"Well, I told her," Bill said at last.

Angelique's eyes lighted up. "What did she say?"

"Nothing much."

Angelique's eyes were very bright now and almost greedy.

"She must have said something. Did she cry?"

Bill looked at her. "Of course not," he said. "Jill never cries. She doesn't believe in it."

"Well, what did she say?" demanded Angelique impatiently.

"Nothing, I told you," said Bill. "She just said okay, that she knew that something had been bothering me. Then she told me to go home." He put the car in gear. "I don't want to talk about Jill any more."

He drove up to Deer Park and stopped the car in the darkest place he could find.

"Aren't you forgetting something?" Angelique asked in a cool voice when he reached out for her.

"What?"

"I never said I'd be your girl."

"But you will," said Bill harshly and pulled her roughly to him. "You will." He began to kiss her. "Say it, Angelique, say it right now."

And all of a sudden she wasn't fighting him any more or acting cool or detached.

"Yes," she said into his mouth. "Yes, yes, yes."

Winter came and that year it brought with it not only cold and ice and snow but poverty such as the city had never known.

The Northeast Manufacturing Company was dead. Just like that, it seemed, the giant had rolled over and died and its death agony had lasted but a single week. One day the mills had been operating as usual and then old Lawrence Archibald's son, Lawrence, Jr., called his workers together and announced that in seven days the Company would close its doors temporarily.

"What is temporarily?" the workers wanted to know.

"Yes. How long is temporarily?"

"Oh, just a week or two," said Lawrence Archibald, Jr., and the workers believed him just as they had always believed his father before him.

The heads of the houses of Archibald, Atwood and Eastman were father figures endowed by the mill hands with the virtues of kindness and truth. The "owners" would take care of their children. Nothing bad could happen to you if you worked for the Company.

But Lawrence Archibald, Jr.'s week or two turned into three or four and then into six and finally into two months as the winter pressed down on the city from under a sky of flat, gray tin.

The people of Livingstone had heard about "the Depression." It had even touched them a little with a flick here and there. Things had been tight, work had been slack and the money had to stretch farther, but no one had really had to worry. The Company would take care of everything; but now the Company had ceased to exist.

It is bad to be poor any time, but to be poor in the middle of a New Hampshire winter is poverty beyond the scope of human endurance. And yet the people endured. The Welfare Office had always been there, right in the City Hall, but most

180

of the people had never known of its existence. Now, all of a sudden, it was the focal point of their lives, for without "the Welfare" there was no food, no clothing, no fuel and no one to pay the doctor or the dentist. Pride became the most luxurious thing in the world because so few could afford it any more.

And still, there were those to whom the Depression meant very little in acutely personal terms. People like Frederick Endicott, for instance, whose job with the Power and Light Company was secure, or those like Monique Bergeron, who did not depend on the mills. Their children did not eat Welfare food nor wear Welfare clothing. In fact, that winter Angelique Bergeron and Bill Endicott were not aware of much besides each other.

As the weeks passed, Bill Endicott seemed to grow thinner and more nervous by the minute. His mother blamed it on the fact that he must be studying too hard.

"You ought to let up a bit, Bill," she said. "After all, there's no need for you to spend *every* evening at the library. And you should get more sleep on the weekends too. Every Friday and Saturday night until one or even *two* in the morning. Honestly, I don't know what you and your friends can find to talk about until the wee small hours."

Bill did not answer his mother. His father didn't say anything either, but no one, least of all Bill, should make the mistake of thinking that Frederick Endicott didn't know what was going on. Fred Endicott had never been anybody's fool. He knew what Bill was doing with his time all right. He'd gone downtown to the library a couple of times, where Bill was supposed to be studying, and Bill wasn't anywhere in sight.

What did his son take him for anyway? All of a sudden Bill needed the car every night and old Fred Endicott knew damned well what he wanted it for. It was to take his little

181

Canuck girl friend out and lay her because it was a sure bet that he couldn't lay her anywhere else. Bill had never once asked to bring Angelique to the house and because of this poor Paula thought that he'd stopped seeing her. Well, that was a woman for you. At least the kind of woman Paula Endicott was. She was a lady and no lady would ever think that her own son would be out in a parked car fooling around with a little Canuck.

It was just as well, figured Frederick Endicott. After all, what Paula didn't know wouldn't hurt her. Boy oh boy, Bill must be getting plenty these nights from the way he looked. He was getting thin as a rail and jumpy as a cat. Too bad the kid was so close-mouthed. Fred Endicott would bet anything that his kid could tell him plenty if he wanted to. Too bad too that he never could bring her around to the house. It had been a long, long time since Frederick Endicott had had himself a good helping of fresh young frog's legs.

Bill's home was not the only place that was closed to him and Angelique that winter. Little by little he had begun to be aware that all his friends were giving parties and not inviting him. Or if they did invite him they always said, "Come stag, Bill. We've got too many extra girls."

"How come we never go anywhere except to the movies?" demanded Angelique. "Ben Russell had a party at his house last Friday night. How come you didn't get invited? I thought he was such a big friend of yours."

"Just because Ben and I played football together doesn't mean that he has to invite me to every party he gives," Bill said defensively. "Who cares about a silly kid party anyway?"

"I do," replied Angelique. "Linda Baker and Jane and Martha and all the other kids were invited. I want to know how come you weren't."

"Well, I just wasn't, that's all," said Bill. "Besides, you know what happens at those dumb parties? Listen, Ben's mother stays in the room all the time. With all the lights on too. The kids can't even play post office." He held Angelique close in the parked car. "Now, isn't this more fun, just the two of us, like this?"

She pulled away from him.

"No."

"Come on, honey," he begged, "don't be like that. Come on. Loosen up. Give us a kiss."

"Stop it!" cried Angelique angrily. "Is that all you ever think about? I bet you weren't like this with Jill Robbins."

You'd lose that bet for sure, thought Bill and wanted to laugh. But he never could quite laugh when he thought of Jill and sometimes he actually longed for her. Jill, who was always agreeable, and not only just about sex either. Whenever he'd said to Jill, "I'll pick you up at eight," she'd always said, "Okay, Bill," not, "No. Make it eight-thirty." Or when he'd asked, "Feel like a movie?" Jill had always replied with a quick yes or no. There was none of that "Oh, I don't know" foolishness, or "Why don't you decide?" met with a negative answer when he finally did. Sometimes Bill counted up the cost of his love for Angelique and more and more the price seemed too high.

Angelique had cost him the approval of his family, the loss of his friends and, worst of all, his own comfort and peace of mind and body. But every time he'd just about decide to break it off with her, Angelique would turn all soft and cuddly and warm and he would be overcome with his love for her. Then she would let him kiss her all he wanted but that was about all she'd let him do. Bill thought of his father's knowing look and smirking mouth and he almost had to laugh at himself. If his father only knew!

Angelique allowed herself to be kissed and sometimes she even responded to Bill's demanding mouth.

"This is soul kissing," he'd told her the first time he tried it with her, and she had let him open her mouth with his tongue and probe deeply.

"Now will I have a baby?" she'd asked when the kiss was over.

Bill laughed. "Are you serious?"

"Of course," she said. "Will I?"

Then he'd laughed harder than ever.

"Oh, my sweet, innocent darling," he replied. "You truly are an angel."

He spent hours explaining the mechanics of reproduction to her and Angelique listened very quietly, being careful not to let her smile show. Bill didn't explain things half as well as her father had.

Sometimes Angelique acted as if she liked to be kissed that way and at other times she pushed him away and said, "For heaven's sake, don't slobber all over me like that!"

Bill never knew how she was going to react from one minute to the next and it made him nervous not to know. A few wonderful times she had let him unbutton the front of her dress and touch her breasts over her brassiere and twice she had actually let him unhook her bra and caress her bare flesh. Both times he had gone almost wild with desire. Her hard little nipples were the sweetest, cleanest, most wonderful things he could imagine and he had bitten at them gently until her whole body writhed in his hands and she moaned and cried out. But the minute he'd tried to put his hand up under her skirt she had slapped him hard across the face.

"Don't," she said. "Don't ever do that."

"Let me, Angelique," he had begged. "You'll like it. Let me show you. You'll like it a lot. I won't hurt you."

"No," she said. "That's for when people are married. No. No."

"Just let me show you," he pleaded his fingers stroking her thigh.

"No."

184

"Why?" he asked, still stroking. "Don't you love me, honey?"

She relaxed and let him continue.

"Of course," she said. "But we have to wait until we're married."

"Honey, we can't get married for years and years. It won't hurt if I touch you there. You'll like it. Let me show you."

"No."

Inevitably the end came.

One night Angelique asked, "When are you going to take me to meet your parents? I mean, if we're going to be married someday, I really should meet them."

Bill tried to side-step the question by asking another.

"How come you've never let me meet your mother?"

But Angelique could not be put off as easily as that.

"That's different," she said, "and you know it. I don't have a normal family like you. My mother isn't well. I've told you that a hundred times and I think it's cruel of you to keep on talking about it. My mother can't help it if she's afraid of strangers. She never got over my father dying. It would upset her to know about us until she's better, but your mother and father aren't sick."

"Well," answered Bill, still dodging, "maybe next week, huh?"

"No," said Angelique. "Now."

"What do you mean, now?"

"Just that," replied Angelique. "Now."

"You mean right now? Tonight?"

"Yes," said Angelique, "right now. Start the car."

Bill sat absolutely still for a long time, staring at the ignition switch.

"Well?" Angelique asked impatiently

"I can't, honey." Bill's voice was so low she could barely hear him.

"What?"

185

"Goddamn it," he shouted, "I said I can't!"

She ignored his tone. "And why not?"

"Because they don't know about us."

"How come?" asked Angelique. "Just where do they think you go every night?"

There was no sense in trying to lie his way out of it. Once Angelique had her mind set on something there was no side-tracking her.

"They think I go to the library."

"What about weekends?"

"They think I go out with the guys."

There was a long, tight, terrible silence.

"You're ashamed of me," said Angelique at last.

"Oh, no, honey," Bill answered, hating himself.

"Give me a cigarette." When he had lit one for her Angelique smoked it until the cigarette was half gone, then she looked at him.

"Oh, yes," she said. "You're an Endicott from the north end and I'm a Bergeron from the south end and never the twain shall meet."

"Honey, don't talk like that."

"I'll talk any way I feel like talking," said Angelique. "You think you're too good for me, don't you? And so does your family."

"It's not that, honey. Honest."

"Oh, Bill, don't be such a liar," she said wearily. "I know how tiny little minds work. I can just hear your parents. You're an Endicott and the Endicotts just don't marry French-Canadian girls from the south end."

He wanted to hit her.

"Shut up!" he cried. "Shut up!"

But she would not let it drop.

"It's true, isn't it?" she asked. "That's what they told you, didn't they?"

186

"Yes!" shouted Bill in his rage and pain. "Yes, goddamn it, is that what you want to hear?"

"Yes," answered Angelique calmly and got out of the car. "Good-bye, Bill."

"Hey, wait," he said. "Wait a minute, honey. They don't make any difference. At least they won't after a while. After I finish school and I can be out on my own—"

She did not even close the door on her side of the car. She just turned away and she walked all the way home with small, stiff little steps as if her feet hurt. Her face hurt too, and when she went into the house Monique looked up from her sewing and then stared at her.

"What's the matter with you?"

"Not a thing," said Angelique and walked right by her and up the stairs to her own room.

But once inside she could no longer maintain her stubborn composure.

Papa! she cried and then the tears came.

It seemed to her that she wept a long, long time before her father's words came to comfort her.

Do not cry, my little angel, said Armand. Don't waste your tears over that foolish boy. He wasn't nearly good enough for you. He didn't understand you, what you are. I hate to say it, *ma petite,* but what did you expect from such an insensitive idiot? They're all alike, those cold fish from the north end, you know. No warmth, no understanding of beauty. Don't cry, my darling. You were much too good for him to begin with. What would he have done with a princess?

But what shall I do? asked Angelique.

Wait, my darling, answered Armand. Wait. Your turn will come.

But I don't want to be stuck here forever, Papa. I want something more than this, living here in Livingstone, never seeing anything, living with Maman.

Wait, my angel. Just wait. You'll see. Everything good will come to you if you only wait. You don't have to hurt yourself by going out to look for it. It will all come to you.

The next evening Angelique decided to walk over to Linda Baker's house. She hadn't seen Linda for a long time and perhaps now was the time to begin mending her fences.

Linda and Jane and Martha were sitting in Linda's room talking and laughing when Angelique arrived.

"Go right up, dear," said Mrs. Baker. "My, we haven't seen you in ages."

The minute Angelique appeared in the doorway, the girls stopped talking.

"Well, well, well," said Linda. "Look who's here."

"Hello," Angelique said.

"Hi," replied Martha and Jane tentatively.

"What do you want?" asked Linda coldly.

Angelique made herself laugh. "Do I have to want something?" she said. "I just came over to say hello."

Linda got up to close the bedroom door and then she turned on Angelique.

"You bitch."

Martha and Jane gasped in unison.

"You rotten bitch," said Linda, enjoying the sensation the word had caused. "Just because Bill Endicott threw you over you don't have to think you can come crawling back to us."

"I'm not crawling," Angelique answered calmly.

Linda was enraged because she had not upset Angelique.

"We don't want you around," she said. "Maybe you could take Bill away from Jill Robbins for a little while but don't get the idea you can come around poaching on one of us. We just don't want you around."

Angelique looked at Martha and Jane.

"Is she speaking for you two?"

"Listen here, you little Canuck," shouted Linda.

188

Angelique turned and slapped her hard. "Don't you dare talk to me like that ever again!"

Linda put a hand up to her cheek.

"How very typical," she said with a little smile. "Just like a little Canuck mill rat. Get out of here."

"Yes, yes," echoed Martha and Jane. "Go on, get out of here."

"Canuck!" yelled Linda.

God, she was cold. Her teeth were chattering and all she could hear was that word, echoing in her mind. Canuck. Canuck. Canuck.

"Angelique! Angelique! What are you doing?"

She looked up as if she were just waking. The voice was coming from outside the locked bedroom door.

"Angelique! What are you doing? Etienne has been waiting for you for over an hour. Are you all right?"

The bath water was ice cold and Angelique drew her legs up to her chest. It was time to get ready.

"Yes, yes," she called. "I'm coming."

The water was cold but the tears that fell on Angelique's bare knees were as hot as fire.

Papa, she wept. Papa.

3

As Etienne de Montigny's brother Christophe put it, he had never remained so dressed up for so long in his life.

"I feel as if I'd been born in this goddamned suit," he said. "I tell you, 'Tien, if your bride is going to be as slow about everything else as she is about getting ready to leave on your wedding trip, you will never have a hot meal, a clean shirt or a child. There just isn't that much time."

Etienne grinned and poked his brother in the arm with his knuckles, but his smile was becoming a trifle forced. Surely it could not take any woman in the world over two hours to change from one dress to another. For the past hour everyone at the wedding reception had been eying Etienne with poorly concealed laughter. He would have to speak to Angelique, and sternly. It did not look well for a man to be kept waiting like a salesman at the door on his own wedding day.

"Well, have some more champagne," said Christophe. "You might as well. God only knows how much longer she is going to be. I'd better see that Maman and the girls get some too. They all look as if they were about to burst right out of their corsets. But look at baby brother, will you? He doesn't mind the wait at all. In fact, baby brother is well on his way to being drunk."

Baby brother was the youngest of the de Montigny children and he had been wearing the uniform of the United

States Army for so long that it seemed to have become part of him. His name was Remy and the general consensus of opinion about him, outside of his own family, was that Remy was not too bright. Oh, he could read and write his name all right; after all, he'd gone to school right up through the fifth grade. But it had taken him until he was sixteen years old to get that far and he never seemed to be able to hold on to a job of any kind. Not that Remy was not a willing worker. He was, as were all the de Montignys, but Remy loved to sing and dance and joke and he pursued these pleasures to the aggravation of every man he'd ever worked for, until each ended up by firing him.

"I swear to God I don't know what I did wrong," Remy always said after losing a job. "I tell you all I did was to sing a little song and maybe do a little jig. Like this."

Remy's older brothers and sisters always laughed at his demonstrations, but Simone de Montigny did not. Especially after Remy turned twenty-one.

"Look here, Remy," said Simone finally. "It is not fair that your brothers and sisters and I should have to carry your share of the load. Do you expect us to feed you forever with your doing nothing in return?"

"Oh, Ma, it wasn't my fault that last job. I swear to you, all I did was—"

"That's enough," replied Simone. "Times are hard enough for all of us without our having to put up with your foolishness. You must begin to be a man."

"But I got no job," protested Remy. "I couldn't help it, I swear to you—"

"You are a strong, healthy man," Simone interrupted. "You can join the Army."

"The Army!" yelled Remy in horror.

"Yes," repeated Simone. "The Army."

So Remy went off with the Army. It didn't pay much of anything but what the hell. He got three square meals a

191

day and he didn't have to worry about clothes or a roof over his head. The Army had even given him a leave in order to come home and attend his older brother's wedding. It was a good life for Remy and if a little laughter seemed to have gone out of the de Montigny household with his departure— well, times were hard and who had time to laugh anyway? Certainly not Simone de Montigny.

Remy may look like the Pichettes, thought Simone, but he is just like his father in every other way. Thank God the others don't take after him.

And they didn't either. Oh, it was true that Etienne looked exactly like his father and that Christophe had inherited his tall slimness, but it ended there. As for the girls—Josephine, Charlotte and Cecile—they took after the Pichettes in every way. They were short and stocky and inclined to run to fat. Bread and potatoes and dishes made with macaroni were cheap and filling and they went a long way. Simone de Montigny had never deluded herself into believing that she had the best-looking family in the world, but she had brought up her children to be decent, self-respecting, hard-working people and they stuck together through thick and thin.

Especially Etienne and Christophe, she thought, as she watched her two sons coming toward her with a tray of full champagne glasses. They were good boys, perhaps inclined to a little foolishness, but never to excess so that they forgot who they were or neglected their work. No, never that.

"Have some champagne, Ma," said Christophe. "It'll put chest on your hair."

"Mon maudit fou," said Simone. "I swear, Christophe, if you get drunk today I won't feed you for a week."

"Hear that, 'Tien?" demanded Christophe. "You are not gone from the house even one day and I have to bear her bad temper all alone."

Etienne held a glass toward his mother.

"Here, Ma."

"Here, Ma, indeed," said Christophe. "Ma, if *you* get drunk today I won't feed *you* for a week. How about *that?*"

They stood in a tight little circle enjoying each other.

They are so close, thought Simone, Christophe and Etienne. There are eleven months between them but they are like twins. If one lies the other swears to it.

"To your great good fortune, 'Tien," said Simone and raised her glass.

"She is coming!" called one of the bridesmaids. "Angelique is coming at last."

Etienne did not take his eyes away from his mother.

"Thanks, Ma," he said and raised his glass to clink against hers.

"Hurry, Etienne. Your bride is waiting."

"Ma?"

Simone's eyes were hidden by the rim of her glass.

"Hurry, 'Tien."

"Ma?"

"For God's sake," said Christophe and gave his brother a little push. "Go."

Etienne and Angelique de Montigny left in a shower of rice and rose petals—of which the latter was considered to be a shameful waste of money by everyone at the reception— and to the tune of the hired orchestra playing "La Valse de la Mariée."

Well, thought Simone de Montigny. Well.

"Ma?" said Christophe.

"What?"

"Ma, do you think—"

"Oh, for heaven's sake, Christophe," said Simone. "Find your sisters and your brother. It is time we went home."

They gathered around her, all of them.

"Ma?" said Josephine.

"What?"

"Nothing."

"Ma," said Charlotte.

"Ma," said Remy.

"Oh, for God's sake," cried Simone. "What have I produced here? A bunch of sheep who can say nothing but Ma, Ma, Ma? Come. It is time to go home."

4

The collar of Etienne de Montigny's starched white shirt was so tight that he felt as if he had a red ring of fire all around his neck, and he aggravated the discomfort every time he turned his head. But how was a man supposed to drive a car without moving? And that was the second thing that was wrong. The car.

"Is this the best you could do?" Angelique had demanded as soon as she saw it.

The car was a green Ford roadster, only two years old. It belonged to Etienne's boss, Jack Engel, who had lent it to him for the honeymoon only after considerable pleading on Etienne's part and a great number of reassurances on the caution and care with which it would be driven.

"Listen," answered Etienne, "I was lucky to get a car at all. What did you expect? A Packard limousine?"

"Yes," said Angelique and turned away to look out of the window.

"Boy oh boy," replied Etienne bitterly, trying to run one finger inside the edge of his collar. "You sure got fancy ideas."

It was true. Like this crazy thing of going all the way down to Boston for a honeymoon when they could just as easily have gone straight to the apartment they had rented and finished furnishing a month ago.

A whole month's rent right down the drain, thought Etienne, just to humor Angelique. Well. It was her wedding and her honeymoon and she'd better take advantage of his good nature now because things were sure going to be different when they got back to Livingstone and settled down. Angelique was only seventeen and much as he loved her, she was going to have to learn the responsibilities of a married woman.

"What was the idea of keeping everybody waiting the way you did at the reception?"

"Oh?" Angelique said calmly. "Did you mind waiting for me, Etienne?"

"You're damn right I did," he replied. "It doesn't look good for a woman to keep her husband hanging around for nothing."

Angelique smiled and moved over closer to him.

"I had to get ready for you," she said. "I had to take a hot bath."

"For two hours?" he asked. But he could not be angry with her when she smiled at him like that and rested her hand on the side of his thigh.

"Etienne," she said, "why don't you undo your collar button? You'd be much more comfortable."

Gratefully, Etienne did just that and reflected that this was just one more example of what he usually called Angelique's contrariness. If he had opened his collar without waiting for Angelique to mention it first, she would have turned on him angrily and said, "Are you trying to shame me, Etienne? A grown man on his honeymoon with his collar undone? Do you think you are in that grubby garage of yours or on your way to Boston?"

Etienne took her little hand in his and raised her fingers to his lips.

"I love you," he said.

"And I love you, Etienne," she answered and leaned her head against his shoulder.

The green roadster sped along the road to Boston and Etienne thought that he was a lucky man indeed. Just as all Angelique's friends said: she'd take a bit of taming, Angelique would, but things were going to work out just fine. He looked down at her and smiled. She looked so lovely sitting there next to him in her little pink silk dress with all that long, blonde hair. She looked almost childlike, no, saintlike. That profile of hers was so delicate, her skin almost transparent.

But she had the makings of a little witch under that sweet-looking exterior. He'd known that from the moment he'd set eyes on her and, remembering, he could barely keep from laughing. She had been so adorable in her pride and anger. Etienne grinned as he drove along and then he put his arm around her and his fingers touched the underslope of her breast.

Mine, he thought. Soon now. All mine. It was only forty-eight more miles to Boston.

The first time Etienne de Montigny had ever seen Angelique Bergeron was one hot, sticky day in August, a year ago. In the middle of the humid, dreary street in Livingstone she had somehow managed to look cool and clean and untouched by the weather.

"This is my granddaughter," Toussaint Montambeault had announced. "Angelique, meet Etienne de Montigny."

"Hi, kid."

Angelique looked him up and down and she did not smile.

"How do you do, Mr. de Montigny."

Etienne laughed and slapped Toussaint across the shoulders.

"Toussaint, you old devil," he said. "Why didn't you tell me that your granddaughter was a princess?"

Angelique continued to look at Etienne, but now there was a little softness in her eyes.

"Do you work with *Grand-père,* Mr. de Montigny?" she asked.

"Look, princess," replied Etienne. "Never mind the mister stuff, okay? And yes, I work at the garage with your grand-father. I don't brag about that though." Again he laughed and slapped the old man across the back.

"Nor I," said Toussaint.

Angelique looked at the two of them, hanging onto each other, laughing. She noted their filthy, grease-covered clothes but under the dirt on Etienne's face she noticed also that he was very handsome indeed. He had a strong, sharp-planed face and his teeth were very white and straight. The dirty work shirt strained across his big chest and shoulders but his hands, although large, were curiously delicate.

Yes, thought Angelique, he is a very good-looking man and he is not a child either.

She wanted badly to know how old he was, but standing there in the hot street she could think of no graceful way in which to ask him.

"And where are you off to on such a day?" asked Toussaint. "Believe me, if I didn't have to work for a living I wouldn't stir out of the house on a day like this. You should be home where it is cool."

"I am going to the library," said Angelique and then she looked Etienne de Montigny straight in the eyes. "And to-night I am going to the band concert in Pershing Park."

Etienne grinned more broadly than ever.

"It should be cool in the park this evening," he said.

"Yes," agreed Angelique. "Well, I must hurry. Good-bye, *Grand-père.* Good-bye, Mr. de Montigny."

Etienne watched her walk away, her tight little behind pulsing up and down and back and forth under the fabric of her summer dress.

198

Oh, she was something all right, this one. Not only that cute little ass of hers but those pretty knockers and that long blond hair and that cool, clean face.

"See you later, princess," he called after her but she did not turn around.

That same evening, after supper, Etienne de Montigny put on a fresh shirt and a pair of clean trousers and he used a lot of water to smooth back his black curly hair.

"What's got into you?" asked his mother, Simone. "I never knew you to get this slicked up in the middle of the week."

"I'm going to a concert in Pershing Park," answered Etienne.

His sisters and his brother Christophe began to laugh but Simone merely looked at him.

"A *concert?*" she demanded. "Well, I really believe the heat has affected your brain at last."

Etienne dried his hands. "No," he said, "it isn't the heat, it's a girl. I'm going to meet her there."

"You and your girls," replied Simone sourly. "I can't keep them all straight in my mind. Which one is this?"

"A new one, Ma," he answered, "and a beauty. Her name is Angelique."

"Angelique," mimicked Christophe. "Ma, notice the way he says the name. As if he were dreaming. *Angelique.*" And Christophe began to mince around the kitchen in an imitation of a girl, while his sisters doubled up with laughter.

"That's enough of your foolishness, Christophe," said Simone. "And as for you, Etienne, don't get home too late. Remember you have to go to work in the morning. We all do."

Etienne kissed his mother on the cheek.

"Don't worry, Ma," he said. "I could stay up all night and still do a day's work. I'm as strong as a bull."

Simone turned away from him. "Get going," she said, "or you'll never get back."

So like his father, she thought. So terribly much like him that sometimes it was frightening.

Etienne strutted down the street, swinging his great arms and returning greetings.

"Hello, 'Tien."

"How goes it 'Tien?"

"Hot enough for you tonight, Etienne?"

He was popular in his neighborhood and he knew it. He was popular with everybody but especially with the girls. Etienne walked toward the park smiling at himself and at the world. It was good to be a man and to feel so alive and to be on one's way to meet a pretty girl.

Hey, hold on, he told himself. How do you know she'll meet you?

Ah, she'll be there all right.

Angelique was sitting on a bench as close to the bandstand as she could get, and Etienne spotted her at once. There seemed to be an area of coolness and cleanliness all around her.

Christ, but she was a beauty, this one.

He moved toward her and sat down next to her. The band was playing something loud with a lot of drums but still she heard him when he leaned forward and said hello.

"Oh, good evening, Mr. de Montigny."

"Let's get out of here," said Etienne. "There's too damned much noise and too many people. Come on."

She turned and looked at him with that piercing look of hers.

"No," she said.

"Oh, come on. Who wants to listen to this stuff anyway?"

"I do," she answered calmly, and turned her attention back to the bandstand.

Etienne could not believe it of himself, but he continued to sit next to her, listening to music that he did not understand

and cared about even less. With any other girl he would have said, "Okay. So long, Toots," but he could not somehow say this to Angelique.

He was very much aware of her long hair as he stretched his arm out across the back of the bench and he had a sudden, crazy urge to touch it, to stroke it, to bury his face in it. There seemed to be a scent of rose petals coming from her and in the light from the bandstand he could see her upturned face, the sweep of the profile, so clear-cut and yet soft. It came to him in a rush that he had never wanted a girl so much in his life. He wanted to undress her, but carefully and gently, and he wanted to feel all her lovely coolness next to him.

Jesus Christ, he thought and crossed his legs quickly.

"Hey, listen," he said. "How old are you anyway?"

"Sixteen."

That does it, thought Etienne. Sixteen.

He wanted to get up and leave right then but he did not move.

When the band had finished playing its selection she turned to him.

"Why?" she asked. "How old are you?"

"Twenty-four."

"So?"

He was acutely uncomfortable and horribly aware of the erection that would not go away.

"I was just curious," he said. "I guess I'm a little old for you."

Angelique smiled and put her hand on his arm.

"You're not old," she replied. "You are mature."

Her fingertips seemed to barely rest against the dark curly hair of his arm but Etienne felt as if he'd been burned.

"I like mature men," said Angelique.

And so it had begun.

There wasn't a week that went by during the months that

followed when Etienne did not swear a thousand times that he was finished with Angelique. She was the contrariest, most aggravating female that he could ever imagine.

"Well, then, why don't you break up with her?" asked Christophe practically.

"I don't know," answered Etienne. "I tell you, I just don't know. Every time I try she turns so sweet and angelic that I realize she is well named."

"Listen, 'Tien," said Christophe. "It's not getting it that makes her mean. Give it to her a couple of times every night and I guarantee she'll turn soft as mush in your hands."

"Look who's telling me how to handle girls," laughed Etienne. "Hell, you didn't even know what it was for until I told you."

"Ah," said Christophe, "but I was a good student. Please notice that you don't hear me complaining about being aggravated by a girl. Any girl at all."

"Angelique isn't that kind," answered Etienne.

"Don't hand me that," replied Christophe. "All girls are that kind."

Etienne de Montigny was the first friend, male or female, that Angelique Bergeron had ever introduced to her mother. When Monique first saw him she turned pale.

"What's the matter, Maman?" asked Angelique.

"My God," answered Monique. "It is unbelievable."

"What is unbelievable?" asked Etienne, smiling.

"You look so much like Angelique's father. I mean the way he used to look, the way he looked when I married him."

"Nonsense," said Angelique sharply. "He hasn't the least resemblance to Papa."

But all the same, Monique thought, it was true. Etienne de Montigny had the same big frame, big voice, laugh, the same dark curly hair and the same white teeth. True, there was a certain delicacy in Etienne that Armand had never had, those long-fingered hands, for example, or the fine line of the cheekbones. But the over-all effect was much the same as that Armand had given as a young man.

"They certainly make a handsome couple," said Monique's sister, Antoinette. "They will make beautiful children."

"Are you mad?" demanded Monique. "You forget that Angelique is barely sixteen years old."

"Since when has age ever made a difference where love was concerned?" Antoinette laughed. "No. They will get married, those two. Wait and see. Angelique has her cap set for him all right."

Antoinette's words were far more accurate than she realized, for Angelique's campaign to get Etienne to marry her was as carefully planned as a military maneuver.

Next June Angelique would be seventeen and she would graduate from Livingstone High School. Within a week after both events, if things went the way she planned, she and Etienne would be married and from that moment on Etienne would begin to be her passport out of Livingstone and into the rest of the world. Etienne was older and he had a good, steady job, and having a good, steady job during the Great Depression was very important indeed. Etienne would never deny her anything, she was sure, and eventually when she found the right man, the one with plenty of money, he would really know how to appreciate her.

Boston, thought Angelique, or perhaps even New York. A penthouse apartment and trips to Paris and nothing to drink but imported champagne.

You wait and see, Papa, she told Armand. It will all come true. I'll have it all. The whole world.

Of course you will, agreed Armand.

Of course, it may take a little time, but I have plenty of that. In the meantime, Etienne isn't a bad catch at all. He's even rather attractive.

In the months of their courtship Angelique managed to keep Etienne constantly, or almost constantly, off balance.

203

When he rebelled, she merely withdrew herself from him altogether. She would not answer his telephone calls or see him when he came to her house. And just once had Etienne really lost his temper. Then he had stood at the bottom of the stairway that led to her bedroom on the second floor and shouted so loud that she had no trouble in hearing him through the closed door.

"You go to hell, you little bitch!" yelled Etienne. "I don't need you."

He slammed out of the house and Monique Bergeron never even reprimanded him for his language. She merely smiled to herself as she went on with her sewing. It was about time that someone had had the nerve to stand up to Angelique.

In the bedroom upstairs, Angelique too, smiled. He'd be back or he'd telephone within the half hour. Etienne had had these little tantrums before and he'd always come back on the run.

But this time two whole days went by and Etienne did not come to the Bergeron house. Nor did he even telephone. Angelique waited, at first in disbelief and then in rage. When the third day passed and then the fourth, her anger turned to the beginnings of fear.

Perhaps this time she had gone too far. Six days went by and Angelique was really frightened. She could not afford to lose Etienne at this stage of the game.

At last, after several false starts, she picked up the telephone and called him.

"Etienne," she said, "I must see you."

"What for?" he asked bitterly. "Just so you can begin cutting me to pieces again? No, thanks. I've had enough of that."

"I didn't mean to hurt you, Etienne," she answered softly. "Honestly, I didn't."

"No, I suppose you never mean to," he said. "But somehow it always happens."

"Etienne?"

"What?"

"I've missed you, darling. Please come to see me."

"What's the sense to it, Angelique?" he asked wearily. "It'll just be the same old thing all over again."

Her rage almost choked her. Who did he think he was, anyway, making her plead like this? But she did not let her anger creep into her voice.

"Please, Etienne," she said. "Please?"

There was a long pause. "All right. I've got the boss's car for tonight. I'll pick you up about eight."

"Make it eight-thirty," said Angelique.

"There, you see?" cried Etienne. "There you go already. No matter what I say, you've got to contradict me. No, Angelique. Forget the whole thing. I'm not coming at all."

She could have bitten her tongue right off. "No, wait," she said. "Darling, all right. Eight o'clock. I had something to do for Maman but it can wait."

"All right," answered Etienne. "Eight o'clock."

But for the first time since she had known him, Etienne was late. He did not pull up in front of the house until eight-twenty and Angelique was so angry she could barely force herself to smile.

"Sorry I'm late," he said as he swung the door open for her. And that was the only thing he said; no explanations at all.

Oh, you'll pay for this, thought Angelique savagely. No one humiliates me and gets away with it for very long. Wait and see, Etienne. Just you wait and see.

But she smiled and put her hand on his arm as he drove. He wanted to see a movie, so they went without any argument from Angelique at all. Afterward he wanted to stop for a drink, so they stopped at Jolly Jerry's, where Etienne drank beer and Angelique drank ginger ale. And after that, without so much as asking her, he drove to north of the city and parked in a dark, narrow lane that ended at the edge of the river.

He did not even speak before taking her into his arms. He took her chin in one hand and squeezed her cheeks together until her lips pursed and then very deliberately he took them into his mouth. He smelled of beer and cigarette smoke and she tried to twist her head away from him but his hand gripped her so hard that she could not move. There was something else she could not do either, and that was to understand the dark little thrill that ran through her at his brutality. His hands were very strong as they tangled in her hair and later they did not fumble when he opened her blouse.

"Stop it," she cried. "Stop it, Etienne!"

"Shut up," he said. "You don't have to worry. I'm not going to rape you. We're going to be married, you and I, and I can save your virginity until our wedding night. But in the meantime I'm going to enjoy you a little. Just a little."

"I said stop it!" ordered Angelique and pushed hard against him.

He did not even bother to unhook her brassiere. The hook snapped under his fingers as she struggled and in the next second her breasts were bare.

"That's it," said Etienne as she continued to fight him. "Arch your back like that again. It makes them stand out straight."

What frightened Angelique as much as anything else was that he was not even breathing hard. In the little bit of light that came from the star-filled sky she could see that he was smiling as his hand played with her and all of a sudden it was she who was panting. When his mouth covered her nipple she pressed her knuckles between her teeth against the whimper she could not control as a sudden hot feeling shot up from between her legs and seemed to burn every nerve in her body. But when he put his hand under her skirt he did not touch her there. Instead he half lifted her until her plump little buttocks rested in his hand and then he began a gentle, rhythmic squeezing and releasing that grew in intensity until she did cry out.

"Please, Etienne," she was saying in a voice she did not even recognize as her own. "Please, please, Etienne. Everything, Etienne. Please, please."

She heard him laughing against her skin.

"Not yet, my hot little French bitch," he said. "Not yet. I can wait."

In the moment when he released her she hated him so much that she would gladly have killed him. This time when she began to cry there was no pretense about it at all. She wept in rage and frustration and Etienne did not even try to comfort her. He leaned back in the seat and lit a cigarette while she sobbed and fumbled in her purse for a handkerchief.

She was still trembling after Etienne had let her off in front of the house. And she trembled as she undressed and got into bed. She clenched her teeth together and her fists and at last her whole body was clenched tight, so that when she finally let herself relax the trembling was gone.

But the shame would not leave her so quickly.

Oh, how could she have let herself be handled like that. And to respond to it, so that he knew and gloried in it. Goddamn him to hell.

Wait, Etienne, just you wait. I'll get even with you if it's the last thing I ever do in my lifetime. You'll pay for this. Oh, Papa, Papa, I'm so ashamed. So humiliated.

Hush, my darling, said Armand. No one can humiliate a princess.

Angelique's eyes itched and burned with the tears she had shed earlier and at last she got up for a cool washcloth.

That's right, Papa, she thought as she lay back down on the bed. No one humiliates a princess. At least, no one humiliates a princess and gets away with it. Just wait until the next time he tries it. You'll see.

207

But there never was a next time. From that evening until the night they were married, Etienne never touched her like that again, and sometimes this was even harder for Angelique to bear. When they kissed she often tried to goad him into losing his head but he wouldn't.

"I can wait," said Etienne.

And now the time of waiting was almost at an end. The lights of Boston appeared suddenly out of the darkness and Etienne took his arm from around Angelique.

"We're here," he said unnecessarily.

"Yes," answered Angelique and began to comb her hair. "For heaven's sake, Etienne, pull over to the side of the road and button your collar. Do you want to shame me in one of the best hotels in the country? And when you register, try to remember to write Mr. and Mrs. Etienne de Montigny. Not Etienne de Montigny and wife."

"I'll remember," said Etienne.

The hotel was even lovelier than Angelique remembered and when the bellboy showed them to their suite she realized at once that it had been redecorated.

But of course, she thought, it would have to be. It's been years and years since Papa and I stayed here.

Angelique smiled as the boy went around opening windows and turning on lights. Etienne stood in the middle of the room as if he didn't know what to do with his hands and she was very glad that she had not told him about her letter to the manager of the hotel. In it she had insisted on this particular suite and if it had not been available for this one night she was sure that she would have found a way to postpone the wedding until it had been available. All Etienne knew was that she had written for the reservations.

It will be our secret, Papa, thought Angelique, and she began to hum a little tune as Etienne tipped the boy and closed the door behind him.

208

"Why don't you call room service and order a bottle of champagne?" asked Angelique. "I have to take a bath."

"Another?" demanded Etienne. "You took a bath just before we left Livingstone."

"But it was a hot, long drive," answered Angelique. "Please, darling, order the champagne. I won't be a minute."

"I know you and your minutes," said Etienne, but he smiled as he reached for the telephone. "You and your minutes. A man would have time to get stinking drunk during one of your minutes."

But Angelique was true to her word this time. She bathed quickly and then put on her nightgown. It was made of white chiffon and had cost a great deal too much money. But when she came into the living room of the suite and saw the way Etienne looked at her she knew that it had been worth every cent of it. He almost gasped as he looked at her and a little bit of champagne sloshed out of his glass and down onto the rug.

"My God," said Etienne. "I always knew you were beautiful but I didn't know how beautiful."

Her skin, flushed from the warm bath, glowed faintly pink through the thin chiffon nightgown and her hair fell smooth and soft down to her waist.

"I'd better take a bath myself," said Etienne and did not even know why he said it. He only knew that he felt as if he was in the presence of someone very special and that he would never dream of touching this vision with soiled hands.

"Yes," replied Angelique and turned away to pour herself a glass of champagne.

As she sipped the wine she couldn't keep from smiling as she heard the bath water running and the sounds that Etienne made as he bathed. And when he came out, it was all she could do to keep from laughing out loud. He was wearing pajamas for what she was sure was the first time in his

209

life and he looked more uncomfortable in them than he had in his wedding suit.

"Sit down and have some more champagne," she urged.

Etienne thought that he could gladly have kicked himself all the way back to Livingstone. He sat down beside her and sipped the wine but he could not think of a single thing to say.

"Perhaps we should order up another bottle," Angelique said and raised her glass.

"A good idea," answered Etienne, in relief, and went to the telephone.

Oh, it was just too much, thought Angelique. Big, rough, tough Etienne de Montigny, struck dumb and awkward as a teenager.

She let him stew until the second bottle of champagne was half gone and then she moved over close to him and traced the outline of his jaw with one finger.

"Tell me, darling," she said. "What are you going to do to me?"

"What?" asked Etienne stupidly.

"What are you going to do to me when this bottle of wine is finished and you take me to bed?"

Etienne felt something begin to loosen inside of him. He put down his glass.

"I don't have to tell you," he answered. "I'll show you. And right now."

Angelique moved away. "No. No," she said, "tell me first. I've never been with a man, you know."

"I know," answered Etienne.

"Well, then. Tell me. So I'll know what to expect."

Etienne wanted to grab her and begin kissing her and touching her but he made himself sit still.

Gently, gently, he told himself. A virgin, after all. I don't want to frighten her. Gently.

"Turn around."

She gave a little laugh. "What?"

"Come on. Turn around."

She turned on the sofa so that she was sitting with her back to him and then he did reach for her. Very gently he moved that marvelous, rose-petal-smelling cloak of hair away from one shoulder and then he began to kiss the side of her neck.

"First," he said, "I am going to kiss every inch of your body."

He held her arms gently and slid his lips along her shoulder and he felt her shiver but almost at once she relaxed again.

He began to stroke her and the thin straps of her night-gown slipped down easily under his fingers.

"When I finish with you," he whispered softly, "there won't be any of you that I don't know."

Angelique could not help herself. She could feel her breath shortening and her skin burning everywhere he touched her with that maddening, slow stroking.

"Know me how?"

He turned her then, so that she was lying across his lap, but he was still gentle as he ran his hand down the side of her body.

"With my hands," he said, "and my mouth and my eyes and my own body."

He began to kiss her mouth with soft little kisses, his lips barely parted, and then he moved his hand to her belly and began to press and caress her there. She could feel her breasts tightening and her nipples actually began to ache with wanting his touch, but she made herself lie quiet and acquiescent. He did not carry her into the other room but took her by the hand and led her to the bed. She stood, unmoving, while he bent down and lifted the edges of her nightgown and then she raised her arms and let him slip it over her head.

"Lie down," he said, and when she had done as he asked he stood for a long time looking down at her.

211

She was like a statue, he thought. Not one line, one curve or indentation was misplaced.

When he let his pajamas drop to the floor and she saw him standing naked over her, she turned her head and put the back of one hand against her mouth.

"Don't do that," he said harshly and knelt beside her on the bed. He turned her head toward him, and then he took her hand and made her put it on him. Her hand tightened on him and she whimpered.

"Are you afraid?" he asked.

"Yes."

He lowered himself to lie beside her. "Good," he said. "It is good for a woman to be a little afraid of her man."

And then it began. The gentleness was gone from him now. He handled her furiously, demandingly, as if she no longer belonged to herself but had become an object for his pleasure.

At last he put a pillow under her hips and his hands were hard on her knees as he pushed her legs apart and knelt between them.

"Open your eyes," he said. "Quickly, right now. Open your eyes."

She saw that he was half smiling and that he was sweating.

"Keep them open," he said. "I want to watch you turn from a child into a woman."

She felt the pain almost at once.

"No!" she cried. "No! You're hurting me."

"Oh, I hope so," he said and the pressure grew and grew. "I hope so. I want you to remember that from now on you belong to me."

She felt as if she were being torn in two, and still he would not stop. His face grew larger and larger over her and it seemed that the walls of the room were falling in on her, crushing her.

"Papa!" she screamed. "Papa! Papa!"

Book Three

1

December 7th, 1941, might well be a day that would live in infamy for some people but when Etienne de Montigny first heard the news that Sunday he felt as if someone had just relieved him of a load that he had been carrying for too long on his back. For the first time since he'd been married, he felt alive and like his old self.

At last, he thought triumphantly. At last the perfect escape route. And escape with honor.

He was big and healthy and strong as an ox. The Army would take him, he knew they would, and then he could get the hell away from here. From Livingstone and his family. From Angelique and her tight-lipped mother, and even from the kids.

Etienne paused for a second when he thought of Alana and Lesley.

He'd miss the kids, he supposed. But he'd get over that in a hurry. This was escape and not escape by running away, as it would have been if he'd deserted Angelique years ago. But honorable, worthy escape. For the good of his country.

Etienne laughed for what seemed like the first time in a long, long while.

He wouldn't tell Angelique until after he'd enlisted. Not that he could have told her that very minute if he'd wanted to, because as usual she wasn't home. Etienne was alone in the house with Monique, the little girls were outside playing. The

215

old lady was in the kitchen, muttering to herself as she usually did these days, and in Etienne's eyes she wasn't fit to be left alone with the children.

"My God, Angelique," he'd shout at his wife. "Your mother can't even remember where she puts her own clothes. How the hell do you expect her to remember that there are two kids around?"

"Don't you shout at me," replied Angelique calmly. "My mother is perfectly capable of looking after the girls. If you don't think so, then *you* look after them."

"You're a no-good bitch, you know that?" yelled Etienne.

"And you are a loud-mouthed vulgarian," Angelique would answer as she went out the door.

Well, after tomorrow little Angelique's wings would be clipped for good, thought Etienne with a great deal of satisfaction. Where nothing else had worked, the Japanese attack on Pearl Harbor would turn the trick. She wouldn't dare leave the kids alone with Monique any more than he did. Now she'd have to stay home and start acting like a mother for the first time since she'd borne their first child.

Etienne laughed again and Monique came to the door of the living room and stared at him.

"What's the matter with you?" she demanded petulantly.

"Nothing." Etienne laughed. "Nothing at all. I just feel good, that's all."

"Well, I'm glad somebody does," replied Monique and disappeared back into the kitchen. "Where is Angelique?" she called, her voice whining as it so often did now.

"She'll be home soon, ' said Etienne, and thought: You're goddamn right she'll be home soon, and home is where she'll be stuck from now on.

God bless the United States, Pearl Harbor and the Empire of Japan.

Watch out, you slanty-eyed bastards, here comes Etienne de Montigny!

On that same Sunday afternoon, Angelique de Montigny was sitting on a green upholstered sofa in Peggy Howard's living room. She was wearing a tight-fitting dress of a dull gold color, which looked well against the green fabric of the couch. It also made her blonde hair look paler than it really was and the wintery air outside had brought a glow to her skin.

The wintery air and two very good daiquiris, thought Angelique, smiling her secret little smile.

She was on her third drink now and rather thought she'd nurse this one for a while. From across the room she could see that Ed Miller was watching her and she didn't want him to think her tight. It would be easy to get just a wee bit tight this afternoon. She felt wonderful. She looked beautiful and she knew it and she knew, too, that before much more time passed, Ed Miller was going to walk over to the sofa, sit down beside her and ask her to have dinner with him that evening. She'd keep him guessing for a little while and then she'd say, yes, slightly reluctantly. Angelique smiled to herself again and sipped at her drink.

Peggy Howard always gave the best parties of anyone in Livingstone. Not that they could compare to a few that Angelique had attended in Boston or New York, but still, they were good parties. Livingstone had its own little smattering of intellectuals and one always saw them at Peggy's.

Suddenly, and for no good reason, Angelique found herself wondering what a good party would be like in London or Paris and she began to feel a little depressed. A small frown appeared between her eyes and she started to feel very much put upon.

A fat chance she had of ever getting to London or Paris so long as she was tied to Etienne. Not only did Etienne have no desire to see either city, but he thought she was crazy even to think of such things.

If Etienne had said it once, he'd said it a million times.

"For God's sake, Angelique. Who do you think we are? I'm just a plain workingman and you are just a plain workingman's wife. Where do you get off with having such crazy ideas? London, Paris, Rome. Good Christ. You must think you're Mrs. Vanderbilt or something."

God, how she hated him!

"I've been standing over there trying to figure you out," said Ed Miller as he sat down beside her. "One minute you're smiling and the next you're frowning. What are you thinking about?"

Angelique was so startled that she almost spilled her drink.

"Oh, nothing much," she said and managed to laugh.

Ed Miller could be important to her, she thought. He was new to Livingstone. Also, he was unattached and quite wealthy by New Hampshire standards. Ed Miller was a stock-broker and his occupation alone was enough to give him a certain glamour in Angelique's eyes.

"Don't kid me," Ed Miller said, smiling down at her. "I've been watching you and you were way off somewhere."

"Oh, all right," replied Angelique and laughed again. "If you must know, I was thinking of Paris."

"Oh, really?" asked Ed Miller. "Do you know Paris well?"

Angelique took another sip of her drink.

"With a last name like de Montigny it would be rather odd if I didn't, wouldn't it?"

"Yes, indeed," said Ed. "Oh, how I love that city."

"Oh, then you've spent time there?"

"Two years. Right after I finished college. By the way, my name's Ed Miller."

Angelique extended her hand. "And I am Angelique de Montigny."

They sat together on the green sofa and talked for almost an hour. Or rather, Ed Miller talked and Angelique listened.

"You know," he said finally, "this is going to sound corny as hell. But I have a few paintings that I bought in Paris and I was wondering if you'd like to see them? Perhaps we could have dinner together and then go to my place."

He held his breath waiting for her outraged refusal. After all, the whole thing smacked of the lecher asking the young beauty up to look at his etchings. But Angelique did not laugh or turn cold on him. She looked him square in the eyes and smiled.

"I'd like that very much."

"I'll get your coat," said Ed.

They were at the front door saying good-bye to Peggy when a man named Ted Lambeth came out of the library and into the living room. Ted was an amateur photographer suspected of having homosexual tendencies. He also drank too much and so now as he clutched the door frame, swaying, his face a dirty-gray color, everyone assumed that poor old Ted had just had a few too many again.

"The Japanese have just bombed Pearl Harbor," he said.

Angelique would remember forever the absolute silence in Peggy Howard's living room for those first few seconds. No one gasped. No one dropped a glass. No one even moved. And then everyone gasped, dropped things and moved and began talking at once.

"When?"

"Are you drunk again, Ted?"

"The radio," he said.

Everyone ran toward Peggy's library where a big console radio stood against one wall.

And then they knew it was true. It seemed to Angelique that the announcer's voice was on the edge of hysteria and that he kept repeating the same words over and over. On her arm she could feel Ed Miller's hand trembling.

"I'll have to get right down to the office," he said. "Sorry, Angelique. Tomorrow the market is going to hell—"

Angelique looked at him with such rage that for a moment he felt chilled to the bone.

"Angelique," he said. "America is at war."

So what? Angelique wanted to scream. Just so the hell what?

But she made herself look at him, solicitously now.

"Of course, Ed," she replied softly. "I guess I'm just so upset that I can't think straight."

"Yes, of course," said Ed and moved away from her toward the door.

Angelique walked home alone. There was no sense hanging around Peggy's any longer. The party was spoiled for sure now.

Goddamn it, thought Angelique furiously, and the tears of anger were hot against her cold cheeks. Goddamn it all to hell. Everything always happens to spoil things for me.

2

The next noon when Etienne de Montigny left the garage to go to lunch he did not go to his regular restaurant. He went instead to stand in the long line that had formed outside the Livingstone Post Office, where the recruiting offices for the Armed Forces had been set up. Along with many other men all over America, he had waited only long enough to hear the President's declaration of war and then he had gone to offer his services to his country.

There was a lot of wild talk going on that day. Some said that the services wouldn't take anybody over the age of twenty-nine. Others claimed that no married man would be accepted let alone anyone with children, while still others joked that the United States was so hard up for manpower that they'd take anybody, so long as he was breathing.

Etienne had decided that he would join the Navy and when his turn came he took no chances of being rejected. He told the recruiting officer that he was twenty-eight years old and unmarried. He was amazed at how ridiculously simple it all was. No one asked him any questions nor seemed to have any doubts about him at all.

The handsomely uniformed Navy man merely filled out a few forms and scarcely wasted a glance on Etienne.

"Report at the Armory for your physical at seven-thirty tomorrow morning," he said as soon as Etienne had signed his name.

That evening Etienne was very good-humored at the supper

table. He even smiled as Monique talked to herself and when Angelique looked at him sharply and asked, "What are you grinning about?" he merely shrugged. "Nothing, my dear. Nothing."

And later, when Angelique got dressed to go out, he did not even ask her where she was going. He merely picked up his newspaper and began to read. Alana and Lesley were playing some sort of noisy game in their bedroom and in the kitchen Monique was washing the supper dishes and mumbling to herself.

Change of life, my foot, thought Etienne as he listened to Monique. The old lady is crazy as hell.

There were a lot of people who agreed with him, especially his mother, Simone.

"It's not right, Etienne," Simone had kept telling him, "two little girls being left alone so much with a crazy woman."

"The doctor says she's not crazy," replied Etienne. "He calls it the menopause."

"Listen," Simone had said, "that's just a fancy name for the change of life. I've seen plenty of women go through it. None of them ever acted like Monique."

When Etienne had reported this to his wife, Angelique flew at him like a wildcat.

"She is *not* crazy," shouted Angelique. "This *is* just part of her menopause. She'll get over it. She's no crazier than you or I. And no crazier than your mother, for that matter. Simone should learn to mind her own business. Does she think she's a doctor or something?"

But one day Etienne had come home from work and heard Monique talking to Alana and Lesley.

"You must understand," Monique was saying, "that I did not really kill him. I only gave him a little drink to ease his pain and that is not really killing anyone."

"What the hell are you talking about?" shouted Etienne.

"Grammy is telling us a story," said Alana.

222

But Lesley did not say anything. Her little face was pale and her lower lip trembled.

Etienne was enraged. "What the hell kind of story are you telling them now?" he yelled. "Who is it that you did not kill?"

"Grandfather," answered Alana matter-of-factly. "Mother's daddy. His name was Armand."

Etienne led his daughters into the living room. Alana stood next to his chair but he took Lesley up onto his lap. The child was shivering.

"Now, you listen to me," he said, "both of you. Your grandfather was a very sick man. He was sick for a long, long time and then God came and took him to Heaven. That is exactly what happened. Nobody killed him or tried to kill him. Understand?"

"But Grammy said—" began Lesley.

"Never mind what Grammy said," said Etienne. "Grammy is—" He'd almost said that Grammy was crazy but he'd stopped himself in time. "Grammy was just making up a story."

When Angelique came home he was still furious.

"You'd better do something about that mother of yours," he said to his wife. "Do you know what kind of crazy story she was telling the kids today?"

Angelique listened intently as Etienne related what he had heard and when he had finished she turned her face away from him.

"I'll speak to her," she said at last. "We can't have that kind of talk in front of the girls."

"She's crazy," repeated Etienne. "I tell you, Angelique, she's crazy as a bedbug."

"No, Etienne, Maman is like me. She is cursed with too much imagination and once in a while she gets carried away. That's all. I'll speak to her about it."

Etienne de Montigny was not an eavesdropper by nature

223

or inclination, but that night he had made himself listen through the door of Monique's bedroom when Angelique went in to talk to her mother. Her voice was low and furious and although Etienne could not quite hear every word, he heard enough.

"What's the matter with you?" Angelique was saying. "Do you want the police down on our heads?"

Monique began to whimper.

"Do you want to go to prison?" demanded Angelique. "Or worse, the crazy house?"

Monique kept saying, "No," over and over again.

"Then you'd best keep your mouth shut about Papa, do you understand? You are never to say one word about him to anyone. Not to the children, not to Etienne, not to your sister, not to a living soul. Do you understand?"

There was no answer, no sound at all except that of weeping, and then Etienne heard the explosion of a single sharp slap.

"Do you understand me?" said Angelique, her voice beginning to rise.

There was another long pause, another slap, and then the one word "Yes," repeated again and again.

Etienne had moved away from the door, his stomach contracting painfully. He went to the bathroom, certain that he had to throw up, but he could not. He sat on the edge of the tub, sweating and gagging.

Etienne had watched Monique more carefully than ever after that, but she told no more stories to Alana and Lesley. She continued to mumble to herself and her ramblings were disjointed and made little sense. Every week Angelique took her mother to see the doctor and there were pills and injections and more pills for Monique, so that at times she was quiet and quite rational. But many nights Etienne heard her weeping in her bedroom and often Angelique had to run to her to awaken her from some screaming nightmare.

224

Finally Etienne, worried about the well-being of his children, had gone himself to consult with the doctor. His name was Myles Gordon and Etienne had never liked him. Dr. Gordon had delivered Alana and Lesley, and the third child too, Etienne's son, who had died at birth. No, Etienne did not like Myles Gordon at all and when Angelique had demanded to know why, Etienne could think of only one reason that he could put his finger on.

"He's a Jew," said Etienne, "and he pretends to be a gentile."

"Now what in the world does that have to do with anything?" asked Angelique.

"If a man is a Jew he ought to act like one," replied Etienne. "It's not right for a man to be ashamed of his religion."

"My God," said Angelique, her voice heavy with contempt. "Look who's turning into a philosopher!"

"I don't care," answered Etienne stubbornly. "It's not right, a Jew going to a Protestant church and eating pork and everything else. It'd be like us eating meat on Fridays and not going to Mass."

"You sound just like your mother," snapped Angelique.

"At least my mother isn't ashamed of what she is."

The next day Etienne had gone to Dr. Gordon's office during his lunch hour.

Myles Gordon knew that Etienne detested him but he was invariably polite to him for Angelique's sake. Dr. Gordon liked Angelique. He liked her a lot.

"Believe me, Mr. de Montigny," said Dr. Gordon as Etienne had sat down alongside his desk, "there is absolutely no basis for your concern about your mother-in-law."

"But she's always talking to herself," protested Etienne. "Are you telling me that's a normal, everyday thing for a woman to do?"

"No, of course not," replied the doctor soothingly, "but it's nothing to worry about. Mrs. Bergeron is having a rough

225

time with her menopause, true enough. But actually she is as sound mentally as any of us."

The doctor continued to smile reassuringly at Etienne but he was remembering Angelique's words.

"You just try having my mother put away somewhere," Angelique had said to him shortly after she had brought in her mother on her first visit. "I'll have your heart on a platter."

"But, my dear child," said the doctor, "she should be placed in a hospital of *some* sort. I'm not saying that she's actually insane, but she should spend some time in a sanitarium, at least until she gets over the worst of this."

"Now, you listen to me, Myles," Angelique had replied. "Livingstone isn't that big a city that people won't talk. If you think for a minute that I'm going to have all my friends saying that I've got a loony mother, you're crazier than she is. Not on your life, darling. You just think about that. And you think about it long and hard."

"Are you threatening me, my sweet?"

"You're goddamned right!" Angelique had answered. "You just remember that old adage about knowing where the body is buried!"

Now, looking at Etienne, the doctor repeated, "You are unduly concerned about Mrs. Bergeron. She will improve with time. I'm very sure that the new pills I gave her last week will help considerably."

"What's in those pills?" demanded Etienne suspiciously. "Dope?"

"Of course not," replied Dr. Gordon, hoping to God that Etienne had never heard of phenobarbital. "They contain a medicine to help her over her difficult periods and that's absolutely all."

"What kind of medicine?"

"A special vitamin," answered the doctor. "Especially useful in female trouble."

And Etienne, who along with millions of other men stood in awe of the words "female trouble," believed Myles Gordon.

"All right," he said. "But I just wish to Christ she'd stop mumbling to herself all the time."

The doctor put a reassuring hand on his shoulder.

"That will pass," he said. "Believe me, Mr. de Montigny, it will pass."

Dr. Myles Gordon had been thoroughly relieved that he had finally managed to get rid of Etienne. As soon as he'd gone, the doctor picked up the telephone and called Angelique. He repeated every single word of his conversation with Etienne.

"Thank you, Myles," said Angelique. "But don't worry. I'll take care of Etienne, with all his little doubts and fears."

"When am I going to see you?" he asked. "It's been a long time."

There was a silence on the wire and then Angelique replied, "Perhaps Friday. Yes, Friday evening."

"Friday is my late night here at the office," protested the doctor. "You know that, Angelique."

She laughed. "Yes, I know. But, Myles, certainly you are clever enough to think up some excuse so your wife won't know that you had a late date. Tell her you have to make a series of house calls."

Then Angelique laughed again and hung up.

But although Etienne de Montigny had been somewhat reassured by Dr. Myles Gordon's words, he could not help feeling a certain uneasiness when the children were left too long alone with Monique. Yet as time passed he made himself believe that things would turn out all right. On this particular evening, his last in bondage, he rattled his newspaper as he listened to the little girls in their bedroom.

Yes, it must be some kind of game about cowboys and Indians, he reassured himself, and smiled.

Monique had finished the supper dishes and now there

was not a sound from the kitchen. Etienne listened intently for several minutes, then tiptoed softly to the doorway and looked into the kitchen. Monique was sitting quietly in the kitchen rocker reading her prayer book.

It will be all right, he told himself, it will be all right. Angelique won't dare to leave the girls alone with her night after night. And I'll write a letter to my mother asking her to keep a check on things while I'm away in the Navy. Everything is going to be all right.

That night Etienne de Montigny put his daughters to bed and then retired himself. He fell asleep almost at once but he dreamed, and when he awoke with a start he couldn't remember what it was that he had dreamed. He only knew that his pillow was soaking wet, as if he had been crying for a long, long time.

3

At seven-thirty the next morning, Etienne presented himself at the State Armory Building and submitted to his physical. In less than an hour it was over and he was a member of the United States Navy.

"That's it, brother," said a uniformed sailor. "Get your affairs in order and report back here next Thursday morning at eight o'clock."

"Next Thursday," cried Etienne. "But that's more than a week away. What's the matter with my leaving tomorrow?"

The sailor gave him a sharp look.

"Look, mate, you're in the Navy now. I said next Thursday morning at eight o'clock. That's an order."

Etienne did not know how he ever got through the remaining days. He went to work as usual. He ate, slept, turned over his pay check to Angelique and waited. But on the last day he could stand it no longer. Right after work he went to a saloon and tried to get as drunk as possible as quickly as possible. It took his brother Christophe less than two hours to find him.

"Angelique called Ma," said Christophe, sitting down at Etienne's table. "She was worried when you didn't come home right after work."

"Sit down and have a drink, for Christ's sake," replied Etienne.

"I am sitting down," Christophe answered with a laugh. "Jesus, boy, you've really been hitting it, haven't you?"

"Well, then, have a drink for Christ's sake," said Etienne and laughed with his brother.

Christophe hesitated. "Nah, I promised Ma I'd stay sober after I caught up with you."

"Let her kiss my ass, the fuckin' bitch."

Christophe jumped up, spilling Etienne's drink.

"Up on your feet, mister," he said furiously. "If you think you can talk about Ma like that, drunk or sober, I'll soon show you."

Etienne looked up at his brother.

"What the hell's the matter with you, Christophe?" he asked thickly. "Who the hell said anything about Ma?"

"You did!" shouted Christophe.

"I did like hell."

"Then who were you talking about?"

Etienne signaled the waiter for two drinks.

"I'm talking about my wife," he said simply.

The waiter placed the drinks on the table and went away. Christophe stared stupidly at his brother.

"Yes," said Etienne, picking up his glass, "I'm talking about my wife. My sweet-faced, whoring Angelique."

"For God's sake, 'Tien." Christophe glanced around apprehensively at the other tables. "Keep your voice down."

"What the Christ for?" demanded Etienne, more loudly than ever. "Probably half the bastards in here tonight have rooted around in her bed."

" 'Tien, 'Tien. You're drunk. Come on, let's get out of here."

He rose and went to his brother and tried to take him by the arm, but Etienne shook him off.

"You're fuckin' right I'll get out," he said. "Right out of the whole mess. Tomorrow."

"What are you talking about?"

"You heard me," said Etienne. "After tomorrow I'll be out. Out of the whole fuckin' mess."

Christophe looked hard at his brother, trying to figure out what lay behind Etienne's words.

"Let's get out of here, 'Tien," he said at last. "There's a place not far from here. I know the guy who owns it. He's got a back room and we can sit there and talk."

"Talk, hell," said Etienne. "I want another drink."

"That too," Christophe promised. "We can get a bottle there. Honest, 'Tien. Come on, huh?"

So they went to the saloon with the back room owned by Christophe's friend, Bob Plourde. The back room was generally reserved for the poker games that Bob Plourde could not seem to live without. But on this particular evening Bob Plourde had found no takers for his dangerous games of stud, so Christophe and Etienne had the place to themselves.

Etienne relaxed with a great sigh in one of the armchairs as Christophe opened the bottle of whiskey that Bob Plourde had put on the table and poured two large drinks.

The short walk in the cold night air had revived Etienne somewhat and now as he reached for his glass he seemed almost sober.

"You never liked Angelique, did you, Christophe?" he asked.

"Oh, come on, 'Tien," protested Christophe. "I never said any such thing."

"You never had to say it," replied Etienne. "I could tell. The girls never liked her either. Or Ma. Well, Ma was right. From the very beginning Ma was right."

"Don't talk like that, 'Tien," said Christophe. "After all, you've made a good life with Angelique. You have a good home, two nice little girls—"

"Oh, balls," said Etienne and poured more whiskey into his glass. He drank in gulps and when his glass was empty

231

he refilled it at once. "I want you to promise me something, Christophe. Promise me?"

"Of course," answered Christophe without hesitation. "Haven't we always stuck together, you and I? What is it?"

"I want you to promise me that no matter how drunk I get, or how bad I feel in the morning, you'll get me to the Armory by eight o'clock."

Christophe stared at his brother. "But what the hell do you want to go to the Armory for at eight o'clock in the morning?"

"I've joined the Navy," answered Etienne gravely. "I'm leaving for boot camp at eight o'clock in the morning."

Christophe was dumfounded.

"Have you gone crazy, Etienne?" he demanded.

"No," replied Etienne, "and I'm not that drunk either, no matter what you might think. It's true, Christophe. I'm going and nobody's going to stop me. Now, do you promise that you'll see that I get there on time?"

"But why?" asked Christophe. "Why have you done this?"

"Do you promise?" insisted Etienne.

"All right, all right," answered Christophe, "I promise. But for God's sake, tell me why, 'Tien. Why?"

Etienne took another drink.

"To get away from Angelique," he said simply.

Christophe sat down next to Etienne and put a gentle hand on his brother's arm.

"What is it, 'Tien?" he asked. "In God's name, tell me what has happened."

How can I tell him? Etienne thought.

In the beginning he had been so sure that his life was going to turn out just as he had planned. He had taken his little contrary wildcat of a wife and tamed her right from the start, which was the way it should be and the way it should have remained.

Years later he could still recall his wedding night in photographic detail and he remembered, with a feeling that was almost exaltation, how she had screamed and tried to twist away from him as he broke into her.

"Papa," she had screamed and Etienne had pushed himself at her as savagely as he could.

"I'm not your goddamned father," he said, his eyes blazing down into hers, "I'm your husband and I've just made you my woman."

And afterward, while she still lay on the bed sobbing, he went to the bathroom and wet a towel with warm water. Then he began to clean her gently, murmuring softly to her the way one does to a frightened puppy. He took a jar of soothing salve out of his suitcase and spread it gently on her until at last she stopped crying. He stroked her and watched her nipples beginning to stiffen again and he felt her whole body begin to swell and throb.

"No, no, no," she whispered, but she strained toward him.

"Yes, yes, yes," answered Etienne and tangled one hand in her hair, forcing her face toward his so that she could not look away. He saw her mouth open and her eyes begin to glaze.

"I can't," she whispered. "I can't."

"Yes, you can," he said. "Any time I want to make you, you can. And you will."

He saw the little film of perspiration that had formed over her upper lip.

"I can't," she said, so softly that he could barely hear her. And then, "I can't fight you any more, Etienne."

He laughed in triumph at the suddenly wildly twisting little animal under his hands. At last, he thought, he knew the secret to Angelique.

Much later, when she was asleep, Etienne sat in the living room of the hotel suite. He smoked lazily, feeling the cool night air against his bare skin, and he could not keep from smiling to himself in the darkened room.

All Angelique wanted, in fact all that Angelique really

233

needed, was to be mastered. Etienne almost laughed out loud.

When I think of it, he mused. All this time when she's been so goddamned contrary and mean, so taken up with her silly little arguments and so bent on getting her own way, all I had to do was give her a good shaking or a swift slap on the behind and she'd have fallen into my arms like a ripened apple. Oh, she wants to put up a fight all right, but in the end what she really wants is to be subjugated, enslaved. Well, I can take care of that any old time.

That whole weekend in Boston had seemed to prove Etienne's theory correct. He could do anything he wanted with Angelique so long as he demanded and did not ask and when he had finished with her she would curl up on his lap and nuzzle against him.

"It will be like this always, won't it, Etienne?" she'd asked.

"Of course, my darling."

"And you'll take care of me always? Just as if I were your little girl?"

"You *are* my little girl," Etienne had answered, kissing her. "My very own precious little angel."

"And we'll live just like a prince and a princess in our own little castle and you'll take care of me forever?"

"Forever," said Etienne.

But Etienne could not resist testing his theory and so one morning he had tried asking.

"Please, darling," he had pleaded, stroking her neck. "Let's go into the bedroom."

She had jumped off his lap and walked away from him.

"For heaven's sake, Etienne," she'd said angrily, "stop mewing like a kitten."

"Please, darling."

"No. I want to go shopping."

"Please come back and sit on my lap."

"No. I'm going to dress now and I suggest that you do the same unless you want me to go out alone."

234

It was all Etienne could do to keep from laughing.

"Don't talk like that, my little angel," he begged.

"And don't call me your little angel," she said furiously and walked into the bedroom.

He went after her and whirled her around.

"You are forgetting something, my little angel," he said. "I'm your husband and I'd advise you never to refuse me again."

"Let go of me!" she cried.

"Take off that nightgown and go lie down on the bed."

"Not on your life," she replied. "I'm going out."

"Angelique," he said patiently. "Are you or are you not going to do as you are told?"

"Never," she said and tried to kick him in the shins.

"Well, we'll just see."

He grabbed her and sat down on the nearest chair. He turned her over his knees and lifted the chiffon nightgown up to her waist. Then he proceeded to spank her until her buttocks were scarlet and she wept with rage.

"Now," he said, setting her roughly on her feet. "take off that nightgown and go lie down on the bed."

She stripped off the nightgown and stood in front of him and her whole body seemed to glow.

"Etienne," she said.

"On the bed," he answered, and watched her move away and then lie down.

She was so excited that he barely touched her before she spasmed under him and even then she begged, "Again, Etienne. Again."

Etienne looked at Christophe, who was looking down into his drink.

It had been like that the whole weekend and it had even lasted for several weeks after they'd returned to Livingstone after the honeymoon. They moved into their tiny apartment, but that hadn't lasted long. Monique Bergeron fell ill, and Etienne and Angelique moved into Monique's house. When Monique recovered, it had just seemed easier to stay on with her than go through all the bother of finding another place.

"Besides," Angelique told Etienne. "I promised Papa I'd take care of Monique. We can't leave her alone now."

Afterward Etienne could never quite remember when things had begun to go sour. It seemed that there was never enough money and that Angelique was always bored.

"It's no goddamned wonder you're bored," shouted Etienne in frustration one night. "For Christ's sake, all you do all day is sit on your ass and read, read, read. No wonder you're bored. Why don't you try giving your mother a hand with the house? She does everything around here."

It was true. Monique Bergeron did everything for herself and Etienne and Angelique, from scrubbing floors to pressing Etienne's trousers.

"If I'd wanted to do housework I'd have got myself a job as a maid!" Angelique shouted back. "If you think Monique is working too hard, why don't you hire a scrubwoman?"

"I can't afford a scrubwoman," replied Etienne, "and you know it as well as I."

Angelique lit a cigarette, which she knew Etienne hated to see her do. She blew smoke in a great cloud and pouted.

"That's not my fault," she said. "I'm bored."

"Well, exactly what would you like to do, princess?" asked Etienne.

Angelique sat up, missing the heavy sarcasm in his voice.

"I'd like to go to Paris."

Etienne could not help himself. He began to shout again.

"Are you crazy? On the money I make? Paris?"

"Well, then, go make some more," Angelique answered, leaning back on the bed and puffing at her cigarette.

"Listen," said Etienne, "the whole goddamned country is in the grip of a depression. I'm working ten hours a day as it is, six days a week, and goddamned lucky to be."

"I could get a job," said Angelique. "There are plenty of people who would be glad to hire someone like me. And not to do housework either."

Etienne grabbed her by the arm, forcing her to sit up, and took her cigarette and ground it out in an ashtray.

"Your place is here in this house," he said. "No wife of mine is going to work so that people can say I'm not able to support a woman."

Angelique looked down at his hand on her arm. Then, very deliberately, she shook it off and lit another cigarette.

"Oh, shut up, Etienne," she said. "And don't ever grab me like that again."

He reached for her again, but she rolled away so quickly that he almost fell against the edge of the bed.

"I said never," repeated Angelique. "Remember this, Etienne. If you can't be a big man with the pay check, don't try to be one in the bedroom."

The following day Angelique went out and got herself a job clerking in a dry goods store. The job paid forty cents an hour, or a grand total of sixteen dollars a week, and Etienne laughed and waited for her to get sick and tired of standing on her feet all day.

But Etienne laughed too soon.

Within two weeks, Angelique was lunching regularly with the owner of the dry goods store and in something less than a month she was sleeping with him every time she had the chance.

His name was Mike Koorkanian and he was one of the ugliest men Angelique had ever seen. He was short and squat with more than a slight suggestion of a potbelly. His complexion was swarthy, his black curly hair was almost kinky and his black eyes protruded slightly from his head. But

Mike Koorkanian also had a tremendously broad chest and huge shoulders and arms that seemed to be made of iron. He exuded an aura of maleness that almost choked Angelique.

Here is a man, she thought. A man who is *all* man.

The fact that he owned and operated a dry goods store did not make him seem effeminate in the least. The store had been left to him by his Armenian grandfather and Mike Koorkanian had never been one to let a good thing go to waste. In his private office in the back of Koorkanian's Fine Fabrics and Dry Goods, he ran a very profitable bookmaking operation. It had taken Angelique de Montigny exactly three days to find out about Mike's secret enterprise and from that moment on she had known that he was going to become her lover.

But it was not easy to carry on a clandestine love affair in a city like Livingstone, New Hampshire. At least without getting caught. And Angelique did not want to lose Etienne. Not yet, at any rate. She was not quite sure that Mike Koorkanian would marry her if she got a divorce and although Etienne was worse than an old woman about spending money, he at least supported her and Monique. Monique was something else again.

Just let Etienne cast her off and Monique was apt to do any number of things with the money that still remained from what Armand had left and which was still accumulating dividends.

No, that money should rightfully come to her when her mother died, and Angelique was not about to do anything to jeopardize it.

Mike Koorkanian had his own apartment, which was located in another part of the city from where Angelique lived, and it was safe enough for her to go there if they were careful. Mike was very generous with gifts of clothing and money, and most of all, he was very good in bed.

He took her again and again with a kind of animal frenzy,

238

a snorting brutality, that excited her, and if Angelique could not be certain that he loved her, she knew very well that he was mad for her body. He never tired of the pale smoothness of her against his own swarthy hairiness and he never took her without every light in the bedroom blazing.

Angelique watched him as he looked down at his dark hands moving over her and when she saw him beginning to sweat and it seemed that his eyes would pop out of his head, she wondered at the lack of revulsion in herself. Sometimes he stroked her for hours, watching his hands and the way her nerves and muscles moved spasmodically just beneath the surface of her white, white skin. She knew he was not touching her like that to stimulate her, but to arouse himself to a point where he was literally helpless to put off taking her for another moment.

"Is this the best, Mike?" she asked.

"Yes, baby, yes."

"Am I, Mike? Your baby, I mean?"

"You said it. My very own sweet-smelling, pink-and-white baby."

It took Etienne de Montigny a long time before he began to be suspicious. But eventually there came an end to the reasons for taking an inventory at the store, another baby shower, a buying trip to Boston, a party for one of the girls, so one night Etienne followed her right to Mike Koorkanian's front door. He watched the lights go on in the bedroom and finally he walked up to the door and knocked. It seemed to Etienne that he had to wait a very long time before Mike Koorkanian, in a bathrobe and barefooted, came to the door.

"I came to get my wife," said Etienne just before he hit him.

Then he stepped over Mike and went to the bedroom to drag a shivering, weeping Angelique to her feet. He watched while she dressed and then he took her by the wrist and pulled her all the way across the city to Monique Bergeron's house.

He dragged her into the bedroom without a word and stripped off her clothes.

"You can start screaming any time you want," he told her, "but it won't stop me. And if you yell, not only your mother but the neighbors, too, will hear you."

Very methodically he took four of his neckties from the back of the closet door and then he held Angelique down on the bed with one knee while he tied her to the four posts.

"There's only one way to cure a wife who runs around," he said. "In fact, there's even an old saying about it. It goes: Keep her barefoot and knocked up."

"No, Etienne," she whispered. "You can't."

He got undressed as calmly as if he were preparing to take a bath.

"Oh, but I can," he replied with maddening calm. "I've listened to you long enough. 'Oh, Etienne,' " he mimicked, " 'we just can't have a baby now. We're too young. We haven't enough money.' "

He fell on top of her and she could not move and when it was over he got up and lit a cigarette.

"Untie me, Etienne," she said furiously. "Let me up at once."

"Not on your life, you little tramp," answered Etienne. "Not on your life. You're not going into the bathroom and do whatever it is you do to yourself to keep from getting knocked up. Not tonight nor any other night, until I'm damned good and sure that I've planted a load for you to carry."

"You son of a bitch!"

"Good night, my angel," said Etienne, and went out of the bedroom, locking the door behind him.

"You seem a little shocked, Christophe," said Etienne de Montigny.

He was very drunk now, and his head rested on his arms, folded across the table in Bob Plourde's back room.

"But every word I've told you is true, you know," Etienne went on, his words slurring badly. "That's how I got my two kids. Little Lesley first, then Alana. Some names for two little French girls, eh? And the one who died, I got him that way too. My son."

"Dear Father in Heaven," whispered Christophe, echoing the words his mother, Simone, used so often. "Dear Father in Heaven, you might have killed her, Etienne. She almost died having the last one."

And suddenly it occurred to Christophe that he was speaking of Etienne's third child the way everyone else in the family did. They always said, "Etienne's son," or "the third child," or "the last one." No one ever came right out and used the name that had been the little boy's for slightly less than twelve hours. Stephen Armand de Montigny. The beautiful, blond-haired, waxen-faced little boy who had bled to death in less than half a day.

"Maybe I still cared enough to want her to die then," said Etienne. "Now I no longer care at all. I just want to get away."

"Listen, Etienne," Christophe said, "there are other ways to get away from her. Let me take you home to Ma. You don't have to run away and join the Navy."

"You promised, Christophe," mumbled Etienne. "You promised me. I'll never forgive you if you don't get me there."

Then Etienne turned his head away from his brother and began to snore.

"Plourde, come in here, will you?" Christophe called.

When his friend came into the back room, Christophe said, "Give me a hand with him, eh? We'll have to spend the night here."

Bob Plourde was nothing if not discreet and he asked no questions.

"Sure," he replied. "We'll put him on the sofa and you can come home with me."

"No," Christophe answered, "I'll stay here with him."

There was not much left of the night, but for the few hours that remained Christophe sat up in a chair tilted against the wall and watched his brother sleep.

The next morning, he and Bob Plourde gave Etienne a few good stiff jolts of brandy and after that Etienne managed to shave and wash. His clothes were a mess but he wouldn't be wearing them much longer anyway.

It was bitterly cold and just beginning to snow as Christophe and Etienne set off for the State Armory Building.

"You can tell Ma, but wait until tonight."

"Okay," said Christophe and his throat hurt.

They stopped in front of the big, cold-looking cement shed of a building.

"Well," said Etienne. "Good-bye, Christophe."

"Yes," answered Christophe and then they just stood there looking at each other.

"Don't worry about Angelique or anything else," said Etienne. "I'll write you a letter after a while."

"Yes." Christophe nodded and then there didn't seem to be anything else to do except punch his brother on the arm as hard as he could and walk away.

Book Four

1

By the time Alana de Montigny had reached fifteen, she was almost entirely the complete cynic she would remain for the rest of her life.

Before she was twelve, she had seen her grandmother Monique committed to the state asylum for the insane and she could tick off the names of her mother, Angelique's, lovers like a bright kindergartener reciting the alphabet.

Alana was the tomboy of the family, while her sister, Lesley, had always been timid and afraid. Alana had learned about boys and sex even before she had reached the age of puberty, while Lesley went right on believing in princes and shining white knights for simply years and years.

It had been much easier for Angelique after Grammy had been put away, because then the house was Angelique's and so was the money. Alana guessed very early that money must be a very peculiar thing. Ever since she could remember it had been "Grammy's money" and now Angelique called it "my money" and the only thing that had changed was that Grammy no longer lived at home but in the crazy house.

Angelique had taught Alana and Lesley to say that Grammy had had a "nervous breakdown" but Alana knew better. She knew that Grammy was as nutty as a fruitcake. Some of her boyfriends had told her so and she was aware of it long before that. After all, hadn't she seen with her very own eyes?

Alana could remember when all that Grammy did was forget where she put her clothes or what time it was. But after a while it got so Grammy forgot to eat with her knife and fork and she forgot to use the toilet and she even forgot that she was supposed to stay in bed at night and took to roaming the streets in her nightgown. Grammy's nightgown always had what Angelique called "nasty" on the back but which Alana and her friends knew very well was plain old shit.

One night a friend of Angelique's dropped in unexpectedly. Grammy waited in her bedroom until he had a drink in one hand and a cigarette in the other and was sitting all comfortable next to Angelique on the sofa in the living room, then Grammy came in in her shitty old nightgown and started to swear at him in French. She called him a whoremaster and a son of a bitch, and Alana, who was listening at the top of the stairs, knew very well what these names meant because a lot of her friends were French-Canadians and had taught them to her.

So the next day Dr. Gordon came to the house with another doctor, whose name was Dr. Henry Goodrich, and a few days later Angelique got all dressed up, even to a new hat. She got Grammy all cleaned up and dressed too. And when Angelique came home alone she said that poor Grammy was going to "a sanitarium" for "a rest" because she had had a "nervous breakdown."

Lesley cried and said, "But when is she coming back home?" Angelique patted Lesley on the head as if she were thinking about something else and replied, "Oh, soon, dear." And Lesley believed her.

But Alana didn't, nor did she cry. Alana knew very well that poor Grammy was going to the crazy house. She tried to tell Lesley the truth one night but Lesley just cried harder than ever and called her a bad, wicked girl.

"To hell with you then," said Alana.

"Oh, oh, oh," sobbed Lesley. "You are a bad, wicked girl and I'm going to tell Mother that you swore at me."

246

"Her name isn't 'Mother,'" answered Alana. "Her name is Angelique. And as for you, you are a dummy and a crybaby. A dumb, dumb crybaby."

But Lesley had her hands over her ears and did not hear her. Whenever Lesley didn't want to hear something, she covered her ears, and when she didn't want to look at something, she shut her eyes. But what was more aggravating than anything was the way Lesley could just do nothing. She could sit by the hour, silently staring out of a window.

"What're you doing?" Alana would ask.

"Nothing," Lesley would answer.

"I can *see* that," said Alana, "but what're you *thinking* about?"

"Everything."

"Oh," Alana would cry in frustration, "you *are* a dummy!"

Lesley was short and rather plump and she had a soft, round little face. Her hair was fair, but not with the pale perfection of Angelique's. Lesley's hair was what Angelique called "dirty blonde" and every time she said it, Lesley looked as if she'd been slapped.

Alana, on the other hand, was thin and wiry and dark.

"For heaven's sake, Alana," Angelique was always saying, "go take a bath. Isn't it bad enough that you *look* like a boy without *smelling* like one?"

Alana could not remember a time when she had not hated her mother. Not that she was conscious of it every single minute. In fact, sometimes hours went by when she did not think about Angelique at all. But sooner or later she would again and then, no matter what Alana did, the feeling wouldn't go away.

If it weren't for Angelique, Alana would think, Daddy would never have gone away. If it weren't for Angelique, Grammy wouldn't be in the nut house. If it weren't for Angelique, Lesley wouldn't always be staring out the window or reading a book or crying so much.

247

Alana's eyes were on her mother every chance she got. She watched the hands, slim, pink-tipped, lighting cigarettes. She spied while Angelique spent countless hours fussing over herself—bathing, brushing, perfuming, preening. She listened to Angelique's silky voice giving orders to the housekeeper, whose name was Maggie Donovan and who hated Alana and Lesley almost as much as Alana despised her.

"Dirty Canucks," muttered Maggie Donovan, but she never said it in front of Angelique.

"Shanty Irish," Alana muttered back, but she never said it in front of Angelique either.

Alana listened to her mother talking on the telephone and she could always tell when Angelique was speaking to a man. Then Angelique's voice would be lower, huskier, silkier than ever.

Alana snooped at night when her mother had company. She had fixed up a comfortable place for herself under the wide staircase opposite the living room. The staircase was not only deep, but it was good and dark back there and when Alana spied she put a couple of pillows on the floor and covered herself with an old blanket. From her hiding place, Alana not only could hear every word spoken in the living room, but she could see almost everything as well, and there was a great deal to see.

When Angelique gave a party, Alana didn't even bother to watch, but when Angelique entertained a man, that was something else again. Then it was well worth all the sneaking around. When Alana prepared to eavesdrop it involved getting her pillows and blanket downstairs and hiding them in the darkest corner under the staircase, and threatening to beat her sister to a pulp if Lesley ever dared to squeal. But worst of all, it meant getting up at daybreak before Maggie Donovan came, so she could get the pillows and blanket hidden again. But when Angelique had a gentleman caller it was well worth

248

it, because then she could watch and listen and not even try to fight the black, black hatred that filled her.

By the time she was fourteen, what Alana had not discovered about sex on the streets and in empty garages, she had learned from watching her mother. From her hiding place under the staircase, Alana found out all about Angelique's lovers and it was from there, too, that she finally found out all about Dr. Myles Gordon.

2

When Angelique de Montigny was finally certain that she was pregnant that first time, she spent a week during which she alternated between weeping, drinking castor oil, running up and down stairs as rapidly as possible and lifting heavy furniture in a series of futile attempts to bring about a miscarriage. When all she succeeded in doing was to make herself so sick that she couldn't even hold water on her stomach, she decided to go to a doctor.

She found Dr. Myles Gordon by simply looking through the classified telephone directory. She liked the sound of his name and the fact that he had his office in what was considered to be the best office building in Livingstone. And when she had made an appointment and seen him, she was delighted to discover that he was possibly the handsomest man she had ever seen in her life.

Dr. Myles Gordon was tall and dark, with the wedge-shaped body immortalized in magazine illustrations. He had blue eyes, the fine-grained complexion of a woman, and long, beautifully shaped hands with short, very clean fingernails. He also had a wife and two children.

Angelique took one look at him and something in the square set of his jaw, in the penetration of the blue eyes, made her decide that in this particular case, honesty might be the best policy.

"I want an abortion," she said to him bluntly.

"Well, you're not going to get one here," he answered just as bluntly.

Angelique had expected that he would be shocked or angry, that he would scold her or try to dissuade her, almost anything except this matter-of-factness. She looked at him in disbelief and his blue eyes looked right back, smiling, tolerantly amused.

"Are you married?" he asked.

"Of course I'm married," she replied angrily. "What do you take me for?"

"A silly, empty-headed woman," he said. "What makes you so sure you're pregnant?"

"I missed my last two periods."

The doctor smiled. "Then you're probably right in your diagnosis," he said, "but let's make sure."

Myles Gordon was thirty-eight years old and had been a doctor for more than ten years, but when Angelique lay nude on the table waiting to be examined, he could not help the sudden sexual feeling that came over him.

She had the most beautiful body he had ever seen outside of an art gallery and she was pregnant all right. Now he could understand why she wanted an abortion. It would be a pity to watch all that loveliness become distorted, to realize, perhaps, that it was disappearing forever. But he wasn't about to turn abortionist, along with everything else. He had too much at stake already.

Another three or four years and Henry Goodrich and I can live on Easy Street forever, thought Myles Gordon. And I'm not going to blow it now. Not even for a body like this one.

"That's it, Mrs. de Montigny," he said crisply when he had finished examining her. "You're pregnant all right, but listen to me. There is no need for you to be frightened about anything. You've got a beautiful big pelvis."

"I have not!" replied Angelique and burst into tears. "I'll die if I have a baby. I know I'll die."

"Stop that," said the doctor harshly, "you're not going to die! You're healthy as a horse and besides, you have me to take care of you."

"But I don't *want* a baby!"

"Well, it's a little late to think about that," answered the doctor. "Come on now. I'll give you some medicine to make you feel better, and I'll give you a diet to follow, and soon it will be over. You'll have a beautiful baby and you'll be the happiest woman in the world."

Angelique blew her nose and gave him a look which she was sure was full of withering contempt.

"You are a fool, Dr. Myles Gordon. I told you I don't want this baby or any other baby. Ever."

"We'll wait and see," said the doctor.

The coming months seemed interminable to Angelique. Her abdomen swelled and her breasts hurt and even her ankles got puffy. She couldn't seem to do a thing with her hair and she even discovered a cavity in one of her back teeth. The first she'd ever had in her life.

Etienne tried to be gentle at first, but Angelique yelled and screamed and cursed at him until he finally gave up in disgust.

"You're not the first woman who ever had a kid, you know!"

"Shut your dirty, rotten mouth, you bastard," Angelique shouted. "You did this to me. The least you can do now is leave me alone."

"I wonder how your Armenian cloth peddler would like you now," Etienne answered brutally.

"You'll be sorry, you rapist!" screamed Angelique. "I'll die having your child. You'll be my murderer."

Actually, Etienne didn't know which was worse—Angelique's tantrums or his mother-in-law's dark silences. Monique glared at him with brooding accusation, but she would speak not one word to him.

252

"Of course she's got plenty to say to Angelique," Etienne said to his mother, Simone. "She's always whispering to her and she whispers loud enough for me to hear. Last night she told Angelique that I was a filthy pig. In fact, she said that *all* men were filthy pigs."

"Go home to your wife," replied Simone, "and don't come crying to me again. I tried to tell you what you were getting into before you ever married her. Now you're stuck. Not only with her, but with her mother and soon a baby. So go home."

"Come on, Etienne," said Christophe, "I'll walk part way with you."

But as soon as they were outside, Christophe turned to his brother. "What I really meant was that I'd buy you a drink. You look like hell."

"Thanks," answered Etienne, "I could use a drink. I can't even buy my own any more. I've got to save every nickel I can get my hands on to pay for that doctor and his goddamned hospital. You'd think that Angelique could go to St. Antoine's and have her baby just like anyone else, wouldn't you? But oh, no. Not Angelique. She has to go to that fancy private hospital. At almost twice what they'd charge at St. Antoine's."

"What hospital?" asked Christophe.

"Ha," replied Etienne, swallowing his drink. "I don't wonder you've never heard of it. It's not for poor slobs like us, you understand. Oh, no. The name of the place is the Myra Gordon Memorial Hospital. That fancy doctor of Angelique's named it for his dead mother. He runs it with some other fancy doctor by the name of Goodrich, Henry Goodrich."

Christophe bought another round of drinks.

"Where is this place?" he asked.

"Up in the north end," said Etienne bitterly, "right up there where all the rich-bitch families live. And that's where my dear wife has to go. The nuns at St. Antoine's aren't good enough for her. She's got to go up to the north end to a fancy hospital where it takes a couple of high-priced doctors to deliver one baby and an army of fancy, starched nurses can wait on her around the clock."

When he got home that night, Christophe looked up the name in the telephone book and sure enough, there it was. Under "Hospitals," right along with St. Antoine's and Livingstone General. Myra Gordon Memorial. Christophe shrugged and supposed that there were a lot of places in Livingstone he'd never heard of. It was too bad for Etienne, though, to be worrying like that about money.

On the first day of October, at eight o'clock in the morning, Angelique gave birth to her first child, a girl, whom she'd decided months ago, over the protests of her husband, mother-in-law and the rest of Etienne's family, to name Lesley. And in spite of a remarkably easy delivery, she insisted on remaining in the hospital for a full two weeks, although she could have been up and back home after six days.

"No, I don't mind," said Dr. Myles Gordon when she suggested it. "If your husband can pay for the room, I don't in the least mind. We aren't crowded right now."

So Angelique stayed and lolled in bed and polished her fingernails and brushed her long blonde hair. She had absolutely refused even to try to nurse her baby, and the first time a nurse brought her Lesley and a bottle, Angelique turned on her in a rage.

"Look here, feeding babies is your job, not mine!"

"But Mrs. de Montigny," said the nurse, "all our new mothers feed their own babies during the day. Of course the little ones on the breast—"

"Get out of here!" screamed Angelique. "As long as I'm paying for this, you can jolly well do your job. And don't disturb me again! If I want you, I'll ring."

Angelique enjoyed the hospital. Myra Gordon Memorial was a rambling, three-story building of natural stone, wood and glass and at one time it had been one of the finest pri-

254

vate residences in Livingstone. Over the years, wings and ells had been added with a haphazardness that should have made the building ugly but instead gave the old place a charm all its own. It looked rather like a house that someone had cared about very much and which had eventually just spread itself out to accommodate a growing family.

Angelique had a large, sunny corner room overlooking the gardens, and as she lay in bed she spent hours pretending that the hospital was her house and that the nurses were her servants. Over the years she had more or less got out of the habit of having long private conversations with Armand Bergeron but now, in this lovely, flower-filled room, she spent hours talking with him.

More coffee, Papa?

No, thank you, my angel.

Shall we take a walk in the garden then?

Anything you like, my darling.

Oh, I almost forgot. We are having guests this afternoon. For tea.

Oh? Who is coming?

Nobody except Etienne and Maman and that crowd.

How tiresome. But you must be gracious. After all, my little princess, *noblesse oblige*.

Yes, Papa.

Angelique wept when the two weeks were up and she had to go home.

"Why are you crying?" asked Dr. Myles Gordon. "This should be a day of rejoicing. You are going home, good as new, and with a beautiful baby besides."

"It's been so lovely here," said Angelique.

"Well, hurry up and get busy on another one." The doctor laughed. "Then you'll be back in no time."

Angelique wiped her eyes. "I don't want to come back *that* badly."

As the taxicab was pulling away from the hospital, Angelique turned for a last look and began to wonder about the place. It was so big and spread out, yet from her walks through the corridors, Angelique knew that there were only five babies in the nursery and five new mothers in their private rooms on the first floor. Two male patients were ensconced on the second floor, one recovering from an appendectomy and the other from a prostate operation, and there was also a woman with her left leg in traction. She knew that the kitchens and the laundry were in the basement. Who, then, occupied all the rooms that there must be on the third floor and in the two big wings?

How odd, thought Angelique, as the cab turned out of the driveway. How can they possibly keep such a place going on so few patients?

She turned to look again but the tall trees that surrounded Myra Gordon Memorial hid the building from view.

From the day that Lesley de Montigny was born, Angelique never once fed her, changed her or bathed her. Monique Bergeron did it all, even to having the baby's bassinet in her own bedroom so that Angelique could sleep.

Angelique spent her time in what she called "recovering her strength after my ordeal." She expended hours doing exercises to firm the muscles of her abdomen. She dieted strenuously and brushed her hair until her arms ached, but by the time Lesley was six weeks old, Angelique could look at herself in the mirror and be assured that from her body no one would know she had borne a child at all.

Simone de Montigny and her daughters, Josephine, Charlotte and Cecile, were outraged.

"What kind of woman," Simone demanded of Etienne, "won't care for her own child?"

"You must allow her time to get her strength back," Etienne replied.

256

"Strength, my foot," answered Simone. "Angelique is stronger than any of us."

"And whenever we go to see the baby," complained Josephine, "Mrs. Bergeron always says that the baby is asleep. Or that she has just eaten, so that we can't even pick her up."

"Yes," said Cecile. "I made a little sweater, all hand knit, mind you, and the old lady wouldn't even let me try it on the baby."

Etienne sighed. "I'll speak to her."

But Etienne's words of reproach fell on deaf ears. Love had come to Monique Bergeron for the first time in her life and she was not about to share it with anyone. It was as if Monique had been hoarding something inside herself and now the time had come to spend it. She spent it all on Lesley without even realizing that the more she gave the more there was to give. Love poured from Monique in a golden, unending flood and the child grew and flourished while Monique herself had never looked better.

One evening, when Lesley was seven weeks old, Etienne went to help Christophe work on an old car that his brother had just bought and when he got home, just before eleven, he found Monique alone with Lesley.

"Where's Angelique?"

Monique shrugged and continued to feed the baby.

"Gone out," she said.

"I gathered that," replied Etienne, "but where and who with?"

Again Monique shrugged. This time she didn't bother to answer.

"Goddamn it, answer me!" shouted Etienne.

Immediately, the baby let go of the nipple and began to scream.

Monique's eyes blazed. "Now, see what you've done," she cried. "You've frightened the child half to death."

She held Lesley close against her shoulder, patting the little back and rocking her gently.

"I don't know where your wife is," said Monique, "and I don't care. I imagine she's out with some man, drinking and dancing and doing whatever women like her do when they are out with men." She paused and looked at Etienne. "You take care of your wife," she added venomously, "and I'll take care of your child."

Etienne waited in the dark living room until one-thirty in the morning, when he heard Angelique's key in the front door. She snapped on the light in the hall and stood blinking rather stupidly in the sudden glare. Her lipstick was smeared and her usually neat hair was mussed and from where he sat Etienne could see that one of her stockings was twisted.

Etienne did not make a sound. He waited until she had gone upstairs, stumbling rather badly, undressed and made her way down the hall to the bathroom. Then he went upstairs to the bedroom.

This time Angelique had had a few drinks and she did not care who heard her screams as Etienne wrestled her onto the bed and tied her down.

Monique came and pounded on the locked door.

"Stop that noise!"

"Maman!" screamed Angelique. "Maman! Help me! He's killing me!"

"Quiet!" shouted Monique savagely. "Do you want to wake the baby?"

Etienne pressed his thumb into her navel when Monique went away.

"Right there, Angelique," he said, and to her his grin was more evil than all the devils in hell. "That's where I'm going to plant it. Right behind there."

Then he held her chin in his hands so that she could not move her head and he bit her lips brutally as he plunged into her.

258

When it was over, he stood by the edge of the bed, drying himself with a towel and looking down at her. Her hair was all over the pillow, blood dripped from one corner of her mouth and her eyes were puffy with weeping and the beginnings of a hangover. Her spread-eagled body bore the marks of his hands and her eyes were glazed.

"My dear little angel," he said, "you look exactly like the great-grandmother of every cheap whore in the world."

It was not as simple this time as it had been the first and afterward Angelique could not remember how many times Etienne had forced her into submission. But in the end she was pregnant again and Etienne seemed to know it even before she did. He stopped touching her completely.

"What the hell do you do," shouted an enraged Angelique, "keep a Quaker calendar?"

Dr. Myles Gordon laughed.

"I remember that I told you to hurry back," he said as he finished his examination in his office. "But I never dreamed that you'd work this fast."

"You've got to help me," pleaded Angelique. "I can't have another baby this soon. Please!"

"Don't talk like a fool," said the doctor. "I told you once, I'm not an abortionist. Besides, you're healthy as a horse. You won't have a bit of trouble."

So it was all to be gone through again. The ugliness, the swelling, the stringy hair and another cavity.

"I know what's in your mind, Etienne," cried Angelique that night. "You're jealous because I'm attractive. Because other men find me desirable. You want to make an ugly old woman out of me."

"No," replied Etienne. "I am merely trying to turn a tramp into a decent wife and mother. And by Jesus I'll do it, too, even if I have to get you pregnant every nine months. You'll learn, eventually."

"I'll kill you, Etienne," she said.

"Try it, you bitch!"

There was no gentleness left in him and he knew it and could not help himself.

Why didn't he just leave her, he wondered for the millionth time? Why did he go to these extremes trying to hold on to her, when it was obvious that she did not want to be held? Was it simply a matter of pride? Was he afraid that everyone would laugh at him if he were a known cuckold?

But sometimes Angelique was quiet, seemingly contented, with the light shining in her hair and her beautiful face almost Madonnalike in its sweetness, and Etienne knew that none of the other reasons mattered. He wanted to hold on to Angelique because he still loved her.

"Brother dear"—Christophe laughed—"you are one old stud, aren't you? Can't stay away from it, eh? And now you're going to be a papa again."

"That's right," said Etienne, but the smile grew stiff on his mouth.

Simone de Montigny did not say anything. She merely looked sharply at her eldest son and she did not like what she saw. Her easygoing, laughing and lovable Etienne was turning into a hollow-eyed, tight-lipped, joyless man. But Simone was determined not to pry. When Etienne was ready, he'd tell her what was bothering him. He always had.

It was autumn again when Angelique returned to the Myra Gordon Memorial Hospital. After less than two hours of labor, she gave birth to her second child, another girl, whom she christened Alana.

"What did I tell you?" said Dr. Myles Gordon. "You see how easy that was? Mrs. de Montigny, you could have a dozen kids with no trouble at all."

"Dr. Gordon," answered Angelique coldly, "there are times when I actively hate you."

Angelique had managed to get the same room and outside her window the chrysanthemums and asters made banks of color in the garden. But this time Angelique did not waste time pretending that the hospital was her house, nor did she have long, charming conversations with her father. Now she lay on the bed, sullen and staring at the opposite wall, and when she talked to Armand it was almost in anger.

Well, Papa, what am I to do now? she demanded.

Doucement, doucement, ma petite, replied Armand Bergeron. We will think of something.

But I tell you this must not happen to me again!

Of course not, my little princess. You should not be made to produce offspring like a peasant. We will find a way.

Yes, Papa, Angelique answered, somewhat mollified.

To Etienne's consternation, Angelique again insisted on staying in the hospital for a full two weeks.

"But, Angelique," he protested, "we can't afford it this time."

Her eyes glittered spitefully.

"Listen, you," she replied, "you're the one who wanted this child. Not I. I carried it for nine months and now you can jolly well pay for it. I'm staying right here for two weeks."

But the hours seemed to drag. She could not keep her mind on a printed page and even the conversations of her friends seemed to bore her. A great restlessness filled her and once or twice she even thought that she might as well go home after all. But no, she wouldn't give Etienne that satisfaction. She would remain until the two weeks were up.

She took to roaming the hospital, chatting with the nurses and the other patients. She even helped arrange flowers and deliver the mail to individual rooms, which was how she happened to notice the door at the end of the corridor on the second floor. It was marked PRIVATE and when she tried the knob she found that the door was locked.

At first she thought that the door must lead to an office or perhaps to the room where the narcotics were kept. But then she realized that the position of the door was exactly like one on the first floor that merely opened onto a stairway, which no one ever seemed to use.

To find out what lay behind that door on the second floor became a sort of interesting game to Angelique, something to while away the time. She explored the stairway behind the door on the first floor and discovered that it only led to the basement. Where the stairs leading up should have been, there was another locked door.

How very queer, thought Angelique. The whole stairway is completely sealed off.

She went down into the basement and made friends with the head dietitian, whose name was Mary Stockman.

"It must be fascinating to work in a hospital," said Angelique to her, smiling. "But, my goodness, you must have to be awfully clever."

"Yes," said Miss Stockman, "it is interesting work."

"May I help with anything?" asked Angelique, looking around. "I'm so bored just hanging around upstairs." She began to walk around the kitchen. "I'm not nearly as smart as you are, Miss Stockman, but maybe I could do something."

"I'm sorry," said Miss Stockman, and she was too. Mrs. de Montigny was so pretty and sweet and nice to talk to. "But it's against the rules. Honestly, I love your company but it'd be worth my job if anyone caught you down here."

"Of course," answered Angelique. "I'm sorry, Miss Stockman. I'll just scoot right back to my room."

But Angelique had seen what she had come to see. There was just too much food in that kitchen for the number of patients on the first and second floors. On her way back to her room she also noticed an elevator marked FREIGHT.

Angelique did not take her sleeping pill that night. She lay awake long after the hospital was quiet, until she heard one nurse say to another, "The coffee's ready. Let's go have it while it's hot."

The two nurses went back into the little office behind the main desk where they could drink their coffee and smoke their cigarettes in peace.

Angelique did not make a sound as she slipped out of her room and down the corridor. The doors of the freight elevator slid open as if they had been soaked in oil and when she pressed the button marked *3* there was only a faint click. The elevator moved upward with an almost inaudible whine. The oiled doors opened silently on the third floor and Angelique stood very still inside the dim cage. Somewhere a radio was playing and she heard a man laugh.

Her slippered feet made no sound on the tile floor as Angelique moved cautiously down the corridor.

In a room halfway down the hall, lights were on, and she made her way toward it, her back pressed against the opposite wall so that she would be in the shadow. She looked into the room and, as she put it to herself later, what she saw made her almost jump out of her skin.

There were five men seated around a table playing poker. On a smaller table, close by, were three or four bottles of liquor, glasses, an ice bucket and a platter of sandwiches. The men were not playing with poker chips; in the center of the table was a huge pile of money. Angelique stared at the faces. Four of them were totally unfamiliar, but she knew the face of the fifth man.

Well, she thought. Well, well, well.

She moved silently back toward the elevator and as she passed the room just this side of it, she heard loud snoring. There was a night light burning in the room and the door was slightly ajar. Angelique pushed it open very slowly.

A man was lying on the bed. He was on his back, his

huge belly making a mountain under the sheet, and his mouth was wide open.

Angelique smiled. She knew that face too.

The next day, when Dr. Myles Gordon made his rounds, Angelique was waiting for him.

"Dr. Gordon, I'm so bored," she said. "Do you think it would be all right if I went home today?"

"You could have gone home the day after you delivered." The doctor laughed. "That's how rugged you are. Sure, you can go home."

Etienne was overjoyed when Angelique telephoned and told him to pick her up when he was through work. As for Monique, she could hardly wait to get her hands on the new baby.

The minute Angelique got home, she undressed and got into bed. Then she told Etienne to bring her all the old newspapers which Monique saved so religiously.

Within half an hour, she had found what she was looking for. The photograph of the man who had been playing poker in the room on the third floor of the Myra Gordon Memorial Hospital was right on the front page. Over the picture was the headline: NEW YORK CITY POLICE HUNT EMBEZZLER.

As for the snoring man with the big belly, practically anyone in the United States would have recognized him. He was called Big Willie Congreve and he was wanted by the FBI for bank robbery.

Angelique de Montigny laughed out loud.

No wonder Dr. Gordon could afford to live in a beautiful house in the north end. No wonder he drove a big Cadillac car and his wife had a full-length mink coat. Dr. Myles Gordon and his partner, Dr. Henry Goodrich, had one of the sweetest rackets Angelique had ever heard of. Who in the world would ever think of looking for big-time hoodlums in a little hospital in a small city in New Hampshire?

Again it took Angelique six weeks before she was satisfied

with her appearance. And then, when her belly was as flat as ever and her hair shone like the sun, she telephoned Dr. Myles Gordon.

"Hello, Myles."

"Who is this?" Dr. Gordon asked, puzzled.

"This is Angelique—Angelique de Montigny."

"Oh, Mrs. de Montigny. How nice to hear from you. Don't tell me you're pregnant again?"

His laugh came over the telephone and she waited until he was quite finished.

"You may call me Angelique," she said, and when he was silent she went on, "Myles, I was thinking. I'd like to have you buy me a drink this afternoon."

"What?"

"I said I'd like to have you buy me a drink. Shall we say around four-thirty in the lounge at the Livingstone Hotel?"

"Mrs. de Montigny—" he began.

"Angelique," she corrected.

"Angelique, surely you must know that such a thing is impossible. I can't be seen—"

"Oh, what a pity," answered Angelique sweetly. "And a friend of yours especially asked me to call you. His name is John Michael Powell. He's from New York City, I believe."

She could barely keep from laughing out loud at the tense silence.

"John Michael Powell is a very dear friend of a type they call Big Willie Congreve."

"Angelique—"

"Shall we say four-thirty, Myles? At the Livingstone Hotel?"

"Four-thirty," repeated Myles Gordon.

Angelique hung up and stood tapping one fingernail against her teeth.

She guessed that she'd wear her little black velvet hat, the one with the veil that came down just below her eyes.

3

Shortly after her sixteenth birthday, while she was still in her junior year at Livingstone Central High School, Lesley de Montigny fell in love, with a boy named Gino Donati, for the first, last and only time in her life.

Gino was twenty-one years old, six feet two inches tall and weighed one hundred and ninety pounds stripped. He had the black, curly hair of his ancestors and their dark-brown eyes as well, and his white, very straight teeth showed often in a wide-lipped mouth that smiled easily. Gino Donati was employed as a driver by the Atwill Express Company—Local and Long Distance Truckers—and with his broad shoulders and thick chest he managed to look every inch a truck driver. But there was a sensitivity in the dark-brown eyes and a gentleness in his big square hands that the casual observer might easily have missed. Lesley de Montigny did not miss these things. She noticed them the first time she ever saw Gino.

She was walking home from school one afternoon in late November. As Alana was always telling her, she was looking everywhere except where she was going, and for heaven's sake what was there to see anyway?

Yet even November could be beautiful in its own way, thought Lesley as she walked.

There was a certain grandeur in the bare, carved-looking trees stretching toward the unfeeling gray sky. Like the Christian martyrs, thought Lesley, or the last tragic act of a grand opera. Not that she had ever seen an opera but she had heard practically every single one on the Saturday-afternoon broadcasts from the Met and she was sure that Milton Cross must be the most intelligent, most wonderful man in the whole world.

"Imagine," she'd said to Alana last Saturday, "just imagine having all that knowledge in your head."

"Oh, baloney," said Alana. "He's probably reading all that junk out of a book or something."

"Sh-h, listen," answered Lesley. "It's the second act of *Carmen* by a man named Georges Bizet. You spell the George with an *s* on the end. Imagine, Alana, to be a composer and hear music like that inside of yourself."

"They all sound like they've got a bellyache to me," Alana said. "Give me Glenn Miller and The Modernairs every time."

"If you're a composer, you must be able to hear music like that all over yourself," Lesley went on dreamily. "In your head and your stomach, even the tips of your fingers."

"You want to come with us?" asked Alana impatiently. "Deenie and Vince and I are going skating up at Dawson's pond."

Deenie and Vince were two boys whose real names were James and Matthew and why they were called Deenie and Vince not many people really knew or cared. They lived down the street from the de Montignys and were considered roughnecks by the whole neighborhood. They were Alana's two best friends.

"What's the matter with you anyway?" demanded Alana. "Don't you ever want to go out and have fun? Don't you *like* boys?"

"Of course I like boys," answered Lesley. "I just don't want to go skating with you and Deenie and Vince, that's all."

Alana started rather forlornly toward the door. "Other sisters do things together."

Lesley looked up vaguely. "What?"

"Nothing," replied Alana crossly.

In the kitchen, Maggie Donovan was loudly banging pots and pans.

"It's enough to drive a body right out of her mind," she shouted. "All that screeching and yelling on the radio every single Saturday that the good Lord brings around."

"Shut up, Maggie," Alana answered. "And leave Lesley alone after I'm gone too. She's not hurting anybody."

"Sixteen years old," grumbled Maggie Donovan. "You'd think a girl her age would be out at the movies with a boy on a Saturday afternoon instead of sitting in there by herself listening to that unholy racket."

"Maybe Lesley isn't as pants-happy as some people I could name," said Alana, going to the kitchen door and staring straight at Maggie.

"You're a bad girl," answered Maggie furiously, "and the devil is going to come and get you."

"Well, you'd be just the one to show him the way, you cock-happy old harpy."

"I'm going to tell your mother on you," said Maggie.

"Go ahead you man-crazy old Irish biddy," shouted Alana. "Thank God Lesley doesn't like boys. She might turn out to be just like you in her old age."

It was not true that Lesley de Montigny did not like boys. It was simply that they did not hold the all-consuming interest for her that they seemed to hold for other girls her age. She did not like having her hand held during a movie, which was why she seldom went with a boy. When Lesley went to the movies she became totally immersed in the story, so that for days afterward she would imagine herself a beautifully gowned Joan Crawford, breaking hearts all over the place, or a tragic Bette Davis, pacing around dramatically, giving up the man she loved, even a marvelously sad-eyed Garbo dying gorgeously in the arms of some handsome actor.

Oh, Lesley liked boys all right, just as she liked most human beings, but they were not necessary to her. She much preferred walking home alone in the November afternoon to having some noisy boy with her who would toss his books in the air or jump over fire hydrants.

Many of the streets in Livingstone were named after trees—Elm, Spruce, Cedar, Pine and Chestnut, Maple and Laurel, though in most cases the names did not fit at all. But this was not true of Maple Street. Here maples lined both sides of the street and Lesley looked up at them now. Tall, wide, beautiful trees which in summer almost hid the sky with their green fullness. But now it was November and the trees stood nakedly bare.

Cover me, begged the trees on Maple Street.

But the gray sky, as if it were a dome of steel, did not change as the trees stood waiting for the opening which would bring the merciful garment of snow.

It's as if the sky were punishing them, thought Lesley, for the orgy of autumn.

She smiled to herself, pleased with her fancy, and then her left foot hit a patch of ice on the sidewalk. Everything seemed to happen at once. Her books went flying in all directions and Lesley went flying too. She landed hard on the concrete, her right leg twisted painfully beneath her. She did not even hear the truck stop or the cab door open and slam shut, because she was too busy fighting off the sickness that filled her throat.

I mustn't throw up all over my new winter coat, she thought frantically.

"Jesus, kid, are you all right?" asked the man standing over her.

Lesley looked up at Gino Donati. "I think my leg is broken," she said and began to cry. "It made such a dreadful sound when I fell."

"You really took a beaut all right," replied Gino and squatted down beside her. "Can you move it at all?"

269

She leaned back on her hand and tried to move her leg.

"I think it's my knee."

Gino put his fingertips on her knee and felt it gently.

"I can't tell," he said, "but it doesn't feel broken."

He looked anxiously up and down the empty street.

"Listen," he said, "I can't just leave you sitting here on the sidewalk. Where do you live?"

"On the next street," answered Lesley. "Four blocks down."

"Well, hang on," said Gino and lifted her gently. "Put one arm around my neck."

As he straightened up with her in his arms, Lesley had an almost overwhelming desire to sob and rest her head against his shoulder.

Gino deposited her in the cab of the truck as if she were made of eggshells, then he went back and picked up her scattered books and papers.

"You could lose your job for this," Lesley said, pointing to the NO RIDERS sticker on the truck's windshield.

Gino smiled at her. "Well, that's the least of our worries right now, isn't it?"

Our worries, thought Lesley, as if they were partners or friends. She sighed and rested her head against the back of the seat.

"Show me where you live," he said.

Gino drove very slowly, avoiding the bumps in the road, all the way to her house, and when they got there he lifted her out of the truck with no more trouble than if she'd been a baby. Again that strange feeling came over Lesley, the urge to rest her head against him, and this time it was irresistible. Just before he pressed the bell next to the front door she put her cheek against his shoulder.

"Lesley!" cried Alana when she opened the door. "What's the matter with you?"

Gino moved past her and into the living room, where he put Lesley down on the sofa.

"She fell and hurt her leg," he said to Alana. "You'd better call a doctor. Are you her sister?"

"Yes," answered Alana. "I'm Alana de Montigny. Who are you?"

"My name's Gino Donati," he replied, "and I found your sister on Maple Street, sitting in the middle of the sidewalk. Hey!" He turned to Lesley. "Here I am feeling like we're old friends and I don't even know your name."

"It's Lesley," she said. "Lesley de Montigny." And for no sensible reason she began to cry again. It wasn't sensible because her leg wasn't hurting her that badly now.

"My mother's not home," said Alana. "I don't know where to reach her."

"Is there a doctor you can call?" asked Gino.

Alana hesitated for only a second. "Yes."

Gino sat down on the sofa next to Lesley and took her hand.

"Don't cry, Lesley," he said gently. "Your sister is going to get a doctor and he'll fix you up good as new. I'd stay with you until he comes if I could but if I don't get the truck back to the garage I'll get fired for sure."

"Yes, of course," answered Lesley and blew her nose. "I'll be all right. Please go. I wouldn't want you to get into any trouble on my account."

"I'll phone you later," Gino said. "Just to find out how everything is."

"All right."

At the front door he turned and smiled what Lesley had already begun to think of as his "wonderful" smile.

"Hey," he called, "how do you spell de Montigny?"

Lesley could not help laughing as she told him.

"A small *d*," she said, "and a capital *M*."

As soon as Gino Donati was gone, Alana went to the telephone table and picked up the pad on which Angelique listed her friends in alphabetical order.

271

"She went to a cocktail party," said Alana. "On Maggie's day off too. We were supposed to fix our own supper."

She called the first three numbers on the list, always asking the same question and getting the same answer.

"Is Angelique de Montigny there, please?"

"No, she isn't."

"Thank you very much."

But after the third call Lesley said, "Alana, please help me. I feel sick to my stomach."

Alana ran and fetched a basin and then picked up the telephone again and dialed.

"Is that you, Myles?"

"Who is this?" asked Dr. Myles Gordon.

"Alana de Montigny."

"Oh, Alana. Well, what is it?"

It annoyed the hell out of him the way this fresh kid called him by his first name. She never did it when Angelique was around. Then it was always Dr. Gordon this and Dr. Gordon that, but the minute Angelique was out of earshot Alana had a nasty little way of looking at him and saying, "Myles."

"Lesley fell down and hurt her leg," said Alana, "and I can't find Angelique."

That was another little habit of Alana's that Myles Gordon disliked intensely. Alana never referred to Angelique as her mother.

"What do you mean, she hurt her leg?" demanded the doctor.

"Just what I said, Myles," replied Alana. "It may be broken for all I know. It's Maggie's day off and we're here alone."

"I'll be right over," said the doctor. "Don't let Lesley move. Do you hear?"

"All right, Myles."

They took Lesley to the hospital in Dr. Gordon's car and after the X rays and what seemed to Lesley and Alana like hours of waiting, Myles Gordon told them that Lesley's leg was not broken. She had sprained her knee badly but that was all. An elastic bandage and a few days off her feet would take care of everything.

"We'll get her to bed and give her a mild sedative," said Dr. Gordon when they got back to the house. "Where did you say your mother went?"

"To a cocktail party," answered Alana. "I don't know where."

"Okay," said the doctor. "You stay upstairs with Lesley until she goes to sleep. I'll see if I can locate your mother."

It was no secret to Myles Gordon, nor to anyone in Angelique's circle of friends, that about three months ago she had taken a new lover by the name of Albert Petrie.

Petrie was an announcer on station WLIV, Livingstone's largest radio station, where he worked erratic hours.

Myles Gordon was furious as he lifted the telephone receiver.

Cocktail party, my ass, he thought grimly. Bedroom party is more like it.

The doctor let the telephone ring and ring, growing angrier by the second. At last, on the seventeenth ring, a guarded masculine voice said, "Hello?"

"Let me talk to Angelique de Montigny."

"You must have the wrong number."

"Listen, you cock-happy bastard, I don't have the wrong number," said the doctor. "Now you tell Angelique to get her ass out of bed and get dressed. One of her kids had an accident."

Upstairs, Alana moved silently toward the room she shared with Lesley.

It must be a new one, she thought, sitting on the edge of her bed. I wonder who he is?

She was still wondering when she heard the taxicab stop out in front of the house and then the door slamming behind Angelique.

Alana moved to the top of the staircase and watched

Angelique come through the front door, the skirt of her black coat swirling around her legs.

She faced Myles Gordon and even from the top of the stairs Alana could see the flash of anger in Angelique's eyes, the red flush on her cheeks.

"What do you mean talking to Petrie the way you did?" she cried.

So that's who it is, thought Alana. Petrie. Albert Petrie, the radio announcer.

She remembered now that he had come to the house three or four times. Never to visit, just to pick up Angelique. And she remembered, too, his thin, nervous hands and the way his voice sounded, like maple syrup poured over vanilla ice cream.

"That, my dear, is typical of you," Dr. Myles Gordon was saying. "Absolutely typical. You don't ask first how badly your child is hurt. In fact, you don't even ask which child. Your first concern is for the feelings of your lover."

"Keep your sermons to yourself, will you, Myles?" replied Angelique. "They're just a little bit sickening. Now tell me what's happened."

"Lesley fell and sprained her knee. I took her to the hospital, X-rayed her, brought her home and put her to bed with a sedative. Alana is with her now."

Angelique removed her little black hat and put it down carefully.

"Is that all?" she asked wearily.

"Yes," shouted Myles Gordon, "that's all, Angelique. Perhaps I shouldn't have taken you from Petrie's warm bed for such an insignificant thing. But since Lesley is your daughter, I presumed that you might be interested in what happened to her."

Angelique went to the small bar at one end of the living room and made herself a drink.

"You're a liar, Myles," she said calmly. "You didn't send for me because of Lesley. You saw a marvelous chance to

274

verify your suspicions of Albert and me, and you took it. You can't bear to think of me with anyone but you, can you?"

Myles Gordon went uninvited to make himself a drink and when it was ready he drank half of it down in one swallow. He smiled as he turned back to face Angelique.

"Isn't Petrie a little young for you, my dear?"

Angelique sipped her drink. "Albert is two years older than I," she said.

"Oh, I know, I know," answered the doctor. "But that's still young for you, isn't it? You usually like your men a bit older, don't you? Fifteen, twenty, twenty-five years older, for instance."

"What have you got against maturity?" asked Angelique. "I find it fascinating."

"Who are you kidding, baby?" asked Myles Gordon. "It isn't the idea of maturity that gets you on your back. It's the idea of a man being old enough to be your father that opens your legs, baby."

He paused and looked her up and down. "I know," he added. "I've been there. Baby."

The red flush was back in Angelique's cheeks and the angry glint in her eyes.

"You know something, Myles," she said. "You are a twenty-one-carat, genuine, complete son of a bitch. You are also a filthy-minded old pig."

"A princess," replied Myles Gordon as if she had not spoken. "A princess, grown up now, but unable to give or receive love. An aging princess, still tied to the kingdom and the king of her childhood."

Angelique stared at him. "Get out of here, Myles," she said and her voice quivered. "Get out of here before I kill you."

Myles Gordon put down his empty glass. "I was just leaving, your highness," he said, and his little laugh was without any humor at all.

275

He closed the front door softly behind him. Angelique finished her drink and lit a cigarette. When she moved toward the staircase, Alana once more moved silently into the bedroom where Lesley slept. Just as Angelique reached the top of the stairs Alana opened the bedroom door and stepped into the hall.

"Oh, hello, Mother," she said. "I didn't hear you come in. Lesley is sleeping. Did Dr. Gordon tell you what happened?"

"Yes," answered Angelique. "I came as quickly as I could but I had a hard time getting a taxi. I'll just go in and peek at Lesley."

"I'm going to get a glass of milk," said Alana. "We didn't have any dinner."

"Missing a few meals won't kill you," replied Angelique absent-mindedly. "It's good for your figure."

As she went down the stairs, it occurred to Alana that neither her mother nor Myles Gordon had thought to ask where Lesley's accident had taken place, or how Lesley had managed to get home with her knee so badly sprained.

Alana looked back over her shoulder to make sure that Angelique was nowhere in sight. Then, very quietly, she lifted the telephone receiver off the hook and casually tossed her sweater over it.

Somehow, she did not want Gino Donati to call while Angelique was in the house.

4

It took Angelique de Montigny more than a year to realize the extent of her daughter Lesley's involvement with Gino Donati. She had, of course, met Gino in the house several times but it had never occurred to her that he was anything more than a schoolmate of Lesley's. She did not realize that he had been out of school and working for almost five years, for the simple reason that she had never bothered to ask. To Angelique, Gino was merely a young, good-looking boy who dated her daughter occasionally. One of Lesley's little friends.

If the telephone rang more frequently for Lesley these days, she put this down to the fact that after all Lesley was seventeen years old now and a senior in high school. It was only natural for her to be getting around more. It was a good thing for a girl to be popular, for if she were ever to make a brilliant marriage she had to meet all kinds of males.

Angelique had had the future of her daughters all neatly figured out for years. They would grow up into attractive, poised young ladies, go to a good college and finally marry rich men. She had told this to Dr. Myles Gordon once and he had stared at her in disbelief.

"Angelique," he'd said, "you can't be serious? Do you honestly believe that bringing up two daughters is as simple as all that? They're people, you know. You can't say, 'All right, you will be this,' or 'You will act thus-and-so,' or 'You will fit into this pigeonhole.' "

"Don't be ridiculous," replied Angelique. "Why shouldn't

things work out the way I've planned them? Why, I've given those girls everything, every advantage. They've had a good home, lovely clothes and the example I've set for good grooming and good manners. So why shouldn't things come out the way I want them to?"

Myles Gordon shook his head. "Oh, Angelique, Angelique," he said. "One of these days you're going to be in for one hell of a shock."

"You *are* ridiculous, Myles," she answered, "but you'll see. In the end, you'll have to admit that I'm right."

She was so convinced of this that when Lesley came home on Christmas Eve with a small diamond engagement ring on her finger, Angelique literally did not believe her eyes.

Every Christmas Eve, Angelique gave what she called a "more-or-less open house." She had eggnog in a big silver bowl and hired Maggie Donovan's two daughters, whom she dressed in black uniforms and frilly white caps, to serve. There was always a huge, beautifully decorated tree at one end of the living room and mistletoe over all the doorways and wreaths at all the windows.

If there were a few things about Angelique's Christmas Eves that seemed peculiar, hardly anyone noticed. Only Alana and Lesley and a couple of Angelique's sharper-eyed friends noticed, for instance, that the Christmas angel on the top of the tree had a porcelain hand-painted face that was an exact replica of Angelique's. It had been made for her by an artist she had met from New York and with whom she had once had a three-week love affair.

And they noticed, too, that the people who came to Angelique's "more-or-less open house" were all of a type. They were the ones who drank too much, swapped husbands and wives on long weekends, bought their children gifts that were far too expensive and had no other place to go on Christmas Eve.

"You're not going to like this party, darling," said Lesley

as Gino stopped his car in front of the house. "I guess Mother's friends just aren't our kind of people. But I want her to know about us. I want everyone to know."

She held up her left hand and Gino laughed.

"You can hardly see that diamond in broad daylight," he said, "let alone in the dark."

He kissed her hand, and then the finger that wore his ring.

"Oh, Gino. Oh, darling, I'm so happy."

He took her face in his hands and kissed her softly.

"I'll keep you happy forever," he said, "and that's a promise."

She sighed and leaned against him. "Oh, Gino, I love you so."

"Half as much?"

"Twice as much."

They laughed together at their secret code, which they used everywhere. In the middle of the largest crowd they could look at each other and one of them would ask, "Half as much?" And the answer was always the same. "Twice as much."

"We'd better go in," said Gino.

"Yes. I want to get Alana alone and tell her first."

"And I'd better get set to cope with your mother."

Gino had never liked Angelique. He thought her selfish, shallow and neglectful of her daughters, and although he had never said as much to Lesley, he had the feeling that Angelique knew exactly how he felt. Now he was nervous and apprehensive about seeing her.

"Why, don't be silly, Gino," said Lesley, surprised. "She'll be tickled to death. Mother's always said that marriage was the only kind of life for a girl."

"Okay, honey," he replied. "Let's go in."

They stood in the front hall until Lesley managed to catch Alana's eye and beckon to her.

"Hi," said Alana, who looked lovely and quite a bit older

279

than her sixteen years in her black dress and high heels. She held a silver cup brimful of eggnog in her hands. "What's with you two?"

"Come on upstairs. I have something to show you," whispered Lesley. "Come on, Gino."

The three of them went up to Alana and Lesley's bedroom and as soon as the door was shut behind them, Lesley whirled and grabbed Alana in a big hug.

"We're engaged!" said Lesley. "Look!"

She held out her hand so that Alana could see the ring sparkling on her finger.

"Oh, Lesley. I'm so glad."

Alana hugged Lesley hard and then went to Gino and put her arms around him.

"I don't have to tell you how lucky you are, do I?" she said, and her eyes were full of tears.

Gino kissed the tip of her nose. "No, you don't have to tell me how lucky I am."

Alana turned to Lesley. "Are you going to tell Angelique?"

"But of course we're going to tell her," answered Lesley.

Alana glanced quickly at Gino, who returned her look.

"Don't, Lesley," said Alana. "Don't tell her."

"Are you crazy?" demanded Lesley. "Of course we're going to tell her. And right now. Come on, Gino."

"Wait," said Alana. "Please wait, Lesley. Don't tell her."

"Alana, what in the world is the matter with you? She's my mother and I *want* to tell her."

Alana shrugged. "So go ahead." She sighed and followed Lesley out of the bedroom. "As for me, I want some more eggnog. And the two of you had better have some too."

"Hello, bay-bee!" cried Angelique as Lesley, holding Gino's hand, came up to her. "Merry Christmas and have some eggnog."

Angelique was slightly drunk—a wee bit tightsy, as she would have put it—and Lesley began to feel vaguely uncomfortable. When Angelique had been drinking she was at first very affectionate toward her daughters, calling them "Baby" or "Sweetie" or "Darling." Later she reached the second stage when she became very dignified and British. Then she attempted to speak with an English accent and during that phase, everybody, including Alana and Lesley, was inferior and beneath her contempt. When Angelique was drunk enough to be British, she was very regal indeed, a true princess in her own eyes, and totally unaware of the smiles and ridicule of her friends or the shame and embarrassment it brought her children.

"And who is this divinely handsome boy?" asked Angelique.

The words divinely handsome were drawled, exaggerated, and Lesley felt herself turning pale.

"Mother," she said as quietly as she could and still make herself heard over the noise in the living room, "you remember Gino, don't you? Gino Donati. You *must* remember."

Angelique focused her eyes on Gino. "Oh. But of course, darling. Gino. One of your little friends."

"Mother," whispered Lesley desperately. "Mother, please. Listen to me. Gino and I are engaged."

Angelique put down her silver cup. "I beg your pardon?"

Her face was very still except for her left eyebrow, which was raised, and Lesley knew, with a horrible, all-gone kind of feeling in her stomach, that her mother was going to turn British any second now.

"We're engaged," repeated Lesley. "Gino and I are going to be married."

Angelique threw back her blonde head and began to laugh. Lesley was trembling and the hand in Gino's was damp. She looked at the beautiful, smooth, white, exposed curve of Angelique's throat, throbbing now with laughter, and all of a sudden all she could think of was how a red line would look across all that whiteness.

281

"Come on, honey," said Gino. "This isn't the time or the place to talk."

Alana came to stand beside Lesley and Gino, and still Angelique laughed.

Everyone else in the room stopped talking, turning toward Angelique, half-smiling, waiting to share the joke. Alana and Lesley and Gino started to turn away when suddenly Angelique stopped laughing.

"Just one moment," she said imperiously and the three stopped, turning to face her. "Now, what was it you said, Lesley?"

"Mrs. de Montigny," said Gino before Lesley could open her mouth, "I've asked Lesley to marry me and she's said yes."

"Lesley," asked Angelique in very British, clipped tones, "what did you say this young man's name was?"

"Gino," whispered Lesley in horror. "Gino Donati."

Angelique looked down the bridge of her nose at Gino and no one in the room moved.

"Young man," she said, "I do not recall having invited you to my house this evening."

"Mother!" cried Lesley.

"Furthermore," continued Angelique, ignoring Lesley's stricken voice, "I don't appreciate bad jokes. And now I really must ask you to leave. At once."

"Mother!" whispered Lesley. "Mother, we're going to be married!"

She forgot that there were other people in the room and that it was Christmas Eve. She forgot everything except the dream that she and Gino had shared for so long.

"As soon as I finish school," Lesley went on, "we're going to be married. The day after I graduate."

Her words stumbled over each other and Gino squeezed her hand.

"Honey, never mind talking to her now—"

"Gino's been saving his money," Lesley continued, talking

282

much too rapidly, "and look." She extended her left hand. "The ring is all paid for and we're going to start buying our furniture right after New Year's."

She wasn't even aware that tears were pouring down her cheeks. "Mother, aren't you happy for me? For us?"

Angelique's left eyebrow was still raised and a hateful little smile of contempt twisted her lips.

"And just how does this"—she waved one hand toward Gino—"this schoolboy intend to support you?" she asked. "Or was he planning to leave that little chore to me?"

"For God's sake, Mother," Alana interrupted, "Gino's been out of school for five years. He's got a job and a good one too."

"Oh?" asked Angelique. "And just what is it that you do, Mr. Donati?"

Gino looked her straight in the eye. "I drive a truck for Atwill Express."

The silence in the room stretched until Lesley thought she would scream, then Angelique turned slowly to one of Maggie Donovan's daughters, who had been standing listening, holding a tray of hors d'oeuvres, as if she were frozen.

"Kathleen. You may bring me a Scotch on the rocks. At once, please."

"Yes, Mrs. de Montigny," answered Kathleen, grateful for the chance to put down her tray and escape to the kitchen. Kathleen, just seventeen years old herself, could have wept with Lesley.

"Right away, Mrs. de Montigny."

Somewhere, at the other end of the room, a woman coughed and a man suddenly began to talk, and someone turned on the record player. But everyone was still very much aware of the way Angelique was standing, looking haughtily at Lesley and Gino.

Kathleen returned with Angelique's drink on a tray and Angelique took a long, slow swallow before she turned to Gino.

"A truck driver. How terribly fascinating."

"Mrs. de Montigny," said Gino, "I'm sure we could discuss this more satisfactorily at some other time."

Angelique swallowed the rest of her drink. "Kathleen!" she called, extending her glass, "fill this again." She turned back to Gino. "As for you, lover boy, just stand where you are."

And then Alana knew, before anyone else in the room, that the third stage in Angelique's drinking had arrived.

"Beat it," Alana whispered to Lesley and Gino. "Get out of here, right now."

"No," Gino answered firmly. "If your mother chooses to talk I think we should stay and listen."

"Ah," said Angelique, taking the fresh drink from Kathleen. "I see he has manners, our little truck driver."

"Run, Lesley," whispered Alana.

"Yes, Lesley. Your greasy little wop truck driver has manners. Or at least he tries to pretend he has."

"Mother—" Lesley began.

"Shut up, you goddamned little tramp," shouted Angelique.

Now, too late, Lesley realized that she should indeed have left when Alana had told her to. When Angelique drank and her affectionate and British stages had passed, she reached a point where she threw things and cursed like a stevedore.

"You fucking oversexed little whore," yelled Angelique. "Tell me, how far gone are you?"

Lesley literally could not move and Gino's face had turned scarlet.

"Mrs. de Montigny—"

"Shut up!" said Angelique, and then she turned to her guests. "The rest of you get the hell out of here. You've spent enough time free-loading off me. Get the Christ out of here. Go drink your own liquor for a change."

Angelique's friends shrugged and began to look around for coats and scarves and handbags. They were not even insulted, for they had seen Angelique in these moods many times. In fact, several of them acted much the same way themselves after they'd had too much to drink.

"Go now," said Alana to Lesley and Gino, "hurry."

"Alana," Angelique shouted, "I'll thank you to keep your goddamned trap shut." She turned on Gino. "And as for you, get the hell away from my daughter, get the fuck out of my house!"

"Mrs. de Montigny, there is no sense in any of this," Gino answered calmly. "I love Lesley and nothing you say or do can change that."

"Love!" screamed Angelique. "You miserable little wop bastard, don't try to kid me. I know all about you and your kind. Love to you is nothing but that big prick of yours!"

Gino, who had spent a lot of time with rough, tough men, was dumfounded.

"And let me tell you something else, you spaghetti-bending son of a bitch," Angelique went on. "If I catch you hanging around Lesley again, I'll have your ass in jail so fast you'll never know what hit you. My daughter is seventeen, a minor child, and don't you ever forget it. Now the best thing for you to do is to get the hell out of here, and quickly!"

She began to move unsteadily toward the telephone.

"Please, Gino," cried Lesley hysterically, "please go now. She means what she says."

"No," said Gino. "I'm not going to leave you here alone with her. She's crazy."

"We'll see how crazy the police think I am," yelled Angelique. "The *carabinièri*. Isn't that what you wop pigs call them?"

"Please, please, please," sobbed Lesley.

Even Alana, usually as tough and resilient as a rubber ball, was trembling.

"You'd really better go, Gino," she said shakily. "You'll just make things worse if you stay."

And finally, under protest, Gino left.

"I'll call you, Lesley."

"No, no, no," cried Lesley. "I'll call you. Tomorrow morning. I promise."

When he had gone there was no sound in the living room save for the maddening click of the record player. The last record had ended and the needle went clickety-clickety-click as Angelique and Lesley and Alana stood and looked at each other.

In the end it was Lesley who moved first. She stepped toward Angelique, her fists clenched, tears still pouring down her face.

"I hate you," she said. And then, "I hate you, I hate you, I hate you!" each time on a rising note, until she was finally screaming.

"And how the hell do you think I feel about you, you stinking little bitch?" cried Angelique. "Laying a slob like that truck driver!"

As Lesley burst out sobbing and ran upstairs, Alana looked at her mother in disgust.

"Jesus, but you're rotten, Angelique."

"Don't you *dare* talk to me like that," said Angelique. "You keep a civil tongue in your head. Haven't I got enough on my mind with one little bum on my hands?"

"Oh, don't worry about Lesley, Angelique," Alana replied, and now her voice no longer shook. "If she *is* pregnant, you'll think of something."

"What the hell are you talking about?" demanded Angelique as she went to the record player and started it again.

The lovely sounds of a Christmas carol filled the room.

"If Lesley were pregnant," said Alana, "perhaps you could get Dr. Gordon to do an abortion on her."

Angelique stopped, a cigarette halfway to her lips.

"What did you say?"

"I said," repeated Alana, "that if Lesley were pregnant,

286

perhaps you could get Dr. Gordon to perform an abortion on her." She advanced toward Angelique and when her face was less than six inches from her mother's she smiled and her words came out in a harsh whisper. "Or perhaps you could wait. Yes, you could wait until *after* Lesley had her baby and *then* Dr. Gordon could kill it."

Angelique turned pale.

"What—" she began and stopped to wet her lips. "Alana— what—"

"Yes," Alana went on in the same harsh voice, but louder now. "Yes. Wait until after she has the baby and then let Dr. Gordon kill it."

"Please, Alana—"

"Yes, kill it," said Alana, "the way he did for you. The way he killed my brother!"

"Come ye, oh, come ye to Bethlehem. Come and behold Him, Born the King of Angels—"

"Alana—"

"Dr. Gordon is a murderer," said Alana, "and you are a murderess. And you're not even smart. Lesley isn't pregnant. She's still a virgin, which is something you probably don't even remember ever being!" She turned and ran out of the room but at the bottom of the stairway she stopped to look back at her mother.

"Killer!" she cried. "Murderess!"

"Oh, come let us adore Him, Oh, come let us adore Him—"

Angelique de Montigny sank down on the floor in front of the record player, her drink sloshing onto the skirt of her dress.

"Something always happens," she whispered. "Something always happens to spoil my parties."

And she began to cry.

287

5

In the three years that Gino had been married to Lesley, she had presented him with two fine, healthy sons, named Giuseppe and Marcello after Gino's father and eldest brother. They were called Joe and Mark, and they had a beautiful, big-eyed sister, named Giulia after Gino's mother, and called Julie. Gino did not notice, and would not have cared if he had, that Lesley no longer wore a size ten dress and that her long hair was no longer always the shining, well-brushed cascade it had once been. He knew only that her eyes lit up in a very special way when she looked at him and that she had a particular soft smile that was for him alone. Gino loved his wife's soft little belly and her full big-nippled breasts and the way she turned at once to his touch, eager and responsive.

Mornings, while the babies still slept and Lesley moved around the kitchen preparing Gino's breakfast, he often walked up quietly behind her, pulling her up close against him, kissing her neck as his hands deftly unbuttoned her pajama top.

"The coffee's going to boil over," warned Lesley.

"Yes," said Gino, his hands full of her, his fingers stroking her waiting nipples.

"I can't do anything when I'm excited."

"Am I helping you to feel excited?"

"Yes."

"How? When I do this? Or this? Or this?"

"Yes."

"Yes, oh, yes."

And more often than not, Lesley Donati would end up stark naked in her kitchen, until her husband would carry her back to their tumbled bed.

"I hope we made a baby this time," Lesley would say afterward.

"What? Again?"

"Yes," she would reply, kissing him with the soft kisses of after passion. "I want to make a dozen babies with you, for you. Two dozen. A hundred."

"All in one morning?" Gino laughed.

"Any morning. Or night, or afternoon."

"If I don't hurry and get to work we won't be able to feed the three we already have," he said, stroking her. "I love to touch you."

"Don't ever stop," answered Lesley. "I'd die if you didn't want to touch me."

"You're everything," said Gino. "Everything I've ever wanted."

And when Gino had gone, Lesley Donati had her blue-and-white kitchen with a row of red geraniums on the window sill, her primrose-yellow bathroom and a living room with a fireplace and a pine-board floor and a hand-braided rug. Her three children were plump and sunny-natured, and they seldom cried, except in what Lesley called their "little Latin temper tantrums."

"Oh, Joe," she would say (or "Oh, Mark" or "Oh, Julie"), "don't tell me you're getting set for one of your little Latin temper tantrums? You are? Okay. Go ahead. Come on, good and loud now. One, two, three. Go!"

And most of the time the children would begin to laugh and to hug her with sweet-smelling, dimpled arms.

Lesley Donati often told herself that she had every single thing in the world she wanted. She had a beautiful house and she knew herself to be well loved. Her husband's family adored her and Gino himself was not only fascinated with her body;

he loved just being next to her, talking to her, being wherever she was. He was kind and gentle, a loving father and a good provider.

The first year of their marriage, Gino had left Atwill Express and gone into business with his father and brothers. Now he was a full partner in the firm of Donati and Sons— Wholesale Fruit and Produce, and he earned a very good living. He could afford to spoil his wife a little, to indulge her.

The one thing he could not understand was Lesley's continued love for her mother, Angelique, and her sister, Alana. It was the only thing that Gino and Lesley ever argued about, but always, one or the other of them put an end to the disagreement before it got out of hand. Still it was always there between them, the one thing in their lives in which they were not in complete harmony.

"Listen, honey," Gino would say, "those two are no good. No good for you, for me or for the kids. They're no good to themselves. They're bums. Look at the way they act."

"Darling, you don't understand—"

"You're damned right I don't understand! And what I don't understand most of all is how you can stick up for them. After all the rotten things they've done to you. I don't see how you stand the sight of either of them."

"Gino, it's my mother, my sister."

"Yeah, I know. And any stranger off the street, who'd never even seen you before, would treat you better."

"You don't understand—"

Of course he didn't understand, thought Lesley. How could he?

The Donati family was the complete antithesis of the de Montignys, and his own family was the standard by which Gino judged.

Lesley smiled to herself. They were something, all right, the Donatis. Something warm and wonderful and as closely allied as the fingers in a hand. Giulia Donati worshiped her big, cheerful husband, Giuseppe, and her sons, Marcello, Gino and Roberto, and her daughters, Sophia and Adrianna, and all of them, in turn, regarded Giulia as the one person in the world around whom the sun and the moon revolved. The Donatis sang, laughed, wept and argued with loud passion and great good humor. After Angelique de Montigny had tried with every means at her disposal to keep her daughter and Gino apart after that fateful Christmas Eve, she accepted defeat but shifted her attack to a new direction.

"Those Italian families are all alike," Angelique would say. "They wallow in each other."

"They are very close," Lesley would admit, attempting to keep a measure of peace between herself and her mother.

"It's disgusting, that's what it is," continued Angelique, "all that spaghetti and cheese and garlic and olive oil. Big fat men and sloppy, slovenly women. You weren't brought up like that, Lesley. Believe me, you'd tire of that sort of in-laws in short order."

After a few such arguments, Lesley refused to discuss the Donatis with her mother. She soon realized the futility of trying to convince Angelique that the Donatis were a far cry from the comic-opera version of an Italian family, complete with fat bellies and hilarious accents. Giulia often cooked Italian food but she also had a rare talent with charcoal-broiled steaks and corn on the cob. And, after having borne five children, Giulia Donati could still fit very nicely into a size twelve dress. As for the girls, Sophia and Adrianna, they both had twenty-two-inch waistlines that turned their non-Italian girl friends green with envy.

No, there was no sense at all in arguing with Angelique, with her narrow-mindedness and her outright lies.

The biggest lie of all, so far as Lesley was concerned, was the one Angelique broached about the Donatis never in the world accepting a non-Italian into their family. From the moment they met, Giulia had shown Lesley nothing but kindness and when Gino announced that he and Lesley wanted to get married, Giulia had burst into tears of joy.

"I will telephone your mother and ask her to come to supper. We must celebrate."

"Please—" Lesley began.

"What is it, darling?" asked Giulia.

"She won't come," said Lesley miserably. "Besides, I haven't told her yet."

"So tell her," protested Giulia. "Go now quickly, you and Gino, and tell her. Then I will call your mother and ask her to supper."

"No, please," Lesley had answered. "I want to tell her on Christmas Eve. She always has a party then."

"Of course, child. Tell her then. After the holidays we can have our celebration."

But after Lesley had gone, Giulia turned to her husband.

"I do not like it, Giuseppe. It is as if she is afraid to tell her own mother!"

"It will be all right," Giuseppe answered comfortably. "The mother will come around to it as soon as she realizes that the children are truly in love."

"Giuseppe," said Giulia, "I have the feeling that Mrs. de Montigny does not know what love is."

"Nonsense," replied her husband and went back to reading his newspaper.

But no one in the Donati household thought that Giulia's feeling was nonsense when Gino brought Lesley home with him on Christmas Day.

Lesley became hysterical all over again when she tried to tell Giulia what had happened at Angelique's Christmas Eve party.

"I showed her the ring," cried Lesley, "and she wouldn't even look at it. She called Gino names. She said—"

And while Giulia held Lesley and tried to comfort her, Giuseppe took his son aside to find out exactly what had happened.

"But this is monstrous," said Giulia later. "What kind of woman would treat her own flesh and blood like that?"

"Perhaps Gino should wait," replied Giuseppe. "If Lesley were of age, perhaps—"

"No!" said Giulia. "The whole thing is idiotic. I will call Mrs. de Montigny and invite her for supper. Perhaps she will at least talk to us."

But when Giulia telephoned and gave her name, Angelique said coldly, "I'm sorry, but you must have the wrong number."

"I did not have the wrong number," Giulia told her husband. "She just did not want to talk to me."

Giulia tried several more times to talk to Angelique and finally she went to her house to call on her. Angelique kept her standing at the front door. She did not even invite her into the house.

"Mrs. Donati, we have absolutely nothing to say to each other. I want your son to keep away from my daughter."

"But Mrs. de Montigny," protested Giulia, "they are planning to get married!"

"Lesley is a child," answered Angelique. "She will soon forget this foolishness."

"But, please, listen to me—"

"Good afternoon, Mrs. Donati," said Angelique and shut the door softly, but Giulia could hear the bolt being slipped into place.

"As if I were a thief," cried Giulia to her husband. "I tell you, she locked her door as if I might force my way into her house!"

"It will pass," said Giuseppe. "Try once more. Write her a note and ask her to supper. Maybe she'll come."

And no one was more surprised than Lesley and Alana when Angelique decided to accept Giulia Donati's written invitation.

"How quaint," said Angelique. "Supper. I haven't heard dinner called that for simply years and years."

"I don't like it," Alana had confided later to Lesley. "I don't like it one bit."

But on the day of the party, Angelique had her hair beautifully done, her nails freshly manicured, and she wore the new black dress she had been saving for Millie Turner's cocktail party. She had never looked lovelier and Lesley told her so.

"But of course, darling," answered Angelique, laughing. "I don't want the Donatis to think that your mother is a frump."

"It's going to be all right," Lesley told Alana just before they left the house.

"Don't count on it, kid."

"Don't be silly, Alana."

"Okay, honey. I hope everything goes off fine."

"Of course it will," Lesley answered.

But then, why, wondered Lesley as she and Alana and Angelique climbed into the taxicab to go to the Donatis, were her knees trembling and why were her hands so wet inside of her white kid gloves?

The Donati living room was beautiful, with fresh flowers and everything shining clean.

And there was music coming from the record player. Not the Italian love songs that Lesley enjoyed so much and that Giulia always played for her, but American cocktail-lounge music. Piano music.

"Ah, Mrs. de Montigny," said Giuseppe, in his most outgoing, jovial manner. "I am told that I make the best martinis in Livingstone. But I'll never believe it until you yourself tell me."

"How perfectly charming, Mr. Donati," replied Angelique, smiling her sweetest smile.

After the second martini, Alana noticed that Angelique had crossed her legs and that one foot was swinging back and forth gently.

Like a goddamned cat, thought Alana. A cat swinging

her tail, ready to pounce. Oh, God, please let it be all right!

"You know, I believe you're right," Angelique was saying as she twirled her cocktail glass slowly in her fingers. "You do make a wonderful martini, Goosep—"

"Giuseppe," he corrected. "A refill, Angelique?"

"Of course, Joosepp—"

"Giuseppe."

"Oh, yes," answered Angelique. "Somehow I never could get the hang of foreign names."

Giuseppe Donati laughed. "Then call me Joe," he said. "That's simpler and it is the same thing."

"Oh, yes indeed," replied Angelique. "It is simpler. Joe, But so common."

Alana could not restrain herself. "What kind of name is Angelique?" she asked. "Old Boston?"

Angelique turned her head slowly and stared at Alana. "Merely because you are in the home of peasants," she said distinctly, "is not reason for you to behave like one. Please remember your manners, Alana."

Oh, God, thought Lesley. It's beginning.

"Lesley," said Giulia quickly, "would you like to help me in the kitchen?"

"Oh, yes," answered Lesley gratefully.

Angelique drank down most of her martini and began to laugh.

"Yes, Lesley, do go to the kitchen and help Mrs. Donati. I imagine that those enormous tubs of spaghetti are awfully heavy."

"Mother—" began Lesley, but Giulia interrupted her smoothly, smiling.

"We're having a roast of beef."

"How very imaginative of you," said Angelique. "Yes, Joe, these are lovely martinis. Another, please."

"But you'll spoil your taste for the wine!"

"Are you trying to cut off my drinks, Joe?" asked Angelique.

295

"Of course not," replied Giuseppe and hastened to fill her glass.

"That's better," said Angelique, "much, much better. You may sit down now."

No one seemed to be able to think of anything to say as Angelique looked, smilingly, from one face to another.

"Now tell me," she said at last. "Just why have you requested this audience with me?"

Again no one spoke and Lesley had the feeling that she was in a bad dream.

"I'll tell you why," replied Angelique, into the silence. "You hoped to persuade me with your miserable little efforts at grandeur that your son is fit to marry my daughter. Well, he isn't."

Giulia Donati turned white. "Now, listen here—" she began.

"Listen here, my ass," interrupted Angelique. "You listen. I don't want any daughter of mine mixed up with a bunch of wops and that's final."

"Mrs. de Montigny," said Gino, "I'm going to marry Lesley, with your blessing or without it. She'll be eighteen in less than five months, and then she'll be free of you forever."

"Shut your big goddamned rotten mouth," shouted Angelique.

"No, Mrs. de Montigny," answered Gino. "You shut yours for a change."

"Gino!" cried Giulia.

"No, Mama," replied Gino. "I knew she would act like this. Well, I don't care. I'm not going to give up Lesley."

"You fucking, greasy little creep," said Angelique coldly. "If you knew what you were talking about you'd be thanking me for saving your dirty neck."

She did not bother to ask Giuseppe for a fresh drink. She walked to the table and filled her glass sloppily from the pitcher of martinis.

"Lesley," whispered Alana, "let's get her out of here! Now!"

But Angelique had turned, leaning against the table, squinting into her glass.

"For instance, greaseball," she said turning to Gino, "has Lesley ever told you that she shouldn't be marrying at all?"

"What do you mean?"

Angelique looked at him. "Well, you guineas are always big for sons, aren't you? I don't suppose Lesley told you that she can never have a son? Or that if she does, he'll be hopelessly handicapped as long as he lives?"

"Mother, what *are* you talking about?" asked Lesley.

"Hemophilia," answered Angelique sweetly. "Hemophilia, Gino. Do you know what that is? Of course you don't. Well, I'll tell you. It's a rare blood disorder passed down to all male offspring by the women in my family. If you marry Lesley and she has your son, he'll bleed to death."

"You're a liar!" screamed Alana.

Angelique ignored her completely. "And that's not all. Oh, no. Not by a shit load. Did you know, for instance, that there's also insanity in the family? Oh, yes, indeed. Lesley's grandmother. Mad as a hatter. Been locked up for years."

"Lesley told me about her grandmother," replied Gino, his face scarlet with anger. "She told me as soon as we knew we were in love."

"I have it on very good medical authority," continued Angelique, pouring another martini, "that insanity runs in families. Oh, sometimes it skips a generation, like in ours, but who knows when it will turn up? In Lesley? In her children?"

"I can't bear any more of this," cried Giulia.

"Look you, don't get emotional with me," said Angelique. "Your wop hysterics won't cut any ice at all. You're the one who invited me here for a little talk. Well, now you're getting it." She turned back to Gino. "So, how do you feel about marrying Lesley now?"

Alana, who had been standing as stricken as everyone else

in the room, suddenly discovered that she could move. It was as if she were alone except for that hatefully smiling face in front of her, as if those glinting eyes and red lips, peeled back from the white, white teeth, were the only things left in the world.

"You vicious bitch!" she shouted at Angelique. "You filthy liar! It isn't true about my brother dying of some crazy disease. You killed him, you and Dr. Gordon. I heard you talking about it. Oh, how many times I heard you! And I saw you too. You with all your clothes off and him touching you and kissing you and telling you how good it was. And you asking him if you were the best he ever had and the two of you with your mouths glued all over each other and rolling on the sofa—on the floor—"

Alana's years of pain and hatred came pouring out of her. All the years of hiding under the staircase, of watching and listening, of being frightened and horrified, of hating and loving and waiting to be loved. All the long, long years of loneliness.

"He told you you were tight, almost as tight as a young girl, and he said how great it was not having to use anything and you asked him if he was really glad that you couldn't get pregnant any more, if he was glad that you were fixed—spayed, darling, you said—and he said, yes, yes, yes."

Angelique de Montigny stared at Alana. She could tell that the girl was screaming at her because her mouth was open, unbeautifully open, but Angelique didn't really mind.

Dear Myles, she thought dreamily. He never gave me any trouble after our first date. Sweet, dear Myles.

She could see him so clearly, with his face almost purple with rage at first, but not for long,

Angelique smiled and smiled and smiled and she could not even hear Alana. It was as if she were not in the room at all.

"For heaven's sake, Myles," she had said, as soon as they had been seated at a dark corner table in the cocktail lounge of the Livingstone Hotel that day, "did you think you could keep your little gangster hideout a secret forever?"

"What do you want, Angelique? Money?"

She looked at him reproachfully. "Do I look like a black-mailer?" she asked with a little pout.

"No, unfortunately," replied Myles Gordon. "You look exactly like a big-eyed blonde angel, sweet mouth and all. No one would ever take you for the black-hearted little bitch you really are."

"That's not nice, Myles," she said. "Not that last part anyway."

"Angelique, I'm a married man—with a family. I can't afford to be seen drinking in here with you. Now for God's sake come to the point. What do you want from me?"

"Nothing, Myles," she replied, "nothing at all. I merely want to be friends. I've always wanted to have a doctor for a friend."

He could not quite believe her and yet he could not help the small feeling of relief that he was beginning to feel.

"Why, Angelique," he said. "You didn't have to go through all this just to become my friend. I've been your friend for over two years now."

"No, you haven't," she answered quickly, "you've been my doctor and I've been your patient. There's an awful lot of difference between that and being friends."

"But, Angelique—"

"Listen, Myles, you know the old saw about a friend in need being a friend indeed?"

"Now what in the hell do you mean by that?" he demanded.

Angelique smiled. "Nothing," she said. "Except that you never know when I might need a friend like you. For some reason or other."

He couldn't help laughing. "You know something?" he said. "We're two of a kind, you and I. A great pair. Each of us looking out for Number One."

"Exactly," she replied and smiled her sweet smile again.

Myles Gordon ordered another round of drinks and leaned back in his chair.

"Tell me," he asked, "have you told anyone else about our little secret?"

Angelique kept smiling even as she put a cigarette in her mouth, and when he bent toward her to give her a light she looked straight into his eyes.

"Of course not," she answered. "The only thing I did was write everything down on a piece of paper and give it to Maman's lawyer for safekeeping just in case anything ever happened to me."

Myles Gordon laughed. "Sometimes you're clever," he said, "but sometimes you can be awfully dumb too. Did it ever occur to you that within one hour I could get rid of all the— shall we call it evidence?—at Myra Gordon Memorial? And what would your paper be worth then?"

"But you wouldn't do that, Myles," she said. "Oh, no. You wouldn't. You're much too greedy."

And Myles Gordon, thinking of the new Cadillac standing out in front of the hotel, and of the new house he had just started to build in the best neighborhood in Livingstone, knew that Angelique had guessed correctly.

"You're absolutely right," he said. "We need each other."

For several months their need for each other was fierce and unrelenting, then like a fire it gradually burned itself out.

They saw each other only occasionally after that. Angelique was moving in an ever-widening circle of friends but sometimes they met at one cocktail party or another. Angelique was always very careful then.

"Hello there, Dr. Gordon."

"Well, hello, Mrs. de Montigny. How are you?"

"I'm feeling much better, thank you, Doctor. Those new pills you gave me are simply marvelous."

"Mrs. de Montigny, have you met my wife?"

"No, I haven't."

"Esther, this is Mrs. de Montigny. One of my patients."

"How do you do, Mrs. Gordon? I can't tell you what marvelous things your husband has done for me. And for my children. Why, we've never been so healthy."

"That's very nice to hear, Mrs. de Montigny."

"Oh, dear. Please excuse me. I see that Pat Condon has just come in and I simply *must* see her. Good-bye, Dr. Gordon. Mrs. Gordon."

"A charming woman, Myles."

"Who?"

"Mrs. de Montigny."

"Oh. Oh, yes. May I get you another drink, dear?"

But, of course, eventually the telephone call came as Myles had known it must.

"Myles? Angelique. I need you."

"What is it?"

"I'll come to your office this evening."

There was no doubt about it. Angelique was pregnant again.

"I told you there would be a time when I would need you, Myles," said Angelique, "and the time is now."

I knew it, he thought, I knew it would come to this.

I will wear my little black dress, Angelique said to herself. And she did.

She came into his office looking like an angel. Angelique. Angelique, the angel. And she said, "Myles, now, now you can pay me. Get rid of it for me."

Dr. Myles Gordon had often heard the expression "sweating gumdrops." He never knew until right now what it meant. Not for my big house, he kept repeating, not for my wife, not for my children, will I become an abortionist.

"Myles," she said, "pay me. Pay me now!"

301

"Well, Angel, get up on the table and let's see what's wrong."

When he had finished his examination, he knew he could easily do what she asked. But no, not for my mother, he thought, not for anyone.

"Angelique, it's too late. It's too late, but I will do this. Go through with it this one last time and I will make sure it never happens again."

"What the hell do you mean by that?"

"Angelique, there are ways. I'll fix it for you so this can never happen again."

"You will make goddamned fucking well sure of it. Because I know where the body is buried and I'll crucify you."

He found it very hard to believe that out of the face of an angel could come words like these.

"We'll do a Caesarian," he said. "It's so simple, Angelique. All I have to do is to take an inch off each tube and it will never happen again."

"Buy me a drink," she said.

"I couldn't right now."

"You can leave any time I say so," replied Angelique.

Thank God, Dr. Myles Gordon thought that day at the operating table, that I have a place where I can do this, that I have my own hospital. But even so he felt harried.

Cut those tubes, Myles! Cut the cord off the baby! Tie it! Hurry, hurry, hurry! Start stitching, boy. Fast!

But I have never seen so much blood.

I think I'll go out and get a drink, he thought, maybe two or three. Everything's fine now, she's fixed. She's stitched and the baby's arrived. The nurse can carry on now. I've done my part.

He turned to the nurse. "Watch that baby," he said. "I want a constant surveillance kept on him."

He had never really trusted Hester as a nurse. She was inclined to be careless. She had gone into nursing because it was a profession and if you had a profession you were somebody.

And Hester had replied, "Of course, doctor."

But there are times when a girl needs a nice cup of coffee and a cigarette.

So Stephen de Montigny lay in his crib with his life dripping out of him—one drop at a time. How many drops of blood are there in a baby?

"What the Christ have you done?" shouted Dr. Gordon when he came back later to see Angelique and looked in at the baby.

But by then it was too late and no one could have saved Stephen.

"For Christ's sake where were you?" he asked Hester angrily. "Couldn't you have watched him?"

Dr. Gordon turned and walked down the corridor towards Angelique's room. Something had made him come back. What? Had he known? But how could he have?

An accident, he screamed to himself as he walked down the long hall. An accident, I didn't mean it. It was such a big field of blood and there wasn't time for everything. I should have checked over the baby before I turned it over to the nurse, especially a nurse like Hester, but suddenly I knew I had to get out of there.

But I came back.

"He's dead. He's dead, Angelique," he said, standing by her bed.

"But I'm alive."

"Angelique, your son is dead."

Angelique shrugged.

She had never wanted a son to begin with and all that she was thinking about was the day when she could go home.

"What have you done?" asked Monique, in her room that night.

"Maman, he died. The baby died."

"Like your father, he died?"

303

"No, Maman, not like that. Perhaps we are fated never to have men around us. Paradise, Maman, I'll tell you what it is—it's having what you want all the time. I don't need any man for that."

Monique just looked at her and thought: Oh, God, what have I done?

"Don't look brokenhearted, Maman. That's the way we wanted it, you and I. The Garden of Eden is one place you don't need a man."

Monique could only look at her and think: I killed him. I killed my grandson.

She just stood there looking at Angelique, the angel.

And Angelique just smiled her sweet smile.

"Angelique, tell me, is it true he bled to death?"

"But of course, Maman. Hemophilia. It is a disease of aristocrats, and if there's one thing I have always been, it's a princess."

Monique couldn't even cry.

"Was there a lot of blood?"

"Well, of course, Maman."

"Like your father?"

"No, Maman, not like Papa. Papa never bled. You know that."

There was no one in the night to hear Etienne crying except Monique. She heard him. That was the beginning of the funny feeling. She couldn't say it any other way except that she felt funny. She'd never felt so funny in her whole life.

So much blood! So much blood, she thought, I will drown in it. But I didn't kill him. I didn't kill him! I didn't kill Armand! I didn't kill Stephen!

Etienne found her on the floor, screaming, "I am dying in an ocean of blood!"

"I heard you," Alana screamed. "Oh boy, did I ever hear you. You can stand there and try to kid Lesley and the Donatis

304

but you're not going to kid me. I heard it with Grammy and I heard it with you, too, every day, every night."

"Please don't do this to each other," Lesley sobbed.

But there was no one to hear her. Alana and Angelique were staring at each other.

"Please, Mother," cried Lesley. "Please!"

Alana suddenly turned on her and said, "I have been listening to you saying, 'please don't do this to each other,' for years. I don't need you or it any more. I have been listening to you for years wanting it nice. You wanted a nice husband, Lesley. Well, now you've got Gino. Get off my back, for Christ's sake! You know what I'm sick of? Not Angelique, but you, yes, of you, sick and tired. I'm going to be one of the takers from now on. I'll just take and take and take. And you know what you will do, Lesley? You'll find fault because I'm not made in the sainted image of what you want the world to be. So who needs an Adam in Eden? We can have an Eden without it, Lesley, so don't say one word."

Lesley could only look at her and say, "Please don't do this to yourself, don't do it!"

"Look," said Alana, "I have had it. Right up to the eyeballs. I told you that. I'm going to remember from now on that the only thing important is no one but me. Me, Lesley, just for Alana, this one time."

She looked around the room. It was as if everyone had been quick-frozen in the midst of a game of charades. Angelique by the martini pitcher, gaping drunkenly. Lesley, her blonde hair hiding her face. The Donatis with a look of confusion on their faces, as if they'd stumbled into a darkened movie theatre only to find that the picture on the screen was not the one advertised on the marquee outside. And Gino, immense and impassive, looking down at Lesley with love in his eyes.

"Come on, Mama," Alana said wearily. "The shit has really hit the fan and since you and I threw it, we might as well go home."

305

6

Alana de Montigny was sitting in an armchair in what she laughingly called the living room.

"Living room, eh?" she sometimes said bitterly. "Listen, in a hovel like this *nothing* is living."

She lit another cigarette and held her glass up to the light.

That was one thing about Bloody Marys, she thought. They were the goddamnedest color.

She wondered briefly where in hell she had ever got such an idea and then she remembered, it had come from her sister. But then, Lesley was always kind of nutty about things.

"Look. Look," Lesley was always saying.

And whenever Alana had bothered to look, it was to see some nutty thing like Lesley pouring cream into a glass of iced coffee.

"Look, look," Lesley would say as the cream fell and then rose to make a swirling pattern in the glass. "Isn't that the loveliest thing you ever saw in your whole life?"

Alana smiled and downed half her drink. That Lesley was a real pain in the ass. Everything to Lesley was either the loveliest, the most stupendous, the most fantastic or the absolute greatest of everything. What a drag. Nuts like Lesley would be better off locked up. But then, you couldn't really blame it all on Lesley. Not when the whole friggin' family was potty to begin with. Who but a real nut like Angelique, for instance, would have christened her daughters Alana and Lesley, with a last name like de Montigny? And Angelique's son, had he lived, would have been Stephen. Stephen de Montigny, for Christ's sake!

"Oh, balls," Alana said out loud.

She finished her drink and went into the kitchen to make another Bloody Mary.

When she came back to the living room and sat down, she threw one leg over an arm of the chair. She could hear her mother, Angelique, who still lived in the old house, say, "Alana, you are a nasty little vulgarian."

"And you, Ma," she answered automatically, "are a whore, a liar, a sneak and Christ knows what else. So leave me alone."

When Lesley had been around, she had always acted as the mealy-mouthed little peacemaker.

"Please, Alana," Lesley would say. "After all, she *is* your mother."

Or Lesley would say, "Please, Mother, Alana is your own flesh and blood."

Oh, we're quite a tribe, all right, all right. The de Montigny tribe. Oh, brother!

She stuck her forefinger into the glass and swirled the ice cubes around lazily.

Yep. Much-married me and nutty Lesley and whorish Mama Angelique and crazy old Grammy Monique. There had been Papa Etienne, who wanted out and had got out, in the middle of the Pacific, in the last days of the war. To say nothing of Mémère Simone and the big fat aunts, Josephine and Charlotte and Cecile, plus retarded Uncle Remy, and the old lush, Uncle Christophe. Yep. Quite a tribe. The de Montigny tribe of Livingstone, New Hampshire.

And of all the people Alana knew in the whole world, the only one who seemed to realize this was Lesley's husband, Gino Donati. Now there was a name for you. Gino Donati.

Alana giggled to herself.

Good old Gino, big, black, curly-headed Gino, with shoulders like a Mack truck, who married Lesley when she was

307

eighteen. Now poor Lesley was twenty-one and already she had a belly from producing three kids in three years. Alana imagined that her breasts sagged too, but Gino still couldn't keep his hands off her.

"A real peasant type," Angelique had said after Lesley's third baby. "She must take after your grandmother Simone."

"Why don't you drop dead, Ma," Alana had replied. "You didn't do so bad yourself, you know. If my brother had lived you'd be even with Lesley. Three brats in three years."

It had always been like that between Angelique and Alana. Two cats in a bag. At least it had been like that since Alana was sixteen years old and had seen what Angelique had tried to do to Lesley.

Strangers usually thought that Alana was the elder of the two girls because she seemed so much wiser in the ways of the world. Well, she'd had a damned good teacher wise her up. She'd had Angelique and before that Monique. And she had watched Lesley almost get her heart broken by the two of them. But Lesley always did go around looking for it.

But not me, thought Alana. Not this little chick. That was why I got out.

She squinted down into her glass. It was empty. Christ, these things disappear fast, she thought sullenly. Oh, well, as long as there's vodka and tomato juice, little old Alana can always make more.

She banged her hip against the door frame going into the kitchen but she barely felt it.

It took her a little longer to fix a drink this time. Nothing seemed to go right and she spilled tomato juice down the front of her clean blouse.

"Shit," she said, "I must be getting buzzed."

Oh, brother, she could hear Angelique now.

"Nasty little vulgarian."

"I must take after my old man, huh, Ma?"

"You certainly do. He was a master vulgarian."

Alana went back to her armchair. She fumbled around the arms for her cigarettes.

I wonder where you are now, master vulgarian, she thought. What about it, Pa, you old master vulgarian? What's new in that tiny grave in the middle of the Pacific? Say, that was an idea.

She stood up and went over to the record player. She shuffled records until she found the one she wanted. She put it on the turntable and after a few minutes of cursing she finally managed to fit the needle into the first groove.

"What's new?" asked the record. *"How is the world treating you?"*

She sat down on the floor next to the phonograph and swayed gently in time to the music as she remembered the last time she had seen her father. He had come home once, on leave, probably just to see her and Lesley. She remembered especially because Lesley had asked one of her usual dumb questions.

"Daddy," she had asked. "What was the happiest day of your life?"

Etienne had a drink in his hand and he looked at Lesley for a long time. Alana knew what poor Lesley was expecting. It was some stupid answer like, "Why, the day you were born, of course."

But Etienne had looked Lesley straight in the eye.

"Why, the day the Japs bombed Pearl Harbor."

Alana had tossed back her head and laughed but Lesley just sat there looking as if she'd been slapped across the face. You couldn't expect Lesley to realize that the old man was half in the bag. Lesley, the dummy, was too busy looking for the bluebird.

"But, Daddy—" Lesley began.

"You're goddamned right," Etienne went on. "Pearl Harbor. I knew we'd go to war and at last I'd be able to get away from Angelique."

What a joke! The day the Japs bombed Pearl Harbor!

"What's new? How is the world treating you—"

Alana de Montigny, whose three husbands had been named Turcotte, O'Brien and Paquin, threw her newly empty glass against the wall. What good had any of them been to her, they or anyone else? She had married the first one, after Lesley moved out, to get away from Angelique, and the second to get away from the first. The third—why had she married Paquin? Well, what did it matter? He was the worst of the lot and all men were the same anyway. At least she'd been luckier than Lesley, who had three brats. In the same length of time she'd had three lovers and now she was free to take another.

Alana threw back her head and began to cry, the way a child does. Loudly and without inhibition. She cried as if she would never stop.

Lesley woke up and she hit Gino with her elbow and she said to him, "Isn't this the loveliest day you've ever seen?"

He reached over and kissed her sleepy mouth. "Baby, you say that every day."

"If you don't cut that out," Lesley said, "you won't get your breakfast today either."

"Why the hell is it," Gino asked, "that you're always so goddamned sexy with your pajamas on?"

"I don't know," she answered. "Is it because you make me this way? Do you know what color the sky is today?"

"Yah, yah, I know."

"Do you know this too? That all the heaven I need is right here?"

"Well," answered Gino, "what about the next time your mother calls? Or your sister?"

"They don't too often, Gino. And Mama's all alone now that Alana moved out. Gino?"

"Huh?"

"Gino, what's going to happen to Mama?"

310

"A bolt of lightning is what should happen to your mother."

"And Alana, Gino? Alana's not like Mama."

"Alana's getting more like her every day," Gino answered.

"Alana was on our side, Gino. Remember how she stood up to Mama that first time at your house?"

"And how long ago was that? Three years? No, nearer five. So all right, she stood up to your mother and then turned on you and belted you around."

"Alana's more like me than Mama, Gino," Lesley said.

"Yah, she's like you all right. You had three kids in three years—Alana had three husbands."

"And Papa, Gino?"

"Your old man was a good joe. Your papa took the dirty brown end of the stick for as long as he could. Then he took a powder. Like remember what he told you that time you asked him what was the happiest day of his life?"

"And what did it get him, Gino?" she asked. "A little white cross on some island in the South Pacific, a number instead of a name, not even a decent Christian burial."

"There wasn't enough of the poor son of a bitch left to bury! And even if there had been, who'd have come to his funeral? Your mother? Yah, to dance on his grave."

"I'd have gone, Gino," Lesley said. "Me and Alana. And you. You'd have gone, Gino."

He shrugged and put his hand up under her pajama top onto her plump white breast.

"I'd rather be here in bed with you, honey."

She shrugged off his hand.

"No, Gino. Not now, I mean. I want to talk."

His fingers felt for her nipple and she shivered.

"I can't when you do that," she said.

"Well, what do you want to talk about?" he asked, feeling her writhe a little under his probing fingers.

"What's going to happen to them, Gino? Alana and Mama, I mean."

"Nothing," he said angrily, "not a fucking thing. It never does. The Angeliques and the Alanas of this world just go on and on, honey. The lightning never strikes. No, they just go on forever, thinking only of themselves, hurting others, taking and never giving. And these are the ones, Lesley, you want to let hurt you, to try and help? They don't want your help, honey. They just want to eat you."

"Angelique is my mother, Gino. Alana is my own sister."

"Some mother, Angelique," he said.

"You know what's the matter with them, Gino?"

"They both got holes in their heads."

"No, really, Gino, you know?"

"Nothing a good bolt of lightning wouldn't cure."

"No, Gino, seriously, I mean? They can't love. They can't, can they, Gino? They have no love to give, only for themselves."

He fondled her breast and the nipple turned hard.

"You can love," he said. "You can give. So give."

"I can, can't I, Gino? We're the lucky ones, you and me."

"Yah, but what about the next time Angelique calls, or Alana?" Gino asked.

"I won't care. I won't care."

And all she could feel was his mouth against her bare shoulder.

"I won't care," she said.

"Yah," answered Gino, "but what about the day after that? What about next week and next month and next year?"

"I won't care," repeated Lesley. "I promise you, darling, I won't care."

"So all right," Gino replied with a smile, "so today you won't care. And if you're lucky, tomorrow you won't care. Why don't we take it just one day at a time?"

"Gino. Gino, I love you."

"Yah. Yah, I know it," he said.

312